PET WHISPERER P.I.:

BOOKS 16-18 SPECIAL COLLECTION

MOLLY FITZ

Editor: Jennifer Lopez, Mistress with the Red Pen
Cover: TM Franklin

PO Box 873543
Wasilla, AK 99687

SCHEMING SPHYNX

It all started when a vengeful seagull with a shady past promised to wage a brutal war against my wedding day. Things snowballed pretty quickly from there.

I always thought my special day would be perfect. Now, all I want is to get through it without any major catastrophes.

And that's pretty hard with four hyped-up cats running underfoot—two who are so desperately in love it makes you want to puke, and two more who very much don't want me as their new stepmother and aren't afraid to tell me so... constantly.

By the time a certain friend shows up with the film crew for her floundering reality TV in tow, I know I'm in big trouble.

Not only could I fail to make it down the aisle, but I also risk exposing my biggest, most intimate secret.

So when all is finally said and done, will I be saying "I do" to the man of my dreams or admitting "I can" when forced to confess to my Pet Whisperer abilities?

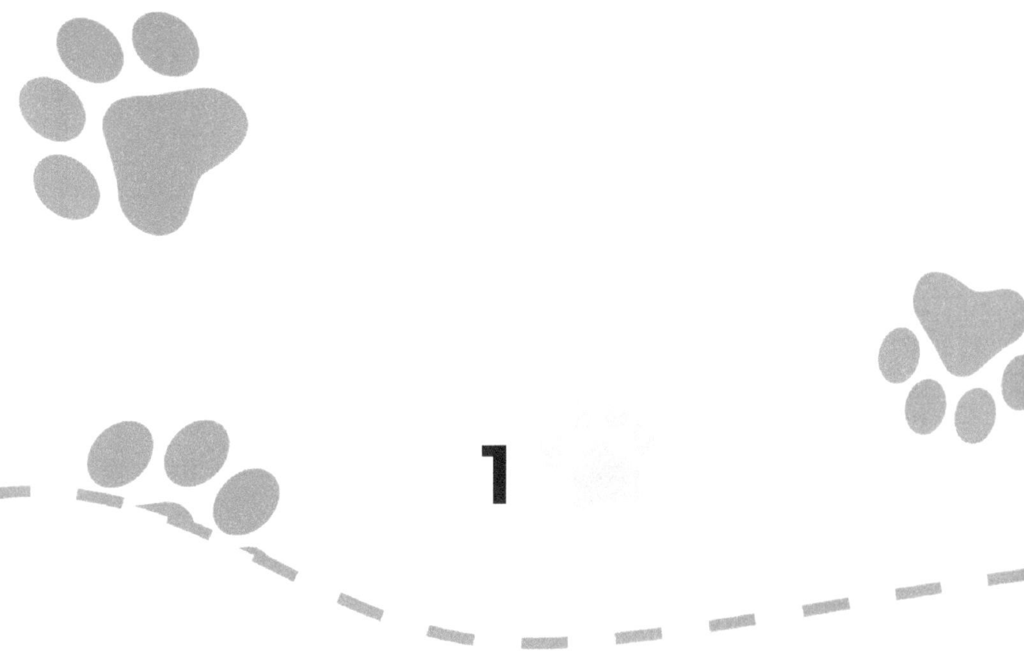

1

My name is Angie Russo, and in just a few short days, I will become Mrs. Charles Longfellow, III. It seems like it's been ages since that first day our eyes met across the office and I instantly fell head over heels for the handsome new law associate from California. Really, though, it's only been a couple years since that fateful day.

And even though I immediately fell in love, it took Charles a little longer to figure out I was the one he'd spend the rest of his life with. It all started when he blackmailed me into helping with a difficult double homicide case. He was the second person to learn of my strange ability to talk to animals—even I was still getting the hang of it then—and rather than gawk at me, he decided to put me to work.

Now we've solved many cases, both together and apart, and in the process we've fallen incredibly and irrevocably in love. He's now the sole partner at the firm, and I've moved on from being a paralegal to working as a full-time private investigator… in theory.

In reality, I primarily live off my cat's trust fund, but I do try my best to find new mysteries to solve, whether or not my help has been requested. Why, just this spring, I solved the murder of my next-door neighbor. Oh, was that one a doozy!

Luckily, we've been light on work in the weeks that followed, giving me plenty of time to focus on wedding planning.

So, that's me. Former paralegal, current private investigator, future bride. Oh, you wanted to know more about the whole talking to animals thing?

Well, it all started when I met Octo-Cat at a rather unusual will reading. This was before Charles had even joined the firm. He was the first one to really trust me to help research our cases. Before that, I was mostly a glorified secretary. And that day, it was my job to make the coffee. Things didn't exactly go well, and let's just say I've had a completely rational fear of that particular appliance ever since.

The unexpected zap messed with something in my brain, and when I regained consciousness, I was met with big amber eyes and stinky tuna breath. Yes, the estate's primary beneficiary was a cat, and when he realized I could understand everything he was saying, he recruited me to help solve his owner's murder.

And thus a lifelong *something* was born. Most days Octo-Cat and I get along just fine, but sometimes he can be a real stinker.

Still, I wouldn't trade him—or really any part of my life—for the world.

My true best friend is my nan. She's the main one who raised me while my parents focused on making the most of their careers. She's not even my biological grandmother, a fact I discovered only recently. And after months of searching and with a little help from a militant flock of seagulls, I was finally able to meet my Grandma Lyn—the one who gave birth to Mom.

Both will be at the wedding, which will definitely be awkward. But we'll have lots of other guests to help keep the two apart as much as possible.

Nan's dog Paisley, a mostly black tricolor Chihuahua she rescued from the pound, is going to be the flower girl at our wedding. Pringle, the raccoon who lives in a treehouse in my backyard, is not invited but will probably crash the party anyway. Our seagull friends Bravo and Abigull have told us they'll be watching from the trees.

Another seagull I know, Alpha, has threatened to ruin the whole affair. He's also recently befriended Pringle and encouraged him to take part in a twelve-step program to help with his behavioral issues. I'm not sure I trust his motives on that one, but the group therapy has definitely been helping Pringle turn over a new leaf.

He's still not invited to the wedding, though.

I'll be plenty busy hosting all the guests we have coming from out of town. Even my old frenemy Bethany Peters is coming up from Georgia along with my cousin Mags to take part in the happiest day of my life to date.

Charles's family is coming out from California, of course, and our friend Sharon is taking a detour on her RV tour of the country to swing on by too. Basically, everyone who's anyone to us will be in attendance—past clients, old friends, distant family... Even my cat's girlfriend's owner is coming all the way from Colorado to offer her well wishes.

In lieu of a bridal party, our three cats will be standing at the altar with us. I've found adorable bowties for Octo-Cat and Jacques and a miniature lace veil for Jillianne. Charles hasn't been owned by cats as long as I have, but he's a sucker for the two hairless sphynxes he inherited from my first dead next-door neighbor, Senator Harlowe.

Over the last several months, I've been giving the two naked felines speech lessons to help them overcome their strange accents—not out of the goodness of my heart, but rather at Octo-Cat's demand. He made it very clear that neither Charles nor his cats would be welcome in our house unless the two kittyfolk stopped communicating in only riddles and rhymes.

It was a tall order, but I'm fairly accustomed to my cat bossing me around, and this demand wasn't particularly unreasonable as far as Octo-Cat goes, which meant I was happy to comply. Plus it gave me a chance to bond with Jacques and Jillianne ahead of us becoming one big happy family.

They weren't too sure about me at first, but now I'm fairly certain I've won them over... At least, I hope I have.

. . .

"Did you pick up my veil from the dry cleaner?" I bellowed at Nan as I rushed down the stairs to answer the door.

"On my list for this afternoon!" Nan shouted back as I flung open the door to reveal a massive pink balloon, which immediately floated forward and bopped me in the face.

"Oof, sorry. That one got away from me." The helium wrangler groaned while hanging on to the rest of his floating bouquet with two firm hands. "Where do you want them?"

"Out back. Let me show you."

As soon as the balloon vendor stepped back, I rushed out onto the porch and down the steps, realizing too late that I'd forgotten to put on any kind of slippers. The cold morning dew tickled my toes and made me shiver, but I was a woman on a mission.

T minus twenty-eight hours until the big *I do*. And I refused to let anyone stand in the way of me and my future husband, least of all some pesky seagull who had vowed to get his revenge on me—even though he was the one who'd ruined his flock; I'd simply uncovered the truth.

That's why, in lieu of flowers, I'd decided to decorate the backyard with hundreds and hundreds of balloons floating in the sky and forming an overhead canopy. That should keep any unwanted avian company away, or at least that was my hope.

"Isn't your wedding tomorrow?" the balloon guy asked as he affixed the balloons to the spot on the massive metal frame I'd just pointed out. “If we get some bad weather in, these will be ruined.”

“No, that won’t happen.” I laughed under my breath. “I’ve already decided that the weather will be perfect both today and tomorrow.”

“But you can’t control the—”

“I’ve already decided that it will be fine,” I said, biting off each word as I spoke it. I’d tried to arrange for the balloon canopy to be erected on the morning of the wedding but couldn’t find a vendor who could work with that proposed schedule. Setting up a day early was the only choice I could make, since I refused to push the wedding back—not when I’d already waited this long to become Mrs. Charles Longfellow, III, now and forevermore.

“If you say so.” He shrugged and got back to work. So much for *the customer is always right*.

I wrung my hands but somehow managed to hold my tongue. I wasn’t usually so high-strung, but this was my wedding. It was the one day I needed to go perfectly right, and I already had at least one strike against me, seeing as a certain murderous seagull has threatened to upend the whole thing.

If I could just control the rest…

If I could just prevent anything else from going wrong…

Oops. I should have definitely known better than to tempt fate. As soon as I rounded the house, I saw two giant RVs sidling up my driveway.

And I already knew that whatever news they brought couldn’t be good.

2

I watched in horror as the RVs parked and half a dozen men scrambled out from the rear vehicle, holding a variety of boom mics, cameras, and other assorted film equipment.

"Excuse me!" I called, wrapping my arms around myself to stave off the early morning cold. I was still barefoot, which didn't help. "Excuse me! What are you doing?"

"Shhh, we're about to start filming," one of the men hissed in my direction before turning back to his team. "And in three... two... one... go."

That's when the door of the front RV flung open to reveal my friend Sharon carrying her white, long-haired cat Chester in her arms. "Oh, what a beautiful day for a wedding!" she exclaimed as the flowing fabric of her princess-cut evening gown swished around her ankles. "Don't you think so, Chessy?"

The group of men moved around her before one yelled, "Cut!"

"I think there might be some confusion. The wedding's tomorrow," I called helplessly as Sharon set her cat down and rushed over to envelop me in a giant bear hug.

"Oh, I know. We all know that. But it takes work to get the right shots, so we figured we'd show up a day early to make sure we get it all on camera. Thank you again for agreeing to this. It will be the perfect finale to the first season of Chessy's reality TV show."

My jaw dropped and practically hit the ground. "I didn't—I mean, I don't— Come again now?"

She lifted what appeared to be a freshly manicured hand to her chest in shock. "Why, it was on my RSVP card. Didn't you receive it?"

"You RSVPed with a plus-one," I ground out, trying so hard not to show my anger in that moment.

"And then I wrote the letters *R* and *V*. Sharon plus one extra RV. Our film crew." Upon finishing her asinine explanation, her face suddenly crumpled at the corners. "We're not unwelcome, are we? I've been talking this wedding up for the last several episodes. It would be a lot of work to remove all that, and then we'd have to come up with a different idea for the finale and everything. If our finale doesn't land just right, we may not be asked to renew for a second season, and we can't have that. Chessy is far too used to the glitz and glamour of celebrity life now. Besides, you knew I'd be filming through the end of June, so I just assumed an invite for me was an invite for the whole crew."

Well, now what in the heck was I supposed to do with all that?

"There'll be a handsome stipend for you, of course. In fact, the producers want to pay for your big day in its entirety."

I gulped down my anxiety and forced a smile. "Sharon, that's wonderful. Thank you," I said, even though I now had one more massive thing to worry about. Forget about ruining the day. If the camera crew caught me at the exact wrong moment, my little secret could be exposed for all of America to see. And that would ruin my entire life.

Yes, I had no doubts that if anyone beyond my very tight inner circle found out about my strange ability to talk with animals, my life would be ruined. No one would ever let me live normally again, and that's not the future I wanted to envision on this, the morning before my wedding.

"What's with the circus?" my cat asked, appearing suddenly behind me thanks to the electronic pet flap on the porch.

I pressed my lips in a straight line, unable to answer without risking a full revelation.

Sharon, of course, wasted no time scooping him up into her thick arms. "Oh, Tubby Tabby! It's so good to see you."

Octo-Cat's eyes widened in horror as our visitor brought her face closer and closer and then placed a kiss smack dab on his whiskered face.

"I will never forgive you for this, Angela. Never," he hissed before taking a swipe at Sharon and then wriggling free and racing back inside.

At this point, I had at least one hundred such threats of him withholding forgiveness into eternity, so I wasn't too worried about this one. Sharon's early arrival with her cinematographers, on the other hand? Definitely a very big problem.

I stared at the ground, doing my best to tune everything out as I thought quickly. "I still have a lot to do over the next..." I twisted my arm to glance at my smart watch. "Twenty-seven hours and eighteen minutes," I announced with a grimace, letting my arm fall back to my side.

"Say no more," Sharon crooned. "Chessy and I are happy to help."

"Actually." I paused to clear my throat. "Actually, it will be easier if I just do it myself. I'm sorry. It's just I have every single minute planned right until the main event. You're welcome to hang out and help Nan while your crew gets their shots, though. In fact, I'm sure she'd be happy for the company. C'mon, I'll take you to her now."

Sharon offered a sad smile that quickly morphed into a huge beaming grin. "I'd love to meet her, and I'd love it even more to have her all to myself. Lead the way." She motioned with a big sweeping gesture, then brought her hands up to pat down the sides of her blonde pixie cut and make sure it was all in place. "I will have to get some shots with Chessy when the crew is done getting their B-footage, but I made sure to get myself ready before we even arrived."

I nodded my approval as I led my overly punctual guest up the porch steps. "You look very nice. Hey, maybe you can show Nan how to make your famous lingonberry pie. She's a baker too, you know."

Sharon's brows furrowed as she shook her head emphatically. "Oh, no, no, no. It just wasn't the same after it cost that Junetta her life. Sure, it wasn't my fault, but well, her death sort of tainted the whole thing, if you know what I mean."

I definitely understood and respected her reasoning on that one, but I didn't really have time to help her and Nan find common ground beyond that. I was already behind schedule as it was.

Thankfully my grandmother was right where I left her, and a few moments later, Sharon and I found her bustling about the kitchen, doing who-knows-what. "Nan, Sharon. Sharon, Nan," I said before running back outside to lay down the law with the newly arrived film crew. Maybe I was becoming something of a bridezilla, but this was a pretty huge surprise to levy on someone right before her big day. A part of me wondered if my avian enemy Alpha had anything to do with the unplanned arrival, but I quickly brushed that concern aside.

Apart from me, the only person I knew who could speak with animals was my long-lost Grandma Lyn. Now that I thought about it, she would be here any minute too. I'd definitely need to pull her aside and explain our heightened risk of discovery. In fact...

I grabbed my cell phone from my jeans pocket and attempted to give my second grandmother a call. No such luck. She was probably already en route, which meant I needed to be extra vigilant.

Suddenly, a hurricane of horrid what-if scenarios swept into my brain, threatening to destroy everything in its path. I stood immobilized as scene by scene of probable mishaps played before my eyes. This was not good. Not good at all.

In fact, was it too late for the groom and I to elope?

Maybe I should give Charles a call and—

"Miss, Miss."

I was shaken from my stupor by the return of the balloon wrangler.

"I'm back with another batch. Is everything all right?"

"It's going to be fine," I reminded him, hating how enraged my usually perky voice sounded. "It's all going to be fine."

He nodded and backed away slowly, then took off to the backyard in a jerky power walk. I'd have laughed if I weren't already about to cry.

3

As I was putting the finishing touches on the seating arrangements for our reception, a soft knock sounded at the door. Nan and Sharon had left to run some errands near an hour ago, which meant it was up to me to answer the unexpected knock.

I tugged the door open to reveal… no one.

Odd.

With a shrug, I began to close the door again, but a small voice stopped me.

"Excuse me. I was hoping we could talk, please, if you don't mind."

Pringle the raccoon stood on his hind legs, clutching a tiny envelope between his clawed fingers. I wasn't yet used to him being polite, but ever since he'd joined AA—yes, Alcoholics Anonymous—he'd really turned over a new leaf. I loved that he was following the twelve-step program to overcome his obsessive and often hurtful behavior, even though I felt quite certain the little creature had never touched a drop of liquor his entire life.

What worried me, though, was the fact that a certain militant seagull had turned him on to the idea, and since I knew that Alpha's revenge would find me at any moment, I'd become suspicious of everything my raccoon neighbor said and did.

Then I remembered that I had one more reason to worry—there was a camera crew currently filming in my yard.

I stepped out onto the porch and glanced every which way to ensure no one saw what I was about to do. When I was satisfied I had a moment's privacy, I pulled Pringle into the house and shut the door behind us.

He immediately turned back. "Oh, no. I am not allowed in the house. If you ever catch me in here again, you're going to turn me into Davey Crockett memorabilia, and I don't think I'd like being a hat."

My chest tightened with guilt. To be fair, I'd made that threat after he kidnapped Nan's Chihuahua, carried her up to his tree fort, and locked her in a live trap as part of his imaginary gumshoe game.

"It's okay when you're invited," I said with what I hoped was a beatific smile.

"Thank you. I shall remember that," the raccoon answered, so unlike his usual self I had to wonder if this was an authentic change or just another one of his role-playing antics.

Pringle bowed, then held up the card he'd brought with him using both hands.

I plucked it from his fingers and examined both sides. It was one of the RSVP cards Charles and I had sent out with the wedding invitations. Each of the meal options was checked off, and a giant muddy paw print filled the left half of the card.

"My invite never arrived, so I figured it must have gotten lost in the mail. I didn't want to bother you, so I waited until I could find a blank one in the trash, and then I filled it out so that you would know I'm coming. I would never miss your big day, Miss Angela."

Sometimes this little trash panda really caught me off guard. I hadn't sent him an invite because he's a raccoon who lives in the treehouse in my backyard—and also because I strongly suspected Alpha would use him in his plot to ruin the whole thing. Still, my heart went out to him. God help him, he was trying very hard to be a good raccoon these days.

"Thank you, Pringle, that's very kind. I see here you will be having the chicken, fish, *and* vegetarian options for your dinner."

His smile widened, showing off those sharp little incisors. "Yes, you planned a perfect menu. I didn't want to miss out on any of it."

I chuckled to myself rather than point out the whole point of having options is that so guests could pick the one thing they liked best.

"Angela!" my cat's panicked cry sounded from the kitchen. "Angela, come here right now!"

Pringle offered me a knowing smile. “Duty calls, I see. If you’ll just open the door, I’ll see myself out.”

I nodded and followed his instruction just as my frantic tabby bellowed my name once more. “Angelaaaaaaaa!”

“I’m coming, I’m coming,” I yelled, moving as quick as I could in his direction.

“What are these vulgar creatures doing drinking from *my* teacup? And eating *my* food?” he demanded, his tail flicking wildly behind him as he stared in horror at our two kitty guests.

“You remember Jacques and Jillianne,” I said, reaching down to pet each of Charles’s sphynx cats between their giant bat-like ears.

“Yes, I remember them, which is precisely why I don’t want them here,” Octo-Cat answered with a sneer.

“I don’t like him staring while we’re trying to have a meal,” Jacques, the smaller sphynx, said with a huff.

“I don’t like him in the same room as us at all,” Jillianne, his large black companion, added.

“And I don’t like them intruding in my home and then acting like I’m not even here!” Octo-Cat shouted right back, the fur on his spine now raised in aggression.

Well, this was not good. One of Nan’s errands had involved picking up Charles’s cats and bringing them here so they had some time to settle in before tomorrow’s ceremony. Seeing as I’d been so immersed in my own to-do list, I hadn’t realized she’d already deposited the two naked felines in our home—their home now, too, since Charles would be moving in, effective tomorrow.

"C'mon, Octo-Cat. I'll get you set up with fresh food and water in your bedroom."

His jaw dropped comically low. I swear it practically scraped the linoleum floor. "Me? You're forcing me to move? Why not them? Need I remind you, this is my house?"

"You know that Jacques and Jillianne will be living here now that Charles and I are getting married. None of this should be a surprise. You know—"

"I don't like his tone," one of the nudist cats interrupted.

"I don't like this place," the other added, and they both shuddered in eerie unison. "I don't like it at all."

It was fantastic that the sphynxes were no longer speaking strictly in rhymes and riddles. If only they hadn't instead defaulted to complaints as their primary method of communication. The two of them were dead ringers for Veruca Salt from *Charlie and the Chocolate Factory* these days, and I did not much care for that.

I turned away from J and J and focused my attention on Octo-Cat. He was rarely reasonable, but I had a better chance of getting through to him than my new step-cats—and here I thought our relationship had been progressing so nicely. "You have to be the one to go because you have your own bedroom that's set up perfectly to your liking. I realize you don't like the idea of sharing the house with other cats, but there's not really anything we can do about that."

The tabby gasped in horror. "You could not marry Up-Chuck

for starters, or we could send those two interlopers to the animal rescue."

"Well, now you're definitely going to your room. You're being very rude to your new siblings and need a time-out." Having said my part, I did the thing my cat liked least. I hoisted him into my arms and carried him up the stairs straight to his bedroom.

"You can come out after you've had some time to think about what you've done," I said, blocking the door so he couldn't run out and end his punishment ahead of schedule.

He chuffed at this. "I've already thought about it, and I still one hundred percent agree with—"

I closed the door between us, not having the time to listen to his spoiled rant. I could hardly take one cat complaining at me day in and day out. How on earth was I going to handle three?

4

Make that four, four complaining cats all under one roof on the day before my nuptials.

Because less than an hour later, Christine arrived from Colorado with Octo-Cat's girlfriend Grizabella in hand. Oh why did I have to invite everyone to stay at my place while they were in town?

True, I've got the space in my giant manor home, but the added complications of catering to all my out-of-town arrivals were not helping with my state of mind. At least having Grizabella there would help to calm Octo-Cat, or so I hoped.

"Come in, come in," I cooed to Christine, giving her a quick hug before practically pushing her toward the staircase. "You two will stay in Octo-Cat's room. Let me show you where that is." Usually I called it the "fish tank" room when talking to outsiders, but if anyone would understand my cat having his own bedroom, it was the show queen Christine and her retired prize Himalayan.

"I'm rather tired from all the travel," the gorgeous new feline arrival explained around a yawn. "Be a dear and fetch my brush. Not the one with the steel bristles. The natural wood, darling. Oh, I must look a wreck. What will my hunka-burning kitty love think of me in this state?"

Clearly my cat was beginning to rub off on her, because otherwise such a refined purebred like Grizabella never would have uttered "hunka-burning kitty love."

Anyway, no time to puzzle over that. I still had a to-do list a million miles long. So I stuffed the two new arrivals into the bedroom, reminding Christine not to admit the two sphynx cats under any circumstances, then ran back downstairs to my post. I'd done my best to stagger everyone's arrivals, but some flights had been delayed whereas others seemed to be arriving early. Definitely not helpful.

Another knock at the door revealed the return of the balloon vendor. "I'm all set back there."

"Great, thanks." I offered him a kindly smile and then shut the door.

He knocked again.

"Yes?" I demanded, perhaps a bit hurried but not unkind.

He took off his hat and wrung it in his hands. "It's just that you said you'd write me a check once setup was complete, and I'd like to avoid another trip out if I can."

"Oh, right, yes, yes. Give me five minutes, and I'll be right back with your payment." I shut the door again and jogged up the stairs toward my office where I kept my checkbook locked in the top drawer of my desk. You can never be too careful, after all.

Christine intercepted me in the hallway. "Angie, do you have any clean towels? I'd love to grab a quick rinse. Wash that plane stink off me, you know?"

"Yes, of course. How are the cats getting on?" I turned on heel to face her, which set me slightly off balance. Luckily, the wall was there to help steady me.

Christine laughed and rolled her eyes as she followed me toward the linen closet. "They haven't stopped grooming each other for even a second. I'm worried they won't be able to breathe!"

I chuckled, happy for them but also happy that I didn't have to watch their over-the-top display of affection. "Here are two towels and a washcloth. Bathroom's fourth door on the right. Need anything else while you have me?"

"A bottle of water?" Christine squeaked as if asking for this small allowance made her nervous.

I bobbed my head enthusiastically. "Yes, yes, be right back."

"You can just show me where it is. I'm happy to grab it myself. I know you're busy."

"Nonsense, you're my guest. I'll just run down and get you a couple bottles from the pantry and leave them in your room for when you're done with your shower, okay?"

I chugged down the stairs again, my breathing becoming

labored as I ran up and down and all around this place. On my return trip up the stairs, my cell phone jangled in my pocket.

I fumbled the water bottles in my rush to answer. "How's my bride to be?" Charles crooned in that lovey-dovey voice of his that has a way of making my knees go week.

"Better now that I'm talking to you," I gushed right back, ignoring the feline lovers as I set the water bottles on the nightstand for Christine and then closed the door firmly behind me once again.

He sighed, and I couldn't tell whether it was swoony or sleepy. His words cleared that right up for me, however. "You sound a bit out of breath. I wish you'd let me come over and help with all these last-minute preparations."

He was right. I was exhausted to the max, but I refused to waste even a second, knowing that everything I was doing now would help form the perfect lifelong memory for the both of us.

Still, I could take a few minutes out of my busy schedule to chat with my fiancé. Couldn't I?

I clomped up the stairs to my tower bedroom, hoping I could get some privacy there. "You know how traditional your parents are. They're not even arriving until tomorrow morning, because they don't want to risk seeing me before the big reveal. Your mother would lose her mind if she knew you got a sneak peek."

"She doesn't have to know," he teased, and I could just picture the mischievous smile stretching across his face.

"Ah, ah, ah," I warned playfully. "Mama Longfellow was very clear. We're not allowed to see each other for a full week before the wedding. That's the only way we can ensure a happy marriage. Don't you want a happy marriage, Charles?"

"I want my Angie," he said with a long-winded sigh. "I miss you."

"I miss you too. I love y—"

My phone began to beep, cutting me off. "Shoot. I'm getting another call. I have to go. Love you!"

"Hello?" a muffled voice rose from the other end of the line. It was vaguely familiar, but not one I could immediately place. "Angie?"

"Yes, hi. What's up?" I asked casually as my nerves once again began to fray.

"This is Reverend Stonehill. I'm so sorry to do this last minute, but I have an out-of-state family emergency, and well..."

I sucked in a deep breath, knowing what was coming next. "I'm not going to be able to officiate at your wedding tomorrow."

I held back tears and bobbed my head, using the repetitive motion to comfort me in this moment of despair. Reverend Stonehill was a man of God, and I knew he wouldn't lie to me. I also knew he wouldn't cancel without a really good reason. Whatever he had going on must have been infinitely more important and more time-sensitive than my ceremony.

"I understand," I said, working hard to keep my voice from shaking, my tears from falling. "Thank you for letting me know." After a brief pause, I decided to add, "I will pray that your emergency works itself out soon." It seemed like the right thing to say, given the situation and the person I was talking to.

We said a quick goodbye, and then I fell back on my bed, letting the tears fall in waves. Soon I'd need to put on a happy face and help my next visitor get settled in, but before that happened, I just needed to let it all out. I tried to picture my tears as a poison being purged from my body so it couldn't hurt me anymore. But not even that helped.

Just one more day, I reminded myself yet again.

One more day to forever. Now it was like a meditative chant.

Instead of *om, om,* I kept telling myself *one, one.*

Just one more day to go, then my happily ever after would begin...

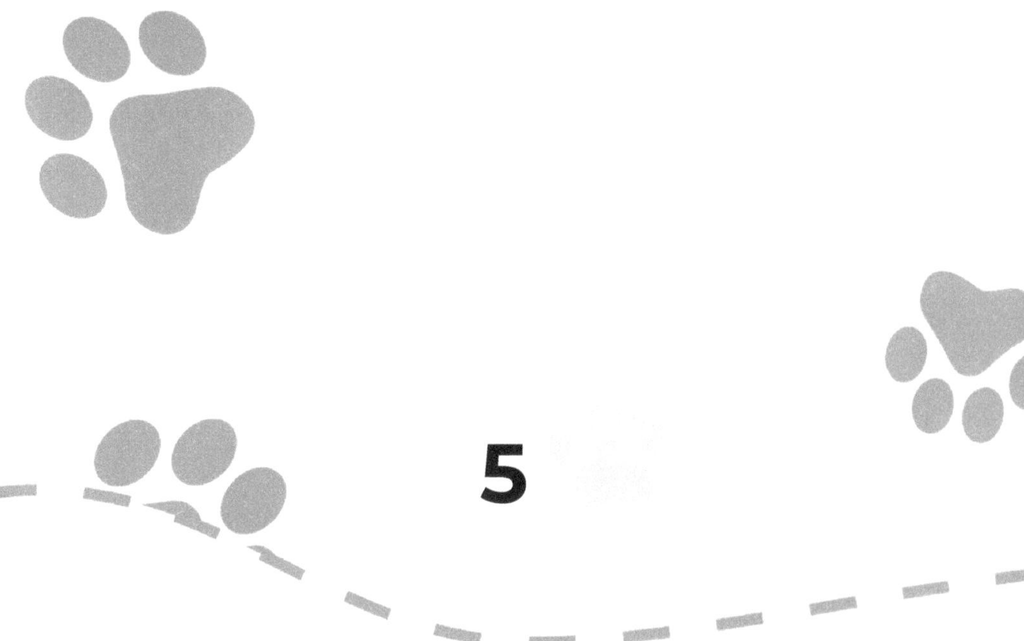

5

A soft scratching at my door pulled me from my woeful funk. "Paisley?" I called as I pushed myself to my feet and padded over to the door. I knew for a fact Octo-Cat was shut in his room, so it had to be our other furry roommate. I hadn't seen Paisley much that day, but her special brand of optimistic enthusiasm was just what I needed to start feeling better so I could get back to work.

But no, Nan's sweet little dog must have gone with her on errands, because Paisley wasn't the one waiting outside my door. It wasn't Octo-Cat, either. My actual visitors were far, far worse.

"I don't like it when she assumes we are a flea-ridden dog!" Jilliane said by way of hello. I was just about to defend Paisley's good, flee-free name when Jacques chimed in with, "I don't like when she closes doors and impedes our access. This is supposed to be our house now."

I bit back a sigh. Step or not, these sphynxes were my cat kids now. I had to make an effort to improve our relationship, no matter how much their complaints grated on me.

So I clasped my hands together and forced a smile. "Jacques and Jillianne, what can I do for you?"

"I don't like being bored," Jacques said with a groan.

"I don't like being cold," his sister added, and on they went with their litany of complaints.

"I don't like being hungry."

"I don't like how this place smells."

"I don't like how—"

"Okay, enough! What *do* you even actually like? Can we focus on that for a second please? I'm happy to help you, but you need to be a bit more specific—and also a bit nicer to me, please. We're family now, got it?"

The two cats sat in unified silence, staring up at me with large unblinking eyes. I stared right back, unsure exactly what game we were playing but also knowing I couldn't afford to lose.

After at least two tense minutes, they turned tail and jogged back down the stairs.

"I don't like her," they agreed in perfect sync. Well, wasn't that just perfect?

I waited to make sure they had gotten to wherever they were going, then descended the stairs myself. I was already way behind on my schedule, thanks to my minor breakdown. I really needed to get back on track. First I would—

"Angelaaaaaa!" my cat called as I passed his bedroom door. Oh, good gravy. More cat drama? Wasn't I the lucky one?

I briefly contemplated ignoring the tabby, but then he added, "I know you're out there, and I know you can hear me. Now come in here. We have something important to discuss."

I hung my head and sucked in a deep breath, hoping it would give me strength for whatever confrontation lay in wait. Then I plastered on a smile and pushed the door open.

"It's about time. I shouldn't have to call more than once when I need you," my cat chastised despite wearing a giant grin on his furry little face.

"What do you need?" I asked, too exhausted to play nice with him for much longer.

"I know you're under a lot of stress right now, Angela, but I have good news to share. I've asked Grizabella to marry me, and she's agreed." He turned to the newly affianced feline and nuzzled her cheek with his.

"That's great, guys," I said, and I really meant it, too. They couldn't really steal my thunder because no one else could understand their words or the change in their relationship status. "Congratulations."

"Yes, Grizzy and I are thrilled to be spending the rest of our nine lives together. We've been talking and—"

I let out an audible groan and began tapping my foot. *Oops.*

Both cats curled up their faces in disgust.

Grizabella hissed.

Octo-Cat said, “Oh, sorr-ree if our love inconveniences you, Angela. I thought you’d be happy for us.”

I signed again. Really, I was only making matters worse here. Why couldn’t I just silently nod and smile until they released me form this room? Me and my big mouth… uh, foot.

“I am. I am. I’m sorry. I’m just stressed about other things,” I begged them to understand.

“As are we, which provides a perfect segue to my next point. The two naked creatures can’t stay here. This is my house, and now we’ll need the space for Grizzy and her human to join us under its roof. I will consent to Up-Chuck’s *cohabitery* since he is your mate, but the nude interlopers cannot stay.” He lifted his chin as if to indicate the matter was settled.

Yeah, right.

I sighed heavily and wrung my hands. “I’ve already told you. Where he goes, they go.”

“Then I guess he goes too. Sorry, I know you liked him.”

I narrowed my eyes in disbelief. “Octavius, you’re being very unreasonable and very spoiled.”

The Himalayan showstopper gasped. “My sweet, does she always talk to you with such disrespect?”

Octo-Cat clucked his sandpaper tongue. “Far more than I would like, I’m afraid. I really need to train my human better.”

The two casts nodded in unspoken agreement.

“Great, well, I’m going,” I announced, stomping back toward the door to let myself out.

"I'm not finished with you yet, young lady," Octo-Cat roared after me.

I immediately turned back to glare daggers at my tabby. "You are not my parent." It was getting harder and harder to keep my voice level. In fact, I felt like screaming at the top of my lungs now. I honestly don't know how I managed to restrain myself.

"And a good thing, too, or you would be living in a constant state of punishment. Anyway, if you refuse to meet our very reasonable demand, then we have an alternate offer." The words came out of Octo-Cat's mouth but sounded far more like Grizabella to me.

"I'm listening," I managed to say without sneering. I hated giving in to this constant bullying, but at the same time, I'd gladly take an easy alternative if it meant getting him to accept the sphynx cats in our home once and for all.

"As you so astutely pointed out, you are *not* our child." He paused to nuzzle his feline fiancée once more. Both their eyes grew wide as they turned back to me. "You are not our child, but we *would* like to start a family. With your help, of course."

Well, this was not what I had expected. I needed to let him down gently if I could. "Um, this is kind of awkward, but Octo-Cat, you're neut—"

He cut me off with a hiss. "Don't say that terrible word. I know what I am, but Grizabella has done some research, and she tells me that it can be reversible in humans who change their mind about starting a family. I'd like to request that mine be reversed too. Grizzy and I would like to start our family right away. And we'd like to try for biological kittens."

"But, Octo-Cat, you're neut—"

"Bah! Don't say that word!"

Heat rushed to my cheeks. This was not a topic I enjoyed talking about with my cat and his girlfriend. Not one bit. "Your, um, procedure, is not reversible. They cut off your, uh, *hairballs* completely."

"I know what they did," he said stonily, staring off into the distance with unseeing eyes. "But Ethel loved me dearly—that was my first owner, darling—and as such, she must have saved them somewhere. Perhaps if you looked in the attic?"

"I..." I began, then, not knowing where to go from there, clamped my jaw shut.

Thank goodness, my phone buzzed with a text. I pulled the tiny screen out of my pocket and read the electronic missive that had just arrived from my mother:

Two minutes away.

A giant, enthusiastic smile bloomed on my face. It was so wide, my cheeks hurt, but I didn't care. I'd been saved from this awkward and un-reproductive conversation, at least for now anyway.

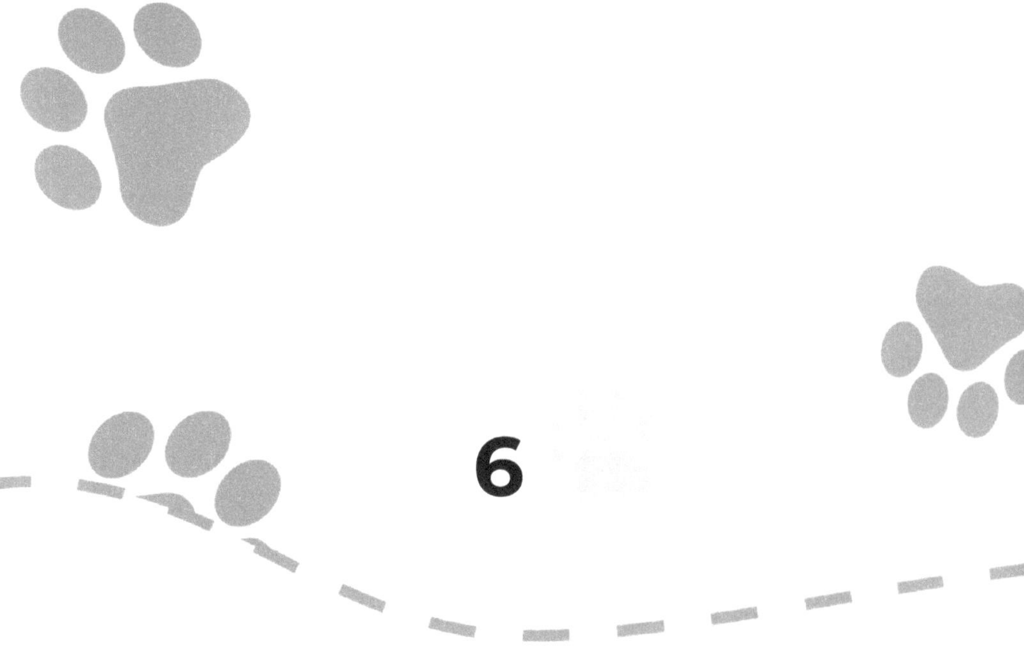

6

I stepped out onto the porch to wait for my next batch of wedding guest arrivals. A quick glance around the property revealed that both RVs had been parked somewhere I couldn't see, while the film crew had ventured into the woods that separate my house from the murder house next door. We hadn't gotten a new neighbor since the last one was murdered, and since two former tenants had been murdered within the last two years, I suspected the house was beginning to get the kind of reputation that would keep it vacant for many more to come.

I wasn't sure what the film crew needed in the forest, but I didn't have much time to wonder about it before a black luxury SUV pulled into my driveway and stopped a few feet from the porch. Dad parked while Mom and Grandma Lyn poured out from the back of the vehicle.

"Look who made it safe and sound," Mom crooned as I rushed

forward to dole out hugs. At this point I was grateful for all the excuses to wrap my arms around the people I love. So what if I'd given out dozens upon dozens of hugs that day? I still needed more to help soothe my tortured bridezilla soul.

Grandma Lyn only lived a few hours away from Blueberry Bay, but she was uncomfortable driving long distances on her own. As such, Mom had readily volunteered to pick up her long-lost biological mother and make an adventure out of it. And since she never went anywhere without Dad, he got to play chauffeur—a role he seemed to take very seriously, given the suit and dark sunglasses he now wore. From the looks of him, I guessed he was serving double duty as their bodyguard as well. I kept my laugh to myself. My family turned everything into a larger-than-life experience, and I was exactly like each and every one of them. I sure hoped Charles knew what he was getting into.

Just as I finished with the first round of hugs and went in for the second, a red Audi coupe zoomed up the driveway, parking right behind the SUV.

"Mommy, Mommy, we're home!" Paisley cried from the open window of the red car. All eyes zoomed to the little dog, sitting proudly on Sharon's lap in the passenger seat.

Grandma Lyn shot me a questioning glance, which reminded me… "Grandma, could you come inside with me for a quick sec? There's something I need to tell you one-on-one. We'll be right back," I promised my parents as Sharon and Nan continued to fiddle with something inside the sports car without exiting.

I pulled Grandma Lyn into the foyer and shut the door behind us. "There's a film crew here," I revealed breathlessly.

"You hired someone to make a video of your special day? Oh, what a great idea!" my bonus grandma said with joyful tears shining in her eyes.

"No." I dropped my voice to a whisper and pulled her close enough to whisper directly into her ear. "One of the guests brought a reality TV crew here. I didn't know until earlier today. We have to be really careful about, uh…" I paused and glanced around like a crazy person. "About what we can do. If they catch it on camera, it will not be good for us."

Rather than looking frightened as I was, Grandma Lyn actually had the audacity to laugh. "Oh, Angie. I've been keeping this secret for decades. Believe me, I can be discreet. Was that all you were worried about, or is there something more you wanted to say?"

"That's all," I said, both loving and hating how simple she made the biggest problem of my day seem.

"Then let's get back to the others." She put her hand behind my back and guided me back to the porch where my parents, Nan, Sharon, and Paisley had now congregated.

"What a lovely family you all make," Sharon exclaimed as I realized too late I should have confided in Grandma Lyn about Alpha and his looming threat to ruin the wedding. "Obviously this is your mother," Sharon continued on as she motioned from my mother to Grandma Lyn. "The resemblance is striking. That means the indomitable Nan must belong to you," she said, referencing my father.

Nobody said anything to that, but I watched as Nan's face pinched tight. She knew how much I loved her. Other than Charles, she was the single most important person in my life—and even then, she and my almost-husband were most definitely tied for first place in my heart. Still, she'd had a hard time since Pringle unwittingly uncovered her big secret: that she wasn't biologically related to either me or my mom. We'd only just recently reconnected with Grandma Lyn, and it had been wonderful to welcome her into the family.

Wonderful for everyone except Nan, who couldn't stop apologizing for playing accomplice to her old friend's scheme and for keeping the secret for so long. In all honesty, she never planned to tell us.

But the truth was out there now and we'd been reunited, making our one, big happy family even bigger and—for the most part—even happier.

"Oh, silly me." Nan bopped herself in the forehead, hard enough to leave a subtle red mark behind. "I forgot to stop off at the dry cleaner. I'll just go run out and—"

"No, the dry cleaner is the first place we went after dropping off those two skinny cats," Sharon rather unhelpfully provided. She blew out her cheeks and made a silly face. "Get it, *skin*ny? You know, since they're hairless and all!"

Nan completely ignored the poor attempt at a joke as she directed her gaze first to the ground and then to the front door.

"Oh, oh, the cats! Yes, I should really go check on them, make sure they're settling in okay."

"Nan," I called out before she could run off. "It's okay. Please don't go."

I thought Sharon understood our unusual family dynamic, seeing as she'd helped me suss out the identity and location of Grandma Lyn, but apparently she had too much in her head to hold on to this one crucial detail. Still, she hadn't meant to hurt anyone's feelings—and she also hadn't meant to upgrade my wedding from a simple circus to a three-ring affair.

I had to remember that.

True friends like Sharon came few and far between; I couldn't say something in anger and risk losing her just because I was feeling a little stressed out.

Grandma Lyn stepped forward and looped her arms around Nan. "We just stopped in to say hello and to see if anyone needed our help," she explained after pulling away.

I met Grandma Lyn's eyes, then quickly glanced sideways toward Sharon, who appeared to be puzzling over what was wrong with what she'd said and didn't notice the unspoken communication happening just in front of her.

"Sharon, was it?" Grandma Lyn piped up. "Why don't you come back with us for a little bit. I'd love to get to know you better."

"Oh, great idea!" I interjected, perhaps a little too enthusiastically.

Our resident reality star beamed. "Sounds perfect as long as I can bring my Chessy. I've already been away for too long, as it is."

"Of course," my mom and grandmother crowed in unison. The words were hardly out of their mouth before Sharon waddled over to the woods and began to call out for her kitty at the top of her lungs.

Well, that explained why the film crew had gone out the way. But why was Chessy canvasing the forest? Could he be in on the seagull's evil plot to destroy my wedding? I definitely needed to devote some more time to doing a bit of reconnaissance, but my day and night were planned down to the minute and I was already running behind schedule as it was.

I wished I could recruit Grandma Lyn to help, but I also couldn't risk hurting Nan's emotions any more than they already were. Plus I was still incredibly worried about the film crew, even though she didn't seem to mind at all.

Would I be like that one day, so comfortable with my gifts I no longer feared discovery?

I sure as heck doubted it.

At this point, I could hardly picture my life one day from now —let alone years and years.

Just one more day. I just needed to keep it together for one more day. Then I could reclaim my life for good.

7

Judging by the forlorn look that remained stuck to Nan's face, she and I needed to have a heart-to-heart, but unfortunately there wasn't any time for one. As soon as Mom, Dad, Grandma Lyn, Sharon, and Chessy rolled out, my cousin Mags and her great-aunt Linda rolled in.

"We're here," my fair-skinned, fair-haired, fair-everythinged cousin announced with aplomb.

"Let's get this party started," Aunt Linda trilled. Thankfully, they'd left their kitty overlord Shadow at home. Honestly, while I considered myself a cat person, I couldn't take even one more demanding houseguest without losing my ever-loving mind.

The arrival of my relatives from Georgia meant the last of the out-of-town guests due in today had now arrived. Everyone else would be coming up tomorrow, including a few who planned on flying. I sure hoped no flights got delayed last minute, because we were now less than twenty-four hours from the main event.

Yes, less than twenty-four hours to go.

This was not a drill.

Charles had invited clients, colleagues, and a few local friends along with his family from California, but most of the guest list came from yours truly. The animals I knew had all agreed to watch from the woods, so as not to arouse human suspicion. My friends Bravo and Abigull—the good seagulls—had done a magnificent job tracking down my former clients, witnesses, and accomplices. They'd even invited Gloria, the mama grizzly we'd helped in Katahdin, although I secretly hoped she wouldn't be coming for the sake of all the prey animals in attendance. Although maybe it wouldn't be such a bad idea to call the caterer and ask for an extra ten fish meals just in case.

"Angie, Angie, are you all right?" Mags asked, concern reflecting in her pale eyes. "You kind of disappeared into yourself."

"Sorry, sorry! Just a lot on my mind," I answered truthfully. Apparently Nan and Aunt Linda had already gone inside, because I now stood alone on the porch with my cousin. "How was the drive up?" I asked politely, even as my mind ran away with itself once again.

A dark shadow swooped overhead, and I craned my neck up just in time to see a flash of white feathers disappear over the house. Alpha, that had to be to him!

"It wasn't too bad. We stopped at—"

I hated to interrupt Mags, but I had no choice. "Did you notice any seagulls following you? Or like an otherwise unnatural volume of seagulls?" I demanded, alternating between watching the skies and attempting to make eye contact with my cousin.

Mags worried her lip before asking, "Are you sure you're all right?"

"I'm fine, so long as the seagulls don't ruin my big day—or one very specific seagull in particular." I groaned and shifted my weight from foot to foot. Everything was hurting now. When was the last time I'd gotten a good night's sleep? I simply couldn't remember.

"I guess that explains all the balloons. I saw them peeking out from the backyard as we drove up," Mags said with a grin as she bumped my shoulder. "One question, though. Why do you think a seagull is going to ruin your wedding?"

"Because he said he would," I told her, thinking back to that tense encounter on the pier. "Or at least he strongly implied it."

"We're all done for the day," a man called before stepping out of the forest. Right, the film crew. I had completely forgotten they were here, which meant I'd forgotten to be careful. If I made it through this ordeal—yes, that's how I'd now taken to thinking of my wedding—unscathed in the end, I'd be truly shocked.

"Great, thanks!" I called out to the reality show guys as Mags studied me curiously. Of course, she didn't know a film crew would be here because I hadn't known either.

"We stay too much longer, the lighting will be inconsistent for our shots today and during the ceremony tomorrow, so we're calling it for the day but will be back bright and early tomorrow."

Okay, okay. I didn't need a whole long-winded explanation. I just needed them gone, and they could take the circling seagull with them. I was just about to tell them as much when their front man asked, "Can you recommend a good restaurant where we can grab some grub?"

"Little Dog Diner in Misty Harbor. World's best lobster rolls," I recommended by rote; it had become such an automatic answer to that question I didn't even need to think about it anymore. At least the thought of my favorite lobster roll brought a brief moment joy and relaxation.

"We'll check it out. Thanks, and see you tomorrow!"

And just like that the moment was gone. I sighed as I waited for them to pack up their equipment in the RV they had parked around the side of the house. The fact I failed to notice it proved just how out of it I'd become.

"What can I do to help?" Mags offered. "Put me to work, even if it's just listening."

And that's when it all came pouring out of me in an angry torrent. I told her everything about the complaining sphynxes, the engaged felines who wanted to start a family, about the awkwardness between my two grandmothers, about the minister having to cancel last minute—

"Let me stop you right there," Mags said, placing a hand on each of my shoulders. "I can marry you."

I rolled my eyes at the suggestion. "That's sweet, Mags, but I'm marrying Charles."

She hit me playfully on the shoulder. "Not like that, weirdo. I can marry you both. I can perform the ceremony."

I stared at her, waiting for her to explain how that could even be remotely possible. Thankfully, I didn't have to wait long.

"Earlier this year, around Easter actually, I was doing this TikTok series where I sold blessed candles as part of our new Holy Smokes line. Well, it was a huge hit, and orders were way beyond what Aunt Linda and I expected. It became easier for me to get ordained than to keep visiting the local pastor every time I finished casting another batch. So, yeah, technically I am now a woman of the cloth, you know, in the loosest definition of the word."

"Mags, that's great." Finally one thing had gone right. Was this a sign the tides could be turning in my favor. "You are a life saver. Literally."

"I know," my cousin said with a proud grin. "I make it a point to be awesome. Now what else can I help with?"

"Actually there is one thing," I admitted before leading her inside. I thought I spotted another flash of white moving swiftly across the sky, but it could have been my mind playing tricks on me.

Anything was possible at this point, and that realization terrified me.

. . .

"So this little one is Jacques, and the big one is Jillianne. They're Charles's cats, and they live here now, but neither they nor Octo-Cat are very happy about it."

"I don't like how all humans look the same these days," Jacques took a break from licking his paw to say.

"I don't like that she's pawing us off on some stranger," Jillianne wanted me to know.

I worked hard to keep my composure as I explained, "The expression is *pawning off,* not *pawing off,* and this isn't a stranger, it's my cousin Mags."

"I don't like Mags," the larger cat said, then took a swipe at me as if to prove her point.

I shot Jillianne a warning look. Honestly, Jacques probably wouldn't be so bad if he weren't always following her lead. But I also had no way of knowing since it was absolutely impossible to separate them.

"They're from France. Their first owner was murdered, so Charles adopted them a couple years back," I continued to explain to Mags. "And basically they will not stop complaining. I figured maybe you could try to help them get settled in. You know, since you can't hear all the nasty things they're saying, maybe it will be easier."

Mags gasped. "They're saying nasty things? Are they saying nasty things… about me?"

"Noooo," I grimaced as I attempted this little white lie.

Mags caught on immediately. "They are, aren't they?" she grumbled, glancing from naked cat to naked cat. "Well, I guess that's fine. I can't understand them, and I can definitely take them in a fight, so there's that."

"I don't like that you're assigning us a babysitter."

"I don't like that she's talking about fighting us." At this point it didn't even matter which cat was saying what. I was so exasperated with both of them.

"Perfect. You're saving my life once again," I told Mags with an exaggerated smile so she knew how much I appreciated her. "Oh, and while you're watching them, could you maybe also just peek out the window every few minutes and let me know if you spot any seagulls hanging around?"

"I can," Mags said slowly, glancing toward the nearby bay window, "but aren't there good seagulls and neutral seagulls in addition to this one bad one? How will I tell them apart?"

Yikes, she was right. "Okay, scrap the seagull thing then. Just make sure you don't let these two out of your sight."

"You can count on me," she promised with a salute.

That left Alpha to me then.

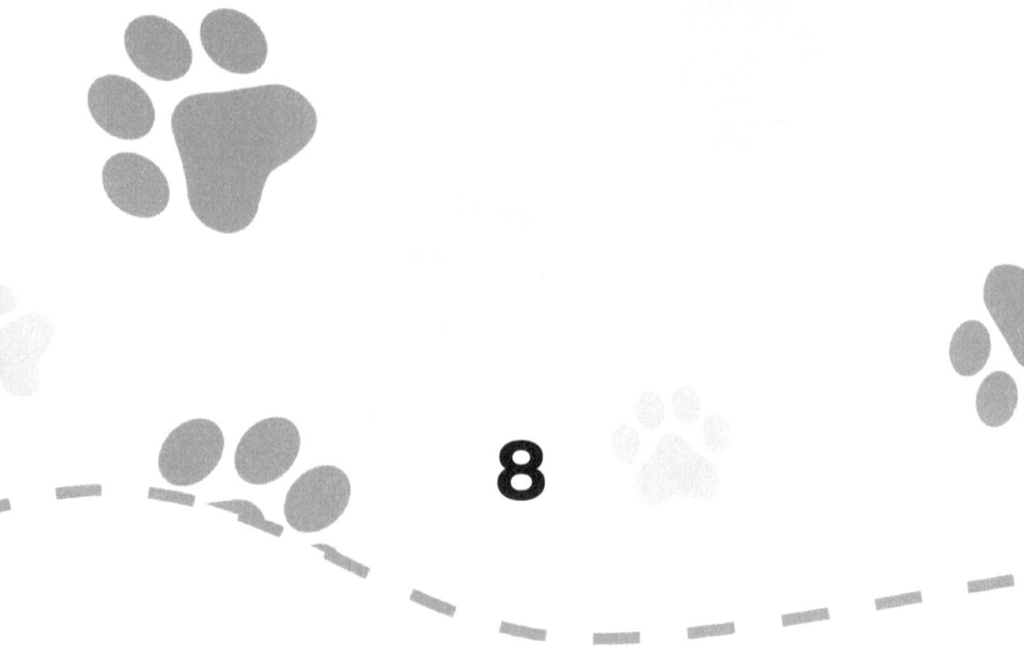

8

"Are you ready to do the final fitting on your gown?" Nan asked later that afternoon. Things had mostly calmed down now that both guests and vendors were done coming and going.

Mags kept an eye on Charles's cats as promised. She locked both them and herself in one of the spare bedrooms, telling me I was not to come in under any circumstances—otherwise I might spoil her special surprise.

Christine floated around the house offering help here and there, but after I declined her assistance a few times, she stopped offering it. It certainly didn't help that whenever she left the room, our Chihuahua Paisley ran over to bark at her and herd her back into the room.

"Am I helping, Mommy?" she asked me brightly, wagging her tail so fast it was a blur.

I nodded in response, just to be on the safe side. The film crew was gone, but Octo-Cat's girlfriend's owner didn't know my secret yet, either. She just suspected I was an over-the-top crazy cat lady, which admittedly was also true.

I'd spent most of the last few hours calling guests and vendors to make sure everyone was prepared for their part tomorrow. Thankfully, I was able to place most of those calls while pacing around the yard outside. Unthankfully, I hadn't managed a sure sighting of Alpha in all that time. I'd just need to remain vigilant.

But first, I had a dress to try on.

"I'm ready," I called to Nan, hanging up with the caterer, having just added those extra fish meals as a precaution.

"You look so beautiful in your mother's gown." Nan handed me the carefully hung garment and gave me a little shove toward the stairs so I could get ready. "This time we'll try it with the veil, too, so we can see the full effect," she added with a sweet smile.

As soon as my mother offered to let me alter and wear her dress, I jumped at the opportunity. Nobody was as happily married as my parents—at least not anyone that I knew. That was part of the reason I became so close with Nan growing up. Mom and Dad were always an item, so wrapped up in each other. That left me and Nan as a de facto couple ourselves. She and I have been best friends as long as I can remember, and that was never going to change even after I became a Mrs.

And I could use this final fitting to tell her precisely that. After the awkward exchange with Sharon on the porch, I knew she needed it. That's probably why I rushed when putting on my dress, not even bothering to look at myself in the mirror before bustling back down the stairs.

"I've been thinking," I began, "and I just want you to know that—"

"Oh, Angie! Oh, dear!" Nan exclaimed, bringing both hands to her face, which was growing pale with horror. "What happened to your dress?"

My eyes searched hers for answers. Was this some kind of joke? Because it wasn't very nice, and it wasn't at all like my sweet nan. Perhaps the stress of the day was getting to her as well? I pursed my lips, unsure of what to say.

Nan raised a shaking finger and pointed to my ivory silk train. I twisted to see better and found that in addition to the lace trim and delicate beading, an unexpected new embellishment had been added—long, angry claw marks tore at the fabric, ripping clean through in several places.

My mother's dress! My dress! My big day! Noooooo!

This time when the tears started to fall I was not the least bit surprised. As the salty signs of my sadness rolled down my cheeks, Pringle entered from the kitchen, carrying with him a snack-sized bag of Cheetos.

My eyes grew wide as I watched the raccoon lick orange powder from his black fingers. "Pringle!" I shouted. "How could you?"

He gulped. "How could I what? Oh, I found these in the trash. Someone started but didn't finish them. I didn't take anything new, I promise. Did you know there was a reality show crew here earlier? It's like all my prayers have been answered. Now I Just have to get them to realize I'm a star in the making, and—"

"Why are you in my house?" I demanded, stomping my foot like a fighting bull.

He smiled, completely unaware of the rage bubbling up inside me. "I was invited. You said as long as I was invited, it was okay to come inside."

I turned sharply, and my dress swirled behind me. "Look at it. It's ruined! Why would you do this to me? Why?"

Now he got it, but he seemed more confused than anything. Probably wondering how he was stupid enough to get caught. Surely, he knew what he'd done was wrong. Yet his words suggested otherwise. "Miss Angela, I didn't touch your dress, I swear. I would never—"

"Out!" I cried, stomping toward the door and flinging it open so hard it hit the wall. "Get out now, and don't bother coming to the ceremony or the reception tomorrow. You will not be welcomed!"

The raccoon intruder dropped the snack bag to the floor and hung his head, then proceeded to stumble toward the door on two legs, looking very much like a depressed *Peanuts* character as he went.

As soon as he was out, I slammed the door behind him. Well, I'd been waiting and waiting, and now this was it. This was Alpha's revenge. The worst part was that Pringle hadn't even realized he'd done anything wrong. I don't know what kind of mind control the evil seagull had managed to exert over the raccoon, but his plan had worked perfectly. He'd recruited an inside man—or at least an animal with relatively easy access to the house—and then he'd gotten him to destroy the one part of the wedding that couldn't be salvaged.

Nan came over and wrapped her arms around me, then hugged me while I shook and cried and cursed the day I ever met that trouble-making raccoon.

"I know someone who can fix it," Nan whispered once my sobs began to slow. "It won't be cheap and it won't be fast, but we can still save the dress."

"In time for the ceremony tomorrow?" I asked, blinking up at her.

She pressed her lips together and shook her head, revealing that tears were shining in her eyes as well. "No, honey, but look at the bright side." She placed her hand under my chin and turned me toward her so our eyes met. "You now have the perfect excuse to renew your vows later—perhaps on your one-year anniversary—and you've also got the perfect dress to do it in."

Instead of having the intended effect, however, that made me cry even harder. I still wasn't sure I'd survive the first wedding. Why on earth would I voluntarily submit myself to a second?

"What do I do now?" I sobbed and accepted a tissue from the box Nan now held out before me. "I can't get married in my pajamas."

She shook her head and pushed a loose strand of hair behind my ear. "Charles loves you. Not some dress. Trust me, honey, it won't matter what you wear as long as you show up at the altar."

I smiled. She was trying so hard to put her own issues aside to help me. At the very least, I could stop worrying about Alpha's revenge now. He'd definitely gotten it, all right. That meant I had no more unknowns to contend with, right? That everything would now go according to plan?

"This is *not* unfixable," Nan insisted, grabbing my hand and squeezing it in hers. "As far as I'm concerned you have plenty of options. Let's see, you could borrow a different dress from your mother. I can stay up all night to make the alterations. I don't mind at all. Or we could borrow a dress from the local theater company. They still have some nice gowns from last month's production of *Fiddler*, and you're roughly the same size as Tzeitel, I'd say. Of course, you could wear a dress you already have, or—oh—we could drive down to the city and do some shopping. We have plenty of time. We can—"

"Nan," I interrupted with a soft laugh. Suddenly I knew exactly what to do. It wasn't the original plan, but I loved it all the same. "I love you, and I appreciate you, but we don't need to do any of that."

"We don't?" she asked, tilting her head in question.

"Nope, I have the perfect idea."

9

It took me a couple hours to hunt down my replacement wedding gown that night, which meant I didn't get to bed until late. I'd hoped to spend some time chatting with Mags, but when I rapped softly on her door, only the sounds of her snoring greeted me. Poor thing seemed just as exhausted as I felt.

I stopped by Christine's room to say good night and make sure the cats weren't being too much trouble, but she just shooed me away. "The cats and I are fine. Go get your beauty rest, wifey!"

Before I could turn to leave, however, Octo-Cat wedged himself in the open door. "We still need to finish our talk," he informed me rather ominously.

"No, no, kitty!" I said in a squeaky baby voice that people tended to use with their pets. "You need to stay in here tonight."

"I will end you," Octo-Cat growled but fell back a few steps, allowing my escape.

"And next time we talk, I won't be so agreeable!" he called after me through the closed door.

Cats. They were so delusional, every single one of them. And now I'd be owned by three—one of whom liked me okay some of the time and two who actively protested my very existence. *Joy.*

After that, I took a quick rinse-off in the shower, imagining all my worries being cleansed from my body and sucked down the drain. I guess I must have inadvertently picked up a meditation technique or two from Nan over the years. Whatever the case, all these visualization tools were definitely helping curtail my anxiety now. Maybe it wouldn't hurt to join her for yoga a couple times a week going forward.

Soon I would probably take any excuse to spend time with my grandmother BFF. As excited as I was for Charles to move in, I would really miss Nan and Paisley. Maybe I could talk to her about setting up a home office for me over at her place so that I'd have an excuse to spend my days with her. Huh, that wasn't such a bad idea. I might actually guilt myself into getting more work done that way too.

With happy visions of days with Nan and nights with Charles playing in my head, I felt surprisingly calm and happy, considering the way much of the day had played out until now. It didn't take long for me to drift off to dreamland, knowing that the next time I opened my eyes it would be on the happiest day of my life.

. . .

I awoke to the sound of hushed whispers. The digital clock on my nightstand had just flipped over to midnight, which technically made it my wedding day.

More whispers invaded my consciousness.

I couldn't tell whether they were coming from outside my window or outside my door. When I got up to check, I saw no one. Hmmm, maybe I was hearing the termites in the floorboards. I hadn't been able to speak with insects before, but why wouldn't my strange gift suddenly grow more powerful at the worst possible time and without any explanation at all?

I strained to hear the whispered words but only grabbed bits and pieces of the conversation. "You go… then I'll… and after that… surprise." Soft giggles punctuated that last bit.

Maybe Mags and Nan were conspiring on that surprise my cousin had mentioned. Yeah, that could definitely be what was going on here. After all, why did strange whispers at night have to mean trouble?

I sorely needed to change my mindset. In fact, I would channel my favorite Chihuahua. I would choose optimism and joy over fear and anxiety.

This was my wedding day, after all, and it was going to be perfect…

Or at the very least, survivable.

. . .

I woke up to the ringing of my phone, but before I could answer it, the power zapped from the screen. Shoot. I must have forgotten to charge it last night. I plugged it in and then drifted downstairs to see what the rest of the household was up to.

After putting on a pot of coffee, I went outside with Paisley for her good-morning pee. Nan either wasn't awake yet or had already headed off on one last-minute errand or another. She'd left a nice quiche warming in the oven for me, so I poured myself a cup of coffee and dug in.

Wait a second...

I put on a pot of coffee.

I poured myself a cup.

I was cured!

Or at least my anxiety over the wedding was so extreme, I'd forgotten all about my other very rational fear. I'd been zapped unconscious by a coffeemaker roughly two years ago—that's what gave me my ability to talk first to Octo-Cat and then all animals. And I'd been too afraid to touch the demonic brew machine since...

Until now, that is.

Well, thank heavens for small wonders—or in this case, big ones.

I decided to take my accidental self-sufficiency as a sign. God and the universe were on my side today, and now Charles and I could get hitched without any further hitches.

I chuckled with an almost manic joy as I poured myself a

second cup of Colombia dark roast, then floated upstairs as if walking on clouds. My phone had gotten enough of a charge now for me to carefully power it back on—and see that I had missed seven calls, all from an unidentified number. Crud.

I didn't have any voicemails waiting for me, and no new texts either. Whatever these calls were about, I hoped they weren't important. Or rather I chose to believe they weren't.

I'd spent all yesterday worrying and waiting for things to go wrong. Today I wasn't going to waste any more energy on it.

Anyway, prep time was officially up for me. I couldn't go out and run random errands to fix things. I was stuck playing hide-away bride until at last that wedding march welcomed me down the aisle.

It felt strange to have nothing to do after spending all week running around like a headless chicken. True, I would have to get myself dressed and made up, but that wouldn't take long, especially not with Nan, Mags, Mom, and Grandma Lyn to help.

Unsure of what else to do with myself, I placed a call to Charles, just wanting to hear his voice. The next time we spoke after this, he would be my husband—*my husband!*

Instead of my intended, however, his mother was the one to pick up the phone. "Good morning, daughter-in-law," she answered chummily. "Did you forget you're not supposed to speak to Charles until it's time to say I do?"

Oops, I hadn't realized they'd be flying in so early. Charles must have been up in the wee hours to collect them from the airport.

"We don't need luck," I said with a dreamy smile. "We have love."

My future mom-in-law chuckled good-naturedly. "Just a few more hours, love, then he'll be all yours for as long as you want him."

We said goodbye and hung up. Even though I was a little irritated by Charles's mom playing gatekeeper to our communications, I could respect her traditions. And she was right. It wouldn't be long now.

The countdown had shifted from days to mere hours. Just three hours and twenty-six minutes until *I do*.

And as excited as I was for the main event, even I could handle that short of a wait.

10

I padded downstairs to see what everyone was up to. Surely, I couldn't be the first one up. That never happened around here.

I didn't find any of our overnight guests milling about the main floor, but I did spot the TV crew floating around the front yard as if one in mind and body. They had their equipment trained on the long-haired white cat while Sharon spoke animatedly from the sidelines. Whether she was trying to encourage her feline or steal attention, I couldn't say for sure. It made me wonder what Chessy thought of all the constant fanfare. I hadn't had the opportunity to ask him and doubted I would find it. If Octo-Cat were the star of his own show, he'd probably love the adulation but hate the intrusion on his schedule. No, if we were to one day share our exploits with the world, he'd probably prefer a different medium.

Maybe a book series.

I smiled to myself as I headed to the kitchen to pour yet another cup of coffee. I'd need all my strength and energy today, no matter where it came from.

"Oh, good. There you are!" Nan shouted, rushing into the kitchen as if I'd been the one in hiding.

"Here I am," I agreed.

"Well, what are you waiting for? Let's get you gussied up." She took the mug from my hands, set it on the counter, and then yanked me toward the main stairway. We went to Nan's bedroom where a host of cosmetic and hair styling supplies had been set up at her old-fashioned vanity. Grandma Lyn stood waiting by the large picturesque window where Nan typically worked on her various arts and crafts.

"We're going to tag team this one. Right, Marilyn?" Nan said, pulling out the chair in front of the vanity and motioning for me to sit.

Grandma Lyn came over and set a hand on my shoulder, watching our reflection in the oversized mirror. "That's right, Dorothy."

It made sense that they'd call each other by their first names, but it still felt weird to hear them speak so formally, yet so chummily at the same time.

"I've got the hair," Nan said, grabbing a curling iron and clicking it like a hungry crocodile.

"And I'll do your makeup," Grandma Lyn supplied without taking up any props to prove her point.

This was a good arrangement. I'd been worried that my former Broadway actress nan would attempt to put me in full stage makeup or use the hot pink lipstick she tended to prefer these days. Grandma Lyn's style was much more understated. It had to be, since she'd been hiding a huge part of who she was for decades.

"Where's your dress?" Grandma Lyn asked as she studied the array of cosmetics laid out on the vanity. "Dorothy told me what happened on our drive over. Such a shame."

I nodded and stretched my neck to either side, enjoying the last few precious minutes of free mobility before I was twisted and prodded and warned to keep still. "I'll put it on after we're done. I want it to be a surprise."

"Don't we get a sneak peek?" she asked with a teasing smile.

"Nope. You'll have to wait along with everyone else." I shook my head, drawing an annoyed tsk from Nan who had just started dragging a brush through my sandy locks.

"I still can't believe the raccoon would do such a thing. I thought you said he was turning over a new leaf?" Nan added with a frown.

"Um." I paused and glanced around the room. "Hey, Grandma Lyn, can you close that window?" I nodded toward it, upsetting Nan's progress on my hair once more. Still, I had to make sure there was no way this conversation could be inadvertently recorded for the reality show finale.

My grandma crossed the room and pushed the window shut, locking it for good measure. "I do always love hearing about the local animal drama. So many similarities, but also so much regional flavor." Her eyes glinted as she returned to us at the vanity.

"Well, Pringle—that's the raccoon that lives out back—he's always been pretty nosy. That's how we found out about..." I was about to say that's how we found out about her, my long-lost biological grandmother, but I didn't want to upset Nan. "Never mind."

I moved on quickly, hoping my faux pas went unnoticed. "He's started watching the local AA meetings through the church window and is going through the twelve-step program."

"That's a good thing, right? If only all raccoons attended such meetings, the world would be a much less chaotic place. When I started renting my last house, I chose a neighborhood far from the woods, hoping it would mean fewer masked gossipmongers, but no such luck."

"Right." I glanced at Nan in the mirror. She appeared to be following along just fine as she began to part and pin my hair. "Well, it would be a good thing, if he hadn't been directed to join by Alpha. He's a seagull I've kind of made an enemy of. And he threatened to ruin the wedding just days before *helping*"—I made air quotes here—"Pringle get his behavior under control."

Grandma Lyn's eyes grew wide as she took it all in. "Oh, so you think the bird is not-so-secretly controlling the critter."

"Bingo." I made a finger gun and pointed to her in the mirror.

"Poor raccoon. Doesn't know enough to know he doesn't know much of anything," Grandma Lyn said with a sigh.

Nan remained contemplative as she worked my tresses. "I just don't know, sweetie. While I can't speak to the animals personally, I feel like I know them well. And Pringle has a vivid imagination, sure, but he'd never intentionally hurt you in that way. He knows what a big day this is for you."

I shrugged. "I don't know what's going on, but we're past it now. You sent Mom's dress to your seamstress friend already, right?"

Nan nodded while Grandma Lyn rifled through the cosmetics and selected a bottle of creamy foundation and a foam beauty blender to get her work started.

I smiled, choosing once again to focus on the positive, lest I allow the anxiety to consume me as it had for much of yesterday. "So it might not all be going to plan, but it is all going well. I'll be fine. The wedding will be fine. At least I don't have to worry about anything else going wrong now that Alpha's gotten his revenge, right?"

I glanced in the mirror expecting to see twin nods of approval, but instead Nan's face blanched right before my eyes.

"You're mostly right, dear, but there is just one last little thing you should know," she mumbled.

Uh-oh. I took a deep breath and braced myself for the bad news I knew I was about to receive.

"Both the rings for you and Charles... Well, they've gone missing, it seems. But we'll find them! I've recruited Christine to help since your cousin is still working on that surprise for you. But if we don't find them in time for the ceremony, I have other rings you can borrow, your grandfather's and mine, actually. So see? It will still be special. And you can use your own rings when you do your renewals wearing your mother's dress, and—"

"Nan," I interrupted, otherwise she may have continued rambling straight up until it was time for me to walk the aisle. My heart dropped, but I quickly picked it back up off the floor. "The rings probably went missing last night, but we didn't notice because of the dress drama. But it's okay. I'd love to borrow your rings. Thank you for offering them."

She studied me for a moment. "Are you sure?"

"Super sure," I said with an enthusiastic grin. "But maybe we could listen to one of your guided meditation tapes while we finish getting ready?"

11

I blinked at myself in the mirror that hung over Nan's antique vanity.

"Well, Angie. Do you like it?" Grandma Lyn asked with bated breath.

Nan held a hand mirror up so I could see my formal updo from all sides. She'd really outdone herself with this one. Soft curls had been worked into a stylish bouffant with sprigs of baby's breath forming a crown around the edges.

"You two could go into business together," I said with a huge grin as I blinked slowly to admire the deftly applied eye shadow. "I don't think I've ever felt so glamorous in my entire life."

Both women clasped their hands together and cooed happily—showing they were more alike than different, just as I'd always known. Maybe they were finally starting to realize that too.

"Now if you'll just let me fit your veil into place..." Nan

jogged over to her bed and lifted the delicate lace accessory from the mattress.

"Your groom is going to lose his mind when he sees you walking toward him down that aisle," Grandma Lyn assured me before both women got to work securing the veil beneath my bouffant.

My heart thrummed with anticipatory bliss. I couldn't wait for the main event, but in the meantime, this moment was its own kind of perfect too. Ever since Grandma Lyn had entered our lives, I'd desperately hoped my two grandmothers could put their divisive past behind them so we could move toward a unified future.

I was just about to say something extremely profound to mark the moment—I'm sure of it—but then my phone rang on the vanity, splintering that picture-perfect moment.

"Oh, could one of you get that?" I begged, realizing I was stuck in place until the veil had been fully secured. "I have half a dozen missed calls from earlier. That's probably them."

Grandma Lyn fumbled for the phone as Nan continued to work with the veil. She put it on speaker, and I said, "Hello?"

"Hey, Angie. It's Dana. We're in route to your place now, but I realized that my assistant forgot that vegan meal you requested in the warmer. If we turn around, I'm not sure we'll have time to complete our full set-up prior to the ceremony, which means everyone would have to wait before we could start the reception luncheon. I'm so sorry about this, but I wanted to call and check in with you before deciding what to do."

Oof, I wasn't sure what to do, but luckily Nan rescued me from having to decide.

"It's fine. I'll go pick something up," she offered with a grunt, a line of bobby pins stuck between her lips.

"Nan? Are you sure?" I pleaded with her through the mirror, not sure what answer I wanted. I did know one thing for sure though. "I don't want you to miss the ceremony."

"We still have plenty of time. Got a friend in the restaurant biz who owes me a favor. Besides, it'll give me a chance to check in on Grant. I haven't heard from him all day, even though he should've arrived at least an hour ago."

"I'll go with you," Grandma Lyn insisted as she plucked the various containers of makeup from the vanity and tucked them away in a nylon carrying bag. "Chores are more fun with company along for the ride."

"Okay," I said with a resigned sigh. "Thanks for the heads up, Dana. We've got it covered."

I only knew one vegan, but he was adamant and one hundred percent committed to his lifestyle choice. I didn't want to leave him out while everyone else got to enjoy their meals. Frank from the pet store was a newer friend and not one I wanted to make feel unwelcome, seeing how socially awkward he was most of the time. I considered it a huge compliment that the die-hard introvert was willing to face his social anxiety to celebrate my nuptials.

We hung up and Nan finished with the veil, then raised both arms over her head and let out a little victory shout. "Success!"

I stood carefully and hugged each of my helpers before

shoving them toward the door. "Thank you. I love you both. Now get out of here. We have less than an hour until go time, and I need to make sure you're both back and ready for the ceremony."

"Okay, if you need anything—"

"If I need anything, I'll ask someone else. Now shoo!"

The two elderly women rushed out, and one tiny dog rushed in. "Mommy, I'm here!" Paisley shouted by way of greeting. "Oh my gosh, you look so beautiful! Like a Cocker Spaniel or—" Her eyes grew wide with wonderment. "Or a Poodle even!"

I laughed. "Thank you, Paisley. I feel beautiful," I admitted. "Think Charles will like it?"

"He will love it! Although I think you look just as beautiful when you first wake up in your pajamas and your breath smells funny." Her tail wagged so hard, her whole body shook, meaning this was an earnest compliment and not a jab at my unpleasant morning breath.

I carefully knelt down to place a pat on her head.

Paisley shivered and shook happily, continuing to wag that tiny, mostly black body of hers.

I picked the happy dog up and stood again, moving toward the window. "What's going on out there? Anything I should know about?"

"There are men with cameras and big sticks, and a lot of people have started arriving. I've made sure to bark at them all for you."

I chuckled. "Thank you for keeping watch."

She stopped wagging her tail for a moment to say, "It is my sworn duty as your guard dog."

"Of course. What else is going on? Is Charles here?"

Her tail started up again. "I smell him here, but I haven't seen him yet."

We both fell quiet as we surveyed the yard from our secret spot in the window. I couldn't see much with the balloon canopy taking up so much of the area, but I could occasionally make out the silhouettes of people passing beneath.

Paisley's fur bristled and her body stiffened, then she let out a sharp, high-pitched bark. The kind she made whenever she saw another dog anywhere near our yard.

I took it to mean Nan's friend Gertie had arrived with her husky mix, Cujo. Yes, I had a lot of cats in my life, but relatively few dogs by comparison. The energetic Cujo was Nan's running buddy. He'd also helped me with a past case involving the former mayor and his kidnapped golden retriever. Ahhh, memories.

"Shh, shhh," I told the Chihuahua in my arms, stroking her back as I spoke. "They were invited, remember? I promise that no one is coming who shouldn't."

Paisley's ears drooped. "If you're sure."

"I am," I said, even though I wasn't. But who would want to crash a small-town Maine wedding in the middle of the afternoon?

Paisley fixed her eyes somewhere in the distance and spoke with a soft, even voice. "Will you still be my Mommy even after I have to move away?"

Ouch, right in the feels.

“Of course, Paisley. I will always love you, and I will always be in your life. But you know Nan is your human, right? She’s the one who adopted you from the shelter, and she’d be very upset if she had to live apart from you.”

“But aren’t you upset that I’m moving away? I am. I don’t want to leave.” These words were whimpered. If I wasn’t careful, I’d start crying too and ruin the makeup Grandma Lyn had worked so hard to set into place.

“I will miss you lots, but I’ll be by almost every day. It won’t change that much.”

“Do you promise?” She stared up at me with large black eyes shimmering with tears, just as they always did, no matter how she seemed to be feeling.

“I—” Before I could say anything, a loud crash sounded from the hall, drawing our attention toward the door.

12

"Do you think anyone heard us?" a voice whispered from the hall. It was the same one I'd heard last night, but who's was it?

"Probably not, but we should be careful just in case," a second speaker chimed in.

"Then we're ready for the next phase of the plan?" Was this a third speaker? It was hard to tell with how muffled the voices were coming through that door.

"Yes, I think so," one of them said, and then nothing.

"Hello?" I called out when the whispering subsided, but the speakers must have already left.

"Could you tell who that was out there?" I asked Paisley before setting her gently on the floor.

"No, I didn't recognize those voices at all," she yipped in apparent irritation with herself for not knowing. Sometimes she took her duty as watchdog far too seriously, especially since no one was ever afraid of the five-pound shivering fur baby.

“Well, let’s go see what all that fuss was about.” I strode to the door and pulled on the knob, but it wouldn’t budge. What the heck?

This was an old house with many updates and additions made over the years. Because of one such update, the door to Nan’s bedroom swung outward while most of the others swung in. I twisted the knob and pushed at the door, but nothing happened.

Okay, this was bad.

Paisley caught on to our current predicament and began barking, “Hey, everyone. We’re stuck! Help!”

I traced the room back toward the vanity and picked up my phone, but it was dead again. Okay, I definitely needed to upgrade to a newer model. This thing was not holding its charge at all lately.

Without a working phone, we were well and truly stuck. But surely someone would notice the bride was missing, right? Someone had to be coming to rescue me and Paisley.

“I don’t get it,” I told her after uselessly attempting the door again. “The knob won’t turn at all. It’s like we’re…”

A horrible realization hit me square in the gut. “Like we’re locked in.”

Nan had fished out the old skeleton key to her room and locked up last night after the disaster with the dress. “We can’t let the same thing happen to your gorgeous veil,” she’d reasoned, and I appreciated her so much for it.

She must have left the key in the doorknob, but who would have locked me in? And why the crash?

"Mags?" I called out hopefully. Perhaps she was still in her room working on the surprise she had for me. "Mags!" I shouted louder.

Well, if she was there, she definitely couldn't hear me. She probably had music on her headphones as she liked to do when she worked.

"Christine?" I tried. "Christine!"

This time I received an answer, though it wasn't from the person I was calling.

"What are you shouting about in there?"

"Octo-Cat!" I cried with relief. "Someone locked us in. Can you get help?"

"Just how is he supposed to do that, dear sweet child?" Grizabella interjected. "The only other person who understands us is currently unavailable. We just saw her drive away with the other old woman."

"I've got it covered, my lovely fluffiness," Octo-Cat said confidently. "Be back with help soon!"

I briefly wondered what my cat had planned, but it wasn't long before a giant commotion sounded outside. I cracked the window open so I could better make out what was going on beneath the guise of the helium canopy.

"Eat my hairballs!" Octo-Cat shouted and then laughed maniacally.

Another cat meowed angrily, then hissed.

"Why aren't you talking? Cat got your tongue?" Octavius teased.

Another low growl followed by a sharp hiss.

"You TV stars are all alike. Beauty without brains." Now Octo-Cat hissed, and soon the enraged utterances of two warring felines filled the air.

"This is gold! Are you getting this?" one of the members of the film crew shouted as the chaos shifted from the backyard to the front.

The front door noisily flew open, then several pairs of feet stomped up the stairs. This was my chance.

"Help! Help! I'm trapped!"

"You, zoom in on the door. You, follow the cats."

"Could you just unlock me?"

"Do you have the shot?"

Whoever he was talking to must have nodded, because at last the door unlocked and swung open.

"Are you okay? What happened?" the lead TV wrangler intoned dramatically, giving me no doubt that this crazed moment would be included in the final cut of their season finale.

"Someone locked me in," I explained, grabbing the key from the lock, then shutting the door between myself and the crew. "Thanks for the help!"

I could still hear them chattering out in the hall. "The bride locked in? Clearly someone doesn't want this wedding to happen. This is even better than I could have dreamed. You got all of that, right?"

The voices receded, and I slumped down to the bed to grab a moment's rest from all the excitement. Paisley must have run out in the commotion because I now found myself completely alone.

Still, leave it to Octo-Cat. His plan had been genius. He must have known the film crew would be unable to resist a good cat fight, and so he picked one with Chessy and then brought everyone up here.

"Hey, let me back in," Octo-Cat called from outside the room, his voice sounding strange. Oh no, I hope he wasn't hurt in all that. I didn't even think about the possibility that Chessy might be able to best him.

I pushed myself off the bed, already missing its comfort, then opened the door just enough to admit the two waiting felines.

Grizabella immediately took up the spot I'd just vacated while Octo-Cat stopped right in front of me and spit something onto the floor at my feet.

Not something. Two somethings.

The missing rings!

I bent down and scooped them up, ensuring they were no worse for the wear. "Octo-Cat, thank you! Where did you find them?"

"Don't worry about it," he said with a satisfied smirk. "I've got your back. Nobody messes with my human's special day."

I didn't point out how taxing his behavior had been just yesterday. Yesterday wasn't the big day, and now today was. I loved knowing he was on my side against any further drama. And even though I still didn't know who had locked me inside the room, I decided that it didn't really matter in that moment.

I could focus on my wedding, or I could focus on this random mystery. And I chose to be truly present so I could remember everything about this day for years to come.

"Nice rings by the way," Octo-Cat said slyly. "Grizabella and I will need something like that to mark our union as well. It's time I made an honest cat out of her."

I sat down on the bed beside Grizabella, and Octo-Cat jumped up too.

I stroked both of their purring bodies and smiled. "I'll be sure to order you both gorgeous bejeweled wedding collars straight away. I'll even let you help pick them out."

The purring intensified, telling me I had gotten my answer just right.

13

Nan and Grandma Lyn returned with the vegan meal twenty minutes before the ceremony was scheduled to begin. They said a quick hello through the door, then excused themselves to finish getting ready. Thankfully, Nan had had the foresight to bring her outfit to one of the guest rooms so she could dress in private—seeing as how we'd co-opted her bedroom as command central for use of its vanity and so I could avoid the second set of stairs that led to my tower bedroom.

With only a short bit of time left to prepare, I put the finishing touches on my gown while Christine and Mags got the cats ready. This included bathing the two sphynx cats, whose tortured howls of protest filled the whole house.

And before I knew it, a soft knock sounded on the door followed by my father's voice. "Are you ready in there?"

I opened the door to my parents' joint expression of love.

They were walking me down the aisle together, just like they did everything else that mattered to them.

"I know it's not my dress," Mom said softly, "But this is just as good. You look incredible."

I handed her the decorative bundle I'd put together last night. "Can you hold onto this for me?" I asked. "Make sure no one sees it though."

She accepted my last-minute arts and crafts project, and Dad offered me the crook of his arm. "Well, let's get this show on the road, kiddo."

My replacement dress didn't have a long train, so it was fairly easy for me to get myself down the grand staircase. Still, both parents fussed over me like I was made entirely of glass. Together we reached the main entrance. I could already hear the music playing softly, waiting to usher me down the petal-strewn aisle.

I hiked my dress up a little to protect it from the freshly mowed lawn, then stepped into the yard. Holding Mom's arm on one side and Dad's on the other, I made my way around the house, then gasped as the backyard came into view.

One hundred white wooden chairs stood in rows, flanking a long aisle. The sunlight streamed through the balloons, creating splotches of color that made the setting look otherworldly, and there, at the very end of the aisle, stood Charles Longfellow, III.

The love of my life, my future, *my husband.*

Tears began to prick at my eyes, but I didn't even care. As the cellist continued her beautiful song, I stepped forward, my parents at my side, all the most important people surrounding me to bear witness to this beautiful memory in the making.

Each step forward was a choice. I was choosing Charles, choosing our love, choosing to leave my old single life to create something new with my partner and best friend beside me for all future steps I would take.

All eyes were on me.

I briefly glanced to either side of the aisle, wanting to remember all the details for later, but it was hard to tear my eyes away from my devastatingly handsome groom. His dark, wavy hair fell in that same perfect swoop it always had, and his bright green eyes sparkled with mirth as he watched me watch him.

Mags stood beside Charles wearing a hot-pink pants suit that she must have borrowed from Nan. She looked incredible and matched the wedding colors perfectly. Nan and Grandma Lyn stood wearing light pink lace bridesmaid dresses, their walks down the aisle already complete. Grizabella's owner Christine was there too, dressed in delicate lace and wrangling the rest of our wedding party—Charles's and my four favorite cats. The boys, Octo-Cat and Jacques, wore hot pink bowties, and the girls, Grizabella and Jillianne, wore delicate pink dresses that coordinated beautifully with the other bridesmaid gowns. The female sphynx seemed quite irritated by the fabric against her skin—she kept nipping at it with her teeth—but Grizabella sat with great poise and obvious pride. The former show cat was no stranger to showing off her beauty for all to admire.

I felt a bit like a show cat myself as the audience oohed and ahhed and murmured soft words of encouragement and approval behind me.

I reached the aisle and took Charles's waiting hands. Mags began to speak, but I didn't hear any of it. My sudden inability to pay attention made me glad the TV crew was here, after all. I could watch my big day on repeat and observe all the tiny details later. Right now, I simply wanted to bask in the moment, in finally having arrived at this place with my very own Prince Charming.

I'd had a crush on Charles from the moment I first saw him, which happened to be when he stopped by the law firm where I once worked as a paralegal to interview for a recently vacated associate position. We started getting to know each other when he caught me FaceTiming with Octo-Cat at work, and he subsequently blackmailed me into helping with a case where a traumatized Yorkie was the only witness to a double homicide.

Speaking of, I'd already spotted both Yo-Yo the Yorkie and her human Mitch in the audience today. I was so glad they could make it, since they'd unwittingly played a huge role in the start of our story.

It wasn't until Octo-Cat was kidnapped by his previous owner's disinherited relatives that our tale turned to love. Charles helped me get my missing cat home safe and sound, and then we'd celebrated that victory with our first kiss. The rest, as they say, is history. It's been a wild ride, but one I wouldn't dream of sharing with anyone else.

"Angela Russo!" Reverend Mags shouted, startling me from

my daydream stroll down memory lane. “Are you listening to a word I’m saying?”

“Oops. Could you repeat that last bit?” Heat rushed to my cheeks while the audience laughed good-naturedly.

Charles chuckled too and mouthed, “I love you.”

“I love you,” I whispered back, forgetting to listen to Mags once again.

She waved a hand in front of my face. “Hello? Angie? Do you have vows or not?”

“Uh…” I had, in fact, prepared very personal, very heartfelt vows. They’d undergone at least nine drafts until I was sure they were perfect, but they also seemed wholly inadequate now that the moment was actually here. On top of that, there was an even bigger issue—I was having a hard time remembering them despite how hard I’d practiced.

“Uh?” Maggie prompted as she rolled her eyes, eliciting more bemused laughter from the audience.

“I just want to hurry up and make this man my husband,” I admitted breathily. “Can we skip forward to the next part?”

The way my guests laughed at that made me wonder if I’d missed out on my true calling as a stand-up comedian.

Mags looked toward Charles for his okay.

“I do,” he said without taking his eyes off me.

I squeezed both of his hands as a thrill rushed through me. “I do, too.”

“Well, I don’t,” rose a voice from behind the object of my

affection. I craned my neck but couldn't see who had dared to rain on my beautiful parade.

"Yeah, I don't either," a second voice chimed in.

And suddenly it all clicked.

The whispers in the night...

The voices I'd heard outside the door right before I got locked in...

I hadn't recognized them because they hadn't been speaking in their usual pattern of complaints beginning in "I don't like."

But this whole time it had been Jacques and Jillianne. At some point, the sphynxes had apparently made it their mission to destroy the wedding, and this right here was their very last chance to do just that.

Unfortunately for them, this bridezilla refused to go down without a fight.

14

I smiled nervously and glanced back over my shoulder toward Grandma Lyn. She was the only one other than me who could understand the animals. Everyone else in attendance just let out a collective *aww* at how cute the kitty bridal party was acting now that they had decided to get in on the ceremony for themselves.

It was good that no one else could hear their protests, but it still hurt my heart all the same. It was especially difficult knowing there was nothing I could do without risking revealing my secret for all our guests—along with all the reality TV junkies in America—to see.

"I don't like this house," Jacques mewled, stepping away from his spot at the altar and crossing in front of me. "And I don't want to live here."

"I don't like your cat, and I don't like you!" Jillianne followed her smaller companion as she hissed, finally alerting the onlookers that something might be wrong here.

Christine, our dedicated cat wrangler, reached for the sphynxes, but they dodged all of her attempts at capture.

I shot Grandma Lyn a pleading look. I didn't want her to miss the rest of the ceremony, but she was literally the only person who could maybe talk some sense into these two naked protestors.

She nodded and moved forward, but before she could cross the altar to the other side, Octo-Cat sprang into action.

"How dare you insult me, and how dare you insult my human on her special day!" he shouted, initiating a cat fight for the second time that day. His hair stood up along his spine, and his tail had grown fat and extra fluffy. "I don't like the two of you either, but I love my human and she loves your human, so that's that. Stop acting like spoiled brats, and fall in line," he growled, then swatted each of the hairless cats in the face.

They stared back at him and wagged their rat-like tails furiously. I imagined that if they had fur, it would also be standing on end.

"Make me say it again. I dare you!" Octo-Cat yowled, wagging his tail now too. I didn't think I'd ever seen him so angry before, and I hoped to never see him this angry again.

Paisley ran over wagging her tail, apparently having no idea what was going on but still wanting to be part of it.

Jillianne reared back and turned toward Paisley.

"Touch the dog, and I will end you," Octo-Cat warned, moving himself protectively in front of the Chihuahua.

"Oh, my man is so brave!" Grizabella swooned, then began licking her paw excitedly.

Grandma Lyn made a grab for Jillianne, and this time she caught the rascally creature. At the same time, Christine yanked Jacques into her arms. Both cats meowed their disdain, but neither managed to break free.

Leading up to the wedding, I'd thought the real threats to my happy day would come from a seagull and a raccoon, but the cats in my life were proving that nobody could out-drama a feline. I'd spent lots of time with Jacques and Jillianne during Charles's and my relationship—and especially since our engagement—trying to bond with the hairless duo. It seemed that all my work had been in vain. As hurt as I was now, I would make it my mission to one day win them over. They were important to Charles, so they were important to me, even if my two step-cats seemed to think I was working full-time to ruin their collective life.

Charles squeezed my hands, and Minister Mags cleared her throat, bringing all eyes back to her. "And that, folks, is why they say to never work with animals or children."

A few strained laughs from the guests punctuated her statement.

"Anyway, let me give you a quick recap of what we've done so far. In lieu of sharing their vows, both the bride and groom skipped straight to 'I do.' So this is the part where I ask anyone with objections to speak now or forever hold their peace."

"I object! Me! I do!" Jillianne shouted from Grandma Lyn's arms and was immediately shushed.

"Okay, no human objections?" Mags quipped, having no idea how right she'd just gotten it. "Then I now pronounce—"

"Wait, not yet, I object!" another voice called from the top of the aisle. Everyone turned as one to view the interloper, but this objection I didn't mind. Instead a huge smile broke out on my face.

"Grant! Where have you been?" Nan demanded from behind me as her boyfriend, the local jewelry store owner, paced quickly up the aisle.

"Dorothy Loretta Lee, it was so hard keeping this secret from you," he sang, striding forward as he reached into the breast pocket of his rented tux and took out a small velvet box, which was hot pink, of course.

"Honey, what are you doing?" Nan stepped forward cautiously and met up with Grant partway down the aisle." You can't just object to my granddaughter's wedding," she scolded.

"I don't object to the wedding happening. I object to it being over before I get my chance to..." He popped open the box to reveal an exquisite ring made of silver, ruby, and amethyst. "To ask whether you'd like to make it a double. Marry me, Dorothy. Right here, and right now."

Everyone watched as Nan lifted her hands to her face and let out a massive sob. Everyone fell silent as they waited to see what would happen next. Somewhere in the crowd, the reality TV guys were probably high-fiving each other over their good luck.

I watched with wide eyes, standing beside Charles, holding his hand as I myself waited for her response. Surely, Nan would say yes any moment now.

"Grant Gable, I am so mad at you," she said instead with a giant scowl. "You're interrupting my granddaughter's big day and stealing her thunder."

"No, no," I cut in quickly, dropping Charles's hand, then pressing a quick kiss to his cheek. "Be right back."

I stepped away from the altar and rushed toward my bewildered grandmother. "This whole thing was my idea," I revealed with a Cheshire grin.

Nan turned toward me with shock plastered across her made-up face. "What?"

"You're my best friend," I told her, as if something so obvious even needed saying at all. "And you know how I've always had a hard time doing anything without you. Well, when Mr. Gable told me he wanted to propose, I suggested he do it today. We already have everyone we love gathered together, right?" I handed her my bouquet and nudged her toward the altar.

"Is that a yes?" her boyfriend called from behind us.

"Yes! Now get up here right now before I change my mind." Nan's words were grumpy, but she wore the most enormous smile of her life.

"What do you say?" Octo-Cat spoke up from near my feet as the two brides, two grooms, and one ordained minister reshuffled themselves at the altar. "Care to go for a triple?"

I smiled and lifted him into my arms, handing him to Charles so that I could hold Grizabella. It was the best I could do for a yes without speaking directly to them in front of the cameras.

“Okay, I think we’re ready to continue now,” I told Mags.

“Never a dull moment,” she said by way of agreement, then returned her attention to the guide she’d printed out from the Internet. “Okay, folks. You’re now getting a two-for-one. Lucky day! Let’s take it from the top!”

15

I did.

Charles did.

Nan and Grant did.

And of course, Octo-Cat and Grizabella did, too. I'd have to make up a special certificate for those two crazy kittens later, but in the eyes of God and one hundred assorted guests, we were all now officially wed.

"You're my husband," I told Charles, rubbing my nose against his after he'd finished kissing his bride to the delight of all who had gathered.

"You're my wife," he answered with a toothy grin before claiming my mouth a second time.

"I said kiss the bride," Mags teased over the growing din. "Not have a full-on make-out session with her."

Charles and I broke apart, then kissed again.

And again.

And—you guessed it—*again.*

Everyone laughed. There was so much laughter that day. It's one of the things I liked best about it.

Grandma Lyn tapped me on the shoulder. "I'm just going to take the cats inside while you do your processional," she whispered in my ear.

Right, the processional. Okay.

I could see some of the guests starting to get antsy as they waited for Charles and me to make our ascent up the aisle. I motioned to my mom. "It's time," I called and gave her a quick nod of confirmation.

She jumped up and delivered the bundle I'd entrusted to her. Yesterday, after purchasing my 90s-tastic gown from the Salvation Army, I'd stopped off at the dollar store to stock up on supplies. The end result was a bouquet of multi-colored sharpies, each with a faux flower glued to its cap. The result was clearly homemade but also really quite pretty.

"You'll be first," I told Mom as Charles and I arranged ourselves beside the first aisle of white wooden chairs.

"First to what?" Mom glanced from me to the markers and back again. "You couldn't possibly mean—"

"I'm a living guestbook," I said, untying the crafty bouquet and fanning out the different colors before her.

"You'll ruin your gown," she warned, meeting my smile with a tense expression.

"Nah, I'll just make it better. This way everyone who was here gets to contribute to this special memento. Besides, it's going to look so cool when it's all signed! Now pick a color, pick a spot, and write on me, Mom." I nudged the markers toward her again, unwilling to flinch on this.

She shook her head and laughed. "You always did march to your own beat, Angie Russo."

"That's Angie Longfellow to you, missy."

We both tittered at this while she selected a place on my torso and wrote in purple marker. When she finished, I asked what it said, unable to make out the script since my sizable chest was in the way.

"That I love you," she said, offering both me and Charles a quick peck on the cheek. "And I'm so, so proud of you."

We hugged, and then it was Dad's turn. He chose red but wouldn't tell me what he wrote. He said I could find out later after I'd gotten changed into something else. When he moved on, Charles let me know that he'd written the classic Dad threat, telling Charles to treat his little girl right... or else.

Nan and her new husband stood beside us greeting each guest along the processional. Nan and I had many of the same friends to begin with, and I'd also helped Grant sneak in some of his friends without her noticing. Octo-Cat and Grizabella had been escorted back inside by Grandma Lyn and Christine, but I think they preferred it that way.

I glanced toward the woods and spotted a few of my animal friends watching from the protection of the trees. Irving the giant buck who had witnessed my former neighbor's accidental death stood with a family of squirrels sitting on top of his head. It was hard to tell for sure from this distance, but I think one of the squirrels was my old friend and helper Maple. It looked like she too had fallen in love and already had a huge family to prove it. Good for her.

A fluttering of white among the trees drew my eyes up just as two seagulls took to the skies. That would be Abigull and Bravo, my friends who had promised to watch from the woods. And so they had.

"You've got yourself a good one," Officer Bouchard told Charles as he clapped him on the back, then selected a black marker from my hands and stooped down to write a message near the hem of my dress.

I loved this.

The ceremony had been all about me and Charles, but now with the processional, I was able to focus on each of my guests in turn. I couldn't wait to celebrate with everyone at the reception. I hoped they were all having a great time, like I was.

It seemed that, excepting a few minor bumps along the way, this whole day had been filled with perfect moments from start to finish. And it wasn't even close to over yet!

"I love you," Charles said suddenly, then grabbed me in his arms and tipped me back as if part of a dance. If not for his strong arms, I surely would have fallen. Instead I got another earth-shattering kiss as I clung to my brand-new husband.

"Congratulations," a voice I hadn't heard in a very long time muttered as soon as we came up for air. It took me a moment to regain my senses, but when I did, I recognized the Calhoun twins —Charles's former girlfriend Breanne along with my one-time crush, Brock, who after being arrested for a crime he didn't commit had decided to turn over a new leaf and change his name to "Cal."

"Thanks for coming," I told them both, even though I wasn't super happy that Charles's ex had shown up on our happy day. I probably should have expected this, but it still mabe me wonder: Was she here to try to ruin something? Well, she could get in line behind Jacques and Jillianne as far as I was concerned.

"You make a very handsome groom," Bree said, placing both hands on her hips and drawing attention to her above-the-knee green dress, complete with plunging neckline.

"And we'll just be going," her brother said, yanking at her before she could try to lay a hug on my new husband.

"Thanks for coming," I yelled after them, even though I'd already said that once before.

Charles pulled me to him and pressed his forehead against mine, creating a little bubble just for the two of us. "Sorry about that. I told you not to invite Cal. He always shows up with her as his plus-one," he said.

"It's fine. She's fine," I said with a soft laugh. Charles had already chosen me over Breanne a thousand times over. I wasn't jealous of her desperate ploy for attention. If anything, I felt kind of bad for her. Hopefully she'd find love of her own someday soon.

I'd stopped paying attention to what she was up to after she and Charles broke up. As far as I knew, she was still in the real estate business and doing well.

Last I'd heard, her brother had given up his handyman gig and gone back to school. He wanted to be a lawyer now, imagine that. I guess being wrongly maligned and imprisoned gave him a deep sense of justice, and I admired him for turning his horrible ordeal into something positive for the world.

"Ready for me?" another familiar voice prompted, drawing Charles and me back to the task at hand.

"Bethany!" I shot forward and hugged my former frenemy tight. I hadn't seen Bethany Peters since she moved to Georgia to look after her delinquent cousin Peter, who had thankfully chosen not to attend today's ceremony.

"How have you been?" I gushed, thrilled to bits that she was here now. All that frenemy stuff had been nonsense. I wished I had taken more time to get to know her when she still lived so close. I couldn't change the past, but I could do better going forward.

Another vow for today, and one I intended to keep.

"We'll catch up at the reception," she promised. "Oh, and I brought you a special essential oil blend I made. It's for wedded bliss. Put two to three drops in your diffuser daily, and you'll live happily ever after."

"I will, thank you," I said as she signed my gown in turquoise. She'd always been oddly obsessed with essential oils, and while I'd never been a fan, I would happily take her up on this promise of wedded bliss.

Even though I highly suspected Charles and I would not be needing any help in that arena.

16

And then it was time for the reception. Thankfully we had a huge yard, so we simply had to shift the party over to where twelve circular tables of eight and one long rectangular head table were already set up and waiting. A bonus table sported a host of wrapped packages and a big basket where guests had dropped their congratulatory cards.

Charles had wanted to create a bridal registry, but I insisted it was way more fun not knowing what people might buy. Since I'd won that argument, I had no idea what types of gifts filled the table, but I knew finding out after our honeymoon would be great fun. One of the presents made me a little uneasy though. It was suspiciously wrapped in old junk mail circulars and not very skillfully at that.

"Do you think it could be a bomb?" the boom mic operator asked his buddies as the film men zoomed in on the odd present.

"Oooh, I hope so. That would be awesome!" another of his crew answered. Well, glad to know they were on my side. Entertainment over excellence, I supposed.

My mom had fully taken over MC duties from Mags now that the reception was on. She was quite comfortable in front of a camera thanks to her job as a big-time local news anchor. I assumed the TV show guys didn't know that—and that she didn't want them to—because they spent very little time focusing on her or my dad, the semi-celebrities in our midst.

They had figured out that Mags was something of an Internet celebrity, though, and had foisted their star feline Chessy into her arms as they recorded the both of them.

"Ladies and gentlemen, please welcome Mr. and Mrs. Charles Longfellow, III!" my mom announced in her reporter voice as Charles and I rushed out onto the shiny dance floor that had been laid in the yard for just this purpose.

Charles spun me to the delight of our guests, then pulled me close to his chest as our cellist began to play "My Funny Valentine." We swayed together, heart to heart, as Charles serenaded me with the song he had sworn would always be ours.

The music ended far too soon for my liking, but at least we still had so many more festivities ahead. Our guests cheered and started clinking their wine glasses, indicating that they wanted us to kiss. No problem there!

A second song began to play, and we cleared off the floor to give Nan and Grant space for their first dance as a married couple. While we'd gone with a timeless classic, they'd selected something hugely inappropriate that I recognized from the current radio hits. I think it was a Cardi B song. Either way, I did not want to know how or why this became my eighty-something grandmother's go-to love song. I did not want to know even a little bit.

When the music ended, Nan pulled me and Charles back toward the house. "C'mon, there's a surprise for you inside. We'll be quick, but I wanted you to see."

Back in my giant manor home, nothing was as I'd left it less than an hour ago. The furniture had been cleared out and a baby gate had been erected at the bottom of the grand staircase.

"Hello and congratulations!" Nan's friends Gertie and Pearl chimed as we went further into the house. Pearl had taken over at the animal shelter after the last director was caught embezzling, and Gertie had become Nan's closest friend thanks to all the visits that followed her early morning runs with Cujo. They stood beside a trio of incredibly tall cat trees that were ringed by several bowls of both dry and wet cat food. Some loose catnip had also been scattered on a large throw rug they'd brought, and I could already see Beans from the pet store rolling around and rubbing himself in the stuff.

"It's a reception for all our animal guests!" Nan announced proudly and with jazz hands. "Didn't want them to miss out on the celebrating."

I heard footsteps on the stairs and turned just in time to see Octo-Cat and Grizabella jump over the baby gate in unison. They walked side by side so close they were touching, then scaled the tallest cat tree and took up post at the very top. The two barely fit up there together, but somehow they made it work.

Nan leaned in to whisper, “I suspected he’d make your day all about him, so I figured we might as well give him a party too.”

I beamed and gave her a wink, letting my grandmother know just how right she was about that. True, she couldn’t speak with the animals, but she understood them all the same. I didn’t see the sphynxes anywhere, leaving me to wonder whether Grandma Lyn had shut them in a room so they could think about what they’d done. I hadn’t known her for long, but that seemed like the kind of thing she might do.

“Thank you for coming to our wedding celebration,” Octo-Cat meowed from the top of the tree. “You may leave your gifts at the entrance. And be warned, nobody look at my beautiful bride too long, or I’ll cut ya!” He flexed his claws demonstratively, and Grizabella nuzzled him with great gusto. Apparently she liked the tough guy act. To each their own, I guessed.

“I love it, thank you!” I gushed, realizing I hadn’t said anything at all. I’d been too busy taking in the spectacle.

“You’re very welcome, Angie,” Pearl chortled and fluffed her short hair. “I hope you don’t mind, but I brought a few adoptable pets too. Maybe you could just make it a point to mention that to the guests? It would be great to find these cats homes. What a way to leave a lasting mark on your big day.”

I agreed that of course I would make an announcement. I wanted the homeless pets to find their place too, but if you asked me, our wedding had already left quite a mark.

"We will do just that," Charles answered for the both of us, lacing his fingers between mine, then lifting our joint hands and placing a kiss on the back of mine.

"I wish EB didn't have to miss out," Grant said with a wistful smile as he talked of his gray rescue lop rabbit named EB, short for Easter Bunny, which is precisely what she was before he rescued her. "But she probably wouldn't enjoy hanging out with all these predators."

Nan rubbed his back and laid a head on his shoulder but said nothing.

"As the first order of business, I would like to uninvite all the dogs. Thank you for coming. Goodbye!" Octo-Cat decreed from his prime perch, then added, "Except Paisley. Paisley can stay."

"He's being a real piece of work again. Isn't he?" Nan whispered in my ear as Charles squeezed my hand knowingly.

I bit back a laugh. Yes, the people in my life definitely understood me, and I wouldn't have it any other way.

17

After our initial dances and a quick visit to the cat reception inside, it was time to enjoy the special luncheon our caterer Dana had prepared. Charles and I fed each other each bite like the love-drunk fools we were.

I did pause briefly to make sure Frank was enjoying his vegan meal after all the special measures we had to take to get it for him. He seemed happy enough with what looked like a mixture of beans and rice and fajita veggies. He caught me staring and offered an awkward wave before returning his full attention to the food in front of him.

I eyed the woods to see if my animal friends were still watching from the sidelines, but they appeared to have cleared out and gone back to their daily lives. I'd have to thank them for coming later. It really did mean a lot that they'd shown.

Pringle, for his part, had stayed away as I'd instructed. A part of me felt bad for exiling him, but I just didn't want to risk him ruining anything else—whether intentional or not. Nan believed he had good intentions, and based on the little show with Octo-Cat at the kitty party inside, she did understand the animals in our lives quite well. Still, I didn't know if I could ever really trust the raccoon again.

"Everything okay?" my husband asked after we'd polished off our shared plate of fish.

I kissed him, which one of our guests saw and began clinking her water glass. Soon a chorus rose up asking us to kiss again. Like I needed a reminder to kiss my husband.

"Everything is wonderful," I told him, still leaning in close. "I'm just thinking about Pringle."

A sudden wave of concern flooded Charles's shining green eyes. "I haven't seen him around. Is he okay?"

"Oh, man. You have missed out on so much, thanks to your mother wanting to keep us separated for tradition's sake."

He nuzzled my cheek, much like I'd seen Octo-Cat do with Grizabella. "Thank you for doing that. It meant a lot to her," he whispered, then kissed me again.

I leaned into him with a happy smile. "Of course. There's just so much to catch you up on, and with a certain film crew roving about, I'm not sure I can do it right now."

"Later then," he said with a dopey smile of his own. "We do have the rest of our lives together, after all."

"Ladies and gentlemen. Honored guests."

I glanced up to find Mags standing beside the cellist after

having coopted the microphone from my mother. "Just because the bride and groom chose to skip their speeches doesn't mean I won't delight you with mine. Buster, roll tape."

I had no idea who Buster was, but apparently he was listening because right on cue, someone set up a projector screen behind Mags, and a film began to play for all to see. It began with a photo of me and Charles taken at the altar, then splintered into hundreds of tinier pictures that showcased Charles and me both together and apart. The Frank Sinatra version of "My Funny Valentine" played in the background, but even after it stopped, the pictures kept flashing by onscreen.

Now that the music had ended, Mags took over narrating. "Big shout-out to Mama Longfellow who provided the pictures of Charles, and to the many, many folks who shared photos of Angie. This one's my favorite by the way."

Everyone laughed at the photo of me and Mags bundled up against the cold sporting red noses and hot cocoa at the holiday festival downtown where two people had been murdered in an ice sculpture garden—they probably didn't know about the murders that happened shortly after this photo op though.

"Aunt Linda is now coming around with some mementos for everyone," Mags boomed next. "Show them what you got, Aunt Linda!"

Maggie's great-aunt waved and then held up a gorgeous candle made in our wedding colors. The bottom layer was hot pink, the middle layer was an understated softer hue of the color, and the top had been cast in white. The finished candle had then been carved carefully to reveal a big cursive *L* protruding from the rest of the design. *L* for Longfellow. That was my name now. Aw, heck yeah.

"I want one!" I shouted, and Mags rolled her eyes. "Duh, I made a ton extra, and they're all yours. Light one each year for your anniversary and think back to this special day. Love you, cuz!"

She then went on to tell me in great detail just how much she loved me and how much richer her life has been since we found each other. Mom and Dad made speeches too, along with Charles's parents. It all boiled down to how much everyone loved us, thought we were a great couple, and wanted us to live a life of happiness and love.

All the speeches made me tear up, but it was Nan's new husband Grant who really pulled at my heartstrings. He took center stage with his bride, pulling her out onto the dance floor and holding one of her hands in his while hanging onto the microphone with the other. His words were projected for all to hear, but his message was clearly just for her.

"I know we don't have many years left, but I look forward to spending every last one of them… every last day, minute, second, with you. I didn't think there was anything left for me in this life, but then I found you and that all changed. I feel like a young lad again, and I'm the happiest I've ever been. Who knew that our golden years would truly be the best of our lives? I love you to the moon and back, Dorothy Loretta Lee Gable, and I will keep on loving you until this old heart can love no more. Until then, every beat will be shouting your name so that the whole word knows exactly who it belongs to. My wife. My best friend. My whole world."

I swear there wasn't a dry eye in the place after that one.

The cellist began to play again, inviting everyone onto the dance floor.

"I love you like that," Charles told me before offering another kiss.

"I love you like that too," I responded, and kissed him again. One day I would have to share the vows I'd written just for him. Maybe I could recite them on the long drive to our honeymoon destination.

The honeymoon was a gift from my parents. For one week we'd be staying at a stately old home in the heart of Richmond, Virginia. The place boasted an enormous garden made private by a tall brick wall around the perimeter. Somehow my parents had managed to book the entire enormous estate just for the two of us. It would be a bit of a drive, but Charles had insisted on road-tripping it rather than flying. We'd sat down together weeks ago and planned each stop along the way to extend our trip into a truly memorable affair.

We'd leave tomorrow morning since we planned on partying late into the night. Nan and Grant would have free rein of the place until our return. Before Nan had realized that she would be married too, she'd agreed to wait an extra couple weeks before moving out so she could pet sit while Charles and I were away.

Once again I found myself torn between enjoying the moment

I currently found myself in and anticipating all the good things that would happen next. First world problems, I tell you.

"Excuse me." Someone poked me in the arm as Charles and I swayed together to another one of Nan and Grant's questionable song choices.

"No cutting in. I'm not ready to let her go," Charles mumbled without even looking at the interloper.

"I don't want to dance," the other man said in a deep, almost threatening voice. "I want to be given what I'm owed, and I'm not leaving until I get it."

18

I stopped dancing and turned toward the man in shock. Charles continued to hold me close, protectively even. It took me a minute to place our unfriendly guest without his wares, but this was undoubtedly the same vendor who had taken several trips out yesterday to set up our massive balloon canopy.

"I'm sorry. What?" I asked, blinking back my surprise. He'd been so amiable yesterday, if also a little put off by my obvious struggle to maintain composure.

"You left me waiting on your porch for almost an hour," he sneered. "I told you I needed to be paid that day, and instead of saying you didn't have the funds, you ghosted me!"

"What? No! I paid you." How dare he show up at my wedding and cast insulting accusations at me like this?

"I don't like how you're talking to my wife," Charles interjected, fixing the balloon vendor with an equally hostile stare. "Either adjust your tone, or leave."

The other man scoffed, refusing to back down. "Well, buddy, your wife didn't pay me, and then she also wouldn't answer my calls."

I gasped as some of the pieces began to click into place. "Were you the unknown number? Why didn't you leave a message?"

"Your voicemail was full. I didn't even get the option. I did a big job for you, and I deserve to be paid for it. Now since you wasted my time by making me take yet another trip out here, I'm afraid I'm going to have to charge you an extra ten percent late fee. And if you don't pay me right now, I'll sue you for all you're worth and get much more."

My lawyer husband bristled at this careless and uneducated threat, but I placed a hand on his chest to indicate that he should hold his tongue.

I thought back through the timeline in my head. I remembered the vendor coming back yesterday and asking for payment. I remembered going upstairs to get the check, and then...

Then I helped Christine with one thing and Octo-Cat with another. I'd called Charles. I'd talked to the reverend who had to cancel. I'd lain on my bed and cried...

But I never actually went back downstairs with that check.

"Gosh, I am so sorry," I cried, and the aggressive vendor's face immediately softened and his words became more kind.

"It's okay," he said. "I could tell you had a lot on your mind, and I know how weddings are. But it's the end of the month, and

I need that check from you to make my mortgage. You understand, don't you?"

"What's the bill?" Charles asked with a sigh, pulling out his wallet. He still seemed rather worked up about the vendor's less than affable approach to collecting what he was owed.

The vendor told him what it amounted to, and Charles handed him a wad of cash. "Keep the extra. Sorry for the inconvenience."

"Thank you! Congratulations!" Now that he was paid, Mr. Helium was quick to depart.

"Why do you have all that cash?" I asked my husband, perplexed by the huge sum he'd had just waiting and ready to go. It saved me from having to run inside to grab my checkbook, but—as the kids were saying these days—was also a bit *sus*.

He shrugged. "Had a client pay yesterday in cash. I was going to take it to the bank, but then thought we could use it on our honeymoon for all the lavish dinners and spa treatments we plan on having."

"I like how you think," I said, relaxing into his embrace as we resumed our dance.

"Mmm" was his only response as he pressed his lips to my forehead. We swayed for a little longer until my cousin's voice rose high above the crowd.

"I already told you. I don't want to do your stupid show!" she practically screamed at the film crew surrounding her.

Sharon, wearing the same gown she had upon arrival yesterday, tried to push into the group and draw attention back to the cat in her arms, but no one paid her any mind.

"You're funny. You're beautiful. And you make honest-to-goodness candles! And fancy videos, too!" one of the reality TV guys insisted. "You could be the biggest thing since *Keeping Up with the Kardashians*!"

"Eww, pass." Mags held up a hand to block her face, but the disgust in her voice made her feelings on the matter clear.

Charles tugged me over to the dramatic scene unfolding across the dance floor. "Excuse me. Is there a problem here? I'm Ms. McAllister's attorney and would be happy to discuss this harassment in a more formal setting."

"We were just going," one of the men groaned, and like magic the unit floated away.

"Sorry about them," Sharon said with a pitiful look on her face. "I thought they were excited about the wedding because of all the cats that would be in it, but it seems like they were just looking for their next big show idea. They were never planning to renew me and Chessy."

I put an arm around her shoulders. "Did they say that?"

She nodded glumly. "This morning, and they've been horrible to me ever since. I have a feeling they're only filming Chessy still so they have enough to wrap up the season and make a good portfolio piece for wooing bigger and better stars."

"I'm sorry. We still think you're a star," I said, and Charles and Mags bobbed their heads in enthusiastic agreement.

"Want me to show you and Chessy how to cast candles?"

Mags offered magnanimously. “We can put it on my YouTube channel. I have more than a million subscribers, you know.”

Sharon’s eyes lit with renewed excitement. “You don’t say? One million? That’s far more viewers than our little TV show ever had. Yes, please sign us up!”

It seemed once someone got bitten by the fame bug, there was no recovering. The Sharon I originally met pre-show had been so quirky and full of life. Now she just seemed sad and desperate for attention. I hoped that after the excitement from the show died down a bit, she could go back to being her normal fabulous self.

Meanwhile I would do my best to keep out of the limelight, secrets and all.

Something moving low and close to the ground caught my eye. Octo-Cat was creeping around the outdoor party and had just swiped a leftover filet of fish from someone’s plate.

“What are you doing out here?” I asked in that singsong voice I used when pretending to be a normal pet owner.

He finished chewing and then gulped the fish down. “Need you inside,” he mumbled, then ran off, expecting me to follow.

I waved to Charles where I’d left him on the dance floor, and he waved back, despite appearing to be deep in conversation with my former boss, Mr. Richard Fulton. He’d been senior partner at the firm before Charles arrived, which meant that this was the first time the two were meeting.

I wondered what they could be talking about. Probably just lawyer stuff.

Well, at least he would be occupied while I checked on whatever it was Octo-Cat needed from me. I knew better than to keep that feline of mine waiting, and I still owed him big for his help finding the lost rings and wrangling the protesting sphynxes during the ceremony.

I'd have expected him to be fully immersed in his new wife Grizabella rather than worrying about the likes of me.

Made me wonder what he wanted now.

I guessed it was time to go find out.

19

Octo-Cat led me inside and up the stairs. Thankfully, Pearl and Gertie didn't notice me, which meant I didn't have to explain what I was doing sneaking around my own house while the party raged on elsewhere. We stopped outside the door to the guest room where Mags was staying.

"We did all our talking through the door, but you can go ahead and open it," my cat informed me.

I carefully let the both of us inside and found Jacques and Jillianne curled up together on the bed to share warmth.

"What's going on?" I asked, glancing from my tabby to my husband's hairless felines.

Jacques stood and stretched forward, revealing the webbing between his toes. No matter how many times I'd seen the way he moved, I couldn't help but be transfixed. The most horrifying thought? That all cats looked this way under their fur, even my Octavius.

Octo-Cat hopped up on the bed, and I sat down too.

"Well, go on with it already. Just like we discussed!" he growled impatiently.

"I don't like that I hurt your feelings," the black-and-white skin-cat said.

"Not like that," Octo-Cat corrected with a flick of his tail. "Speak like a normal cat, or don't speak at all."

Jillianne growled in defense of her little brother, but Octo-Cat quickly shut her down with another stern glance.

"I'm sorry," Jacques mewled pitifully. "We were bad kitties."

Jillianne remained pointedly quiet, so I kept my focus on Jacques. Now that he was being nice to me, he was kind of cute, actually. All those wrinkles were endearing, and the fact that he had a light fuzz on his feet and ears but zero fur on the rest of him was also charming.

"It's hard for us to be back here after the senator died. We still feel guilty about what happened, and we really miss her," little J continued.

Yes, their former owner had been the first corpse to turn up next door. After Octo-Cat and I solved the case, Charles had agreed to give the two pedigreed cats a new home with him so they wouldn't need to spend any time in the rescue or risk going to separate families.

"Why do you hate me?" I asked, never understanding what I'd

done wrong when I was the one who had proven their innocence and had worked so hard to bond with them since.

Jacques shook his head. "We don't hate you, but we don't want things to change. It was hard after the senator died, but eventually we started to feel happy again with Charles. Now everything's changing. New family. New house. We're scared."

"You don't have to be scared. And you can always tell me how you feel. I want you to be happy here. And I want to help however I can."

"Told you," Octo-Cat sang with a satisfied smirk. "She may be just a human, but she's the best one there is."

I puffed up with pride at that. I would never stop being shocked and delighted by my cat's somewhat rare shows of affection. He was really spoiling me today, too.

I reached a hand toward Jacques, and he stretched into my palm, letting out a rumbling purr. He felt like a warm peach, not entirely unpleasant but definitely not anywhere near normal.

Octo-Cat crossed the bed and nudged Jillianne with his paw. "Now you."

"He already said it. Why do I have to?" she groused.

Octo-Cat swatted her again, this time with claws.

"Fine," she snarled, then rose to her feet. "I'm sorry. Everything Jacques said is true, okay?"

"And what else?" my cat prompted with another flick of his tail.

Jillianne sighed and mumbled something I couldn't quite make out.

Octo-Cat grabbed her by the skin of her neck and flipped her over while still holding on with his teeth and all four of his legs. "We can do this the easy way or we can do this the hard way," he mumbled, his mouth full of kitty flesh. "It seems you've chosen the hard way."

The black lady sphynx breathed heavily, her eyes wide.

"Just do it, Jilly," Jacques said softly. "We already tried being bad, but it didn't work. Let's be good now. Pretty please." Even though I knew Jacques was three years old, he sounded like a baby then as he pleaded with his older and much crankier sibling.

"Fine," Jillianne spat. "Now let me go."

Octo-Cat held on for another few seconds to really get his point across, then released her.

"I'm sorry for the things we did," she recited tonelessly.

"Which was what exactly?" I asked, even though I already had an idea.

"We created a scene," she began with a bored expression, then smiled as she delved deeper. "And locked you in the room. And stole the rings. And ruined the dress."

Hearing her confirm my newly formed suspicions really twisted my gut. I'd blamed Pringle for things he had no part in. I'd forbidden him from sharing in the most important day of my life. I'd treated him like a criminal, even though he'd done nothing wrong.

Instead of asking *why*—Jacques had already explained that, after all—I wanted to know, "How?"

"There was a key in the door," Jacques answered. "Jillianne gave me a boost, and I was able to turn it with my sphyngers before I fell back down."

Sphyngers. Huh. Now that these two were actually talking to me, it seemed I'd have a whole new lingo to learn.

"That lady who was supposed to be watching us yesterday was pretty distracted. It was easy for us to slip in and out without her noticing us," Jillianne added, apparently enjoying the villain's speech portion of their apology. "The rings were easy to nab from the top of the dresser and hide in our blanket. And we saw you let the raccoon in and listened when you told him it was okay if he was invited. We also saw how annoyed you were with him and figured it would be easy to frame him. So we invited him back inside right after we ruined the dress."

"That was a horrible thing to do!" I shouted, then remembered that I needed to keep quiet if I wanted to avoid inviting more company into this room before we finished our conversation.

"We're sorry," Jacques said again and rubbed against my arm. "We'll be good now."

Jillianne rolled her eyes but offered no verbal argument.

"I appreciate you sharing all this with me. And your apologies, too." I paused and chewed on my bottom lip. "But are we done here? There's someone I really need to apologize to."

"Good kitties," Octo-Cat said with a sage nod. "Now that you've done as promised, I'll keep up my end of the bargain. Let me show you where to get the fish."

I opened the door where Grizabella sat waiting in the hall.

The sphynxes ran out of the room and down the stairs, meowing excitedly the whole way, but Octo-Cat hung back.

"Thank you for that," I whispered.

He nodded again. "We still need to have that serious discussion about our future," the tabby told me.

I sucked in a deep breath, hating to do anything to ruin his big day when he'd done so much to save mine. But a reverse neuter simply wasn't possible. That wasn't something I could magically change, unfortunately.

Before I could say anything, Octo-Cat continued. "We need to have that talk, but it can wait. Grizabella and I have the rest of our nine lives together, and so do you and I, Angela. We'll talk when you get back. Now enjoy your honeymoon, okay?"

Once again, I cried big weeping tears of joy. I was really becoming quite the softie these days, but that's just what happened when a person was well and truly happy with their life.

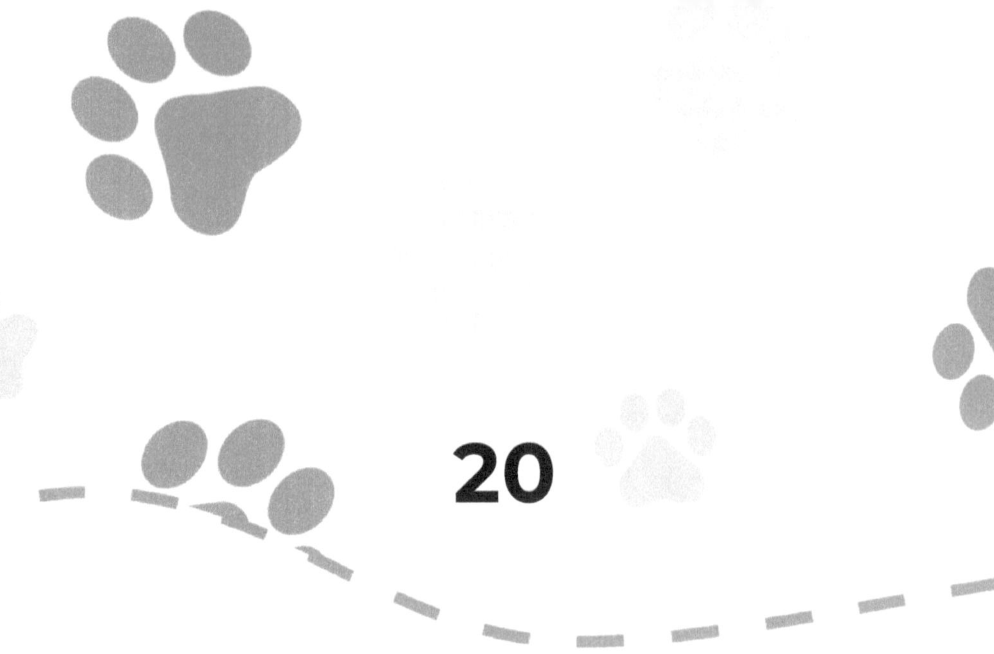

20

"Cover for me while I pay Pringle a quick visit in his treehouse," I pleaded with Mags, knowing she hated the attention of the TV crew but unable to think of another way to get the privacy I needed when going to speak with the raccoon—and hopefully make amends while I was at it.

She reluctantly agreed, and I took off power-walking as stealthily as I could.

I found Pringle sitting in his primary tree house—he had two, after all—with his head pressed into the corner where two walls came together.

"Pringle?" I whispered as I finished climbing the ladder and situated myself on the wooden floor.

He wouldn't even turn to look at me, but at least he was willing to talk. "I was bad. I'm sorry. I ruined the day, and I hurt you. I hurt my very best friend."

My heart broke for him. I'd been so sure he was helping Alpha sabotage my big day that I'd inadvertently sabotaged it myself. I'd closed off someone I love, and now I would never get the chance to include him in the memory of our ceremony. I did have a chance to do something special with him now though—just the two of us.

"I'm your best friend, huh?" I asked with a smile as I crossed my legs beneath my billowy gown.

"Of course you're my best friend," he practically exploded as he finally turned around to face me. "You do so much nice stuff for me. You got me my tree houses and my TV and Carla and everything. We always have so much fun together, even though sometimes I spoil things by being a bad raccoon."

I shook my head sadly. I'm the one who brought him to this point—me and only me. "You're not a bad raccoon, but I've been a bad friend. I'm sorry. Somehow I got it into my head that Alpha was using you to get to me. When he helped you join AA so soon after threatening to ruin the wedding, I was certain that you were a big part of his evil plan."

Pringle crept out of his corner on all fours and tilted his head in question. "Who's Alpha? I don't know any Alpha."

"You specifically told me, by name, that Alpha had suggested you join AA. Don't you remember?"

"Oh, I must have misspoken then. It wasn't Alpha, but it was a guy with a military-type name. You know the one who always comes around with his daughter, Abigull? Remember how I rescued her and saved the day? That was one of my great moments." He stared into the distance, as if remembering fondly.

"You've had a lot of great moments," I told him, unable to believe what he was revealing to me now. "But back up a sec. Are you saying it was Bravo who helped you? Not Alpha?"

"Yeah, I don't know an Alpha. Or, oh wait! Was he the guy who killed all of Abigull's flock? If so, that dude is bad news! He's definitely not allowed in our yard. If I saw him, I would chase him off or—or I'd shoot at him with Carla!" Carla was his Nerf gun that he used for causing trouble more than anything else. It probably wouldn't hold up as an actual weapon, but I did like that he was trying to look out for me. Still, I couldn't believe that all my paranoia and cold-shouldering had been because of a simple confusion over names. I should have known better, and I should have trusted both Pringle and Nan when they told me he wasn't to blame.

"Can you ever forgive me, Pringle?" I asked, unsure whether I actually deserved a fresh chance with him.

"Of course I forgive you!" the raccoon shouted happily, rising to his hind legs. "I was never mad. Just my feelings were hurt is all. I really thought we weren't best friends anymore."

I reached out my fist, and the raccoon bumped it with his much smaller hand. "We're still besties. Maybe one of these days you can tell me more about your twelve-step program and how you're making amends. Seems I could take a page or two from your book, Mr. Pringle."

He jumped up and then scampered to the other corner of his fort. “Which book? I found this one in the trash a couple weeks ago!” He waved a copy of a book with a blue cover called *Merlin the Magical Fluff*. “Seriously, I don’t know who would throw this beauty away. Look at this awesome cover! You can borrow it if you want.”

“Haha, thanks,” I said, accepting the paperback. I wasn’t sure how much time I’d have to read on my honeymoon, but I could always read it after. Then I got an even better idea. “What if I read it to you so we can enjoy the story together?”

Pringle steepled his fingers and looked up at me with what could only be described as puppy-dog eyes. “Really? You would read it to me?”

“Of course. It doesn’t look like the chapters are very long, so we can start right now with the first one if you’re ready.”

His pointed smile widened, but he shook his head. “No, not right now. It’s your big day. Besides, you still have to open my present!”

“Your pres—” I stopped short. “I think I saw it on the gift table. It was the one wrapped in tra—um, in newspaper, right?”

He pointed at me and nodded. “Right-O. So what do you think? Can you open it right now?”

“There are a lot of people around who shouldn’t know that you and I can talk. It could put us in danger, but if you want, you can tell me what it is,” I suggested. The last gift Pringle had given me was a diamond ring, so really this could be anything.

He jumped up and down with excitement. "Good, because I can't wait any longer. It's been so hard keeping this a secret from you, bestie!"

I laughed at his enthusiasm. It felt good to be here with him and put all my doubts and worries behind me. I'd been so mean to him, and yet he harbored no ill will. All he'd wanted was my approval. Animals were better than us in that regard.

"Tell me," I prompted, knowing I'd love whatever he'd gotten for me since it had truly come from his furry little heart.

"It's my namesake," he exclaimed.

I kept my expression neutral as I tried to puzzle it out. "A can of Pringles?" I guessed.

"Not just *a* can of Pringles, *the* can of Pringles. I was pretty much born in that can. My mother had just fished it out of the trash when she felt me and my two sisters getting ready to be born. She took the can and ran into the woods, but she didn't make it to the den in time. She had us right then and there, and then she packed us into this baby and carried us back to our home, safe and sound."

"Pringle," I gasped. "That's a beautiful story. But are you sure you want to give me something so important?"

"Surer than sure," he agreed. "My mom might not be here anymore, but the day after she and my sisters were hit by that speeding car, I found the hole under your porch and moved in. I was so sad missing them, but then I met you, and my life got happy again."

"I'm glad you found that hole under my porch," I said tearfully, both from the kindness of this gesture and the tragedy of his backstory. I'd never heard it before, but now that I knew about his past, I thought I understood him a little better than before. And I definitely knew I could try harder to live up to the lofty title he'd entrusted to me.

Best friend.

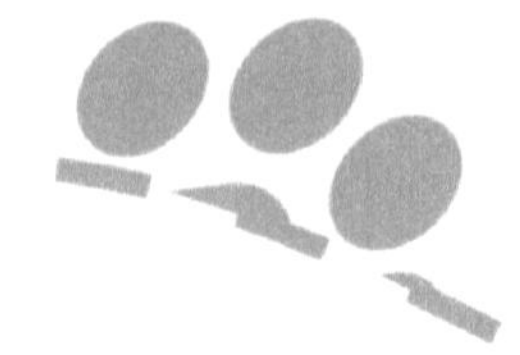

EPILOGUE

I woke up the next morning floating on a cloud. A lady doesn't tell, but let's just say the wedding night more than lived up to expectations.

I was more in love with my husband than ever and couldn't wait to spend the next ten days with him, free of work and family obligations as we kicked off our new life together.

We'd spent last night in his house so we could have some privacy, but I wanted to swing back and say goodbye to everyone at my place before we officially took off.

Everyone was up and waiting, eager to show me all the wonderful photos they'd snapped the day before. I looked forward to seeing them, but it would have to be later. At least ten days later.

"I love you," I told the group that comprised Nan, Grant, Grandma Lyn, Mom, Dad, Mags, Sharon, and Christine, plus five mostly happy cats and one very excited little dog. "But we'll have to catch up once I'm back. Bye!"

Charles picked me up in his arms and carried me over the threshold—albeit moving in the wrong direction of what tradition dictated, the goof. He delivered me to the passenger side of his car and opened the door with a sweeping, knightly gesture. "My lady."

I giggled as I clicked my seatbelt into place.

My husband started up the car, and everyone gathered on the porch to wave. Nan even waved Paisley's little paw for her. Best of all, I could see Pringle hiding just around the side of the house, jumping up and down and waving with both arms.

"Shall we, Mrs. Longfellow?" my husband asked from beside me, a huge grin gleaming on his handsome face.

"We shall, Mr. Longf—Aaaaah!" I shouted in surprise as a giant blob of white hit the windshield right in front of me.

I unbuckled myself, opened the door, and bolted out just in time to see a flash of white flying over the house. "Hahaha," Alpha cawed in victory as he moved out of sight. "Nailed it!"

Well, poop.

It looked like he'd gotten his revenge, after all.

HONEYMOON HEARSAY

PET WHISPERER P.I.

The old stone mansion Charles and I have booked for our week-long honeymoon seems to be something straight out of a fairytale.

That is, until it all starts to fall apart. *Quite literally.* My poor husband plunges straight through the staircase on our first night--and it's a real wonder he didn't need serious medical intervention after that.

I want to find another place to stay, but Charles insists he's okay and that he'd like to see the week out. Of course, we become stucker than stuck when we stumble upon a lost kitten crying for her missing mama in the back garden.

We can't just leave her, but we also can't stay here, especially once deadly rumors begin buzzing in the garden... What happened to Charles wasn't a mistake, but he also may not be the intended target.

Time to find the kitten's mama and skedaddle. I just got married; I'm definitely not ready to become a widow!

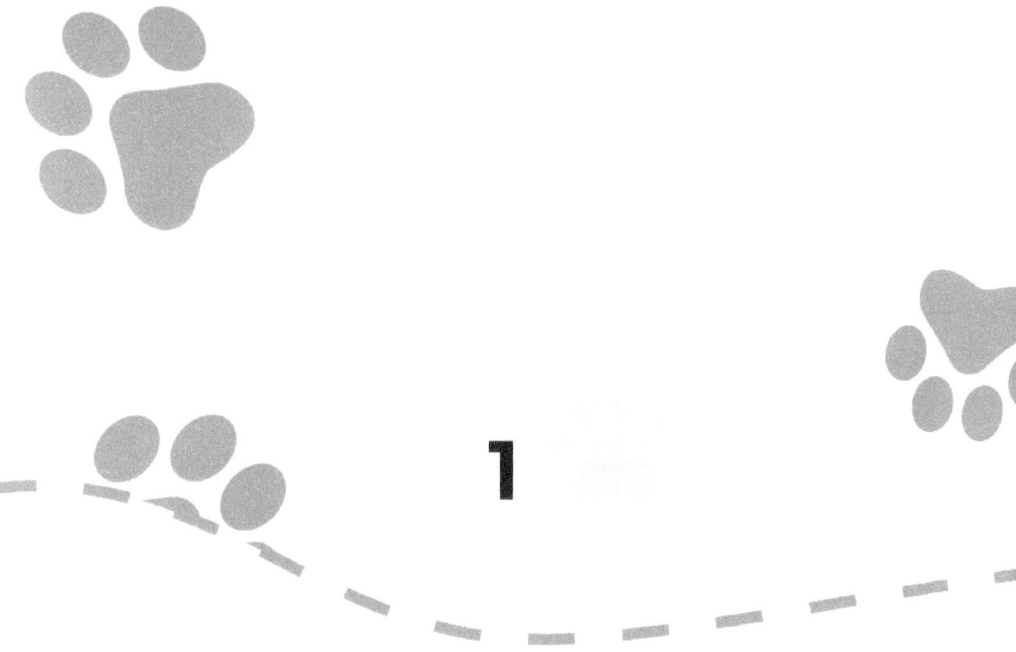

1

My name is Angie Longfellow. Yup, it's official as of the day before yesterday. I'm a married woman, who is currently headed toward a luxury honeymoon destination with new hubby at her side.

I still can't believe it really happened.

Getting married is probably the most normal thing I've done with my life, yet it also feels like the biggest adventure so far.

And that's saying something, considering I racked up seven associate degrees as I struggled with academic indecision, started my own business as a private investigator, and can secretly talk to animals.

Oh, you're wondering about that last part? Well, allow me to explain...

It all started with a will reading at the law firm where I used to work as a paralegal. The same law firm where I met my new husband—*eep!*—but I digress.

As a glorified secretary, it was my job to make the coffee. The partners hadn't sprung for new appliances in quite some time, and the coffee maker was more than a little worse for wear. When I tried to plug it in, the darned thing zapped me unconscious.

I woke up a short bit later to the smell of tuna and the sound of someone addressing me in a very condescending manner. I didn't know it then, but that someone was the deceased's beloved cat Octavius. He told me his owner had been murdered and that he needed help to prove it and thus get justice for the old lady he'd loved so dearly.

If you know cats as well as I do, then you know that Mr. Octavius refused to take "no" for an answer. With no choice but to comply, a partnership was born.

We solved the murder together and became friends while doing it. I was asked to adopt him by the estate's trustee, and I eagerly agreed—even before I knew a certain tabby had a generous trust fund attached to him.

I took to calling him Octo-Cat, and together we moved into his former owner's enormous manor house at his behest. Now the two of us are partners in crime... make that partners in *solving crimes.* Yes, we run the P.I. business together. We don't always agree, but one way or another, we always get the job done.

And it's because of my strange ability to speak with animals that I really got to know my new husband, Charles. He overheard me trying to sneak in a FaceTime call with Octo-Cat at work—

and proceeded to use this knowledge to blackmail me into helping with a difficult case he'd just landed.

That all worked out too, even though honestly he could have just politely asked for my help rather than resorting to blackmail. I already had a huge crush on him and would have jumped at any excuse to spend more time together. And time is all we have on our lengthy two-day drive from Maine to Virginia.

My mom and dad managed to book a gorgeous private mansion for our honeymoon, and we'll have the entire place to ourselves for a whole week to usher in our era of newly wedded bliss. It's the same place they honeymooned more than thirty years ago, which bodes well for us, seeing as the two of them are still crazy in love.

I'll miss everyone while we're away for the week, but I know Nan will keep everyone back home in check. Lucky for her, she won't be able to understand all the complaints Octo-Cat and Charles's two hairless cats, Jacques and Jillianne, are sure to send her way. She'll also have her sweet rescue dog Paisley to keep her company and her brand-new surprise husband Grant, along with his Holland Lop bunny EB. It's a full house for sure!

I'm sure I'll still call at least once per day to play translator and mediator for whatever problems arise, but it's nothing my scrappy grandmother can't handle... Provided our resident raccoon Pringle behaves himself. Lately he's been turning over a new leaf with the help of a certain twelve-step program, and we recently shared a very heartfelt bonding moment, but his natural tendencies still encourage him to gossip and thieve whenever possible.

But no, I'm sure it will all be fine—just fine.

I need to stop worrying about everyone we left in Maine and focus on the wonderful week in Virginia ahead. It's my honeymoon, and my new husband deserves my full attention. It will probably be good for me to have this little break from all the drama and chaos of the busy household back home. I can put out any fires when I return next week.

This week is all about celebrating my new marriage, and that's exactly what I plan to focus on.

"Look at the trees," I remarked, pointing out the side window as Charles and I entered the final hour of our big road trip. We were getting very close to the old stone mansion where we'd be spending the next week, and I was jittery with excitement. "They're changing."

"We've got a long way until autumn," he answered while fiddling with the radio.

I shook my head and pointed again. "No, like they're a completely different type. We don't have trees like this back in Blueberry Bay."

"Touché." He laughed. "Leave it to you to notice the forest *and* the trees."

"You can take the detective out of the agency..." I laughed too. "But no sleuthing this week. Promise."

I grabbed Charles's hand from the radio while he used the other to guide the steering wheel. "The next seven days are about you and me, and only you and me."

"I like the sound of that," he said flirtatiously before raising our linked hands to kiss the back of mine. "And we're almost there. Our turn-off is in less than thirty miles, and from there it's a straight shot to our little Southern slice of paradise."

"So what should we do first once we get there?"

"Oh, I think you know, Mrs. Longfellow." He glanced toward me for a second, then winked before returning his gaze to the highway.

Heat rushed to my cheeks. I was still very new at being a wife and not yet comfortable with all the intricacies that came with the role. Especially with talking about them.

So I redirected the conversation a little bit. "I mean, *after?* I've been reading about the area on Trip Advisor. There are all kinds of historical tours, and some really nice restaurants, and..."

Charles squeezed my hand. "This is our honeymoon. It's not about seeing the sights. Let's just relax and enjoy each other's company."

I wriggled in my seat. "Relax, right. I can do that."

He chuckled good-naturedly. "Yes, you can. If your workaholic husband can enjoy some time off the grid, then so can you. Besides, we'll have each other, and that's all we really need, right?"

"Right," I said, nodding my head sharply, which only sent us both into another fit of giggles. "This week is only about us, but we can still try some of the local restaurants, right? I might die if I don't get true authentic Southern-made biscuits and gravy for breakfast at least once this week."

"Of course! We'll have them every day if you'd like. We'll need something to keep up our stamina between… well, you know."

I blushed like mad at the implication and tried to hide my hot cheeks behind my palms.

"Oh, Angie Longfellow, I love you. Never change," my husband said before releasing my hand to casually rub my shoulder.

Never change. Now that I could do. But could I avoid all my usual worries and busy-bodying for one whole week?

I guess time would tell on that one.

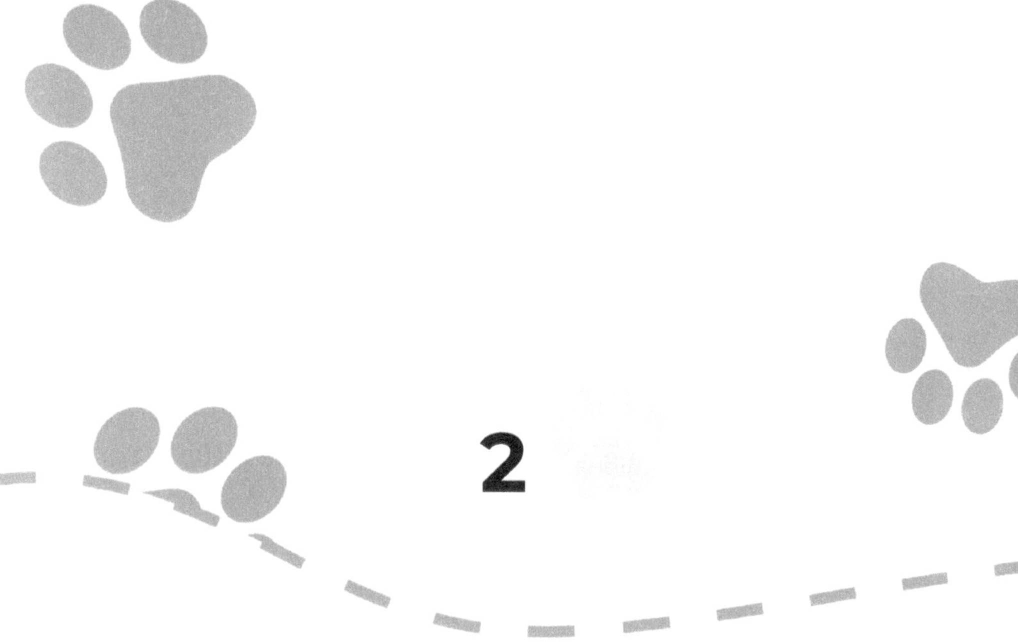

2

"There it is!" I exclaimed as the old stone mansion loomed into view. Even though we split the trip into two days, we'd still driven a long way to reach our destination, and now that we were here, I couldn't wait to get out and stretch my legs a bit.

"Are you sure this is the place?" Charles slowed the car to a crawl as we both gawked at the property ahead. "There seem to be a lot of cars, and we're supposed to have the place to ourselves."

I waved off his concern with a quick sweep of my hand. "I'm sure it's just the staff getting it ready for us. Make sure you give them a nice tip, so it's not awkward."

"Right, okay." He pulled into the small gravel lot beside the mansion and parked next to an old truck, then took out his wallet and thumbed through it for some cash, which he tucked in his front pocket so it would be ready.

I squealed as I hopped out of the car. "*Eee!* I can't believe we're really here."

Charles climbed out of the driver's seat and popped the trunk so we could grab our luggage. "Well, believe it. Only the best for my wifey."

I wheeled one large suitcase behind me while Charles balanced two overstuffed duffle bags. "Look at this garden. It's even more beautiful than my mom described. Is that hydrangea? Look how big and puffy!"

"We can eat your biscuits and gravy out here and watch the sunrise. Want to try for tomorrow?"

"That sounds great, honey, but tomorrow, I'm sleeping in. Let's do it the day after, though, for sure." When I turned back to look at Charles, I delighted in the enormous smile that decorated his handsome face.

"I can't believe the size of this place," he noted, eyeing the mansion. I turned back to study the domicile in all its refinement and grandeur. It appeared to be a mishmash of architectural styles, landing somewhere between a Scottish castle and a Colonial. Whoever had ordered this house to be built clearly had a very creative mind. I wouldn't be surprised if we ran across a few trap doors or secret passages during our stay. I couldn't wait to explore.

We reached the doorstep and paused to collect ourselves. I tucked a loose strand of hair behind my ear as I studied the bright green front door. "I guess we just knock? Or do we head right in? Mom didn't have any information about a key exchange, and I couldn't find this place on Airbnb when I looked."

Charles stepped forward, cleared his throat, and thumped on the door.

And someone pulled it open almost immediately, a little old lady with blue hair and thick glasses. She smiled at us, then turned toward the interior of the house and shouted, "Billy, the honeymooners are here!"

A middle-aged man with a pot belly shuffled out and grabbed my suitcase, leaving Charles to handle his own duffle bags. I stood on tiptoe to kiss my husband's cheek in excitement. "This is it! The place is all ours!"

"What was that, dearie?" the old lady shouted my way.

"Oh, sorry. We're just excited to have free rein of this gorgeous house for the whole week," I explained with an awkward smile.

"You don't exactly have free rein," the man whom she'd called Billy informed us. "The third floor and attic are off limits to guests, and obviously you'll need to keep to your room or the communal places on the property."

"Wait. *Our room?*" I squeaked, not knowing what else to say.

Charles immediately jumped into lawyer mode. "I think there may be some misunderstanding. This is our honeymoon, and my wife's parents expressly reserved the entire property for the week as a gift to us."

"There's no misunderstanding on our end," the old woman piped up, taking her glasses off to clean them on the hem of her shirt. “Costs a lot of money to maintain a place like this, especially since it belongs to the official register of historical homes in the area. And that garden? Quality gardeners don’t come cheap, dearie.”

My heart sank as I filled in the blanks. “So you turned it into a B&B to help pay the bills?”

“About five years back now. Your mother hasn’t been for a while, I’m guessing. I can’t believe she assumed she was reserving the whole place for the cost of a single room. Ha!” She hunched over and slapped her knee.

“There are no refunds without at least two weeks’ notice, so you’re out of time. Do you want your room or not?” Billy sniffed indifferently.

I looked to Charles for a decision since we obviously weren’t going to be offered any privacy to discuss our options.

“We want it,” he said decisively, shooting me a meaningful look that I had a hard time deciphering just then.

Billy nodded and headed toward a narrow staircase. “Very well. Let me show you the way.”

We followed the man up the stairs to a locked door at the far end of the hall. “You only get the one room, but it’s our best room,” he offered almost apologetically as he turned a key in the lock and pushed the door open.

And immediately I gasped as I took in the oversized canopy bed and soft lace curtains. The entire room was something out of a time capsule, transporting us straight to the early days of our nation and showing how the one percent lived in ornate luxury.

Blue flowered vines danced along the wallpaper, and the honey oak hardwood floors appeared to be original. Best of all, a stone fireplace sat opposite the bed with a gorgeous antique love seat positioned comfortably before it.

"Nice, huh?" Billy grunted as he tossed my suitcase onto the bed.

"I love it," I confessed as I turned in a circle to take it all in.

"Thanks for your help," Charles said, shaking our guide's hand and probably slipping some money into it for a sly tip.

"Dinner's at eight p.m. sharp. It's included in the cost of your package, if you want to join us."

This caught my attention. "What's on the menu?"

"No menu. This isn't a restaurant." He narrowed his eyes at me, leaving no doubt the hospitality industry was not Billy's first choice for a career. "We all eat the same, so if you're gluten-free, nut-free, dairy-free, or meat-free, you're free to go grab your grub elsewhere. If you're not too fussy, then you'll love Madame Blue's cooking."

I blinked back my surprise at the way he delivered this invitation. "Madame Blue? Is that…?"

"Yup, you already met her downstairs. She's a much better cook than she is greeter. That's why she keeps me around."

Right, because Billy here was the paragon of hospitality.

"Okay, thanks again." Charles moved toward the door.

Thankfully, the other man took the hint and followed. "The name's Bill. If you need anything, just give a holler."

I smiled and waved goodbye right before Bill took his leave and thumped the door closed behind him.

Charles turned toward me with a bemused expression. “So things are a little different than we expected,” he prompted with a sigh. “I figured we should at least take it for now, so we have a private place to discuss our options. I’d be happy to go somewhere else, if you’d rather.”

“Honestly, it’s fine. You wanted to spend most of our time in the room anyway, right?” I sank down onto the bed and patted the mattress beside me. “Now get over here, Mr. Longfellow.”

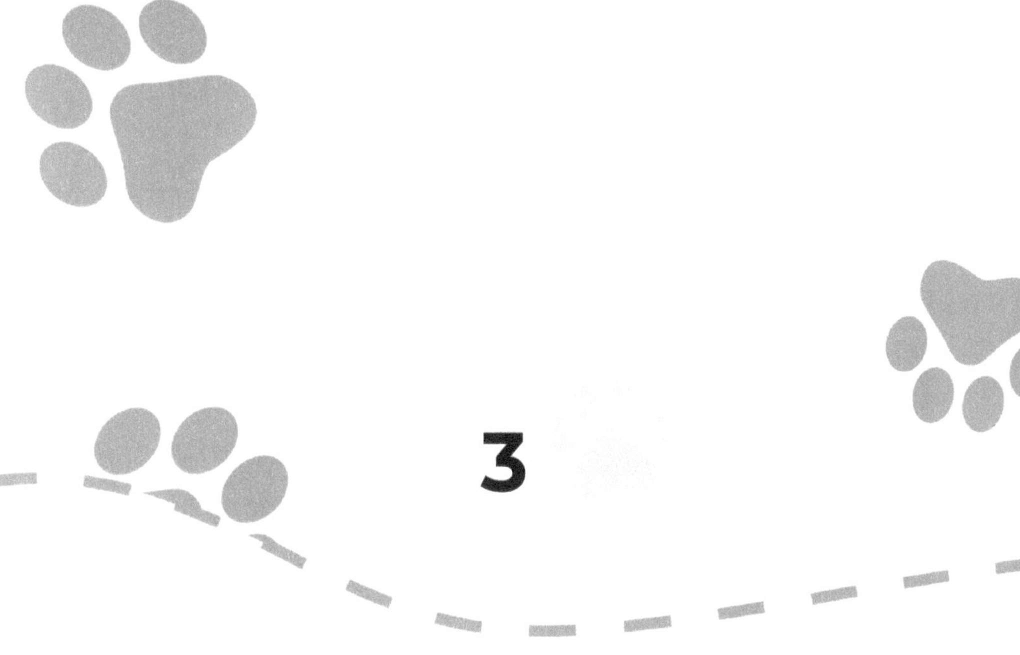

3

After a bit of time to ourselves, Charles and I decided to take a look around the garden. We headed outside hand in hand, swinging our arms between us as we strolled up to a pair of stone cupid statues that stood amid a bed of bright yellow roses.

"I should do more with our yard back home," I said, stooping down to breathe in the sweet fragrance, startled when a fat bee buzzed out from between the petals. I jolted back, hoping I hadn't already upset the creature.

"Oof, careful. I'm allergic to bees!" Charles cried, taking a giant step back and waving his arms about.

"Really? How did I not know that?" I cocked my head to the side as I studied him.

"Because we don't have any gardens back home. Probably best to keep it that way too."

"Better bees than shellfish, I guess. Octo-Cat would never forgive you if we had to stop getting his favorite lobster rolls from Little Dog Diner." I smiled thinking of my crabby tabby back home. Darn it, I missed him already. "Do you want to go back inside?"

Charles shook his head. "I'm not deathly allergic. Well, not unless I get stung by a whole hive. My wife wants to enjoy the gardens, so let's enjoy the gardens. I'll just take some Benadryl when we go back inside, and worst case, I have an EpiPen tucked into the front pocket of my duffle."

"An EpiPen?" I frowned as I looked up at him. "That sounds pretty serious."

"Just a precaution. You know me, always prepared like some kind of overgrown Boy Scout." Charles caught my look of horror and backtracked quickly. "I'm fine. I promise. Look, there are those hydrangeas you saw coming in." He pointed and took off toward the puffy pink flower balls.

I shook my head and followed. Why was he only confiding this allergy in me now?

Mom had spent most of her time describing the beautiful landscaping when she told us about this place. At least that hadn't changed, even if the larger establishment had.

Grassy paths guided us through the generous display of collected plant life. We saw so much diversity in size, color, and type, I seemed to find a new favorite every time the winding path led us to a new bed of blooms.

As we approached the red brick wall that flanked the property, I had a thought that caused me to pull out my phone and do a quick web search. I paused to read through the information on the screen while Charles continued to wander ahead.

A few minutes later, I glanced up ready to share my findings, but my husband was nowhere to be seen. "Charles?" I called, craning my neck to search the area.

"Over here," he called softly, popping up from the ground and waving his hand.

I wasted no time striding right on over. "There are all kinds of non-pollinating flowers." I revealed the fruit of my research labors as I walked swiftly his way. "We can still have a garden, as long as we're careful about what we—"

"Shhh," Charles said, raising a finger to his lips then pointing toward the ground.

I fell quiet, moving as fast as I could to see what this was all about. As I drew closer, his wide smile grew in size.

"Do you see it?" he whispered and pointed toward a patch of clover near the brick wall.

I narrowed my eyes just in time to see a tiny black paw stretch into the air. "Is that—?"

"A kitten," he confirmed, squatting back down to watch it sleep.

"What's it doing out here?" I demanded, even though he clearly didn't know, either. "Do you think it's a stray?"

He reached his fingers forward carefully and scratched at the little white patch of fur on the sleeping kitten's chest. "No idea. You could ask it though."

Now there was a thought, but still I hesitated. "Are you sure you don't mind? I thought we were both leaving work back home."

"Your bond with animals is a part of who you are. It's not something you can turn on and off at will. Besides, I want to know what he's doing here, too."

"Not he. *She.* It's a girl," I clarified, watching that fuzzy little chest rise and fall with each breath.

"How can you tell?" He looked from me to the kitten and back again.

"I don't know. I just can. Should I wake her up to say hello?"

He pushed himself back to standing. "Go ahead. I'll keep watch to make sure no one stumbles by and gets curious."

"Good idea," I murmured, but Charles had already moved to the end of the nearest path, giving me and the kitten some time to ourselves.

Despite the saying being to let sleeping dogs lie, I normally knew better than to wake a cat. Octo-Cat had taught me that lesson the hard way—and many times over at that. But this kitten seemed so small, and it could very well need our help. As a baby, hopefully it didn't have the same reserve of colorful kitty curses to call upon.

I placed a hand gently on its side and felt a rumbling purr through my fingers. That was an encouraging sign.

"Hello, little one," I said softly, waiting for any form of response. But the kitty remained fast asleep.

I stroked her fur softly. "Hi. My name is Angie, and I'm a

friend," I continued, applying increasing pressure with my strokes to wake her gently.

Finally, two little yellow eyes blinked open. "Where's my mommy?" the baby mewled, and I swear my heart broke in two.

"Hi there, sleepyhead. I can help you find your mommy. Where did you last see her?"

The kitten remained lying on her side. She looked weak. "She told me to wait by the fence, but she hasn't come back. It's been a really long time."

"Do you have any brothers or sisters? Are they around here somewhere, too?" I was already going into full-on rescue mode. Thankfully, I knew Charles would want to help the baby, too. After all, he was the one who'd discovered her.

The kitten drew in a deep breath before answering. "It's just me and my mommy now. My brothers and sisters got taken inside a house by a nice lady while Mommy was off hunting. I was scared so I hid."

"You don't have to be scared of me," I offered with what I hoped was a kind smile. I made sure to only use closed-lip smiles with animals, since the sight of teeth often sent them on the defensive. "And we'll look for your mommy together. But before we do, are you hungry?"

This got the kitten to rise to her feet and perform a series of stretches. "Yes, very much so."

"Then let's go see if Madame Blue has some milk she can share," I said, impressing myself with my ability to remember the old lady's name after hearing it only once. "Before we go inside, though, would you tell me your name?"

"My name is Charlene," she answered around a yawn as she finished her stretches. "And my mommy's name is Mommy. I really miss her. Do you think we'll find her soon?"

"I'm going to do everything I can to help you find her, but first let's get some food in you. You'll feel better once your tummy's full."

The kitty nodded. "Okay."

"Do you mind if I carry you to the house?" I asked. Charlene had clearly been born a stray, and I didn't want to frighten her by picking her up without first getting permission.

"Okay, but please be gentle," she squeaked.

I leaned down and carefully lifted her into my arms. She was so tiny, she could practically fit on the palm of my hand. "It's okay. I've got you now, and I won't rest until I know you're safe."

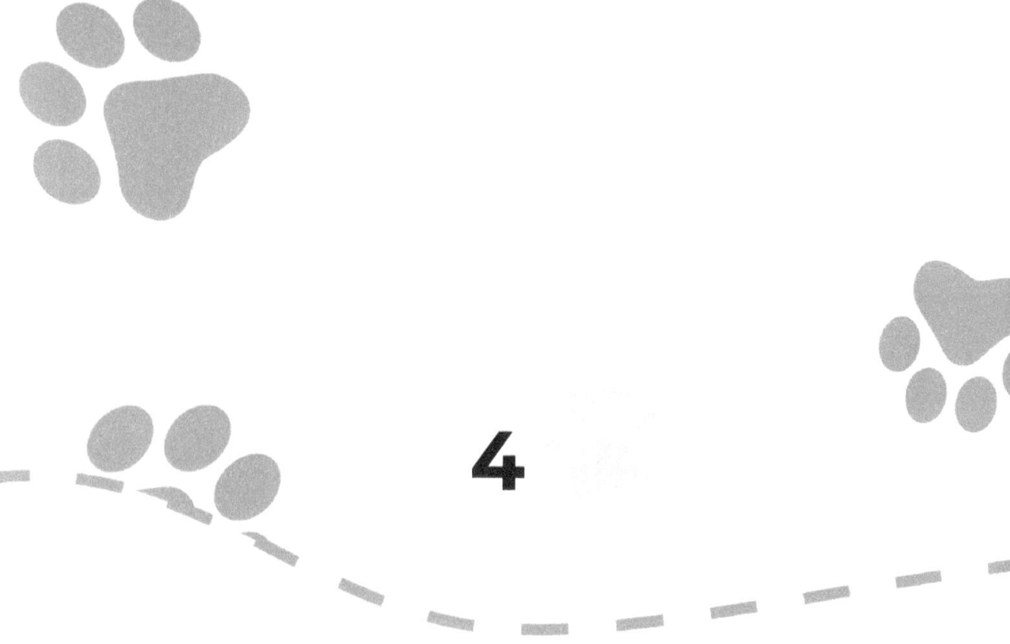

4

I wasted no time introducing Charles to the kitten he'd found sleeping in the garden. "Hi, Charles. This is Charlene. She's lost her mother, but we're going to help her find her."

"Oh, of course, we are," Charles cooed, running his knuckles over the kitty's head the way his Sphynx cats liked.

"What is he doing?" Charlene cried, pressing herself into my chest.

"He's just saying hello," I assured her. "Charles is my husband. He's the one who found you."

She scrunched up her nose as she considered this. "Why is his name like my name?"

I chuckled. "I don't know. I guess that's just a fun coincidence, but shhh. We're heading into the house now, and I won't be able to talk to you once we're inside."

"Why not?"

"Because most other humans can't talk to cats. They'll think it's weird and get scared if they hear us talking to each other. And we don't want to cause a scene. We just want to get you fed and then find your mommy, okay?"

Charlene appeared to think about this for a moment before letting go of some of the tension in her tiny body and saying, "Okay. I'll be quiet."

I reached down to stroke her head as Charles pushed open the front door. "I think the kitchen's back there," I told him, heading decisively to the right.

"I thought you said not to talk," the kitten cried out.

"Hush, little baby," I cooed like a mother singing a lullaby. The only time I could get away with talking to animals in the presence of those who didn't know my secret was when using a cutesy baby voice to say very basic things—the way most people did with their pets, not expecting them to be able to talk back. Charlene didn't know this, but I hoped my words would soothe her all the same.

Sure enough, she said nothing more and we found the kitchen easily. The old woman Charles and I had met earlier now sported an apron tied around her slim hips as she began to work on that night's supper.

"No guests in the kitchen!" she shouted upon noticing us.

The kitten shrunk back in my hands, but I strode forward with confidence. "Sorry to trouble you. We found this little one outside in the garden, and she seems to be missing her mother. I was hoping we could have a spot of milk to offer her. She appears to be quite hungry."

"No pets are allowed on the property," was her only reply. She didn't even bother looking at the poor needy creature.

I refused to give up. Surely this woman had an ounce of kindness somewhere in her cranky soul. "She's not a pet. We just found her outside, and she's very hungry. Could we please have that milk, if you don't mind?"

"I do mind. The historical society is just looking for any reason to remove me as caretaker, and the last thing I need is guest complaints about little black hairs in their dinners. Now shoo!" Madame Blue used her small body to force us back toward the doorway, waving a wire whisk at us to really get her point across.

"Well, that didn't go great," I said, letting out a breath of frustration.

"I'll run into town and grab some supplies. Do you want to stay here with Charlene?" my husband offered helpfully once we were out of earshot of the kitchen.

"She said no pets allowed on the premises," I reminded him with a pout, but he was undeterred.

"Well, good thing Charlene isn't a pet." He reached out to rub his knuckles over her head again, and this time the kitten leaned into him. "She's just a friend we're helping out. Probably best you keep her hidden though."

"Thank you." I leaned in to hug him. "Will you be able to make it there and back by dinner, though?"

He checked the time on his phone and frowned. “Probably not. You go down without me. I’ll feed Charlene once I’m back with the supplies, then I’ll come down and join you. I’ll grab some snacks while I’m out too, just in case Madame Blue’s cooking is terrible.”

“Right?” I smirked at his sneaky jibe. “I thought the special ingredient in Southern cooking was supposed to be love. She definitely missed that memo.”

“It will be fine,” he assured me, stroking the kitten lovingly while I held her. “If our host is still being horrible by the time we find Charlene’s mother, we can book the rest of the week somewhere else, okay?”

I smiled at that. I loved how little he let these kinds of setbacks bother him. “Okay,” I agreed with a huge smile. “Now give me a kiss goodbye before you go.”

My husband happily obliged this request. “Now get upstairs quick,” he urged, pushing me toward the narrow staircase. “Before that crotchety old lady comes back out to yell at you again.”

Well, I didn’t need to be told twice. I jogged up the stairs, taking extra care not to jostle my precious cargo as I went. Once inside our room, I locked the door behind me and set Charlene on the plush bedspread.

“This should be a more comfortable place to nap for now. Do you want me to stay here with you, or go outside to see if I can find your mommy?”

Charlene glanced around the room with a shiver. “I don’t want to be alone. Will you stay?”

"Of course I'll stay." I smiled at the sleepy baby as she explored the large bed and finally curled up on one of the pillows with her tail tucked tight around her body.

"Will you tell me a story?" she asked, a bit more upbeat now that she'd gotten comfortable. "Mommy always told me stories before I go to sleep."

"Sure, uh..." I racked my brain for a story that a young feline might enjoy. "Oh, I've got it! Once upon a time there was a very spoiled cat named Octavius."

Charlene stretched her paws before her. "Is this a true story?"

I bobbed my head enthusiastically. "Yes, it's very true. It's about my very best friend in the whole world. He's waiting back home while Charles and I are on our honeymoon."

"What's a honeymoon?" she asked, tilting her head to one side.

"It's like a special vacation two people take after they get married."

"I don't know a lot of the words you use, but I like the sound of your voice," Charlene said with a twitch of her whiskers.

I chuckled softly. "Should I keep going with the story? I can try to use easier words."

"No, I like hearing the new words. They make me smarter, right?"

"Definitely."

"So use all the biggest words you know, and I promise not to interrupt again."

"Okay, here goes..." I paused to make sure she was ready and listening.

Charlene's wide, unblinking eyes focused on me. Time to shine.

"Once there was an incredibly pampered feline by the name of Octavius," I continued, using a dramatic old-time voice. "Octavius believed himself to be the most exquisite cat who ever lived and often told others of his greatness. For the longest time, nobody understood his not-so-humble boasts, but one day, thanks to a shoddy coffee maker, he met a human woman who did understand..."

I let my voice fade away when I noticed that Charlene had already fallen fast asleep. I sat and watched her for a little while, debating the urge to go search the gardens for her mother while I had a bit of free time. But by then, it was fast approaching eight o'clock, and even though I didn't look forward to any more interactions with the unfriendly caretaking duo, I couldn't deny the way my stomach grumbled upon smelling the delicious blend of savory scents that wafted up the stairs from the kitchen.

Charles would be back soon to leave a saucer of milk and some soft food for our little visitor, which meant she wouldn't be alone for long—and she'd wake to a nice meal waiting for her.

Now it was time to see about a nice meal to fill my own belly. I just hoped the food would be worth the uncomfortable conversation that would surely be accompanying it.

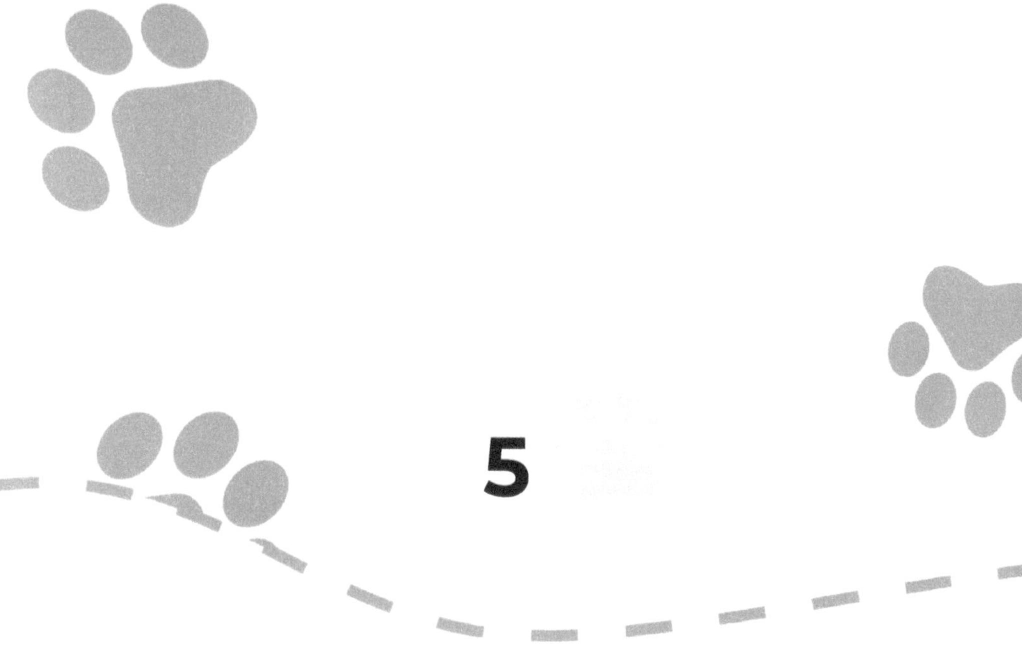

5

I wandered into the dining room five minutes before eight, not wanting to risk upsetting Blue or Billy by being late. I was the first to arrive in the gorgeous dining room that came equipped with a mahogany table to seat at least twelve situated beneath a stunning crystal chandelier.

Charles and I had only checked in a few hours prior but hadn't happened upon any other guests during that time, leaving me to wonder if we were the only ones here besides the staff. I couldn't decide whether that would be a good thing or a bad one. Other guests meant that the rude caretakers would be less fixated on us, but it also meant more people who might intrude upon moments Charles and I preferred to keep private.

That concern was cut short, however, when a young woman with rainbow-dyed hair and a smattering of freckles sat down across from me. "You weren't here last night," she noted with an indifferent expression.

I smiled and sat up straighter in my seat. "My husband and I just came in this afternoon. We're on our honeymoon."

She eyed the empty chair beside me and shrugged. "If you say so."

"No, really. He ran into town to get some supplies, but he'll be here soon." I forced another smile, all the while wondering why I cared what this stranger thought of me or my marriage.

She grabbed an apple from the fruit platter in the center of the table and spun it in her hands. "You don't have to prove anything to me. I had a fight with my boyfriend and decided to stay here until he comes back to his senses. Name's Blaire, if that matters to you."

"Angie," I answered with an awkward wiggle of my fingers. "Nice to meet you."

"Yeah, sure. Whatever." Blaire brought the apple close to her face and stared at it for a few moments before returning it to the platter.

An elderly couple shuffled into the dining room just seconds before the grandfather clock in the hallway chimed eight.

"Good evening!" the man crowed, pulling out a chair for his partner. They were both dressed in khaki shorts and Hawaiian shirts, very obvious tourists. Probably retirees too.

"Isn't it a beautiful evening?" the woman asked Blaire, who simply shrugged and turned away.

"It's lovely," I chimed in, feeing bad about how rude the rainbow-haired twentysomething was being, even though I wasn't responsible for her. "Tomorrow, I'll have to watch the sunset in the garden before dinner. I bet it looks absolutely stunning above all those gorgeous flowers."

All eyes zoomed to me. The man's jaw fell open, and the woman shook her head before folding her hands in her lap.

"Sorry, I didn't mean to speak out of turn. My name's Angie," I said, trying to salvage the interaction.

"Her *husband* and her are here honeymooning," Blaire supplied, making sure to add air quotes around the word *husband.*

The woman curled her lip before offering the fakest smile I'd ever seen in my life. "Well, it's nice to meet you, Angie. Although I suspect you're the reason we were denied our favorite suite despite being very loyal customers to this here establishment."

Heat rushed to my cheeks and I turned my eyes to the table in front of me. "Sorry about that," I murmured.

"I'm sure you wouldn't have stolen our room if you'd known, honey. All is fine." She offered me a saccharine expression that made me feel sick to my stomach.

Thankfully, Madame Blue and Billy chose that precise moment to enter the dining room, each carrying a large silver platter piled with food.

"Salisbury steak," the old woman announced, plunking her tray down before the lone male at the table.

"Mashed potatoes." Billy added his tray to the center of the table, then both returned to the kitchen. When they came back, they delivered a bowl of buttered peas and freshly baked sourdough bread.

"It smells so good," I gushed, sucking in a deep lungful of the savory scents as I reached for the dish nearest to me.

"No, honey. It should be age before beauty," the tourist woman said, shooting daggers my way.

I shrank back from the platter and waited for the others to serve themselves before I risked a second attempt. Tomorrow Charles and I would definitely be grabbing all our meals at a restaurant. Somehow the guests here were even worse than the staff, but I wouldn't let them spoil my honeymoon.

Improvise, adapt, and overcome. That's what my dad would say if he were here.

Plus this place was special to my parents, and I wanted to experience firsthand all the good memories they'd carried with them over the years. It would be rude to turn our noses up at their gift and book a chain hotel for the week when this place was already paid for. Besides, our room was to die for. I couldn't blame my cruel dining companion for being upset over losing it, but then again, she shouldn't be blaming *me* either.

Once I'd piled my plate with food, Bill and Madame Blue each took a seat at the heads of the table.

"Where's your fella?" our cook asked several notches too loud on the volume scale.

"He just ran into town for a couple supplies. He'll be back soon," I answered meekly. Thanks to the onslaught of sarcasm and snide remarks from the other guests, I was no longer feeling in the mood for conversation of any sort.

She frowned at the bowl of peas. "Supper is at eight p.m. sharp. Didn't you tell them, Billy?"

"Yes, that's the first thing I told them," he said, bobbing his head. "I can share the rules, but I can't force anyone to follow them."

She huffed but said nothing more as she served herself scant portions from each dish.

I made it my mission to finish my food at record speed, hardly taking the time to appreciate the perfect creamy consistency of the mashed potatoes as I shoved them down my gullet and swallowed hard. If Charles wasn't back soon, he'd miss out entirely, but I didn't think he'd mind when I filled him in on what I'd experienced.

I'd finished eating everything except for my last few bites of steak when the lights flickered out, ensconcing the room in darkness.

"Oopsie daisy!" Madame Blue shouted, the same way she shouted everything else. "Billy, grab the candles while I go futz with the fuse box!"

Her cries were met with silence. The older tourist couple seemed to whisper amongst themselves, but I couldn't make out what they were saying.

"Billy?" Blue shouted again. "Billy? Oh for Pete's sake, I'll get the candles myself." Her chair noisily slid out from the table as she continued to grumble to herself. "Honestly, what's the point of hiring paid help if they're never around when you need help?"

I grabbed my phone from my pocket and turned on the flashlight. Unfortunately, I'd had it angled too high and the light shined directly into Blaire's eyes across the table.

"Ahh, are you trying to blind me or what?" she groused, moving her hands in front of her face.

"Sorry, gotta go," I murmured, quickly making tracks back to the staircase. They didn't need me to fix the lighting, but if Charlene woke up to a dark, empty room, she'd be terrified.

I had to get to her—and fast. I just hoped Charles would be back with the two of us soon. I needed his strength and positive outlook now more than ever.

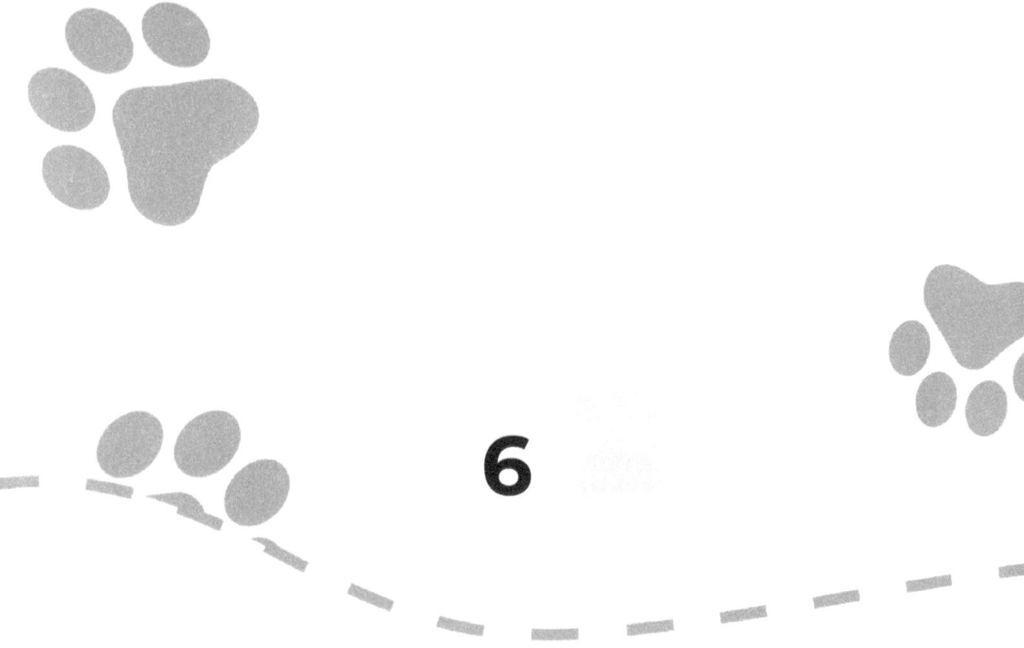

6

I returned to a dark room and sleeping kitten. Of course it took a bit of searching with the flashlight on my phone before I finally spotted her snuggled beneath one of the pillows near the headboard of the bed.

Seeing as she was still sound asleep and Charles had yet to return, I spent some time reading a new book from my favorite series on my phone. I managed to squeeze in three full chapters before my husband returned with the supplies.

"Why are all the lights out?" he asked upon entering, his arms encumbered by two large paper grocery bags.

I closed my e-reading app and shone my phone's light toward him in the doorway. "Good question. It went out during dinner. That was more than half an hour ago."

"How hard is it to flip a switch in the fuse box?" he grumbled as he made his way over to me. "Maybe I should go offer to help."

"I wouldn't," I said before filling him in on the details of the quickie dinner party.

"It sounds like each person we meet is worse than the last," he remarked, setting the bags on the loveseat by the fireplace. "I think I met Blaire, assuming she was the rainbow-haired girl slinking around downstairs. I almost ran straight into her when I came through the front door."

"Yup, that would be her. I wonder what she was doing downstairs while all the lights are out, though."

"No idea. She said something about me being the prodigal husband and laughed before turning around and going the opposite direction."

Well, at least now she knew he was real. Not that it mattered —or at least it shouldn't have.

"Is Charlene up?" Charles added while crinkling the bags, presumably as he searched through them.

I shook my head, then realizing he couldn't see me at present, added, "Nope. Not yet."

"Well, let me see if I can start a fire to give us a little more light." More crinkling noises followed.

I came over holding up the flashlight to help light the area while he examined the hearth and surrounding area.

He bent down and poked at the wood waiting in the fireplace. "Darn, these logs are fake. I think it's just meant to be decorative."

I sighed at this. "Welp, no fire for us. Seems about right, given how everything else has been since we arrived."

"It's okay. I can keep you warm," he growled flirtatiously. He grabbed me in his arms and settled for a not-quite-so-quick kiss.

"Stop it. We have a baby in the room with us, remember?"

"Oh, yeah. We really need to make quick work of finding her mother, huh? Should we wake her up to feed her?"

I nodded, still wrapped in my husband's embrace. "Probably a good call. Let's take her and the supplies outside. At least there we have the moonlight."

"And we can kill two birds with one stone by searching for her mother while we're out there," he added before pressing his lips to my forehead and then letting me go.

I scowled at him, illuminated by the bright light of my phone screen. "Charles, you know I hate that expression."

"Oops. I forgot." His features pinched in apology. "Guess it totally changes meaning when the birds are friends of yours."

"It's okay." I kept the flashlight trained on him as he grabbed a few supplies and then held them up with a grin.

"Ready when you are," he said a few seconds later.

I padded over to the bed and tried implementing the same gradual awakening from before, but Charlene was out—just like all the lights. I frowned. "Maybe we should take her to the vet to get looked over. I'm really starting to worry about her."

"Everything will be closed up for the night by now, but let's get some food in her and see if she perks up. If not, we can go first thing in the morning," Charles said from where he waited near the door.

"Good idea." I leaned down over the bed. "I'm going to pick you up now," I whispered, then did just that.

Charlene sighed and stretched, offering proof of life, but she still didn't wake up.

"Let's go," I said, balancing the kitten and my phone light as best I could while we made our way to the garden.

Sure enough, it was easier to see outside, but I still needed my light to avoid trampling any of the beautiful flowerbeds by accident. We wove along the trails until we reached the bricked property line, close to the spot where Charles had first discovered the kitten.

"If her mother is going to come back searching for her, she'll check here first," I reasoned, shutting off my flashlight and settling myself on the lawn with my legs crossed beneath me.

"Do you think she'll be back?" Charles whispered, almost as if he were afraid to speak the words.

I placed a hand on Charlene's back to make sure she was still sleeping and breathing both. When I was certain she hadn't stirred, I whispered back in answer to my husband's question. "It's not looking good," I admitted with a soft sigh. "But we'll keep trying. Charlene says she's been gone a long time, but that could mean anything. It may have only been a couple hours when we found her for all we know."

"She's very weak for having only been on her own for a little while," he pointed out with a sad expression.

"Well, all we can do is try our hardest and hope for the best," I answered while thoughtfully stroking the smooth black fur.

"I'm going to get her dinner together," he said after we both sat in silence for a few minutes. "I wasn't sure how old she is and what she can handle. Plus I remember hearing cats shouldn't have cow's milk. Something about them being lactose intolerant. But I found special cat milk and some soft food made specifically for kittens." He grabbed a pair of small stainless steel bowls and poured the specialized milk into one. "It took a while to find a pet store that was still open, but I managed to sneak into one a few minutes before closing."

"I'm sure Charlene will appreciate it. She's gotta be starving."

Charles pulled the metal ring on the kitten food can next.

"What's that smell?" the kitten mewled from my lap almost immediately.

I chuckled. All cats are the same, whether young or old, pet or stray. "We have some dinner for you," I enthused, setting her on the ground in front of the two bowls just as Charles finished plopping the kitten pate into the second dish.

She went straight for the tuna-flavored mush, making yummy noises as she snarfed it down as quickly as her tiny mouth would allow.

"Would you look at that?" Charles remarked, his green eyes fixing on the baby lovingly. "Looks like I did good."

"You did great," I said, reaching over to rub him on the shoulder. Charles and I both thought it would be best to wait a couple years before starting a family, but at least now I saw he would make a truly fantastic dad when the time came. Maybe that would be sooner rather than later, after all.

7

Charlene finished half of her wet food before moving on to the milk, which she proceeded to lap up just as enthusiastically. Her ability to eat solid foods was encouraging. Perhaps she wasn't as young as we'd initially feared. But the fact that such a tiny thing was eating so much at one go suggested she'd been on her own for far too long. It's a good thing Charles and I found her before some predator had.

"You stay here," I told my husband, carefully pushing myself to my feet. "I'm going to search for Charlene's mother."

I flipped my phone light back on and started my hunt. I really needed to get more information from the kitten about what her mother looked like, but I also didn't want to upset the frightened little thing any more than I had to. That meant right now I was simply looking for a cat—any cat.

"Here, kitty, kitty!" I called softly, unsure whether this strategy would even work. But what choice did I have?

I moved closer to the house, checking for any hidey holes that might attract an animal in search of shelter. "Hello?" I called.

No one answered. Of course no one did.

I moved around the house to the backyard. The gardens back here weren't as neatly kept as those out front, but still very impressive all the same. I stopped to admire a small vegetable patch and wondered if this was where supper's buttered peas had originated.

After only a very brief pause, I carried forward, making clicking noises that I hoped would entice any cat who might be listening.

Zip! A fast flash of movement on the periphery caught my eye, and I spun around. Whatever I'd noticed had already disappeared from view, however.

"Hello?" I called, voice shaking. Was this the missing mother cat or a roaming murderer? I shuddered again and vowed to stop watching so many true crime documentaries in the future.

Swallowing down that sudden lump of fear, I moved decisively in the direction of the movement. And my senses screamed at me—specifically my sense of smell.

"What is that?" I groaned, waving a hand before my face to help dissipate the awful aroma. With one hand pinching my nose, I used the other to wave my light around until it landed on a huge leafy green plant. Yup, that was definitely the source of the smell. *Gross.*

I snapped a quick photo before turning tail and moving as fast as I could in the other direction.

When I returned to Charles and Charlene, I found that both bowls of food had been licked completely clean. Now a full-bellied fur baby was resting on my husband's lap and purring so loud I could hear it from several paces away.

"Any sign of her?" he asked hopefully, but I just shook my head.

Charlene stopped purring. "Why hasn't my mommy come back?" she demanded, her eyes roving across the garden. Unlike us she could see perfectly in the night. Her hearing beat ours too, which Octo-Cat had reminded me several times over the years—along with every other way cats are superior to humans.

"We haven't found her yet, but we aren't giving up," I assured the little one, taking a seat beside her and Charles. "Can you maybe tell us a bit more about her?"

Charlene closed her eyes and purred softly as she called upon the memories of her mother. "She is the nicest mommy ever with very soft fur for cuddling and very sharp teeth and claws for hunting. I want to be just like her when I grow up!"

"What does she look like?" I prompted gently.

The kitten closed her eyes again, whiskers twitching as she thought. "She's black with brown spots, long whiskers, and a very pink tongue."

I got out my phone again and did a quick web search. "Kind of like this?" I asked, showing her a photo of a tortoiseshell cat.

"That's not my mommy," Charlene cried, offended for a

moment before softening in defeat. "But I guess she looks a little like that."

"Okay, I'm going to show you some more photos, and you can let me know if any of them are your mommy." I typed in *animal rescues near me* and then began scrolling through the photos of adoptable cats, pausing over any mostly black cats to share the photos with Charlene.

But none were a match for the missing mama cat.

"My eyes hurt," the kitten squeaked, squinting them tight. All that blue light must have been bad for her. Oops. So much to learn about babies before I had any of my own.

"We'll stop for tonight," I said tenderly, "but we'll start looking again first thing tomorrow morning."

"You promise?" she asked meekly, her ears falling flat against her head.

"Of course, I promise." I scratched gently at her tiny forehead to reassure her. "Are you okay spending the night inside our room with us?"

Her ears lifted, but she still appeared to be on high alert, ready to run off at any moment. "I think so. You promise not to eat me, right?"

I laughed. "Yes, I promise that too."

"And he won't either?" she asked, turning to look up at Charles with sudden suspicion.

"Neither of us eat cats," I assured her very firmly. "You're safe with us."

As we headed back toward the house, the lights finally flickered on.

"About time," Charles remarked as he concealed Charlene in his large hands.

I glanced up at the house and saw a dark figure backlit in one of the bedroom windows upstairs. It looked like it could be ours, but surely I just had my wires crossed. I wasn't the best with directions, even when I had a GPS to help me. And from my count, there were at least eight bedrooms on the second story, which meant the figure was more than likely occupying one that wasn't ours.

Still, the eerie sight sent a chill straight through me. I glanced toward Charles, but he just kept striding swiftly ahead, completely unaware.

When I looked up at the window again, the figure had vanished, leaving me to wonder if my mind was simply playing tricks on me.

"Careful," Charles warned, his eyes staring straight down as he held the door open for me. "There's mud everywhere."

Sure enough, fresh, wet mud had been tromped across the downstairs. It was too messy to discern clear footprints, but that was clearly the source.

I sucked air in through my teeth. "Oh, Madame Blue is not going to be happy about that."

"Well, just as long as she doesn't blame us," Charles grumbled.

I made extra sure to avoid the filthy rug at the base of the stairs so there would be no question that another guest was responsible for the mess.

But suddenly I found myself feeling a bit guilty about keeping a secret pet on the premises. Madame Blue had been very clear about the rules, and she obviously had a lot to worry about, given her constant grumblings. I didn't want to contribute to her problems, but the lost kitten needed help and I refused to turn my back on that.

I guess it wouldn't be a problem as long as we didn't get caught... At least that's what I told myself as we tucked in for the night.

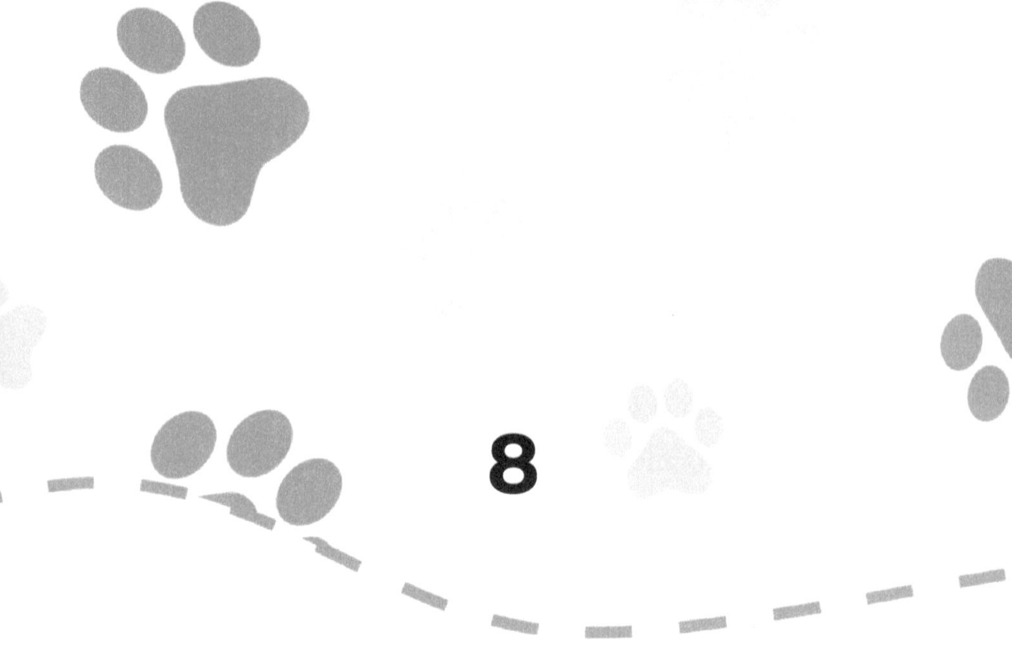

8

"AAAAAAAAH!" a rough scream jolted me from sleep the next morning.

The kitten beside me jumped at least two feet straight into the air and hissed as I grabbed my robe from the love seat near the non-functioning fireplace and ran out into the hall to see what had happened.

"Is everything okay?" I asked a confused-looking Blaire, who hadn't bothered to cover up before stepping into the hall. She rubbed at her eyes and then pointed to the narrow staircase where my husband crouched midway down the steps. No, he wasn't crouched. He'd *fallen* partway through. Splintered wood shot up in jagged spikes all around him. I couldn't see his face, but I assumed he wore an expression of great pain.

"Charles!" I shouted, rushing forward to the edge of the broken staircase. "What happened?"

He grunted and attempted to turn toward me, but shifting his weight caused him to fall a few inches farther into the hole. He let out a long groan before saying, "I was going to surprise you. With biscuits and gravy for breakfast at sunrise," he murmured with the back of his head facing me.

"We have to get you out of there!" I shouted, spinning around in search of someone other than Blaire, who clearly didn't have the strength—or the inclination—to assist us. "Billy? Madame Blue? Can someone please help?"

"Now what's all this fuss about so early in the morning?" the man from the tourist couple asked, pulling open his bedroom door and breezing down the hallway in our direction.

"My husband!" I cried, pointing frantically. "He fell through the stairs and needs help getting out!"

He turned to look and actually had the audacity to chuckle. "You're right. That's quite the pickle he's gotten himself into." He raised his voice to call to Charles. "Hold your horses, son. I'll grab Bill and be right down to help you out."

"This is not how I wanted to start my day." The man's wife appeared wearing another Hawaiian shirt and khakis get-up along with a look of consternation. "Nothing like this ever happened during our other stays."

I bit my tongue to avoid saying something I'd regret.

"So cringe," Blaire said with a laugh before returning to her room. She reappeared a few seconds later holding her phone out before her. "I know just the sound to use with this video, too," she said, leaving no doubt that she was turning my husband's misfortune into a TikTok meme.

"Charles, are you hurt?" I called, choosing to ignore the other guests and focus on what was really important here. "Should I call 9-1-1?"

"More startled than anything," he answered with a sharp grunt. "Knocked the wind right out of me, but nothing's broken."

"Well, let's get you out first, then we can see if we need to visit a doctor." My anxiety had gotten so bad, I wanted to curl into a ball on the floor and start crying—but Charles needed me to be strong, so that's what I tried to do.

"Shoot, what a mess!" Billy said, arriving on the scene with a worn leather tool belt clinched around his waist. "You're going to have to pay for this to be fixed, and it won't be cheap."

"Can you please just get him out of there?" I begged rather than fighting against his ridiculous claim. Right now, he was our best bet for getting Charles back on solid ground.

"We're on it," the tourist man said, appearing at the bottom of the stairs beside Billy. I hadn't spotted a second staircase, but clearly they'd gotten down there somehow, and now they set straight to work on their mission.

Everything seemed to happen in slow motion as Bill and his helper worked to free Charles. For a while I was worried that they'd fall into the hole with him, that the whole house would crumble around us, but eventually they managed to pull him free.

As soon as he was out, I ran down the hall until I found the second set of stairs and bolted down them. When I returned to the base of the broken staircase across the house, I hugged Charles tight. “You had me so worried.”

“Angie, I’m fine. Just a couple of Tylenol and a hot bath, and I’ll be right as rain.” He pulled out of my hug to study me with a piteous expression. “We missed the sunrise, though. And breakfast.”

“I’ll order some delivery. Let’s just get you taken care of first.” I slung an arm around his waist in case he needed the extra support while walking. “Come on, there’s a second staircase over this way.”

“Not so fast, honey,” the tourist woman called from above. “I personally don’t feel safe with you two staying on the second floor. What if your oaf of a husband breaks the other stairway? Then we’ll all be stuck up here for who knows how long? And, well, it makes much more sense to move the two of you than to have to move us and that other young woman with the crazy hair. Don’t you think so, Madame Blue?”

“Better safe than sorry, I suppose,” the elderly caretaker shouted back with a scowl, then dropped her voice to grumble to herself. “But either way, the historical society is not going to take kindly to this mishap.”

She turned toward me and Charles with a frown. “We do have a room on the first floor. Billy, will you unlock it and help them move their belongings down?”

The tourist woman stood with arms crossed and an enormous smirk on her face. “Thank you for taking such good care of us. And if it’s not too much trouble, once you’ve had a chance to clean out the grand suite, could Fred and I move in? We were originally supposed to have that room anyway, so it works out great for everyone."

"Sure, Madeline. Whatever you want," Madame Blue answered with a sigh before ambling off.

Blaire kept recording the whole scene, but nobody paid her much mind. She did shoot a sympathetic glance my way, though and said, "This really sucks for you."

Honestly, I couldn't have said it better myself, even if I'd tried. And right now I just didn't have the energy.

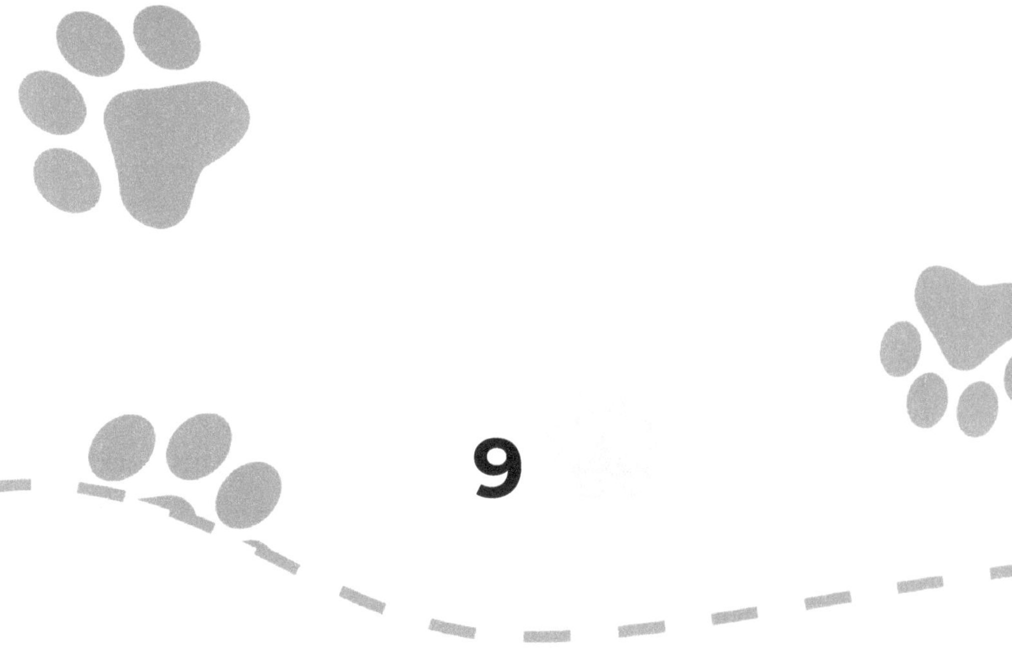

9

"We could sue them for negligence, seeing as I was injured on their property," Charles told me once we were by ourselves again. The other guests had all gone back to their rooms while Billy worked on seeing to our change in accommodations, and Madame Blue was off doing who knows what.

"But you said you weren't hurt," I reminded him gently. Even if we were in the right, I didn't want to waste any more time with these people when it would be so much easier to just move on with our lives.

"I'm not planning to open a case, but it's just the principle of the matter. Especially if they're going to ask for the cost of repairs. That's definitely not legal." Charles pulled out his phone and opened the search window, ready to jump into lawyer mode despite his claims.

I pushed his hand down and shook my head. "They really seem to be in dire financial straits. I wonder what else isn't to code. Charles, that was really scary. I'm not sure if I feel safe staying here for another night. Let's focus on that rather than researching legal action you don't plan to take."

He nodded and tucked his phone back into his jeans pocket. "I understand, Angie. We can't leave, though. Not until we find Charlene's mother."

"Shoot, Charlene!" I cried. Even if Billy and Madame Blue were in the wrong when it came to Charles's accident, we were in the wrong too by willfully disregarding their rules.

"I have to get back up there and hide her before Billy moves all our things and locks us out. I'll meet you at the new room as soon as I have her, okay?"

Charles gave me a peck on the cheek. "I'll wait here and see about getting some breakfast ordered."

"Love you," I called before heading back up the second, unbroken staircase.

When I reached the room, Billy was already there gathering our things for relocation. The tourist woman—Madeline, apparently—was also there, observing the fireplace. "It won't be any problem to get this lit for us tonight, would it?" she said to the porter, not really making it a question.

"Um, excuse me," I barked, not even trying to be polite with them anymore. "Until we're moved, this room still belongs to me and my husband, and we'd appreciate some privacy." I returned the same daggers Madeline had thrown at me over dinner last night.

She narrowed her eyes before switching to a tight-lipped smile. "Whatever you say, honey. It will be ours soon enough." Thankfully, she saw herself out after having stated her piece.

Once she was gone, I stepped into the bathroom where Bill was haphazardly tossing our toiletries into a plastic grocery bag. "Um, Bill, we appreciate your help, but can I please pack up my own belongings? I don't really like the idea of a stranger handling my toothbrush… or my underwear."

"The lady of the house wants it all moved ASAP," he explained, continuing his work undeterred. "Between you and me, she doesn't want to deal with the Mackenzies any more than you do."

"I understand that, but could you just wait out in the hall for a few minutes? I promise I'll get it done quick."

He nodded, handed me the plastic bag, and left, clicking the door shut behind him.

"Charlene?" I whisper-yelled once I knew for sure we were alone.

A moment later, she pushed her little black head out from beneath my pillow. Oh, thank goodness!

"I don't like it here," she growled, surprising me with her deep rumble. "Too many scary people."

I nodded in understanding. Frankly, I found them a bit scary too. "Charles and I will keep you safe until you're back with your mother. You have my word, Charlene. We won't let anything bad happen to you."

"I thought I heard my mommy calling to me last night, but it was just a dream." This sweet kitten kept breaking my heart.

"Dreams do come true," I offered, running my hands over her fur. "But right now we have to get you out of here. They're making us switch rooms, but after that, we'll head back outside to look around, okay?"

She responded by purring and asking to be picked up.

"Perfect. Let's go." I quickly shoved all our loose belongings—along with Billy's plastic bag—into one of Charles's duffle bags, then grabbed a spare sweater to wrap the kitten in while I moved her downstairs.

"Ready for you now. Thank you, Bill," I said as I left the dream room behind. With how terrible everyone had been since we'd arrived, Bill was the only one to show even the slightest glimpse of compassion—be it exceptionally brief. "We appreciate your help."

"Your new room is just off the kitchen. It isn't much. We usually only book it if all the rooms are already spoken for, which hasn't happened in a really long time. But you can easily sneak anything you need from the fridge, so there's that," he offered apologetically. "I'll meet you in the kitchen. Just give me two shakes of a lamb's tail."

"Thank you," I said again before heading back down the long hall and toward the second staircase. As I passed, Madeline and Fred Mackenzie watched me from their doorway with matching expressions of glee. I hated that they were getting what they wanted after such gruesome behavior, but there wasn't a thing I could do about it.

"They're putting us by the kitchen," I told Charles when I joined back up with him, motioning toward the bundle that concealed Charlene with my chin.

"Excellent," he answered calmly. "I am more than ready for those Tylenol. And that bath."

"No bathtub in your new room," Billy said, coming up behind us with one duffle balanced on the suitcase and the other slung over his shoulder. "No bathroom at all, actually. You'll have to use the communal on the first floor. Thankfully, we added a shower stall to it a few years back for just such emergencies."

That was when I finally lost it. My husband had been grievously injured and all he wanted was a hot bath. Why were they making that impossible for us in a literal mansion with multiple accommodations?

"Surely, you see how ridiculous this is?" I hissed, no longer playing nice. "Charles isn't a liability, he's a victim. And my parents paid for your best room, thinking they were reserving the full property, but now you're shoving us into your smallest room because of some other guest's unfounded complaint?"

Billy shrugged, unmoved and apparently unsurprised by my outburst. "If it upsets you, give us a bad review. It's no skin off my back. It's only Madame Blue you'll be hurting, since she's the owner and all."

"You said we'd have to pay for the damages," I reminded him, the rage continuing to build.

He clicked his tongue in disagreement. "I said that to keep my job. I knew that old biddy would be listening."

"If you hate her so much, why do you work here?"

"Hard to beat a job that includes room and board in this economy. Now, after you." He pushed the door open to reveal a room that barely contained the lone queen-sized bed. A tall dresser stood in the corner, and a folding TV tray had been topped with a lamp and doily as some kind of makeshift nightstand. Otherwise, that was it.

"You're kidding me. This is barely more than a closet!" I protested as Bill set our bags by the dresser, taking up almost half of the unoccupied floor space.

"At least the garden is nice," Charles said once the porter had left us to our own devices.

"Most of it, anyway," I shot back, remembering the foul patch of greenery I'd stumbled upon the night before. "Oh, I didn't show you what I found last night." I set Charlene on the new bed, then pulled out my phone and thumbed through the camera roll.

"Here," I said, shoving the screen toward him. "I found this around the back when I was searching for Charlene's mother last night. It smelled terrible."

His face lit with amusement. "Like a skunk?"

"Yeah, actually. How did you—?"

"That's skunk cabbage. Doesn't make much sense to have it in a garden that's as well maintained as this one. Then again, given the condition of the stairs, maybe the garden isn't as well maintained as we once thought."

"What is going on with this place? It's nothing like my mom described, and I doubt it's anything like she remembers. Almost as if everything that could go wrong has."

"Shhh, you'll jinx it," Charles said with a playful wink. Well, at least I had the best possible company for my week in hell.

10

I fed the kitten inside our downsized room while Charles grabbed a quick shower in the first-floor communal bathroom. When he returned, claiming to feel much better, we both got dressed so we could head outside to further investigate the gardens.

"I couldn't find a place that delivers this far out," I revealed as Charles pulled on his shoes. "So let's eat some of the snacks you brought last night and then we can go to town for an early lunch after we've spent a few hours searching."

"Fair enough. I'll grab the snacks," he offered without complaint.

"I'll grab Charlene." She'd wasted no time in sandwiching herself between the mattress and pillow of the new bed.

After a brisk walk across the property, Charles and I settled ourselves at an iron bistro table that stood flanked by two ornate chairs.

"Doritos and beef jerky for breakfast," I quipped, eagerly digging into the snack food. "Living the high life."

"Only the best for my wifey," Charles teased, crunching into a bright orange tortilla chip. "And if you're really good, I'll share my Oreos with you."

"Can't refuse an offer like that," I joked right back.

The two us ate in companionable silence as the three of us kept our eyes and ears peeled for Charlene's missing mother.

"Do you hear that?" I asked after a short while had passed.

Charles straightened in his seat. "What? A cat?"

I strained to hear more clearly but was met with little more than a stream of hushed whispers from across the garden. "I'm not sure. There's multiple voices. They're quiet, though. I can't hear what they're saying."

"Well, let's go find out." Charles stood and brushed his hands together to rid them of the flavor dust.

I sucked each of my fingers clean, then we headed back toward the yellow roses that had so enchanted me the previous afternoon.

"Do you hear them? The voices?" I asked, glancing around but still not finding the speakers.

He shook his head. "Must be an animal. You know I'm useless when it comes to that."

"You're not useless," I insisted before glancing to the kitten in my arms for aid. "Do you hear anyone, Charlene?"

"No, sorry," she mewed sadly. Huh, that was weird.

"Hello?" I called hesitantly as we continued toward the yellow roses.

Finally the words started to make sense. "And that's another thing. I know the lights went out, but if they couldn't see, they should have stayed put. Someone trampled the flower beds out back. They almost stomped right on the queen. The queen!"

"Humans, they're the worst. Almost as bad as that pesky skunk," a second mystery speaker agreed.

"Hear, hear!" several voices chimed at once.

"Hello?" I tried again. "Who's there?"

"What are those two humans doing so close to our hive? Should we sting them?" one of the soft voices ground out.

"Please don't sting me," I cried, now understanding without a doubt whose conversation I was overhearing. "I'm a friend to all creatures. Including bees."

"Is she talking to us? No human has ever done that before." A confused buzzing followed.

I lifted Charlene closer to my face and asked. "Are you sure you can't hear anyone?"

"Nope," the little kitten confirmed. Usually animals had no problem understanding each other, but then again, I'd never spoken with insects before. I'd never heard them until now. I swear, this honeymoon of ours just kept getting stranger and stranger.

With my companions unable to offer assistance, I pressed forward all on my own. "Hello, bees. I'm talking to you. I'm sorry about the trampled flowers and that someone almost hurt your queen. I can help, if you'll talk to me."

I waited as the voices whispered amongst themselves, clearly not wanting to be overheard until they reached some kind of unanimous decision about me.

Finally, one plump bee flew out to greet me face to face. "Greetings, human. I am Aldrin and this is Lightyear." He waited as a second buzzing insect joined us.

"Hello. I'm Angie." I stayed stock still, but Charles jumped behind me.

"Oh boy. More bees. I'm just going to go grab my EpiPen, just in case. I'll take Charlene too." As soon as I transferred the kitten to his arms, my husband took off like a shot.

"You do not fear us, human," Aldrin noted, bobbing in the air.

"Angie," I reminded him with a gentle voice. "Call me Angie."

"Apologies. We have not spoken to any human before. Are you the one who lives in the house?" I couldn't tell whether this came from Aldrin or Lightyear. I wasn't sure that it mattered, since the bees all seemed to act and think as one.

"No, I'm just here on vacation." I chose not to point out that Madame Blue and I looked nothing alike, seeing as she was several decades older, much shorter, and much louder as a general rule. I'd guess that all humans looked the same to bees, the way all bees tended to look the same to humans.

The two bees buzzed back and forth to each other, communicating with a series of movements rather than words. When at last they seemed to agree, they spoke to me again. “Then would you share our complaints with the human who does?”

“I can try,” I answered truthfully. I could barely share my own complaints with Madame Blue and Billy, and I was a paying guest. I didn’t think they’d agree to do anything to help the bees, but I would at least try.

“Good enough for us,” Lightyear decided, and both bees bounced up and down.

Aldrin was the one who delivered their list of grievances. “Our gardens used to flourish, giving us an abundance of delicious honey, but lately the landscape is looking bleak. Some of our favorite flowers are disappearing, only to be replaced with poor substitutes.”

“The skunk cabbage,” I said, thinking back to last night plus Charles’s later identification of the plant.

Both bees zigzagged in a frenzy before calming down enough to speak again. “Skunks are natural enemies of bees. Someone is attempting to threaten us, and we do not take kindly to it. Our honey is also being over-harvested, and it’s not leaving enough to nourish our hive. We are happy for humans enjoy the fruits of our labor in moderation, but now our sustenance is being stolen right from under us. We work hard and yet our bellies remain empty into the next day.”

“I’m really sorry. That sounds horrible.” I sympathized with them even though I had little basis for understanding the secret lives of bees.

"It is quite horrible," they said in unison, moving in a synchronized aerial dance.

"I will see what I can do for you," I assured them. Maybe if I asked some questions about the skunk cabbage I'd found and where I could buy some local honey, Madame Blue would inadvertently open up to me.

"That is all we ask," one of the bees said before both flitted back to the hive somewhere out of sight.

Charles and I had come to this old stone mansion nearly a thousand miles away from home to get away from it all. Yet somehow we found ourselves plagued by mystery after mystery. If it weren't for one very sweet kitten needing our help, we would already be gone. But since we were stuck for the time being, we might as well try to solve a couple of these mysteries and hopefully leave the place better than we found it.

11

Once the bees left me, I decided to wander the property line in hopes of finding Charlene's mother. The entire yard was marked with a red brick fence running around the perimeter, but there was plenty of nature on the other side of the fence, too. Maybe we should expand our search to the neighboring properties as well. I'd ask Charles for his thoughts on the matter when he returned with his EpiPen.

Halfway through my second circle around the garden, Blaire barged out through the front door, shouting into her phone. The sunlight reflected beautifully off her multi-hued hair, making me wonder if I could pull off such a bold look myself.

I tried not to listen to her conversation as I quietly continued my search, but Blaire's voice carried across the open space.

"Maybe I don't want to come home! Did you ever think about

that?" she practically snarled while I busied myself inspecting the hydrangeas.

A few moments later, she laughed bitterly. "You really think that, huh? Do not—I repeat, *do not*—come here. I don't want to see you right now, Dylan, and at this rate, I'm not sure I ever want to see your stupid face again!"

I stole a glance at Blaire and found her freckled face now covered with red splotches, too. The poor thing. She was so young to have such intense domestic troubles. Should I offer to help somehow?

She caught me staring and scowled my way.

I quickly averted my gaze.

"I've gotta go," she said much more quietly to the person on the other end of the call—presumably a boyfriend named Dylan. "There's some nosy lady listening in. And besides, I have nothing to say to you anyway."

She ended the call and then let out a primal scream before rounding on me. "Enjoying your daily dose of *schadenfreude*?" she yelled before marching straight back inside and slamming the door behind her.

Well, at least it seemed like Blaire could take care of herself, even if she was no great fan of mine. Hopefully, she knew not to go back to a boyfriend who wasn't treating her right.

One day she would find her Charles.

I took a moment to luxuriate in the love I had for my new husband, only to realize I hadn't seen him for quite a while. He'd left when I was speaking with the bees, promising to be right back after he'd grabbed his EpiPen. He definitely should have returned by now.

Unless something bad happened?

Oh my gosh, it was the broken staircase all over again. Generally, I wasn't a very superstitious person, but we were definitely living according to Murphy's Law since arriving in Virginia. Everything that could go wrong was—and then some.

I quickened my pace, suddenly desperate to find Charles. I ran to the base of the broken staircase first but couldn't see him there. I did, however, hear a faint pounding from the back of the house, so I ran that way next.

"Charles?" I called, tracing my way through the kitchen toward our new bedroom.

"Angie? Is that you? I'm locked in!" he called glumly through the door.

"Locked in? What happened?" I grabbed the doorknob and attempted to turn it, but it was definitely stuck. *Ugh!*

"I don't know," my husband's tired, muffled voice answered. "It took me a couple minutes to find my EpiPen since our stuff was all mixed up from changing rooms. By the time I found it and went to leave, the door wouldn't budge. I've been calling for help a while now, but nobody's answered."

I knew that Blaire had been occupied by her phone call, but where was everyone else? Why wasn't anyone helping? Well, at least I was here now—for all the good that did.

"I can't get it to open, either. I'm going to find help!" I shouted, hating to leave him there.

Billy had been more or less gracious about helping us earlier, but what would he think now that we had a second crisis on our hands within the span of just a couple short hours? If he'd heard Charles calling, he'd chosen to ignore him.

I searched the house for any sign of life—I even attempted knocking on the guest rooms upstairs, but nobody answered my cries for help, even though I swore I could hear Blaire moving about in her room, not that she'd be able to offer much help anyway.

Having exhausted my options inside, I swung back by our room to tell Charles I was still searching for someone to open the door, then stormed outside quickly reaching my rope's end. I remembered seeing an old toolshed on the far edge of the property; maybe I could find something to help me take the door off its hinges. Right now that seemed like the best option, because nobody else was here and I certainly didn't trust myself to pick a lock.

I'd stalked halfway to the shed when the same old pickup truck we'd parked beside upon arriving rumbled into the driveway. I turned back to the lot and watched as Madame Blue parked and then hopped down, spotting me almost instantly.

"Yes?" she shouted unhappily. "What is it now?"

My cheeks grew hot with embarrassment. "Well, Billy switched our bedroom to the one downstairs, and now the door won't open. My husband is stuck inside."

"Stuck? Oh, for crying out loud. If it's not one thing, it's the other. Can't even leave for one hour to run an errand in town.

Things like this are exactly why the bank denied my loan. They don't think the place is worth saving, and sad to say I'm starting to agree." She shook her head and fumbled with her keys.

I could see she was in no mood to be bothered, but I also needed her help to free Charles, leaving me no choice but to press her further. "I'm really sorry to bother you with this. It's just that he's locked in there with no food and no bathroom."

"Yeah, yeah, I'm coming," she groused, pulling her purse strap high over her shoulder as she marched past me and into the house.

When she tried the doorknob and found that it was, indeed, stuck, she returned to the kitchen to grab a step stool. After setting it in front of the door, she climbed on top, then swiped her hand over the doorframe and pulled down an old brass key, stuck it in the knob, and pushed the door open.

"Now, if you don't mind, I'm behind on preparing the day's lunch," she huffed, leaving me and Charles to stare at each other with bemused expressions.

"I didn't know there was a key," I told him with a wince before falling into his arms to offer a giant hug.

He stroked my hair to soothe me, even though he was the one whose safety had once again been compromised. "Somebody must have locked me in, but why?"

"That, my dear, is a very good question."

He was right. Somebody was definitely out to get him, and I needed to discover who before anything else bad transpired.

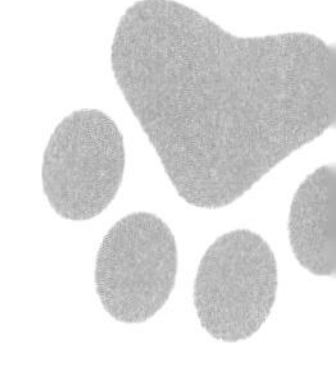

12

Charles's stomach growled as we were resting on the bed together.

"I guess assorted snack food doesn't exactly make the best breakfast, especially since you missed dinner last night," I told him while Charlene snoozed tucked into his side.

"Yeah, but no one delivers out here, and we can't exactly leave Charlene." He paused to run his hand over the kitten a few times before turning his attention back to me. "Madame Blue mentioned making lunch, right? Maybe we should just brave another awkward meal with the others. Once we find Charlene's mother, we can go into town for a massive nine-course meal."

"And we could book a new place to stay while we're there," I added with a sigh, rolling over onto my side to face him. "But are you sure about waiting to leave?"

"What better option do we have? We can't leave this baby on her own, and we can't exactly trust anyone else here with her."

"We could take her with us to the new hotel," I suggested, already knowing that wasn't really an option.

Charles's green eyes bored into me. "But then we'd have no reason to come back to the property. You and I both know Madame Blue would kick us out in a heartbeat."

"True." I picked at the skin on my elbow, a nasty nervous habit. "I'm just worried something else bad will happen."

He shook his head, also shaking off my concern. "We'll be fine."

"I know I will be, but what about you?"

"I'll be fine too," he assured me despite loads of evidence to the contrary, but he had a smile on his face again. "Now let's go eat before my stomach starts making some truly terrifying noises."

I still felt unsure about joining the others but had to admit we were in a pretty tight spot. Reluctantly, I joined Charles, making sure to swipe the key from the top of the doorframe so nobody else had access to it while we were staying inside. We found Madame Blue, Billy, and the Mackenzie couple eating pastrami sandwiches and what appeared to be potato salad.

"No Blaire today?" I asked casually as Charles and I took our seats.

"She does intermittent fasting. Some trendy Zoomer thing," Madeline Mackenzie explained with a huge grin pointed my way.

She seemed to be in a far better mood now that she had the room she wanted. Good riddance.

Charles pulled the platter of sandwiches across the table and helped himself to two on rye, leaving the sourdough for me.

I spooned big heaps of the salad onto each of our plates while he polished off the first triangle of his first sandwich. Something green mixed into the creamy potatoes caught my eye, causing me to take a closer look at the lump on my plate. Yup, capers.

That was one food I truly despised, and there would be no eating around them. The bitter little balls ruined anything they touched—especially my taste buds. *Bleck.*

Charles finished his first sandwich and then dug into his potatoes with great enthusiasm. After taking that first bite, he turned to me and I nodded. A second later, he grabbed my plate and transferred all of my salad over to his. Ah, he knew me so well.

"My cooking not to your liking?" Madame Blue shouted from the other end of the table.

"The sandwiches are delicious," I enthused, pointing toward my plate with one hand and giving a thumbs-up with the other. "I'm just not a fan of capers."

"No class," she muttered to herself, though it was loud enough for everyone to hear.

Mrs. Mackenzie snickered, but then her husband put his hand on her arm and she fell quiet.

Charles seemed to eat even faster after that, wanting to free us quickly while still satisfying his stomach. By the time I finished my sandwich, crusts and all, he was ready to go.

He placed his napkin on his plate and rose to his feet. “Thank you for a delicious meal.”

I got up too, then scrambled after him as he strode swiftly toward our room, which was now very close to the dining area.

At the door, Charles’s stomach gurgled loudly.

“Didn’t you get enough to eat?” I teased.

He grimaced and placed a hand to his belly. “Just need to make a quick trip to the bathroom. I’ll be back with you soon.” He bent to offer me a kiss, but then quickly changed his mind and took off power-walking in the direction of the communal restroom.

I shrugged and let myself into the room to check on Charlene.

She woke up when I joined her on the bed. “Where’s your mate?” she asked, searching the small room for Charles.

“He’ll be back soon. How are you feeling?”

“Still sad about Mommy, but I’m not so sleepy anymore.” She licked her paw and ran it over her head.

“That’s good!” I enthused as the kitten settled herself on my lap.

“Yeah,” she said with a heavy sigh, falling over onto her side dramatically in true cat fashion. “But now I’m bored. Would you tell me more of the story of Octavius?”

I chuckled at how wide her bright eyes were when she made this request. “You like that story, huh?”

“Yes, very much.” She bobbed her head, already picking up our human gestures after such a short acquaintanceship.

Then I had an idea that I was sure would be a hit. “Want to see a picture of him?”

“Yes!” she squeaked in pleasure, jumping back to her feet and glancing around the room in confusion. “Where is it?”

“On my phone, one sec.” I pulled out my cell phone and flicked through the camera roll, settling on a photo I’d snapped of Octo-Cat and Grizabella on my wedding day, which had somehow turned into their wedding day, too. He looked very handsome in a pink bowtie while she stood at his side with a bow of her own and a fancy lacy veil.

“Wow, I’ve never seen a cat like that before.” Her eyes were trained on the Himalayan, a former show cat and true beauty.

“That’s Grizabella. She’s his mate,” I explained, then pointed to the other side of the photo. “And that’s Octavius.”

Charlene looked at Octo-Cat briefly before her eyes darted straight back to Grizz. “Does she live with you too?” the kitten wanted to know.

“No,” I answered with a sad smile. Of course my cat fell in love with someone on the other side of the country, because life could never be easy. “She lives very far away.”

“I bet he misses her when she’s not around. Just like I miss my mommy.”

“I think you’re right about that. Want to see more photos?” I offered, since like every cat owner in the history of existence my camera roll was filled with candid snaps of my furry roommate.

“I want to see all the photos!” she cried, drawing a happy chuckle from me in response.

Charlene was absolutely enamored with my spoiled tabby, asking many questions as we browsed. Finally she squinted her eyes tight and reported that the light was hurting them again. "But we can look at more later, right?"

"We can even call him if you want to meet him. When your eyes are feeling better."

"I would love that very much, but right now I'm feeling sleepy again." She wasted no time curling back into a tight little ball.

"Good night, Charlene," I said, placing a light kiss between her ears.

13

Charles remained in the bathroom for a worryingly long time. At one point, I even got up to check if he'd somehow gotten locked in again, but he assured me—through a tightly shut door—that he was fine and would be out soon.

I tried not to worry, but this was odd behavior for my new husband. Another hour passed before he finally returned to our room, looking absolutely worse for wear.

"I think someone poisoned me," he whispered cautiously.

"Poisoned!" I couldn't help but shout.

"Shhh," he warned, putting a finger to his lips to emphasize the point. "We don't know who's listening. And poison might be too strong a word, but I do suspect there were laxatives mixed in with the potatoes. You're fine, right?"

"Fit as a fiddle." I spun around with my arms in the air to give him a look at me from all angles, then dropped my arms and frowned. "But do you really think someone slipped you something? That's awful."

He held his stomach and dropped onto the foot of the bed so as not to disturb Charlene who was sleeping near the headboard. "Yeah," he groaned. "Someone's definitely out to get me."

I lay across the middle of the bed between the two of them, turning onto my side to face Charles. A theory was forming in my head.

"Maybe not you specifically," I said, giving that a second to sink in. "If they slipped something into the potatoes, they could have meant to get the both of us. Same with the stairs. They had no way of knowing you'd be first down in the morning. And the room, that could have just as easily been me—or both of us—inside."

Charles thought about this for a moment. "So someone's out to get us. They just keep getting *me* specifically. But why would anyone even want to? We just arrived last night, and nobody knows us here."

"Your guess is as good as mine, and I have no guesses at all. We do, however, have a fairly limited pool of suspects."

"Madame Blue, Billy, the rainbow-haired girl—"

"Blaire," I provided.

"Right, Blaire, and that older couple who nabbed our room right out from under us." His expression turned sour. "My money's on them."

"The Mackenzies are pretty unpleasant—I'll give you that—

but our culprit could really be anyone here. Blaire's made it no secret she doesn't care for me. But it's Billy and Madame Blue who have the best access to everything. Let's assume the stairs were an honest-to-goodness accident. Someone still had to purposely lock you in and lace the potatoes with laxatives."

Charles's eyes lit with understanding. "Madame Blue is the one who prepared the food, which makes her our most likely suspect."

"Maybe, but maybe not. When the lights went out during dinner, she called for Billy to help with the candles, but Billy wasn't there." I just now realized Charles hadn't been there with me during that ill-fated supper. He didn't have all the same first-hand information I did, and I hadn't thought to share these details last night, assuming they were simply minor caveats. Now they could be our biggest clues.

"You think Billy's the one who cut the power?" Charles summed up.

"Honestly, I don't know what to think at this point. The only thing I know for sure is that we're not safe here." A shiver tore through me. I hated to think what might happen next. Poor Charles had already been through the wringer and didn't deserve even a drop of additional trouble.

"But we're stuck until we find Charlene's mother," he said.

We both gazed lovingly at the snoozing kitten.

"One good thing, we have the key to our room now." I pulled it out of my pocket with a grin. "If we spend most of the day in the garden searching for mama cat, we can lock our room whenever we're not in here."

He took the key from me and studied it for a moment before tucking it into his front pocket. "True, and I can go into town around dinner to pick up some takeout and stock up our food supplies again."

I frowned at the thought of him leaving yet again. We weren't supposed to spend even a second apart this week. "I'm sorry our honeymoon has turned into such a downer."

Charles reached for me and pulled me tight to his side. "Angie, dear, we have the rest of our lives together. We'll have a million opportunities to do the big romantic vacation thing some other time."

I forced a smile. I knew he was right, but still, this trip was turning out almost the exact opposite of what I'd anticipated. "Well, at the very least, this trip is becoming quite unforgettable." And Charles and I weren't fighting or turning on each other—that was important, too.

He bobbed his head encouragingly. "We'll laugh about it one day."

"Provided we both make it out of here alive," I added gloomily.

"Stop it." Charles brushed a thumb across my cheek. "We'll be just fine. We weren't suspecting any mishaps earlier, but now we're on high alert. We have a plan."

Yes, we had a plan. "I just hope it's the right plan."

14

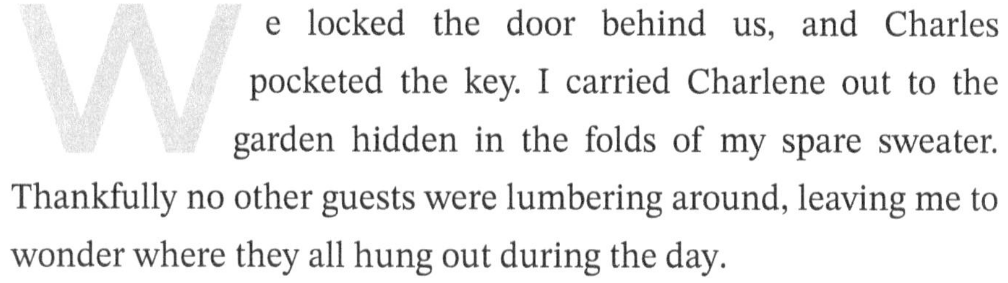

We locked the door behind us, and Charles pocketed the key. I carried Charlene out to the garden hidden in the folds of my spare sweater. Thankfully no other guests were lumbering around, leaving me to wonder where they all hung out during the day.

"I think we should start with the bees. I want to ask them if they've seen any other worrying occurrences—things that may be related to the series of misfortunes you've faced since arriving," I explained once I was sure nobody else was around.

Charles dug into his pocket and pulled out a bright yellow tube with an orange cap. "Got my EpiPen, although I should probably teach you how to use it, just in case."

I remained quiet as he talked me through how I could save his life in case of a severe allergic reaction. "I really don't like this," I told him. "It's scary to think of losing you, especially with the kinds of *accidents* that keep happening."

He placed a kiss on my hairline. "You won't lose me. I'll take Charlene to another part of the garden while you speak to the bees. Oh, and while you're talking maybe you can ask them not to sting me?"

"Good idea." Charles headed toward the back of the property with Charlene in tow while I tracked my way back to the yellow roses, knowing the hive was hidden nearby. "Aldrin? Lightyear?" I called out. "Hello, bees? I'd like to talk to you again please."

When nobody responded, I began searching the flowerbeds and trees for any sign of their hive. My search took me farther and farther away from the gorgeous yellow flowers. I finally found a white wooden box hidden in some bushes near the foul-smelling skunk cabbage. "Aldrin? Lightyear?" I tried again with my nose plugged. The cabbage didn't smell nearly as bad today as it had last night, but I still wasn't taking any chances.

"Greetings. How may my colony and I help you, human?" I turned to see an enormously plump bumblebee sitting on a black-eyed Susan nearby. Given her size and the fact that she was a female, this had to be the queen.

Not knowing the slightest about bee social etiquette, I curtsied —just in case. "Your majesty."

"Please just call me by my name. That shall suffice."

"Yes, your maj—uh, what is your name?"

"I am Bey." *Queen Bey,* of course.

"Hello, Bey. I am Angie. What are you doing out of your hive?" Carefully I lowered myself to the ground and hunched over so that I was closer to eye level with Bey.

She rubbed her front legs together as she spoke. I was now close enough to see that. "My worker drones are hunting for a new location to build our hive. We cannot tolerate being so near this wretched plant."

We both glanced toward the skunk cabbage. "I can't say I blame you there. Do you need my help moving your apiary?"

"No, we will make our own hive, so that the humans can no longer over-harvest our honey. We'll be solving both problems in one action."

I thought of the expression I hated—two birds, one stone—and decided to use a saying I quite liked in its place. "That idea sounds like the bees' knees," I announced proudly and overly amused by myself.

Bey looked down at her plump forelegs, confused. "I do not understand."

I chuckled at her look of bewilderment. "Don't worry about it. Just a silly human expression."

She made a sharp buzzing noise that I took to be a sigh—or maybe a scream. "You may be silly, Angie, but lately other humans have become a danger to us."

"Aldrin and Lightyear told me about the over-harvesting and the new plants," I offered, recalling the earlier conversation.

Bey circled slowly on the flower before settling down again.

"Were it not for tradition, we would leave this place altogether. But this lot is where my mother lived out her rule, and her mother before her."

"This garden has sentimental value. I can understand that. What can I do to help ensure you can stay?" I really did want to help. I hadn't spent much time in conversation with bees before now, but I knew from the news that their populations were at risk and that their survival was important to the whole planet. Surely I could do my part to save this one hive while given the chance.

"Keep the other humans away," Bey commanded, her voice haunting. "I do not wish to sacrifice members of my colony to communicate our displeasure via stings. But I fear we are close to that point."

"Oh, yes, that reminds me, please don't sting my husband. He is a good man, and very allergic."

Bey made a strange shrill buzzing sound again. "Sadly, I cannot tell one human from another. I will not even recognize you, should we meet again."

I nodded subtly, not wanting to overdo my motions when speaking with such a tiny creature. "While I have you, then, have you noticed any other strange goings-on in this garden or its house?"

"Strange how?" Bey's voice was growing weak, exhausted. It probably wasn't good for her to spend so long out of the nest. I would be quick with my questions, but first I needed to take a few minutes to catch her up on all the trouble Charles had faced since our arrival.

She sat motionless on the flower, listening with rapt attention. "You humans are a danger to yourselves even more so than us."

I sighed. "That is sadly quite true."

"I can offer no help, other than to tell you much has changed during my reign. These gardens were once the envy of all, but more and more, their glory has been compromised. Not from neglect, but from willful destruction."

"Someone is bringing in the bad plants," I summarized.

"And removing the good ones. Over-harvesting our honey and causing a great famine."

I clucked my tongue at this. "I'm sorry. That's awful."

"We are not the paragon of hard work without reason. Starting today, my workers will be constructing a new hive, and together we will usher in a new era of prosperity. Until then I will endure and put on a strong face for my colony."

"You are a good leader," I assured her.

"As all queens should be."

"Be, ha! Get it, *bees* should *be*?" I couldn't help it. The unexpected pun brightened my mood once more. Hopefully Bey saw the humor in it too.

"You are a strange human, but a kind one. Good luck with your problems."

"Good luck to you with yours. I'll talk with the owner of this house and see if she can offer any help."

"I do not hold out much hope but appreciate your efforts all the same. Farewell, Angie." Queen Bey kept her place on the dark flower center, telling me I had been dismissed from her audience.

Now to find my husband and our temporarily adopted kitten to tell them what little I had learned from our talk—and to see if Charles had any ideas for helping the colony while we were still here at the old stone mansion that held many mysteries within its walls and gardens.

15

We let Charlene prowl around the garden on her own four feet for the next hour, hoping it might encourage mama cat to make contact. We kept close watch to ensure she remained safe and undiscovered by Madame Blue and the other guests.

While she explored, I showed Charles the patch of skunk cabbage and told him how the bees were moving from the apiary to a new self-made hive as a result. “It doesn’t smell as bad today, but I’m sure it’s still terrible for the bees.”

“Let me see here.” Charles bent down to examine one of the thick leaves. “Someone trampled it fairly recently. That’s probably why it smelled so bad last night but is getting better today.”

Shame flooded my chest. “Oh, I hope I wasn’t the one to run into it. I’d feel awful for causing all that trouble for Bey and her colony.”

"I don't think it was you. Look here." Charles shook his head, then pointed to another section of the cabbage patch. "It's only been flattened in a few spots around the edges. Someone who accidentally ran over it would have left a much more obvious trail."

"So you think someone stomped on it on purpose?" I summarized.

"Well, someone planted it here on purpose," he argued, rising to his feet and then brushing off his palms.

"True. We should probably look around and see if we find anything else that seems out of sorts."

"We can take pictures and reverse image search to figure out the identity of each flower and plant," Charles suggested, pulling out his phone, ready to jump deep down the research rabbit hole. "Perhaps that will be more telling than looking for visual cues."

"Oh, great idea!" I pulled out my phone, too. He and I both loved intellectual challenges, and this was a doozy. "I think there's an app that helps identify flowers too. Let me download it real fast."

For the next hour or so, we took photos of each plant we found on the lot, trying our best not to attract attention as we catalogued the garden.

"This is tough," I ground out once we'd snapped the last one. "There are so many different sub-species. Like how do we know if this little guy is a Shasta daisy or an ox-eye?" I ran my fingertip over the delicate white flower and sighed.

Charles, however, was still in high spirits. With a focused

expression, he tapped on his phone and flipped through a couple articles. "My money's on ox-eye."

"Why?" I leaned over to see what he'd pulled up on his screen.

He handed me the phone while he explained. "It's an invasive species. It looks like a flower, but it's really a weed, famous for destroying the work of inexperienced gardeners in many climates, including this one."

"But Madame Blue isn't inexperienced," I argued. "When my parents honeymooned here, the garden was perfect, and that was decades ago. Presumably she was the owner then, too."

"My guess is someone swapped the plants out on purpose so that they could destroy the garden from within."

"But who would do that and why?"

Charles shrugged, then joined me in a sigh. "Who would lock me in our room or sabotage the potato salad?"

"I really don't like this." I hung my head, feeling more confused than ever as the clues continued to stack up.

"Me, neither. But I have an idea that should make you feel better."

I looked up, waiting for him to reveal his latest grand idea.

My new husband met me with a loving smile. "Let's call home. I know you've got to be missing everyone there. Talking to them will make you feel better."

"But this week is supposed to be about just us," I argued, shaking my head and grabbing his hand.

He squeezed my hand and then let it go. "I know better than

to keep you from your nan. Besides, we'll have the rest of our lives to spend time together just the two of us."

"I like the sound of that," I admitted, biting my lower lip as I thought. "Okay, let's call."

"I'll go find Charlene," he offered, blowing me a kiss as he trounced away.

I wasted no time pulling my phone right back out and placing the call. I really missed my grandmother. She'd been my best friend as long as I could remember, and it was weird to even go a couple days without seeing her shining face.

She answered my FaceTime call after a few short rings. I couldn't see much of her, but she appeared to be lounging in bed while wearing hot pink silk pajamas and an enormous grin.

"Angie, darling!" she exclaimed, her smile widening even further. "How's married life treating you?"

"Married life is great. I'm not so sure about the rest of it, though," I confessed, trying to keep my expression bright for her benefit.

"I'll be right back, Grant," my grandmother whispered offscreen before returning to me.

"Tell me all about it," she said, moving through the house until she landed in the kitchen. "I'll just put on some tea."

And so I told her everything, concluding with, "But please don't share any of this with Mom or Dad. They were really excited to give us this gift, and I'd hate for them to hear how much trouble this place has been giving us, especially when they both have such fond memories from its heyday.

"Oh, dear. That's terrible," Nan said, steeping a tea bag in a mug of hot water.

"Yeah. I hope your honeymoon is going better than ours?" My words lilted up at the end, seeing as I was almost afraid to ask.

"Well, our honeymoon is next week after you get back. Grant booked a surprise cruise in Alaska!" she gushed, fluffing her hair with one hand like a fancy lady.

I laughed at her show of enthusiasm. You could take the actress off Broadway, but that dramatic persona remained even decades after retirement. "What? Why do you want to go somewhere so cold?" I insisted, now with a genuine smile. Talking to her always made me feel so much better, no matter what else was going on in our lives.

"Oh, *pffft.*" She blew a raspberry, making me giggle. "Grant says they have harsh winters but the most lovely summers in the whole world. We're having a good time here too, though. I never thought I'd remarry after losing your grandfather, but I'm so glad I have Grant now that you're all grown up and starting a family of your own."

"I'm glad you have him, too, but Charles and I are not starting a family just yet," I reminded her with a stern expression.

She waved away my concern with her hand. "You know what I mean, dear."

"I have gotten some unexpected experience with motherhood this week, though." I proceeded to tell her all about Charlene, then added, "Man, you really have missed so much."

"It sounds like it! Many memories in the making, both good

and bad, I'd wager." Her eyes held a knowing glint. She and I both knew that some of my worst experiences had turned into my best memories. Like meeting Octo-Cat after my traumatic near-death experience at the hands of a faulty coffee maker.

"That reminds me," I said suddenly, growing excited. "Is Octo-Cat around? Charlene wanted to meet him. She's kind of a fan."

"Uh-oh." Nan's face blanched. "You remember what happened last time that cat had a fan. Pringle entered all of our lives."

"He's not so bad," I said with a smile, remembering the special moment we'd shared on my wedding day.

"Okay. One second, then." The screen grew dark, but I still heard Nan loud and clear. "Paisley, find the kitty!" she shouted in a high-pitched baby voice.

A few moments later, a sharp string of barks rose on the other end of the call. "I think that's my cue," she said with a chuckle, heading up the stairs—not just once, but twice—all the way to my tower bedroom. Charles and I had talked about moving into the master now that he'd be joining me in residence, but I'd become quite attached to my tower.

Apparently, Octo-Cat had, too. Even though he had his own bedroom, complete with a fish tank and everything else a spoiled feline could ever want, he was still hanging out in my room while I was away from home.

While Nan went to get him, I flagged down Charles to tell him I was going inside, then hurried to the privacy of our accommodation.

I'd only just shut the door behind me when Nan held the phone in front of that furry little face I missed so much.

"Aww, what are you doing in my room? Do you miss me?" I cooed, partially teasing but mostly delighted.

His ears pressed down against his head. "Don't be so—"

"I miss you, too," I interrupted so he would know the feeling was mutual. "It's okay to admit you love me, even when nothing bad is going on."

"What do you mean nothing is bad? *Everything* is bad. My Grizabella has gone home, and now I am stuck missing her," he growled as if the whole thing were my fault. To be fair, this was their honeymoon period, too, and they were spending it apart. Despite all our misfortunes, at least Charles and I still had each other.

"I'm really sorry," I said and meant it. "We'll book a trip to go see her in Colorado soon, okay?"

"I'm not okay, but what choice do I have? We can't help who we love, and that darling kitten has my whole heart and soul." He sighed and flopped over onto his side, tail a-swishing.

I think I swooned a little at his declaration of love. Cats—when they showed you love, it was like you became the queen of the whole universe.

As I thought about what I might say next, the door to our room swung open to admit Charles.

I motioned for him to join me on the bed. "Speaking of kittens, there's someone here who would like to meet you," I said, positioning the screen in front of the little black kit-kat.

"So this is my replacement for the week," Octo-Cat intoned, then let out a soft chuff that told me he was just joking.

"Hello, Mr. Octavius. I like your pictures and your story." Charlene appeared unsure of herself as she heaped praises on my tabby back home.

But Octo-Cat ate the praise right up. "The human's been bragging about me, eh? Can't say I blame her."

"Yes, she loves you very much. And your mate is the most beautiful cat I've ever seen in all my life." Yup, Charlene definitely knew how to get on his good side right from the start.

He smiled wide, teeth and all. "Yeah, kid, you're absolutely right. Hey, Angie, can I talk to you in private for a sec?"

"Sure. Be right back," I told Charles before heading for the communal bathroom and shutting myself inside.

"That kitten is hardly old enough to be away from its mother. What are you doing with her?" he demanded, concern reflecting in his amber eyes.

"She's lost," I explained quietly. "We've been searching for her mother almost non-stop, but so far no luck."

"If you haven't found her yet, she's probably not coming back," he said with eyes lowered, telling me he hated to be the one to deliver this somber news.

"I know, but we have to try."

"Good luck, then. She seems like a sweet kid. I hope it all works out for her."

"Yeah, me too," I said before ending the call.

16

When I returned to our room, I found Charlene bouncing on top of the mattress showing great excitement.

"That was awesome!" she cheered while Charles took a video of her adorable antics.

We really needed to get back outside to look around for her mother some more, but our search was beginning to seem more and more hopeless. And right now the young kitten was so happy that I hated to upset her by abruptly changing the subject. So instead I stood with Charles and watched her celebrate meeting her newfound hero.

When she tired herself out enough to fall back to sleep, we snuggled together while watching a movie on my iPad. Once that was over, Charles ventured into town to grab dinner and some more supplies while I hung back with Charlene, continuing to search local rescue groups for any sign of her lost mother.

That night, we ate dinner in bed, enjoying the simplicity of each other's company. After that, we spent some more time outdoors, hoping Charlene's mother would find us—but no such luck.

We went to bed, the day ending much better than it had started, thanks to our caution. Still, even if we managed to survive the rest of the week at the mansion, we were still facing a ticking clock when it came to reuniting the kitten with her mother. I really hoped this week would have a happy ending for the sweet girl, seeing as Charles and I had already gotten ours.

I woke up sometime during the night to the sound of heavy footsteps treading outside our door.

Charles slept deeply beside me, his soft breaths making it obvious the sounds hadn't disturbed him in the slightest. Well, that just left me to investigate. I refused to be a sitting duck while someone planted some new trap for us to fall into the next day. Poor Charles had already been through more than enough.

Tugging my robe around me, I padded out into the dark kitchen and flipped the light switch on.

A shock of rainbow hair greeted me.

"Blaire, what are you doing out here?" I glanced at the digital clock above the stove. "It's two o'clock in the morning!"

"I know what time it is," she told me flatly, shutting the fridge before her, but not without first taking a jug of milk in hand.

"I thought the kitchen was off limits," I pointed out sassily, too tired to try to play nice with someone who wouldn't even meet me halfway.

She rolled her eyes. "Which is why I'm here in the middle of the night, duh."

"You've done this before, haven't you?" I asked as she headed to one of the cupboards and grabbed a glass, seeming to know exactly where she'd find it. "Are you the one who slipped laxatives into the potato salad at lunch?"

Blaire couldn't hide her spurt of laughter, not that she tried to.

"It's not funny," I seethed, then grabbed the glass of milk from her before she could bring it to her lips. "Would you please take this seriously? You poisoned the potatoes, locked him in his room, sabotaged the stairs. When will enough finally be enough?"

Her eyes widened as she ran her fingers over the milk jug's handle. "Calm down. I didn't do any of that, okay? I literally do not care enough about you or your husband to attempt to poison you."

I nervously picked at the skin on my elbow. Was I wrong in accusing Blaire, or was she simply denying her misdeeds now that she'd been caught?

She placed the milk back in the fridge, then asked, "Do you really think someone sabotaged the stairs?"

I nodded emphatically. "Yes, and he could have been seriously injured. In fact, it's basically a miracle that he wasn't."

She frowned, for once showing some small sign of concern for other people's problems. "That's pretty serious. Maybe you should talk to Mademoiselle Blue or whatever her name is."

"But what if she's the one doing all this stuff?" I pointed out in a hushed whisper.

Blaire frowned and shook her head. "No. I mean, why would she?"

"Why would anyone? We know absolutely no one here. None of this makes any sense." I sighed, becoming more and more frustrated as I thought about everything that had transpired since our arrival.

"Why did you think it's me?" Blaire asked, her eyes meeting mine for a second before glancing back toward the counter.

"You're here in the middle of night, right outside our room, and you laughed this morning over the accident on the stairs, then laughed again when I told you about the laxatives."

"Because things like that are funny when they're happening to someone else," she said, rolling her eyes at me a second time.

"It's not funny." I thrust her glass of milk at her, then crossed my arms, incensed. "And for that matter, I still don't know whether I can cross you off the list of suspects. You are here right outside of our room in the middle of the night."

Now Blaire dropped her voice. "It's not what you think, okay?" A pleading expression took over her usually smirking features.

"Then what is it?" I demanded, cocking an eyebrow in question. She could either tell me right now or deal with an increasingly uncomfortable interrogation. I wasn't above tattling to Madame Blue, either.

Blaire must have sensed this because she threw her hands up in the air and growled. "Ugh, you are so annoying. Do you know that?"

I met her with a deadpan expression, refusing to budge.

"Fine, come with me. I'll show you what I've been hiding."

I followed Blaire upstairs to her second-floor bedroom, which happened to be at least three times larger than the one Charles and I were currently occupying.

She flicked on the lights, then moved across the space to the attached bathroom. "Follow me," she instructed.

I watched as she stooped down by the sink and poured her glass of milk into a China bowl. A flash of movement from the bedroom caught my eye, and I turned just in time to see a black cat racing toward us.

No, not black. *Tortoiseshell.*

"Charlene's mother!" I exclaimed. "You had her this whole time."

The cat turned toward me with wide eyes. "You found my baby?"

At the same time, Blaire asked, "Uh, what? Who's Charlene?"

"Oh, we found an abandoned kitten and decided to call her Charlene while we searched for her mother," I answered flippantly, trying to hide my screwup.

"What makes you so sure this cat is her mother?" Blaire challenged, eyeing me suspiciously.

“I am her mother! I am! Will you bring her to me?” the torty pleaded, coming over to rub her head against my knee.

I couldn’t exactly admit that the kitten had told me and that her cat had just confirmed it to boot. Blaire would think I was crazy, provided she didn’t already. I decided to play off her question instead. “I mean, what are the chances of you finding a cat and us finding a kitten so close together?”

“How do you know I found her? What if I brought her here with me?” Blaire was not letting me off the hook.

I just had to meet her confidence with some swagger of my own. “Did you?” I lifted an eyebrow.

“No, but that’s not the point. You’re making a lot of assumptions here. Just like you assumed I did all that stuff to your husband.”

“Okay, I get your point, but something tells me this is the kitten’s mom. They’re both mostly black, if that helps prove anything. Can I bring the kitten up here to introduce her? We should know by how they interact if they belong together.”

“Yes, yes! I want to see my Charlene!” the torty cried, now pawing at my knee enthusiastically. “I’ve missed her so much!”

Blaire just shrugged, completely oblivious to the pleas of her new feline friend. “I guess. If it will get you off my back,” she said, and I rushed out of there to grab the kitten before the rainbow-haired woman could change her mind.

17

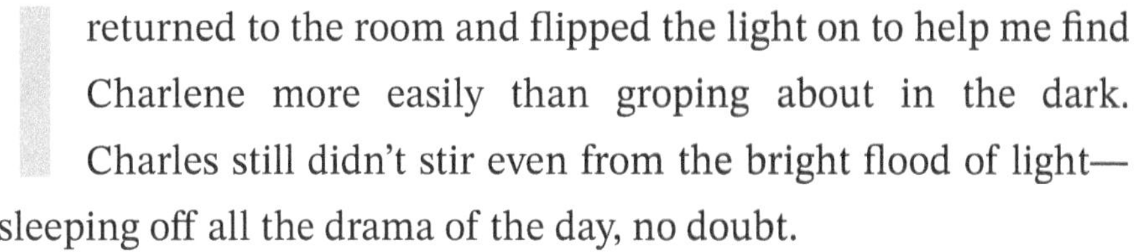

I returned to the room and flipped the light on to help me find Charlene more easily than groping about in the dark. Charles still didn't stir even from the bright flood of light—sleeping off all the drama of the day, no doubt.

"Charlene," I whispered when I didn't immediately spot her. "We found your mother. C'mon."

The little kitten jolted out from beneath my abandoned pillow. "Really? Let's go!" she squeaked happily.

"You've got it, boss." I scooped her up, turned out the light, and jogged back up the secondary staircase to reach Blaire's room upstairs.

As soon as I'd returned, the mother cat came running. Even before I could set Charlene on the floor, she was pawing at my legs and shouting, "My baby! My baby!"

"Mommy!" Charlene mewled in matching excitement. "It's really you!"

Blaire stood back and watched this happy reunion from the bathroom doorway. "Okay, so they probably do belong to each other," she admitted. "I wasn't planning on keeping two cats, but I guess it's fine."

"You're keeping Charlene's mother?" I asked, not sure why I hadn't pieced that together already but still surprised all the same.

"Her name is Socks," Blaire corrected, creeping over to join me and the cats.

"That's not my name," the mother said as she busily groomed Charlene with her sandpaper tongue. "But I don't mind."

"Why Socks?" I wanted to know. I supposed most pets had their names changed by humans once adopted, but this one made zero sense. "She doesn't have any. Her feet are all black."

Blaire smirked at my question. "That's the point. It's ironic. *Duh.*"

"Well, then hello, Socks." I ran my hand over the tortoiseshell cat's back, and she lifted her tail happily.

"Charlene is a dumb name. I'm changing it," Blaire said a few seconds later.

Neither cat seemed to pay her much mind as she ran through a list of possible names. "I think I'll call her Snowball," she landed on after at least a dozen such *ironic* possibilities. "And don't you dare point out that she's not white. That's the whole point."

Stupid names aside, Blaire did seem committed to the feline mother-daughter duo. Still, something nagged at me. "You'll take good care of them, right?"

She seemed offended by my innocent question. "Of course I will," she practically snarled at me.

I said nothing, focusing my attention on Charlene. This was really goodbye, and I couldn't even talk with her properly while Blaire was watching. I'd sure miss the little fluff ball, but she got what she'd wanted this whole time, and she would have a home, too. I felt much better, knowing she'd be off the streets.

"I guess I should let you all get back to sleep." I pushed myself back to my feet, hesitant to leave but also knowing it was for the best. "We have some supplies for Charl—um, Snowball—in our room. I'll bring them by in the morning. Let me know if you need anything else by then, okay? Charles and I will probably be checking out to grab a hotel in town."

She perked up instantly. "On account of someone trying to kill your husband?"

"I don't know about *kill,* but yes. We don't exactly feel safe here."

"Well, at least you have somewhere to go. I have two cats and no home." She glanced up at me with tear-rimmed eyes, an unexpected display of emotion from the mostly stoic girl. "Dylan and I broke up today. I'm only staying here until the old lady realizes I can't pay and kicks me out."

My heart went out to her, especially since I was in the exact opposite predicament. I was literally here celebrating my honeymoon. "Do you need some money, Blaire?" I offered gently.

She snorted. "I need a job. I met Dylan at work, so naturally I quit. I can't stand the thought of having to see him every single day. It would be too awkward."

"Well, I'm sure something will turn up." My well-intended optimism was not well-received.

"Okay, Boomer," she practically barked. "I'll just walk into an office and immediately land my dream job without so much as an interview, then I'll get a mortgage on a three-bedroom house by batting my eyelashes and promising not to default. All I'll need after that is a white picket fence, and I can live happily ever after. I'll pass on the whole Prince Charming facade, thanks."

Okay, that was pretty harsh.

"I am nowhere near old enough to be a Boomer." I tried to keep the upset from my voice, seeing as the girl was having a rough time already. "But I have a good feeling about your future, even if you don't."

With that, I left.

Charlene was so caught up in the reunion with her mother, she didn't even see me go. Oh, well. It was for the best, right? Even if Blaire had nothing else, she would at least have the love of two very special felines.

I trudged slowly toward the staircase, trying to come to terms with how I was feeling in that moment. For the last day and a half, Charles and I had been focused almost solely on finding the missing mother cat, and now that we had… I was really going to miss that kitten.

Maybe I was more prepared to be a mother than I originally thought. Or maybe I just really liked cats.

Who knew?

Certainly not me.

I paused to look out at the garden from the window beside the secondary staircase and was startled to spy movement outside. I squinted in an attempt to clarify the picture, but it was all so dark.

Past midnight was no time to work in the garden. Could whatever was happening out there somehow be related to all the trouble Charles and I had been facing since our arrival? Was that the guilty party right outside the window already working to sabotage us yet again?

I honestly didn't know, but I certainly had to go out there to take a closer look.

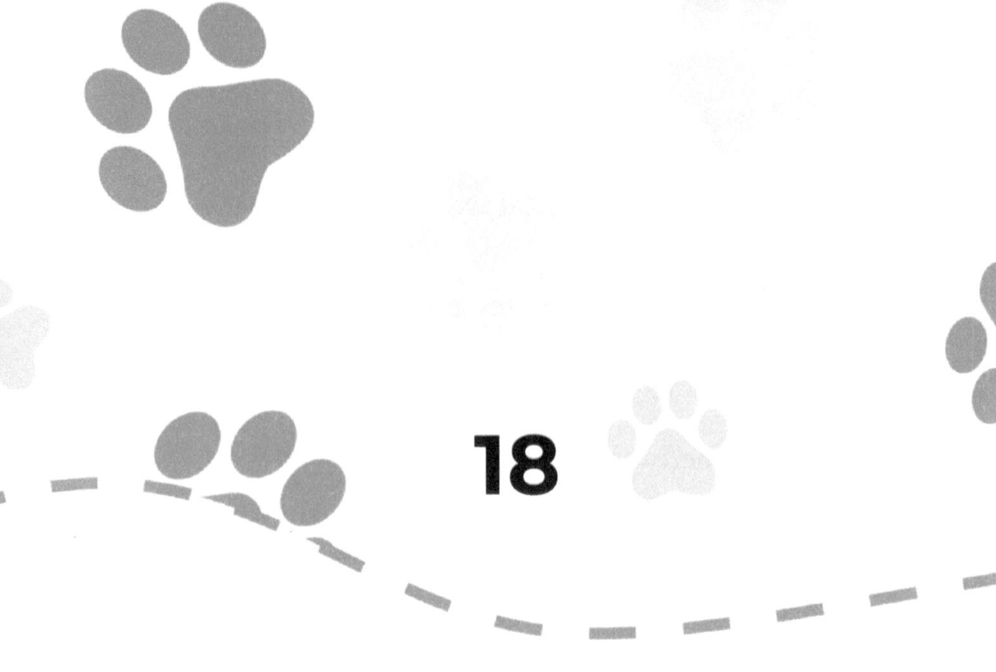

18

This time I did wake Charles. It took several good shakes, but finally his eyes blinked open.

"What time is it?" he groaned, covering his eyes to block out the light.

"Late," I confessed with an apologetic wince. "I'm sorry. It's just I found Charlene's mother, and now there's something going on in the garden. I'd feel safer if you were with me."

He struggled to sit up in bed. "You found Charlene's mother?" This was followed by a sharp gasp of pain.

"Oh, sweetie." I reached over to rub his shoulders.

He leaned into my touch. "I guess that fall hurt me more than I initially realized. Let me just pop a couple Tylenol and—"

"It's okay. You should rest." And I should have known better than to wake him. Of course he was putting on a strong face after that horrid accident. He didn't want to worry me, and now I'd only made things worse by disturbing him while his body was trying to heal.

He shrugged off my concern and practically leapt out of bed, as if to prove a point. "And miss the action? No way."

I waited as he swallowed a couple capsules dry.

He clapped his hands together to signal his readiness to proceed. "Let's go see what's happening. And after that, you'll tell me about finding Charlene's mother?"

"Definitely. I can even take you to meet her in the morning, but I don't know how much longer that person will be outside."

Charles locked the door behind us, then shot me a worried glance. "A person is out there? Doing what?"

"I don't know. That's what I want to find out."

"Fair enough," was the last thing either of us said before quietly moving through the house and very quietly letting ourselves outside.

We held hands as we moved toward the dark figure to get a better look. The sound of a shovel breaking the soil rang out through the night.

"What was that? Do you think someone's burying a body?" I whispered, fear surging through my body.

"I think..." Charles said, leaning down to whisper in my ear. "That my wife needs to stop watching so many true crime documentaries."

"Who's there?" a man called into the chilly night air. Apparently, we hadn't been quiet enough. I blamed our extreme sleepiness for us being careless enough to get discovered in our covert spy operation almost immediately.

Charles let go of my hand and moved in front of me to shield me from the stranger. “We were just coming out for some fresh air,” he announced, creeping closer with me behind him.

“Who are you, and what are you doing here?” I shouted, my voice quaking.

The man clicked on a flashlight and shone it beneath his face, creating a ghoulish affect. “It’s me, Bill.”

“Gardening at night a habit of yours?” Charles’s voice was light and airy, conversational. He was an expert at questioning witnesses and suspects alike.

“Usually, no, but there was no time during the day, what with the fiasco on the stairs and all the room switching. Tomorrow will be another busy day, so I figured I’d just knock this out now, before the old lady realized I’d fallen behind on my chores.” He took a step back, releasing a familiar foul smell into the air.

“Is that skunk cabbage?” I asked, immediately moving to pinch my nose.

Billy swept his flashlight toward the freshly planted cabbage. About half the gorgeous yellow roses had been uprooted to make way for their highly undesirable replacement, and this made me quite sad. The bees loved those roses and were likely planning on constructing their new hive nearby. Now the same plant that had driven them from their apiary would ruin this new location, too.

“Why would you tear up flowers and plant skunk cabbage in their place?” Charles asked, sounding genuinely curious. I knew him well enough, though, to see that he was just two steps away from levying a serious accusation the porter's way.

"It's all these darned bees," Billy complained, lifting a hand to wipe sweat from his brow. "They're scaring the guests. Madame Blue suspects they're to blame for our lack of return bookings. She needed the money, so she wants them out of here. Obviously we can't kill them, so I'm trying to drive them away using more natural means."

"But you're ruining the garden in the process," I argued, protective of the place where we'd spent so much time over the last couple of days, the place my parents still remembered so fondly from decades past.

Billy swung his flashlight toward the uprooted roses. "These guys? Nah. I'll move them to pots for the time being, then return them to this soil once the bees have left. No harm, no foul."

Except this was incredibly harmful to the bees. They would be forced to leave their ancestral land, just because Madame Blue didn't realize her unfriendly staff and deteriorating house were the real reasons so many guests never returned.

Charles and I, for one, couldn't wait to get out of there.

19

The next morning, Charles and I were up early despite our strange night-time excursion. He was excited to visit Charlene and her mother so we could all say goodbye before we packed up and headed to a nice, safe, *boring* hotel chain in town. I would take boring all day long if it kept my husband from facing any more misplaced misfortunes.

The only problem was that we had no idea what time Blaire might wake up, and I didn't want to be the one to roust the cranky young adult from her sleep. So Charles and I busied ourselves by grabbing showers in the communal bathroom and packing up our luggage. When that was done, we scarfed down some protein bars that Charles had picked up on his latest supply run.

"After this, it's only the finest Southern dining for the rest of the week," he promised, pulling me into his side for a snuggle.

"Laxative-free, too, right?" I joked before offering him a peck on the cheek. He needed a shave, but I also liked this laidback vacation version of my new husband. The scruff made him appear even more handsome. Maybe I could convince him to grow out a beard.

He dropped a hand to his stomach in memory. "Ugh. I sure hope so."

I quirked a brow. "Too soon?"

"No, it's just..." His words fell away. "Did you hear that?"

Both of us directed our gazes toward the closed door, where the sounds of soft but persistent scratching rose to meet our ears, then suddenly fell away.

"Do you think it could be Charlene?" I asked, filled with joy at the thought. I assumed we'd have to wait at least another couple hours to see Blaire and the cats, but maybe I was wrong.

Charles was grinning like a maniac, too. "Only one way to find out."

We both moved swiftly toward the door. Charles was the one to pry it open. When we looked down, however, nothing was there.

"*What is this?*" Madame Blue shouted from a couple paces away, holding our kitten up by the scruff of her neck.

Charlene twisted and writhed but couldn't break free. I stomped right over to them and grabbed Charlene from the horrid old woman's clutches. "Why are you so mean?" I demanded.

"You knew the rules. No pets allowed!" she huffed.

"She's not a pet. She's just a poor lost kitten who got separated from her mother."

The sound of footsteps stomping down the stairs diverted everyone's attention before Madame Blue could offer a rejoinder. We all turned to see Blaire racing toward us rather breathlessly.

"There you are, Snowball!" she cried, stopping to rest against the counter.

"Is this your pet?" Madame Blue insisted.

"Yes," Blaire claimed, proudly raising her chin in defiance.

"No pets allowed," the old woman shouted, her face growing red.

"Oops," was all Blaire said before taking the kitten from my protective arms.

Madame Blue huffed, apparently unsure of how to respond to Blaire's complete inability to care.

Charlene squirmed in Blaire's arms and turned to face me and Charles. "I'm sorry if I caused trouble. I was coming to find you. I missed you!" she mewled sadly.

My heart broke for her, but I was also still incredibly livid.

"What happened?" Blaire mused, stroking the kitten in her arms as she faced the woman. "Cat got your tongue?"

"Young lady, I will not be disrespected in my own home!" the proprietress fumed.

"Yet you disrespect all your guests constantly. That's why we're leaving," I shot in, hands on my hips in a power pose. "Ever since we got here, it's been one problem after another. You don't even care that my husband fell through the stairs due your negligence in keeping up the property. You forced us to change rooms, locked him into the bedroom, slipped laxatives into the potato salad. And to top it all off, you hate animals, first with the bees and now with this sweet kitten."

The old woman blinked several times hard. "What a string of accusations! All false, of course."

"Really? Then maybe you should explain yourself," Charles urged from my side. His voice was much calmer than mine, which I guess made me the bad cop in this scenario.

Blue placed her hands on the counter to steady herself, her voice shaking with rage that matched my own. "I have the house appraised every five years so that nothing falls into disrepair. The stairs were fine as of our last inspection about two years back, so that accident was not on behalf of my negligence. I've practically bankrupted myself keeping this house to code to appease the historical society. As for getting locked in the room, old doors stick sometimes. These are the originals after all, and I came and helped you out just as soon as I got back that day. And my cooking? How dare you insult my cooking to accuse me of putting laxatives in the potatoes, when the rest of us ate them and were just fine. Maybe you have traveler's diarrhea, I don't know, but again, not my fault. I already explained why pets aren't allowed. This is a place of business and it's my right to make the rules. What if a guest was deathly allergic, huh?"

"What about the bees, then?" I challenged, prompted by her comment on allergies, which made me realize she hadn't addressed that part yet. "Why would you intentionally drive them from the property?"

Madame Blue appeared quite taken aback by this. She even literally took one step back as if she'd been slapped. "I am not trying to drive the bees away. I love them. I use their honey in my tea every morning and had planned to expand this dying business by selling their honey at the local farmer's market. It's why I was at the bank that day, trying to get a loan. I hate dealing with ungrateful, self-important guests, but I love those bees."

"Then why are you planting skunk cabbage and ox-tail daisies and other things that will choke out the garden?" Charles wanted to know. I admired how calm he was able to remain. It was probably the only reason Madame Blue was willing to explain herself at all.

"I am not doing any of that! The garden is my pride and joy, but ever since I took a spill last winter, I haven't been able to get around as well as I used to. That all falls to Billy now."

"We saw Billy last night, close to three a.m.," Charles revealed. "He was outside digging up the roses and replacing them with skunk cabbage. He said it's what you wanted because the bees were scaring off the guests."

We all watched Blue for her reaction, which was one of genuine shock.

"He couldn't possibly have said that. It's not true!" she insisted, shaking her head emphatically.

Charles sighed. "Perhaps you better take a look in the garden, then."

After that, we marched outside, Blaire and Charlene in tow, and together Charles and I pointed out the spots where skunk cabbage had been both planted and systematically trampled. We also showed her the place where daisies had been swapped for a lookalike invasive species.

"I can't believe any of this," Madame Blue said in a jarringly quiet voice. It was the first time since our arrival two days back that any of her words hadn't been yelled.

"Looks like Billy has some explaining to do," Blaire said with a smirk before setting her phone to record video. That girl lived for the drama.

Me? I just wanted a happy resolution for all involved, especially the bees who depended on this garden for their livelihood.

I couldn't wait to hear what Billy had to say for himself.

20

We marched in a straight line to the third floor of that old stone mansion.

"Billy! Get out here right this instant!" Madame Blue yelled through a closed door.

He grumbled something I couldn't quite make out, then pried the door open, seeming to have forgotten to put on a shirt. "What is it? I don't start work for another hour, and you know that," he complained. His eyes grew wide as he saw the entourage that joined his employer—me, Charles, Charlene, Blaire, and Blaire's phone, already recording.

"Let me put on a shirt," he muttered, shutting the door on us.

We all waited in silence until the door popped back open and Billy ushered us in. His room was small, just like the new one we'd been moved to on the first floor. It felt incredibly crowded with all five of us standing in the space, but nobody wanted to leave before getting answers.

"Well?" Billy demanded with a snide expression on his grizzled face. "What's so important that it couldn't wait one hour?"

The old lady marched right up to him and poked him in the chest with her finger. "What's this I hear about skunk cabbage and bees?"

"What about it?" Billy answered smoothly. "You asked me to find a way to get rid of the bees, so I opted for a natural method."

"I did not ask you to get rid of the bees!" Madame Blue stomped her foot in frustration. "You and I both know how much those bees mean to me."

Billy's featured pinched. "But you did ask me, Bluebell. Why else would I try to drive them off?"

"Lies!" the old woman hissed.

"Not lies," Billy countered calmly. "Let me get dressed, and I can drive you into town to see your doctor. We both knew this day was coming."

"If you're trying to suggest I'm senile, you've got another think coming. My hips are bad, hearing's gone, but my memory is just fine. I did not ask you to scare off my honeybees."

They both seemed so sure of their position, it was hard to know who was telling the truth.

"Knock, knock," someone called from out in the hall. Before anyone could answer, Madeline Mackenzie let herself into the room. She was wearing yet another Hawaiian shirt. How many did this woman have in her wardrobe?

"I heard shouting and just wanted to make sure everything was all right." She shot Billy a meaningful glance, and that's when it all clicked into place.

"You!" I rounded her, pointing a finger in accusation. "You're the one who caused all those accidents. You locked my husband in our room, and I'm willing to bet you messed with the stairs, too."

"That's ridic—"

"The game is up, Madeline," Billy interjected, obvious relief coloring his expression. "Just admit what you did."

Everyone waited for someone to confess, but nobody did.

"You wanted the house for yourselves," I explained. "You were willing to do anything to get it, including endangering the other guests."

"Silly and offensive!" Mrs. Mackenzie shouted.

I came right up to her and poked my finger into her chest, same as Blue had done with Billy. "And true!" Now we were all shouting.

"I didn't do any of those things," she fumed, crossing her arms over her chest.

"Okay, can you prove that you didn't?" Charles posed calmly.

She growled but didn't respond with any words.

"I think maybe I can," Blaire said, coming forward with phone in hand. She handed it to me.

"You know how I've been sneaking around at night to take things from the kitchen? I didn't put two and two together before, but look at this." Blaire hit play on the video, and my eyes grew wide as I watched the scene unfold. She'd managed to catch footage of Mrs. Mackenzie and Billy meeting by the broken staircase before it had been broken.

"They didn't see me, and I thought this was some kind of midnight lovers thing despite the obviously enormous age gap."

"Why would you record that?"

She shrugged. "I record everything. Thought this would either turn funny, disgusting, or into good blackmail fodder. Since I didn't have money to keep staying here, I thought maybe I could convince one of them to foot the bill in exchange for me keeping their secret. I just hadn't hit that point of desperation yet."

I watched as they talked for a while, pointed at the stairs, talked some more, then hugged and wandered off in separate directions.

"What were they saying?" I asked, confused as to how this was the smoking gun we needed.

"Just stuff about plans and being ready. Again, I thought it was about an affair, but maybe they were plotting something else. Maybe they were working together to sabotage your stay."

Neither Billy nor Mrs. Mackenzie said anything in response to this accusation. That's when Mr. Mackenzie joined us.

"What's all this talk of having an affair?" he asked good-naturedly, clearly thinking it was out of the realm of possibilities.

"We think—" I started, but Blaire cut us off.

"Sorry to be the one to break it to you, but your wife is cheating on you with that guy!" Blaire pointed to Billy.

He looked from his wife to Billy, then burst out laughing. “No way. That’s our son. Didn’t you know?”

“What?” Madame Blue shouted. “How come nobody said anything to me?”

“I guess it slipped our minds,” Mrs. Mackenzie said with a wave of her hand.

“Or you didn’t want her to know,” I suggested, unmoved by this shock twist. If anything, it made the pieces fit together more perfectly. “How long ago did you hire Billy to help out around here?” I asked Madame Blue.

“About two years ago. Why?”

“That was after your most recent inspection, right?”

“Just a couple months after, yes. It was the enormity of the repairs needed that made me realize I couldn’t do it all on my own anymore.”

“Madame Blue, you’re not losing your memory. You’ve been double-crossed,” I revealed dramatically.

“Of course I’m not losing my memory. I’m sharp as a tack, but what do you mean about double-crossed?”

“These two”—I pointed at the mother and son—“were working together to sabotage your business. She has a special place in her heart for the house but can’t buy unless you put it for sale. Billy has been her inside man. He’s been secretly damaging the house, ruining the gardens, and encouraging guests to leave bad reviews,” I added thinking back to how nonchalant he was while we were changing rooms, even going so far as to suggest we leave negative feedback online. "Scaring off the bees was probably meant to be the last straw, since you love them so much. He thought that you'd have no reason to stay with everything that was going wrong."

Mr. Mackenzie did not look happy about any of this. "These are very serious accusations you're making."

"Yet somehow they're true."

"You can't prove anything," Billy said flatly.

"Well, my friend, you messed with the wrong guests," I said with a smirk of my own. "My husband's a lawyer and I'm a private investigator."

"And I record almost everything," Blaire added.

"I'm sure with a little digging we could piece together a timeline of events, uncover receipts for repairs that never happened, and even get a clean bill of health from Madame Blue's doctor to prove her memory is just fine."

"We should get another inspector in too. To check out the stairs and see if there's been any obvious tampering."

"There's no need to do that," Mrs. Mackenzie said. "We'll leave. That's what you wanted, right? You want the good room back?"

"This is about so much more than a room."

"Did you really do what they're saying, Madeline? Billy?" Mr. Mackenzie asked with a crestfallen expression. "I know we wanted this place, but we all agreed to wait until the old woman died. Goodness knows that should happen soon enough."

"Billy, you're fired," Madame Blue growled. "Get off my property."

"Before you go." Charles stepped forward with a business card in hand. "I'll be representing Madame Blue in a suit to reclaim damages due to willful destruction of property. Expect a call from me soon."

EPILOGUE

FOUR DAYS LATER

"Mmm," I moaned as the creamy goodness filled my mouth. "So worth the wait."

"Cheers to that," Charles said, holding up his fork to bump it to mine as the sun rose over the garden.

"Ready for another round?" Madame Blue asked, hovering nearby with a Pyrex dish half-filled with the delicious homemade biscuits and gravy.

"We should save some for Blaire," I suggested, daintily wiping at the corners of my mouth as if I weren't making a huge mess of myself already. "She'll be hungry when she finishes replanting those roses."

This was the last day of our stay at the old stone mansion so beloved by my parents. Now that Billy and his parents had gone, it was a perfectly lovely place to vacation. The inspector had come out yesterday to assess the house and its property. We were still waiting on an official report, but he noted at least sixty thousand dollars' worth of new damages since the last inspection.

Charles had wasted no time in letting the Mackenzies know that they were expected to pay for all the damages in duplicate—or he would file a suit over the accident he'd suffered on the tampered staircase, and he would be sure to win.

Madame Blue still needed the help, of course, and since Blaire still needed a home, the two decided to help each other. And Blaire was already teaching her new employer all about how social media could help her increase bookings. They'd even submitted a listing to AirBnB and already had a couple stays booked for later in the month.

It seemed to be a match made in heaven.

Blaire's only request was that Socks be allowed to stay on the premises, despite the no pets rule.

Just Socks.

Charlene would be coming home with us.

It turns out our time spent helping her led to all of us being quite attached, which is why she'd snuck out of Blaire's room to come find us.

"I love my mommy, but I'm old enough to be on my own now. Or at least to be with you," Charlene had said when she asked us to become her family.

Socks also gave her approval. "It's what cats do, and it's a mother's greatest delight to know her child is truly happy in life. Thank you for loving my sweet baby."

And that was that.

“Her name being so much like mine was a sign,” Charles said. “We always belonged together.”

I liked that, and I hoped Octo-Cat, Jacques, and Jillianne would be accepting of the new baby when we brought her home, further blending our household. Now we had my cat, Charles’s cats, and one that was both of ours. Soon I hoped we would be a cohesive family unit, but these things took time… especially when cats were involved.

“Ready for a break?” Madame Blue shouted across the yard.

Blaire stood and tore off the oversized gardening gloves. “I’m starving,” she said before striding over to join us.

“You didn’t have to wake up so early for our benefit,” I reminded her.

“Maybe not, but I wanted to make sure to see you off before you left,” she said with a smile. Yes, Blaire visibly liked me now. I considered it one of my greatest achievements from this week.

“When is the apiarist coming by again?” Madame Blue asked. Now that she would be receiving a generous stipend from the Mackenzies, she had enough cash to expand operations, just as she’d always wanted. The apiarist would be consulting on a new bee house and inspecting the current colony so they could talk about how best to introduce even more bees to the lot.

Queen Bey’s reign would be one for the history books. You know, if bees had history books.

“Did you have a good week?” Charles asked just as we were about to climb into the car and head back to Maine, Charlene in tow.

"The best," I answered before we shared one final kiss. "I can see why Mom and Dad like it so much."

"Me, too." Charles smiled and let out a wistful sigh. "We should come back for our first anniversary. Just eleven months and some change to go."

"I can't wait," I answered with one last look back at the enchanting stone mansion where we'd made so many memories.

"Bye, Mommy!" Charlene shouted happily, and with that, it was time to move on to our next adventure.

ANIMAL ACCOMPLICE

PET WHISPERER P.I.

The jig is up. Someone knows my secret.

What starts as mild online harassment soon turns much more dire when my blackmailer reveals irrefutable proof of my ability to talk to animals, promising to expose me whether I like it or not.

I've always lived life on my own terms, but if word were to get out about my secret superpower, I know better than anyone that things would never be the same... for me or anyone I love.

With the stakes higher than ever, Octo-Cat and I decide to take on one last case. First we must reveal the identity of my anonymous bully, and then we'll have to ask ourselves the hardest question yet: Where do we go from here?

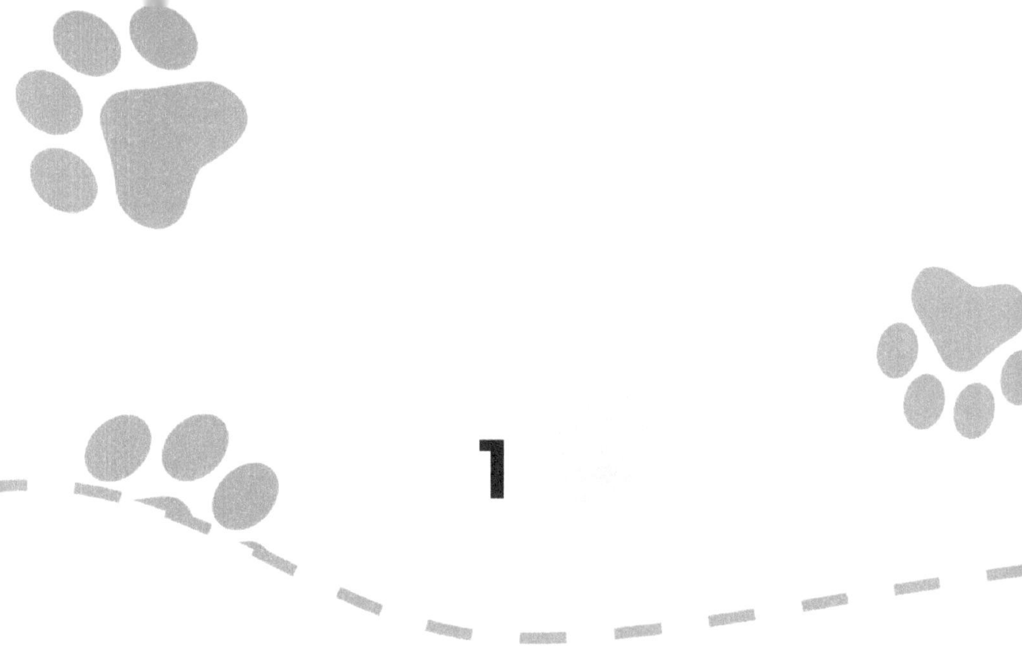

1

My name is Angie Longfellow, and I lead a pretty great life. For the longest time, I had trouble finding my path, racking up associate degrees and building my resume like nobody's business.

I never would have suspected my crummy job as a paralegal for the local law firm would have led to my happily ever after, but it brought me both my husband and my very special, *very secret* ability.

So, yeah, I can talk to animals, a fact that more or less rules my day-to-day life.

It all started when a faulty coffee maker zapped me unconscious at a will reading, only for me to be awoken by the deceased's cat—who also just so happened to be her primary beneficiary. With vile tuna breath, he informed me that his old lady had not died of natural causes and that it was up to me to help him solve the murder and bring her killer to justice.

At first I could only talk to him—to Octo-Cat—but now I can talk to pretty much any animal or insect that is willing to talk back. My regular entourage includes that original talking tabby, my husband's two hairless cats Jacques and Jillianne, our newly adopted kitten Charlene, and Pringle the raccoon who lives in a swanky set of tree houses in the backyard.

Paisley the rescue Chihuahua moved out when Nan went to live with her new husband Grant. I miss having her in the house, but I still see her nearly every day, along with Grant's rescue bunny—a Holland Lop named E.B.

It's strange not living with my grandmother anymore, but I do love married life. Charles works long hours as the senior partner at the law firm, and I don't have much to do, given that my P.I. business rarely has any clients.

So in the meantime, Nan is teaching me to be domestic. I'm pretty good at cleaning the house, but my cooking leaves much to be desired. Still, I have a lot of time to figure things out since Charles works such long hours.

To fill my time, I also read several books per week, which is kind of a dream come true. Except it's starting to wear on me.

I love reading about others' adventures—don't get me wrong—but I also want to live my own. I was the main character here, not some simple spectator. Lately, though, my life doesn't have a whole lot of plot.

Strange how having all your dreams come true can turn out to be so boring. It's like I have nothing left to strive for, that I already have everything I've ever wanted—and then some.

Between Charles's cushy paycheck and Octo-Cat's trust fund, we're more than covered financially, but still, I'd like to make my business a success for my own satisfaction.

There's just two problems with that. First, Nan and my mom took it upon themselves to register my firm with the state government as Pet Whisperer P.I., which means I'm stuck with the name. Second, I'm not the sole owner. Octo-Cat is my partner, and he's not always the easiest to work with.

In fact, he doesn't want to do any work at all, not since he piggybacked on my wedding to marry his long-time, long-distance girlfriend, Grizabella, the former show cat. Then right after that, we subsequently adopted Charlene, the little lost kitten Charles and I found on our honeymoon.

Now our Octavius is a full-time doting dad and a constant critic of yours truly. I have a feeling *that* will never change, no matter how much I might want it to.

"You're slouching," Octo-Cat growled shortly after entering our shared office.

I straightened my spine then let out a long, frustrated sigh and clicked my laptop shut. Twisting in my desk chair, I turned to face my feline partner. "Where's Charlene?" I asked with one eyebrow quirked in question.

Octo-Cat sat and idly licked at a paw. “The nudists have her for late-morning classes.”

“I really wish you’d stop calling the Sphynx cats that.” I groaned. Still, I found it adorable that the three cats had rallied around our new arrival, even going so far as to homeschool her. I had no idea what they taught her during these catting lessons, but everyone seemed more or less content, so I didn’t pry.

He dropped his paw to the ground and stared at me with wide amber eyes. “Do you prefer I go back to referring to them as the interlopers?”

“But you’re all getting along now,” I argued, drumming my fingers on my knee as I thought about how I might turn this conversation around before my kitty partner became too agitated.

He just shook his head. “Thus the new nickname. You can’t deny the fact they’re naked, Angela. If they wanted to grow fur, they would have done it by now.”

I chose not to acknowledge that with anything more than an exacerbated eye roll.

Octo-Cat shifted his eyes toward the desk then back to me in the chair. Thankfully, it was he who changed the subject, although it was definitely one I didn’t care for. “Are you really done with work already? It’s hardly past breakfast time.”

“I’m just not making any progress, and I feel bad spending Charles’s money when the ads clearly aren’t working.”

“You never felt bad about spending my money,” he pointed out with a holier-than-thou expression.

Heat rushed to my cheeks. “That was different,” I admitted,

glancing down at my lap before returning my gaze to him in embarrassment.

“Oh?” Octo-Cat tilted his head to the side as he studied me. “Then go ahead. Please do tell me how.”

“Well, you’re my business partner, and it’s not exactly like you work for your income,” I mumbled meekly; my confidence could never match his and that often became a problem.

The tabby scoffed at this. “I don’t work? Ha. Is that so? I’ll have you know that I work very hard keeping tabs on you all day.”

I pressed both palms to my thighs and then stood. “Look, I’m not trying to start a fight or anything. I’m just feeling discouraged is all.”

“I already told you. You’ve been doing the work for free for far too long. Nobody wants to pay for it now.”

I sighed. Octo-Cat was a pretty good sleuth, but he was a terrible businessman. I wasn’t much better, but I still knew I could learn. My cat seemed to think he was infallible in this and all things.

I stopped at the door and turned back to him. “It’s not that—”

“Not to mention, the one time you did have a paying client, you pinned the crime on him!” he shouted as if it were the silliest thing he’d ever heard.

“He was guilty,” I argued right back. Frankly, I was done with this conversation, but I knew Octo-Cat wouldn’t drop it until he was satisfied, meaning I was stuck for the moment. “Was I supposed to turn a blind eye just because he was paying us?”

My cat shrugged. "It was a bad business decision. That's all I'm saying."

Was my cat right? Was I hopeless at this whole business thing? Well, it wasn't like I could go out and find another private investigation firm to hire me on salary. This kind of work was pretty much freelance, which meant if I wanted to continue as a detective, I'd have to get a whole lot better at the business side. *Ugh.* Perhaps it was time to simply admit defeat. All my other dreams had come true, so why did I continue to cling to the only one that hadn't?

"Maybe I should ask Charles for some paralegal work," I admitted with a sigh. "I was good at that. Plus, having something to do with myself would make it so I don't feel quite so useless."

My cat growled at me. "You are not leaving me here alone all day. What if I need fresh water? What if someone comes to the door? What then, Angela?"

I ignored him and headed down the hall in the direction of the grand staircase. Perhaps I'd feel better about this whole failed businesswoman thing once I'd had a bit of lunch.

Was ten a.m. too early for my second meal of the day?

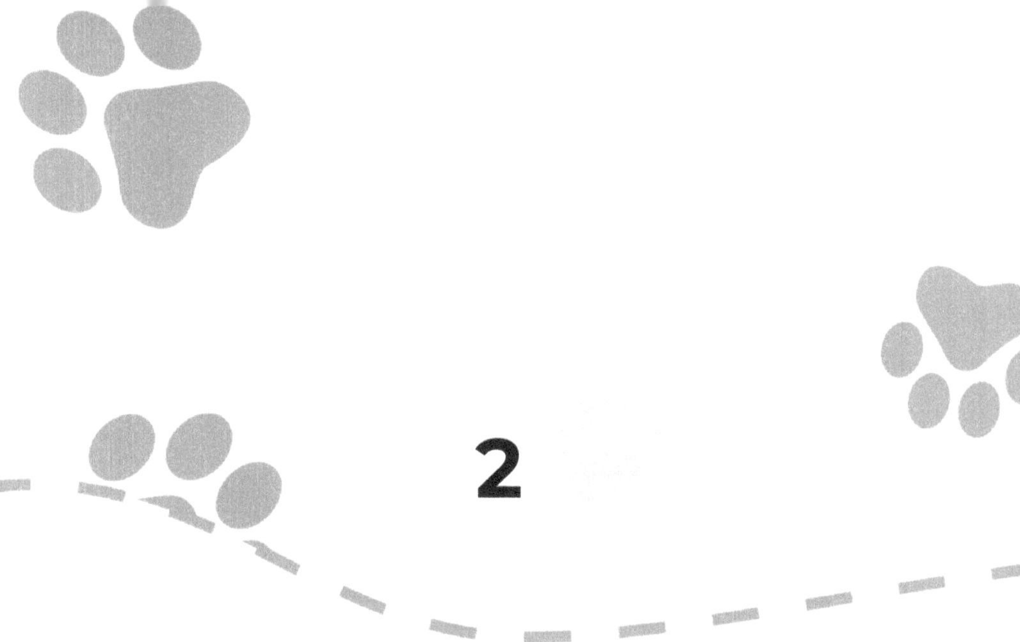

2

After heating up some frozen waffles and slathering them with both butter and blueberry syrup, I felt a little better. But once I'd managed to finish eating them, I found myself with a slight stomach ache.

Note to self: *ten is, in fact, too early for lunch. Also you are not a hobbit, so no more second breakfasts.*

Octo-Cat now lay snoozing in a sunbeam while Jacques and Jillianne looked after Charlene, which gave me a bit of time to myself. I'd just finished my current read last night, so instead of starting something new, I decided to do a little extra work at my desk. After all, I'd only stopped earlier because of Octo-Cat's intrusion.

With a quick prayer to the heavens, I lifted the lid of my laptop and did the same thing I always did when starting a work session—checked my messages for any new client inquiries.

And just like always… digital crickets.

I sighed and moved on to scroll my newsfeed. I'd started a new profile for the business and made sure to follow other private investigators only. Seeing what was working for them was meant to inspire and motivate me. Instead, it only made me feel more hopeless with regards to my own floundering firm.

I was just reading an article detailing how a P.I. duo in the Midwest added murder mystery dinner parties to their repertoire, when a little red notification popped up on my screen.

Excitement surged through my veins.

Was this it? The new client who would turn my entire practice around?

I clicked eagerly and waited while the social media site pulled up one of my geo-targeted ads. Someone had left a comment.

I'd clearly listed my info and availability in a pinned post at the top of my page, but maybe this person was so desperate for help, they skipped researching me and went straight to reaching out.

Yeah, I liked that. My services weren't only needed, they were now in demand.

Dancing in my seat, I dragged my eyes down the page to read the comment from my brand-spanking-new client and possibly my new biggest fan.

The username was Charm—no last name—just Charm, and the comment said: *I know who you are. I know your secret, and soon everyone else will too.*

Dread roiled in my gut. Who was this Charm, and why had

they decided to mess with me? Surely, this whole thing was just some stupid coincidence. Granted, I hadn't always been as careful as I should when it came to protecting my secret ability, but...

No, no way.

I clicked on Charm's name to open their profile, but the privacy settings had been cranked all the way to the max, and the profile snapshot of an ocean told me absolutely nothing.

With shaking hands, I navigated back to my ad. I should have simply deleted the comment, blocked the user, and moved on with my day.

But I couldn't.

I had to know more.

Who are you? I typed, waited for a beat, then added, *And what are you talking about?*

The response was almost immediate: *You don't know me, but you do know what I'm talking about.*

I bit my lip and slunk back in my chair. What were the chances that Charm was making everything up? And how could they possibly know my secret if they didn't even know me?

And most importantly of all, what on earth was I supposed to do now?

Third breakfast seemed like a truly terrible idea and I knew Charles was busy at work, so after a few quick minutes to calm myself, I decided to call Nan.

"You say someone is threatening you on the Internet?" she asked as she frowned at me through the FaceTime app.

I nodded emphatically. "And I have no idea who or why."

Nan's expression softened, not just in sentiment but also because she had started messing with the beauty settings and filters on the app. "I wouldn't worry about it too much, dear. They probably just have you confused for somebody else," she assured me as rainbow unicorns danced over her head in the frame.

"Maybe," I agreed while picking at the skin on my elbow to calm my nerves.

"Just try to relax and enjoy your day," my grandmother suggested from beneath a sky of twinkling pink stars. "Grant and I are catching a matinee, but I'll see you after for tea?"

"Yeah, sure." My throat was dry and my voice sounded terrible, but I was a grown woman. I needed to learn how to solve some problems on my own.

And this was a doozy.

Charm could very well be some rando just messing with me for fun, or they could be an enemy fully intent on ruining my life. I'd sent more than one person to prison in my days as an investigator. Maybe one of them had been released and was now looking for revenge. In any case, it wouldn't hurt to do a bit of research on their whereabouts.

I grabbed a pad of sticky notes out of the top drawer of my desk and wrote down the first bad guy I'd helped catch—my former friend, Diane Fulton. We'd been pretty close back when I worked at the law firm, but that hadn't stopped her from trying to kill me when I found out the truth about what happened to Octo-Cat's previous owner, how *she* was the one at fault.

I tore off the sticky and attached it to my desk then returned my attention to the pad. Enemy number two was a realtor from Misty Harbor, Sandra Lyn. She was responsible for a double homicide and had almost let an innocent man endure life in prison at her expense. It seemed unlikely she'd be out of the cage or have access to social media within it, but I would still need to do a bit of research before crossing her off my list. I placed her name next to Diane's.

My third enemy was my former boss, Richard Thompson. He'd murdered my former neighbor, a beloved senator with a soft spot for protecting the environment. To add insult to injury, my cat had peed on him while the cops had him restrained on the ground.

I tore off the sticky note and added it to the growing collection on my desk. *Hoo, boy.* Despite being out of work for most of my career as a P.I., I had sure managed to amass quite the list of enemies—and I was only just getting started with my task of enumerating them all.

I paused to shake my hand out before racking my brain for the next suspect. Considering my ads were geo-targeted, I should probably be looking specifically for someone who was still residing within the Blueberry Bay area, right?

No, I probably shouldn't rule anybody out. The sooner I uncovered Charm's secret identity, the sooner I could get back to my very full schedule of… nothing.

Sigh.

Well, at least I now had something to keep me busy.

Thanks, Charm.

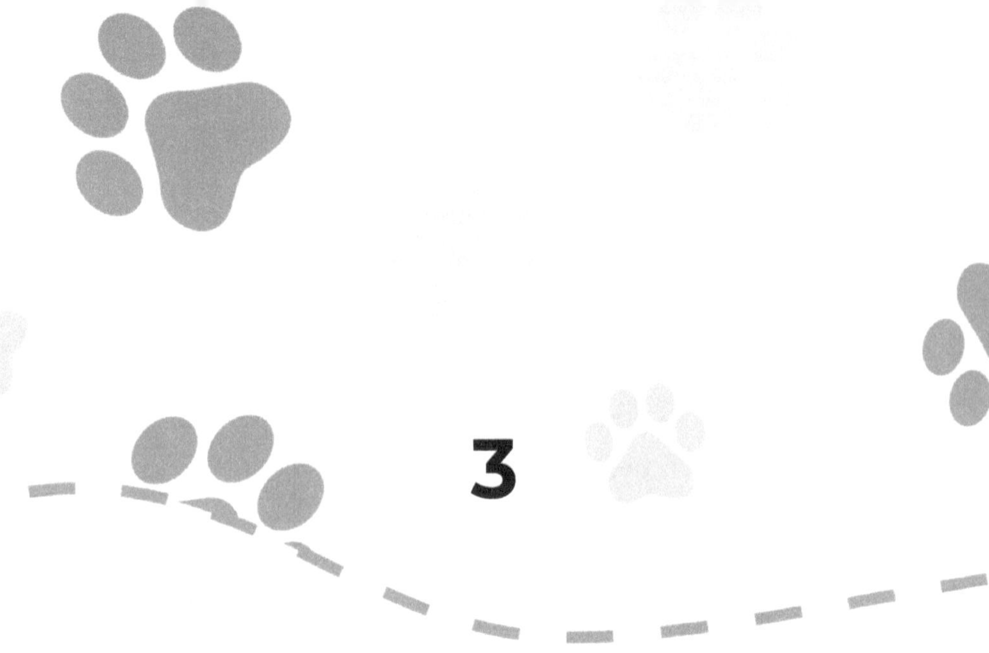

3

"Whatcha doing?" Charlene, our little black kitten, jumped up onto my desk to investigate. At this point I had so many sticky notes, I'd recently started affixing them to the wall as well.

"Making a list of suspects," I answered distractedly as I scrawled *Sara Stevens* onto a hot pink Post-It and tore it from the pad.

Charlene moved to study the writing. "Suh," she sounded out slowly, then "ah," "ruh," and another "ah" as in *apple*.

"Sara," I supplied, then looked up at her with wide eyes. "Wait, are you learning to read?"

She plopped her rear onto the desk and lifted her chin with pride. "Papa Octo-Cat is teaching me. He says I'm a very smart young lady."

I reached out to stroke her head and was met in turn by a rumbling, contented purr. "Charlene, that's fantastic."

"I want to be brilliant like Papa Octo-Cat when I grow up and beautiful like Mama Grizz," Charlene informed me as she leaned in to each stroke of my hand.

I laughed at that. Of course Octo-Cat referred to himself as *brilliant*. *Smart* just wasn't high enough praise. "Seems you're well on your way. What about your aunt and uncle? Do you want to be like them too?" I asked, referring to the Sphynxes who seemed to love Charlene every bit as much as her adoptive parents did.

"Auntie J and Uncle J are fun!" Charlene enthused while bobbing her head up and down.

Fun was not the word I'd use to describe the two hairless cats, but they'd only taken to me after a significant amount of hesitation and threats from Octo-Cat to really drive the point home.

"What are you learning from them in your lessons?" I asked, more curious now than when I'd first heard of their special homeschool arrangement.

The black kitten shook her head. "I'm not allowed to tell. Cat class is for cats only."

"But you told me you're learning to read?" I pointed out.

She scrunched her face up and thought about this for a moment before breaking out in a relieved smile and saying, "That's an extra-circular, so it's okay."

"An extra*curricular*?" I offered with a slight giggle. "Like outside of your normal studies?"

“Exactly. An extra-circle-ular.”

I patted her head again. I knew Charlene had to grow up, but I hoped she would never change. Her pure joy and wonderment often helped me see the world through new eyes myself. I certainly felt better about investigating my online bully since she’d joined me in the office.

Charlene stuck around, keeping me company while I finished making my list and attempting to read each name as I placed it with the others.

“Your handwriting is very sloppy,” she told me at one point, proof that Octo-Cat was, indeed, teaching her how to be a cat in every sense of the word.

Rather than scold her or defend myself, I let her remark slide, hoping the casual insult was a one-off. Besides, I was too distracted by the task at hand to jump into full-on lecture mode.

When I’d finished, I had a total of fourteen sticky notes with fourteen names—and no idea where to start.

The doorbell rang, announcing Nan’s arrival.

“Coming!” I called at the top of my lungs, scooping Charlene into my arms and shutting the office door firmly behind me.

By the time I reached the top of the staircase, Nan had already let herself into the house and was shrugging out of her light windbreaker.

“Did you have a nice time out with Grant?” I asked and her cheeks immediately grew rosy.

“I’d forgotten how much I love being married,” she admitted, fluffing her hair demurely then coming in for a hug once I had reached the bottom of the stairs and set Charlene onto the hardwood floor. The kitten immediately raced toward the kitchen, presumably in search of the other cats, leaving Nan and me to ourselves.

"Where's Paisley?" I asked, glancing around the foyer. Nan and I always had lots of animal company. It was strange that we didn't now.

"I came straight from the cinema," she informed me, unbothered by the absence of furry companions. "Grant dropped me off because you seemed so distressed when you called earlier."

"Distressed is putting it lightly," I admitted, chewing on my bottom lip as I thought back to those initial messages that had set me on edge.

"I'll put on the kettle while you catch me up on the finer details." Nan floated toward the kitchen, and I ran upstairs to grab my laptop.

"See," I said pointing at the screen once I'd pulled up the ad and its comments.

"You don't know me, but you do know what I'm talking about," my grandmother read aloud and then tutted. "What a rude individual this Charm is. Kind of ironic, don't you think?"

I didn't want to debate whether the username fit the user. I wanted to figure out who was on the other side of that screen. "Do you think they know my secret? Or what I can do?" I asked, hoping to refocus my nan.

"How would they? This is probably just some crazy person trying to get a rise out of you. The Internet is full of them, you know." She shook her head and said nothing more. Why wasn't she getting what a huge deal this whole thing was turning out to be? It could ruin my whole life if I wasn't careful, if I didn't act fast.

"I haven't always been as careful as I should," I argued, averting my gaze toward the floor. It physically pained me to think back over all the times I'd been careless with protecting my secret. Those times easily outnumbered my list of enemies at least a dozen to one.

And what if Charm wasn't an enemy at all? What if they were just some random person who had stumbled upon what I could do and was now trying to extort money from me?

"What do you think they want?" I asked Nan, glancing from her to the screen and back again.

Nan grabbed the computer from my hands. "Well, why don't we ask."

I watched as she typed in slow motion, one finger at a time: *What do you want?*

For as slow as Nan was, Charm's response came instantaneously: *I want the truth to come out.*

"Well, that's not good," Nan said as I stared at the threatening comment over her shoulder.

"Not good," she agreed with a slight shake of her head before turning to face me. "But not necessarily bad."

"How can this be anything but bad?" I whined.

"This Charm character probably doesn't know anything. They're just trying to get a rise out of you."

"And if Charm actually knows my secret? Then what?" I demanded, taking the laptop back and hugging it to my chest.

"Then what's so bad about coming out with it? Talking to animals is a huge part of who you are. Why hide it?" Nan shrugged as if this recommendation was one I could actually take, as if my entire life weren't currently on the line.

"Do you not recall how it ruined Grandma Lyn's life?" I challenged with one eyebrow raised.

She simply shrugged again. "True, but people are more open minded these days."

"I don't want to become the punchline to some poorly told joke. I just want to live a normal life," I whined. I hated that I was whining or groaning all my words today but I couldn't help it given my current state of distress.

Nan blinked up at me with wide eyes, a sly smile blooming on her face. "My dear sweet Angela, when has your life ever been normal?"

4

Whether or not Octo-Cat wanted anything more to do with the sleuthing business, he was still half owner of Pet Whisperer, P.I.—and I needed his help now more than ever.

After Nan left, I searched the house until I found him sitting in his bedroom watching the fish swim about his 140-gallon aquarium.

"Yummy is looking particularly plump today," he noted as I entered. "Maybe I'll just try a quick bite."

Of course, he'd named all his fish various synonyms of the word "delicious." I thought he did it mostly to get a rise out of me, since every time he hinted at eating his pets, I rushed to buy him fresh shrimp or his favorite lobster rolls from Little Dog Diner.

"Not today," I warned with a stern look.

That got his attention. "Keep your voice down. The child is

sleeping." He motioned toward his red silk cat bed where Charlene was dozing tucked under a pillow that was almost as large as the bed itself.

"Can we go somewhere to talk?" I whispered, kneeling down to bring myself closer to his height. I locked eyes with him and then put every ounce of desperate passion into my next words. *"It's important."*

Octo-Cat abruptly turned away from me, speaking back over his shoulder. "I don't like your tone of voice today, Angela," the tabby complained. "Maybe we can talk once you've had a chance to gain control of your emotions?"

"I am not being emotional," I shouted and stamped my foot in frustration. "I am having the proper anxiety response to a very big, very new threat, and I'd feel better if I could just talk to you about it!"

Across the room, Charlene mewled and popped her head out from beneath the pillow. Oops, I'd forgotten the need to be quiet. Maybe I really was a touch emotional over everything that was going on. I wouldn't be nearly as perturbed if my business partner and supposed best friend would just listen to me.

"Now you've really done it," he growled and rushed to lick the head of his beloved adopted daughter. "There, there, sweet pea. Papa is here. The mean old lady was just leaving."

I refused to accept being called "old," and frankly, Octavius hadn't seen mean yet, but if he kept this song-and-dance up, he soon would.

"What's wrong?" Charlene asked me with a soft voice and

wide golden eyes as Octo-Cat continued to snuggle her protectively.

For a moment, I considered how much I should reveal in front of the youngest member of our household. I didn't want to frighten her, yet I didn't want to hide any important truths from her either.

Ultimately, I decided to reveal everything and use gentle language to do so. I took a deep breath before launching into my slightly censored explanation. "Someone is sending me messages online, saying they know I can talk to animals, and they're going to tell everybody about it."

There. It really didn't sound nearly as bad when I put it that way.

Octo-Cat stared at me as he flicked his tail back and forth, presumably deep in thought. At least I hoped so, seeing as I could really use his perspective on this whole thing.

Charlene, however, spoke up immediately. "Who is saying those things to you?"

I forced myself to shrug nonchalantly. "I don't know. It's a mystery."

Charlene rose to her feet and stretched, shaking off her father's continued attentions. "Isn't that what you do best? Solve mysteries? You found my mother when she was missing and figured out who was hurting your mate, remember?"

Of course I remembered. All of that had happened just a couple weeks ago, but I refused to be snarky with a kitten, especially one who was just trying to help.

"You haven't been careful," Octo-Cat decided with a low rumbling in his throat that fell somewhere between a growl and a purr.

"I should have been more careful," I admitted. "But I can't go back and change the past, so how do we fix this in the here and now?"

"We could build a time machine!" Charlene cried, jumping into the air so that none of her four feet touched the ground. "That would fix everything!" she added once she'd landed.

"Time machines aren't real," I said with a soft chuckle as I reached out to stroke her fur.

"But Papa Octo-Cat said—"

Octo-Cat put a paw in front of his daughter's mouth. "Some knowledge is for cats only. You must never share what you learn during cat lessons," he said gravely.

"Not even with Angie?" the little one squeaked.

"Especially not with Angela. She already knows too much, as it is."

"Um, hello, I'm still here," I said, turning their attention back to me. Honestly, I didn't even want to know what they were yammering on about. Time machines? What ridiculous nonsense.

"Can we please redirect our attention to the problem at hand?" I begged, having completely discarded any lingering sense of pride long ago when it came to this situation.

"But I was—" Charlene began, but stopped abruptly when Octo-Cat shook his head.

"Proceed," the elder feline said with a wave of his paw in my direction.

"The person threatening me goes by the name of Charm. Really, they could be anybody, but I thought we could start by going over a list of suspects I made."

"All the pretty papers with words!" Charlene cried, all the pieces finally clicking into place for her. "You said that was a list of suspects."

"Yes, that was my list of suspects, and it includes anyone whose nefarious plans we've thwarted over the years. Unfortunately, it is not a short list."

"So what do you want me to do about it?" Octo-Cat asked with another flick of his tail.

My heart dropped. He knew how important maintaining my secret was to me. Did he really not care? "Help me," I enunciated slowly before adding, "You are my partner, after all."

He sighed and shook his head. "I told you, I'm a family man now. I don't have time to go on any more wild goose chases with you, Angela, especially not any that could be dangerous."

"But Octavius, this isn't just some throw-away case. This is my life." I brought my hands together in supplication, praying the haughty kitty would take pity on me and agree to lend his brain to the investigation. *"Please. Octo-Cat, I need you."*

Octo-Cat remained silent, but it seemed my appeal had gotten through to at least one of the cats.

"We've got to help her, Papa," Charlene insisted, coming up to me and rubbing her body against my arm. Moving to Octo-Cat, she did the same, claiming him with a friendly snuggle. "She helped me when I was scared and lost, and look how sad she is!"

I pouted my lower lip and made my eyes extra wide to drive home the kitten's point.

Charlene and I both stared at Octo-Cat, knowing that he needed to be the next to say something.

After several tense moments passed, he finally let out a long sigh and said, "this is the last time." His stony gaze fixed on mine as he added, "The very last time. I mean it."

"Thank you," I mouthed, overcome with a tremendous sense of relief.

If I couldn't turn the business around, this would be the last time, regardless. And if by some miracle I managed to save us, then I could worry about convincing Octo-Cat when the time came to take on our next case.

Either way, I needed to get to the bottom of this whole Charm thing before they made a mockery of both the business and my life.

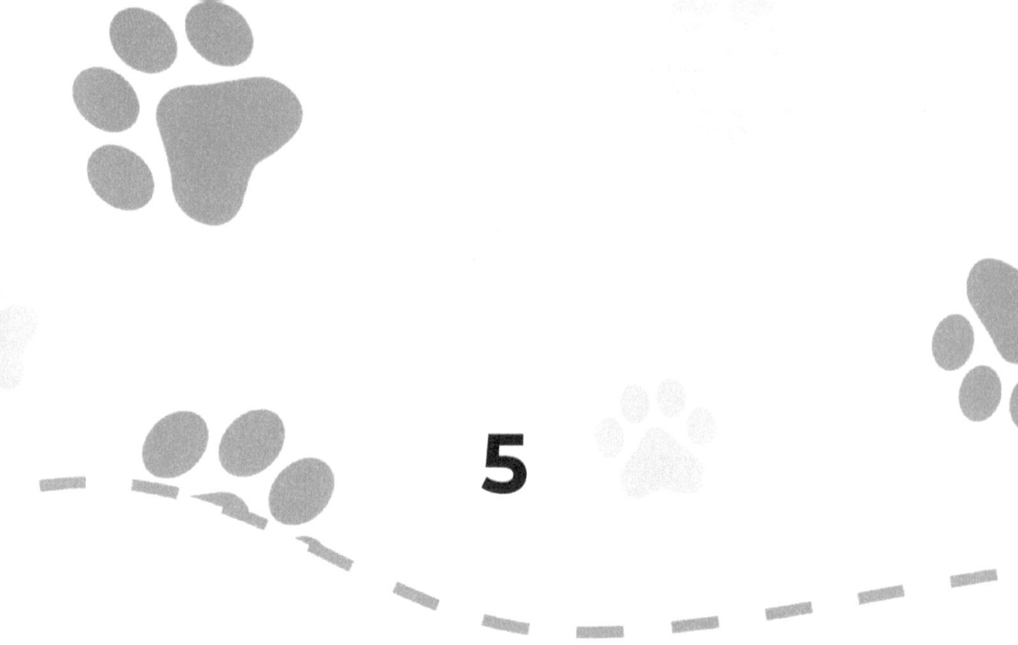

5

"So we're assuming Charm is a human, correct?" Octo-Cat asked after reviewing my hastily scrawled Post-It note suspects. And honestly I hadn't even considered that it might be an animal messing with me, until he suggested otherwise. How would an animal even be capable of typing out those messages—and so quickly? Then again, what if I overlooked the true identity based on making sweeping assumptions like that?

"Uh..." I really didn't know how to answer him. Luckily, Octo-Cat had much more to say on the subject.

"A cat is above all this," he pointed out drolly. "And a dog isn't smart enough. Wild animals wouldn't have access to the Internet. That leaves humans."

"Fair point," I conceded with a nod. Was it really that easy? See, this was why I needed him.

"I also think you can cross any murderers off your list." He pawed at the note with Diane Fulton's name scrawled across it, wrinkling his nose in disgust. "Why would they stoop to making idle threats when they've killed before? If they truly wanted revenge, Angela, they'd just off you."

"That's... not a comforting thought," I murmured as my heart sped to a gallop in my chest. My throat also seemed to be closing in on itself. Maybe my cat was right; maybe Charm wasn't a murderer, but did that mean there might actually be someone else out there plotting my demise?

"It's a good argument, though." Octo-Cat turned his nose up, oblivious to the effect his candor was having on my mental health.

"Do you think Charm is someone we've interacted with more recently?" I asked next. The sooner we narrowed down our list, the sooner I could start investigating each lead. "I mean, why would Anne Fulton, for example, come out of the woodwork now?"

Octo-Cat shuddered. "Don't ever speak that name in my presence again." Anne was the one who had kidnapped him and held him for ransom in a last-ditch effort to contest the will that left him almost everything. It made sense that he didn't have fond memories of her. Then again, that's how I felt about basically every single name under consideration.

"I don't really know," Octo-Cat confessed, resettling himself on the desk. He'd taken Charlene back to the Sphynx cats for kitten-sitting while we worked on our newest mystery, but I could tell he was eager to return to his charge. "It could very well be someone you haven't even thought of yet."

I sighed and leaned back in my chair. "That's what I'm afraid of. Until I figure out who Charm is, I can't really trust anyone."

Octo-Cat sneered at me. "I'd be careful about making such general statements. You can trust me, Charlene, Charles, Nan..."

I raised an eyebrow in interest. "You didn't mention Jacques and Jillianne."

"I still haven't forgiven the exhibitionists for the mess they caused at our wedding." A light growl sounded in his throat at the memory.

"I don't think they're behind this, though," I said softly, not wanting to create drama where there needn't be any. "Everyone's been getting along so well lately."

Octo-Cat sighed and nodded his head in concession. "And I remain convinced a human is to blame this time, so we should probably cross them off the list anyway."

"Maybe we can make a second list, one for everyone who already knows my secret?" I groaned and reached for my sticky pads again. "At least it will be shorter than my list of enemies."

"Remember that weird author we met on our road trip? Melissa something?" Octo-Cat said, his eyes closed up tight while he thought. "She knew because Nan had been blabbing to her friends on the Internet."

Dread roiled in my gut. "You're right. There's no telling how many people found out that way. But that was more than a year ago. Ever since Nan and I had our talk, she's stopped gossiping on online message boards. She even removed all her old posts."

"So?" the cat challenged, opening his eyes again to stare at me coldly.

"So it doesn't make sense for one of those people to be messing with me now. Too much time has passed." Right? Right? That had to be the case.

"What if that person suddenly needs money or a favor?" Octo-Cat raised both whiskered eyebrows. "Maybe they hadn't needed to threaten you before, but desperate times and all that."

"So our suspect list is every human with the Internet?" I glanced at my desk with trepidation. I didn't have anywhere near enough Post-It notes—or wall space—for that.

One of Octo-Cat's fangs came out to rest on his lower lip, giving him a comical appearance. His words, however, were anything but. "Well, as you pointed out, it's been a long time. Even people without Internet may still have come into contact with the info by other means."

"Which means our suspect list is every human in the entire world?" God help me, I didn't have the strength for this.

Octo-Cat nodded. "Every living human."

I groaned and threw the notepad down onto my desk. "This isn't helping."

"You're the one who's forcing me to be here," my cat challenged.

"Fine, then go," I barked out, trying not to let any tears spill from my burning eyes.

Octo-Cat rose to his feet, but paused to study me. "It's going to be okay, Angela," he offered as parting words. "One way or another, it will all work itself out. But if Charm doesn't want us to know their identity, I don't see how we're going to figure it out. Maybe you should stop trying to figure out who they are and instead start focusing on what you're going to do once your secret comes out."

"Please just go," I said between clenched teeth. He was already assuming I would fail. I didn't need that. Couldn't handle it, either.

I kept my head bowed toward my lap as I struggled to work through my emotions. By the time I raised my eyes again to glance around the room, my cat had gone. It was times like this I really missed Paisley and her eternal optimism. I knew Octo-Cat was being a realist here, but I also needed to live in my secret fantasy world just a little bit longer—especially if Charm was going to come and pull the rug out from under my feet any second now.

If Octo-Cat wouldn't help me and Nan refused to see the problem, that meant I had to find someone else to confide in. Of course, I knew Grandma Lyn would be a good person to go to. She could talk to animals too, but when she tried to share her secret with her husband at the time, he not only left her, he stole her baby away too. Being honest about what she could do ruined her life.

Sure, times had changed and my husband already knew and

accepted all parts of me—including this one—but what if something awful still happened as a result of Charm outing me?

Octo-Cat said that if my bully didn't want me to know their identity, then there was no way I'd be able to figure it out. But he was an amateur on social media… at best.

And while I myself wasn't the greatest, I did have someone else I could turn to—someone who not only understood the intricate ins and outs of the Interweb but also made a living at it.

Yes, I decided. My cousin Mags would know what to do, and it was just about time I gave her a call.

6

I grabbed my laptop and headed upstairs to the tower bedroom that Charles and I now shared. Crossing my legs beneath me, I opened the computer and messaged Mags an *SOS*.

Almost as soon as I pressed send, my phone buzzed beside me. "Hello?"

"What's the emergency? How can I help?" my cousin asked breathlessly, leaving me to wonder if she had just stopped a workout on my account.

Well, might as well just come straight out with it. "Someone's threatening me online, and I was hoping you could help me figure out who."

Mags's breathing slowed to a more measured pace. "Oooh, a bit of digital sleuthing? I'm in, although I definitely don't like that someone's picking on you. How bad is it?"

I closed my eyes to hold in the tears. "They say they know what I can do, and they're going to tell everyone."

Mags took a long, slow breath on the other end of the line. "Okay, okay, that could mean anything."

"Yeah, but we both know what it *does* mean. Are you near your computer? I can do a screen share, so you can see everything."

"I can be in five minutes," my cousin promised. "Want me to stay on with you until I get home?"

"Yes, please." Hearing her voice brought a much-needed smile to my face, and I wasn't willing to let that go just yet—not even for a single second.

While Mags power-walked back to her house, I filled her in on the details I had so far as well as some of my guesses for who might be behind Charm's messages.

"I'm home now. Just booting my PC. Shoot me a Zoom link on messenger."

I dutifully did as requested and waited for Mags to join the meeting room before we hung up on the phone and switched to this new means of communication.

A moment later, Mags's face appeared bright and rosy; her hair hung in a loose ponytail at the nape of her neck.

"I didn't mean to interrupt your exercise," I said, feeling bad about how little I actually worked out myself.

Mags shook her head and waved her hands in front of the camera. "But this can't wait. I'm glad you called me. Now, show me the comments."

I shared my computer screen and navigated back toward the ad, so Mags could see everything for herself.

“Hmmm,” was all she said.

“Is that a good hmm or a bad hmm?”

“Right now it’s a curious hmm. Click on the profile.”

I watched the tiny window with Mags’s video feed as she leaned forward and squinted. And once again I did as instructed. Charm’s profile was still locked due to their high-level privacy settings.

Mags groaned when she saw that. “They’re giving us nothing. Not even a location.”

“Well, it has to be someone local, right? Otherwise they wouldn’t have seen my ad. I only targeted people within a twenty-five mile radius.” I still felt proud that I’d figured the ads thing out all by myself. Not that they’d brought me any clients, but still.

“Actually...” Mags shared her screen, which in turn minimized mine. I watched eagerly as she clicked around on my page and then brought up the same ad where Charm was leaving nasty comments. “See, anyone can find your ads if they know where to look.”

“So we’re back to my suspect list being basically everyone on planet Earth,” I ground out in defeat.

Mags’s blonde brows pinched together in confusion. “What?”

I waved a hand dismissively. “Just something Octo-Cat was saying.”

“Okay, well...” Mags stopped sharing her computer screen,

and her flushed face once again filled the picture window. "You made a list of your enemies, right?"

I nodded.

"And a list of everyone who already knows your secret?"

"Well, I started to, but then Octo-Cat pointed out that Nan had been pretty free about sharing my secret online about a year ago. Those posts are gone now, but anyone could have seen them while they were still up."

Mags shook her head, then said, "Hmm. That's a me-feeling-bad-for-you hmm by the way."

"Thanks" was all I could manage to say in response. At least I had her sympathy, if nothing else.

We sat in silence for a few beats before Mags's face lit up anew. "Okay, here's what we do. So far we've been focused on brainstorming who you know that might say these things based on your past encounters. But we shouldn't be focusing on the past."

This admittedly confused me. "We shouldn't?" As a private investigator, focusing on the past was all I did as I tried to piece together what happened and save the day.

But Mags was insistent. "No, we need to focus on the here and now. We don't have much on Charm, but everything we do have is a clue."

"I'm listening." I moved my hands to my lap to avoid fidgeting while she explained.

"Go back to Charm's page and enlarge that profile picture," my cousin commanded, staring intently at the screen.

Once we'd returned to the profile, we both stared at the photo of a tranquil ocean. I, for one, had no ideas.

"Okay, so I just did a quick reverse image search, and nothing is coming up. Or rather, too much is coming up. The photo is too generic to match, which means that could be any ocean anywhere," Mags explained, her shoulders slumping. Was she also ready to admit defeat, just like Octo-Cat?

"Do you think Charm lives by the ocean?" I prompted, still unwilling to let her go.

"I have no idea. I was hoping I'd find something, but no such luck." She shook her head before pointing at me in the screen. "But there's still more we can look at. Their comments—what they say and how they say things."

"So far there hasn't been anything that stands out. At least not to me."

"Me neither, but maybe we can trick Charm into revealing himself—or herself."

"Should I ask them a question?" I waited, hands poised over the keyboard.

"I'm thinking of the right way to word it. Unfortunately, since their profile is set to private, the only way for you to reach out is very publicly through that ad. We have to be very careful about how we proceed."

I blinked hard. Everything about this made me super nervous, but what other choice did I have? At least Mags was ready and able to help.

Mags sat straight again, her face glowed with the promise of a new idea. "Oh, I've got it. Type this."

I wrote out Mags's response word for word: *Let's meet to discuss this. How about the Little Dog Diner tonight at five?*

"Good thinking," I enthused as a wave of relief rushed over me. "That will help determine if Charm is local."

"And if they're willing to put their money where their mouth is," I added.

"Exactly?" Mags bobbed her head before suddenly pausing to ask, "What money? What mouth?"

I laughed at that. "Sometimes you're as bad as the cats. You know that?"

Mags blew a raspberry at me. "Hey, you're the one with all the fancy idioms. Not me."

Mags and I chatted back and forth as we waited for a response, but ultimately none came. I glanced at the time in the corner of my computer screen and sighed.

"Guess I better get ready to head out. Thanks for all your help, Mags."

"Keep me posted," my cousin cried before her face disappeared from the screen, leaving me completely and utterly alone.

Now that the moment was nigh, I found myself equal parts excited and terrified. Was I really on the way to meet my accuser? Could this really all be over before my husband even made it home from work?

Oh, how I hoped so.

7

I sent Charles a quick text to let him know I would be picking up lobster rolls for dinner, then hopped behind the steering wheel and began the long drive to Misty Harbor.

As I navigated the streets of the area I'd called home my entire life, I began to wonder how any of the friendly people here could want to ruin me. True, we had our fair share of murderers and other con artists, but I'd only ever tried to help people—to put good out into the world.

And now someone was threatening to bring that to an end once and for all.

Was I endangering myself by meeting with this person face-to-face? By asking to talk about things, I was also all but confirming whatever they believed to be true. What were the chances they'd been hinting at something completely unrelated to my ability to talk to animals? What if they actually assumed something far worse about me?

Nope. I did not like this situation one bit.

At least Mags took my concern seriously, but it hurt that Nan and Octo-Cat both remained largely unbothered. And, yeah, I probably should have told Charles by now, but he was so busy at work, making up for all the time he took off for our honeymoon.

I'd tell him tonight, though, over our favorite meal from our favorite diner to soften the blow.

These swirling thoughts of fear, self-doubt, and indecision kept my mind busy until I reached my destination.

When I entered my beloved diner, the waitress on duty caught sight of me immediately. "Four lobster rolls to go, darling?" she asked with a huge smile as she wiped down menus with a wet cloth. She was newer and I couldn't quite remember her name, but she definitely knew me and my order.

"Actually…" I coughed into my fist, suddenly very nervous. What if Charm was already here? What if they were watching me right now? I desperately glanced around the establishment as my pulse pounded in my ears.

"Actually?" the waitress prompted with a reassuring nod when I didn't immediately continue.

My eyes zoomed back to hers, and I jammed both hands into my pockets to hide that they were shaking. "I'd like to stick around for a little while before I grab those rolls to go. May I have a table? And a Diet Coke?"

"You've got it, babe. Sit anywhere you'd like. I'll be right with you." She seemed relieved to bring our awkward exchange to an end—or at least to put it on hold.

Once I was seated, I glanced around the other patrons of the diner a second time. Almost everyone was closer to Nan's age than my own. Did I really think that sweet old man wearing coke bottle glasses and polka-dotted suspenders was capable of Charm's heinous behavior?

The waitress brought me my soda, and I sucked it down while continuing to catalog the other diners. No one paid me any mind, except to smile politely or give a quick nod of acknowledgment.

None were Charm. I was sure of it.

"Waiting for someone?" the waitress asked kindly after stopping at a nearby table to distribute entrees.

"Yeah," I said, my voice suddenly hoarse.

"If they'll be here soon, I can put in an order," she offered with a grin. "Or I can at least bring you a refill on your Diet Coke."

How long did I want to commit to waiting for someone who might never show, someone I was less and less sure I actually wanted to meet as time droned on?

"Um, I'm actually not sure when they'll be here. Let me just check my phone." I smiled awkwardly at the waitress as she waited, tray held high. With shaking fingers, I scrolled to the ad where all my interactions with Charm had taken place.

Nothing.

This was stupid. I had no reason to believe they were actually coming. I should have stayed at home rather than driving all the way out here. And yet, I just so desperately wanted the whole thing to be over.

Well, we can't always get what we want, I supposed.

"Everything okay?" the waitress asked, lowering her tray and tilting her head to the side.

"I'll take those lobster rolls to go now," I answered with a forced smile.

"Be back in a jiff," she assured me before floating off toward the back kitchen.

I nodded, but I just couldn't tear my eyes away from the phone's tiny screen. Even though I knew better, I couldn't help but type out a new reply: *You're not here.*

This time Charm responded promptly: *I never said I was coming. Someone seems pretty desperate to meet up though.*

After the words, Charm posted three skull emojis.

What was *that* supposed to mean?

I decided to send a quick screenshot to Mags and ask her.

Dead came her immediately reply. *Likely dead laughing. They're making fun of you.*

I bristled. Glad this was all one big joke to Charm. Meanwhile, my entire day had been spoiled, and I was still no closer to figuring out who they were or what they really wanted.

A few minutes later, the waitress set a white paper bag down before me. "Tada, four lobster rolls to go!"

Oops. I'd forgotten to modify my usual order to reflect the current members of our household, but I also had no guarantee that Charlene, Jacque, or Jillianne would even like the food. It was weird enough that Octo-Cat did.

I handed the waitress a wad of cash, thanked her for the help, and then bolted out that door. No one there knew what was going on, but I was still thoroughly embarrassed by the ordeal.

It all felt so hopeless.

I felt hopeless.

I'd barely gotten back in my car when my phone rang. I let the Bluetooth route the call through my speakers, and Charles's voice wrapped around me like a warm hug.

"I'm home, but where is my beautiful bride?" he wanted to know.

"I'm about thirty minutes away," I said, checking the GPS for an ETA. True, I knew this area like the back of my hand, but sometimes I got so wrapped up in my inner thoughts that I missed my turn-off.

"You sound…" My husband started but then abruptly switched gears. "Everything okay?"

"It's been a day," I admitted with a sigh. "I don't want to trouble you with it." I don't know why I said that. It wasn't true at all. I very much needed someone on my side, someone who wasn't a thousand miles away like Mags.

"Hey, I knew what I signed on for when we said 'I do.' Half your problems are now my problems, so let's hear it. Maybe I can help."

It was then I finally began to cry. I cried so hard I had to pull over on the side of the road until my vision cleared enough to continue the drive. And I told Charles everything right from that first introduction to Charm all the way down to the row of skull emojis and everything in between.

"Honey, honey, it's okay," he said. Charles had taken to the nickname after the whole fiasco with the bees on our honeymoon. "We'll figure it out together. If nothing else, I can send a cease and desist. That often scares people enough to make them stop whatever it is they're doing."

I let out a long, shaky breath. "Yeah, okay."

"I wish you would have called me when this first started."

"But you're busy with work. I didn't want to distract you," I argued, at the same time regretting that I hadn't. Charles always knew just what to do, no matter how big the problem.

"Work is work, but Angie, you're my whole life."

"I love you," I said with another sob.

"I love you too, but…" His voice switched from soft to stern in an instant. "I don't love that you tried to meet this person by yourself. That could have been really dangerous."

"I know," I confessed. I deserved his ire, there was no denying that. "I was just so desperate for it to be over."

"Leave it with me," he said decisively. "Do you mind if I use your laptop? I have some questions for this Charm."

"Have at it," I said, then blew my nose loudly in a tissue.

"Drive safe," was the last thing Charles said before ending the call, and then I was alone again.

8

Thirty minutes later, I marched through the front door, lobster rolls held out in front of me like some kind of sacred offering.

"Finally," my cat yowled, jumping from the bottom step of the grand staircase and trotting briskly toward the dining room.

"What do you mean *finally?* You didn't even know I was going out!" I huffed.

The only response was the jaunty swish of Octo-Cat's tail as he departed.

"Is that my wifey?" Charles's voice sounded from above.

I turned back toward the staircase and watched him race down the steps, holding on to my laptop with a tight grip.

I was almost afraid to ask. "Any luck?"

The corners of Charles's mouth tilted down as he revealed, "It's Blaire."

"Blaire," I parroted in bewilderment, then it hit me. "Blaire from-our-honeymoon Blaire?"

"Look at this." Charles motioned me to join him at the table, then set the laptop before us and pressed play on a video I'd never seen before.

In it, I stood in a beautiful garden having a conversation with a queen bee named Bey. That whole scene had played out sometime between two and three weeks ago at our honeymoon in Virginia. The recording only showed my side of the conversation. I guess Bey's quiet buzzy voice just couldn't be captured on film.

"Aldrin and Lightyear told me about the over-harvesting and the new plants," my likeness said. The camera wasn't particularly close, but you could still see the hint of a sympathetic expression on my face.

Video-me paused while Bey responded, and the person taking the video attempted to zoom in on the queen bee who sat perched upon a flower. I only knew she was there because I'd been there too. For viewers, she was much too small to see.

"This garden has sentimental value," my recorded self continued. "I can understand that. What can I do to help ensure you can stay?"

The camera panned out, bringing me back into frame.

"Oh, yes, that reminds me, please don't sting my husband. He is a good man, and very allergic."

Another long pause.

"While I have you, then, have you noticed any other strange goings-on in this garden or its house?"

The video cut off abruptly even though I knew the conversation continued for some time after that.

"Well, that isn't so bad, right? I mean, you can't even tell who I'm talking to, really. Nobody will accept this as any real kind of proof," I argued, waiting for my husband to agree.

He did not.

"Yeah, but then there's this one too," Charles informed me, clicking on a second video while I was still trying to process the first. Now I sat inside cross-legged on the floor as I visited with Charlene and her mother cat, the one we'd worked so hard to find during our trip. That was our last day in Virginia before we headed home with the kitten in tow. I remembered it vividly. I had asked Blaire for some privacy while I said goodbye. The rainbow-haired girl had adopted the mother cat and named her Socks, despite the fact that Socks was a tortie with not a drop of white on her.

Blaire had left us alone then, but must have set up a secret camera somewhere first. She already knew what I could do since the conversation with Queen Bey had happened days earlier. I should have known better, too. I'd caught her recording when Charles fell through the staircase, and it was her secret recording of a midnight meeting between Mrs. MacKenzie and Billy that had revealed the true culprits behind everything that had gone wrong at the inn. Blaire always had that phone in her hands, and she was always recording. Of course she'd recorded me. Of course she had. And yet…

I let out a long sigh. "I don't get it. We helped that girl. We arranged for that job and a place to live. Why would she suddenly blackmail me like this?"

"Why don't you ask her directly?" Charles suggested, tilting the laptop toward me on the table. "I asked her to private message the page, by the way. None of those videos were posted publicly as far as I know."

Well, that was a relief, but it's the only thing that was. Now that I knew Charm's secret identity, I felt even worse. I'd never hurt her in any way. She had no reason to threaten me like this.

My fingers hovered over the keyboard as I thought of what to say. I decided to just be direct:

Blaire, why are you doing this?

Her response came rather unexpected. *Don't you want to be famous?*

"No!" I shouted at the computer, leading Charles to place his arms over my shoulder in support. "This is ridiculous."

"Just talk to her. It's the best chance you have of putting an end to all of this."

I want to live a normal life. What will it take to convince you to delete your videos and leave me alone?

"Even if she deletes the original videos, they're still probably backed up to the Cloud," Charles reminded me gently, proving I would never be safe even if I got Blaire to agree to silence.

What Blaire said next seemed to suggest we were having two different conversations.

Think of it. Endorsement deals. Reality shows. You could even become a TikTok influencer. And I'll manage the whole thing. For a cut.

She punctuated this with three wide eye emojis. The skull emojis from earlier probably should have clued me in that my bully was a member of Gen Z. A Millennial like myself would have used the cry-laughing emojis in that situation.

But I don't want any of that, I typed back furiously, then watched Charm's ocean profile pic bounce up and down as she typed. *Look, I'm offering you a chance to get in on the ground floor here. I already have the footage. It's mine to do what I want with.*

"Give me that," Charles said, practically tearing the computer away from me.

"Actually," he said every word aloud as he typed it into the chat. "Sharing these videos without Angie's consent is illegal. At best, it's an invasion of privacy. At worst, if you use the videos to garner endorsement deals or even just to monetize your feed, you're violating Angie's right of publicity, which is an even more serious charge. Is your address still the same? I need to know where to send the cease and desist letter."

I gave Charles an excited high five. Gosh, I loved being married to an attorney. He always knew just how to scare people into compliance.

There was a long pause before Blaire started working on her response, and then: *Ah, you must be the "husband." Well, tell our girl that I was just trying to help her, but if she wants to be a wet blanket, that's on her. Stay poor for all I care.*

I let out a frustrated groan. "But we're not—"

Charles placed his hand on my shoulder and squeezed. "Don't say anything more. She should be done bothering you now. Just in case, we'll grab screenshots of this conversation and her comments on the ad."

It was true that Blaire knew Charles could get results. That was what had saved the inn back in Virginia and gotten her that job in the first place. I just couldn't believe she would throw it all back in our faces by trying to force me into some warped celebrity status so she could collect a side income. *Gross.*

I closed the laptop and turned toward my wonderful husband. "So what now?" I asked; already my heart was slowing back to its usual pace. My breath was coming easier, too.

But not everyone was relieved in that moment.

"For the love of all things fluffy," Octo-Cat shouted at top volume. "Is anyone going to feed me?"

I laughed as I unwrapped a lobster roll for each of us.

And that first decadent bite? It tasted just like victory.

9

Charles and I had a great evening snuggling with the cats as we caught up on our Netflix to-watch list. I always felt so much better when he was home with me.

"I'm sorry I've been so busy with work lately," he mumbled when we were both brushing our teeth before bed. "There's been a rush of cases lately, but not enough to justify bringing on another attorney. You just never know what you'll get with small towns. There's either too much work or not enough."

Honestly I couldn't ever remember his workload falling under the "not enough" umbrella. Lately, though, it had risen to a whole new level. I was proud of my husband and his successful career, but I also sometimes wanted to hide him away from the rest of the world so that he could be just mine, even if just for a few hours.

I finished brushing, spit my toothpaste foam into the sink, and gave Charles a peck on the cheek. "It's okay. I understand. I just miss you."

He leaned into my kiss for a moment before returning to his nightly ministrations. "I miss you too, honey. I love my job, but I wish I didn't have to work so much. I feel like I'm always missing out on things at home. Like this whole thing with Blaire..." He shook his head. "I should have been here."

"Seriously, don't worry about it. Today was an anomaly. Not much happens otherwise."

Charles glanced up to study my reflection in the bathroom mirror. "Are you sure you're okay?"

"I'm fine, or at least I will be. Just a lot of changes. Good changes, but they still take getting used to, you know?" I shrugged and applied some moisturizer to my face. Normally I didn't put any on at night, but I needed to keep my hands and mind busy as we chatted.

More than anything, I missed Charles, and I missed Nan. Sure I still saw both of them every day, but it just wasn't enough. I hated being on my own, and it so often felt like I was. Even Octo-Cat kept himself busy apart from me, considering he now had his daughter to look after. And I missed him, too.

God help me, I missed having my cranky cat criticize me! I was seriously starting to lose it here.

I needed to get my life figured out—and soon.

Unable to shut off my brain, I lay awake that night, lost in my thoughts while Charles dozed beside me. Maybe I could go out looking for mysteries to solve. While it would be great to make my business successful, more than anything I just needed something to keep me busy, to reignite that passion within me.

Feeling somewhat satisfied with my plan to roam the downtown area the next day, I at last fell into a fitful sleep. And by the time I awoke the next morning, Charles had already left for the office.

Bored, so bored.

And yet I had no energy to get ready and drag my sorry butt into town. It didn't really matter if I wore pajamas all day, did it? Or whether I brushed my hair?

It was funny that having nothing to do somehow made me want to do even less with myself. But I had no one to impress, so what did it even matter?

I puttered around on the computer for a while, mostly playing match-four games instead of actually doing anything that resembled work. Hmm. Maybe I should go back to school. Get another associate degree, or even go for my bachelor's. I'd always liked school. That's why I'd done so much of it.

Hey, maybe I could sneak into Charlene's cat lessons. Yeah, that would be something to do, and then I wouldn't be alone all day.

My mind made up, I shut down my computer and then slowly padded around the house in search of my feline roommates. It didn't take me long to discover that the Sphynxes had claimed Nan's old bedroom as their own, and that's where they'd created the makeshift classroom for their pupil.

I cracked the door and gave a listen: "If you have two dead mice but only one is really, truly dead, how should you reduce your treat intake to prevent flabbiness?" Jillianne asked in a rhythmic, lilting voice so unlike the one she used with me.

"Trick question!" the kitten cried in response. "Treat intake should never be reduced. Besides, I got lots of good exercise hunting those mice!"

"Very good!" the professorial cat mused. "Now if you'll—

Her voice dropped off at once as she spotted me in the doorway. "May I help you?"

Drats! I hadn't understood their odd mix of nutrition and algebra, but I had found it quite entertaining. "Sorry," I blurted out, opening the door the rest of the way and stepping into the room. Immediately, I noticed an odd collection of objects laid out on the bed between the cats: missing socks, trash, plants from outside, and some kind of furry carcass.

"No humans allowed," Jacques, the smaller of the two hairless cats, shouted, marching right up to me and then taking a swipe at my ankle. "Cat classes are for cats only. Now out! Shoo!"

"I don't mind if she stays," Charlene argued but was quickly overruled by her elders.

"What happens in cat school must stay in cat school," Jillianne decreed as her brother pushed me back into the hall.

Well, so much for that idea.

After that failed attempt at educating myself in the ways of catdom, I decided to go outside and take a walk about the property.

I'd barely managed to step off the porch before Pringle discovered me and quickly scampered over.

"Are we having story time early today?" the raccoon asked, rubbing his hands together like some kind of furry addict. "I can't wait to see how Merlin is going to defeat that mean, old ghost."

And because it was as good an idea as any, I nodded. "Sure, let's spend some time with Merlin, Gracie, and the gang."

Pringle leapt into the air with great vigor. He'd come so far since our first meeting, and it wasn't until very recently that I'd come to acknowledge his personal growth. If Octo-Cat didn't want to help with Pet Whisperer anymore, I knew Pringle would happily take over the role.

But was that what I wanted?

This gave me something to think on later, but for now, I'd lose myself in the magical mysteries of our favorite book series. I could figure out the mystery of my life later.

10

By the time Nan and Paisley turned up for lunch, I was beside myself with boredom and frustration. Octo-Cat had showed up unbidden at one point to give me a lecture about my intrusion upon Charlene's cat lessons, even going so far as to claim my innocent curiosity could disrupt the entire balance of the universe.

Yeah, sure. Sometimes my cat's inflated sense of self really wore on me. And sometimes it made me thankful that he kept busy parenting Charlene instead of constantly nagging me.

At least I had Nan and Paisley for a couple hours nearly every day to break up the monotony of my new life.

"I missed you so much!" Paisley cried out, wagging not just her tail, but her whole body as she slathered me in kisses and provided quite the contrast to my cat's attitude about me. It had only been one day since I last saw the good-natured Chihuahua, but I had felt her absence quite keenly during that time.

I scratched behind both of her ears and smiled. "I missed you too, baby dog." Then looking up at my grandmother asked, "How was your morning, Nan?"

She sashayed past, carrying two very full looking reusable grocery bags straight to the kitchen and calling out her answer as she went. "Grant and I started doing Tai Chi in the park downtown with some other seniors. This morning we were already there and halfway through our workout by the time the sun rose. It was magnificent."

Sounded like torture to me.

Nan poked her head through the kitchen doorway and smiled. "Are you sure you don't want to come along?"

"Nan, I'd be the youngest by at least forty years." I groaned as I drifted into the kitchen with Paisley scampering closely behind.

"So what's the big deal about that?"

While it was true I needed to find my place, I doubted that was with a group of health-nut octogenarians, and before sunrise at that. This was Nan's thing. I needed something that was all my own, another reason I so desperately wanted to turn Pet Whisperer P.I. around.

When my only response was an uncomfortable grimace, Nan waved her hand and returned her attention to the baking supplies. "Today I thought I could teach you how to make my famous blueberry scones," she explained as she unpacked first one bag and then the other. It looked as if she'd brought half the spice aisle with her.

"I was thinking about maybe going back to school," I mumbled, just to see how the idea might be received. I already knew I made a hopeless baker, which made it hard to pay attention. I had a lot of mental baggage I still needed to unload, too.

Nan paused and turned very slowly to look at me. "But you love being a detective. And you're so good at it."

I shrugged, attempting to appear nonchalant. "Nobody wants to hire me, and Octo-Cat wants out anyway. Then there was that whole thing with Blaire yesterday."

"I still can't believe that girl would throw everything you've done for her back into your face." My grandmother's face turned red; her voice shook with rage.

"She was just trying to help—mostly herself—but hey."

"Awful, awful," Nan tutted while returning her attention to the groceries.

"It was pretty stressful yesterday, but at least it was something to do. I've been feeling adrift lately."

"The post-matrimonial blues?" she suggested. "That's not as uncommon as you might think. Your life is changing a lot right now. It's natural to feel off-balance."

"I love Charles. No regrets there. But he is so busy at work each day, and I have very little to do here. Plus the cats all keep to themselves and with you and Paisley gone, I just..." I shrugged. "Well, that's why I thought going back to school might be a good idea."

Nan nodded as she lined up the various jars of spices in a straight row. “I understand now. Do you have an idea of what you might like to study?”

The corners of my mouth turned down. “Honestly, I’m not sure. I love solving mysteries. I wish I could keep doing that.”

“You could do it on the side if you have to. Maybe you’d enjoy being a policewoman?”

“Maybe,” I said, even though I could never picture myself carrying a weapon on the regular. I’d been threatened one too many times to ever feel comfortable with that kind of power on my person.

Nan placed a hand on my upper arm and waited for me to meet her eyes before speaking. “You’ve been the Pet Whisperer for nearly three years now. You never stuck with anything else that long. It seemed this career was truly it. You’re something special.”

I sighed heavily. She was right. She was so right, but it was also no longer enough. “All good things must come to an end.”

“Pish-posh. That’s just what unhappy people say.”

“Yeah, *me.* I mean, I’m mostly happy with my life. I just need more. Does that make sense?”

Nan placed a quick kiss on my cheek. “You’ve always been too big for this world, Angie. It’s the thing I love most about you. I also have no doubt you’ll find what you’re missing—and soon. But right now, let’s bake some scones. Could you preheat the oven for me?”

I loved Nan, but I also didn’t think she understood the crux of my problem. She'd lived an adventure-filled life for twice as long as I'd led my comparatively mundane one. Nan had always been my best friend, my closest confidant, but this particular problem just didn't seem to be connecting. She and her husband were both retired and got to spend all day doing wonderful things together.

She also hadn't understood my anxiety over the whole Charm situation the day before, which made me wonder if our bond might be fraying a little bit.

We still saw each other most days, but not living together really limited our contact. And I was no longer the most important person in her world—her new husband Grant had stolen the spotlight from me.

Maybe I was finally growing up, standing on my own two shaky legs.

With little else to keep me occupied for the rest of the afternoon, I decided to call and check up on Grandma Lyn. Now that the Charm situation had resolved itself, I wanted to get her insights on having been ridiculed for her secret—the same secret I now shared.

"And she threatened to expose you?" Grandma Lyn asked with a gasp once I'd finished relaying all the details.

"She said she wanted to make me famous. Isn't that so silly?"

"Well, Dr. Doolittle was a very popular movie. The original, not this new CGI nonsense with that Ironman fellow."

I smiled to myself as I pictured the look on her face. It had to be a doozy to match the disgust that laced her usually sweet voice.

"Do you think people would be more accepting nowadays?" I ventured while picking at the skin on my elbow.

Grandma Lyn thought about this for a moment. "The world has changed a lot in recent years, but I just don't know, Angie. I wish I did, but it's impossible to guess what might happen if others were to find out."

"So far everyone has been very accepting of it. Nobody ever spoke bad about it until Blaire. And even she wanted to monetize my ability, not ridicule it."

We both sat silent for a moment. What was I trying to convince my grandmother of? Was it something I'd already decided for myself? I hadn't gotten this far in my conversation with Nan, but try as she might she would never understand—not the way someone who shared my ability could.

"Do you ever have regrets about what happened back when Mom was a baby?" I asked gently. I'd been curious for ages, but had never gathered the courage to ask. Until now.

Grandma Lyn didn't hesitate with her answer. "All the time. It's tough not to wish the past was different, but at the same time, I'm very happy where we've all landed in the present. If your mother hadn't grown up, she never would have met your father. Never would have given the world its greatest treasure—you."

And I was crying again.

Great.

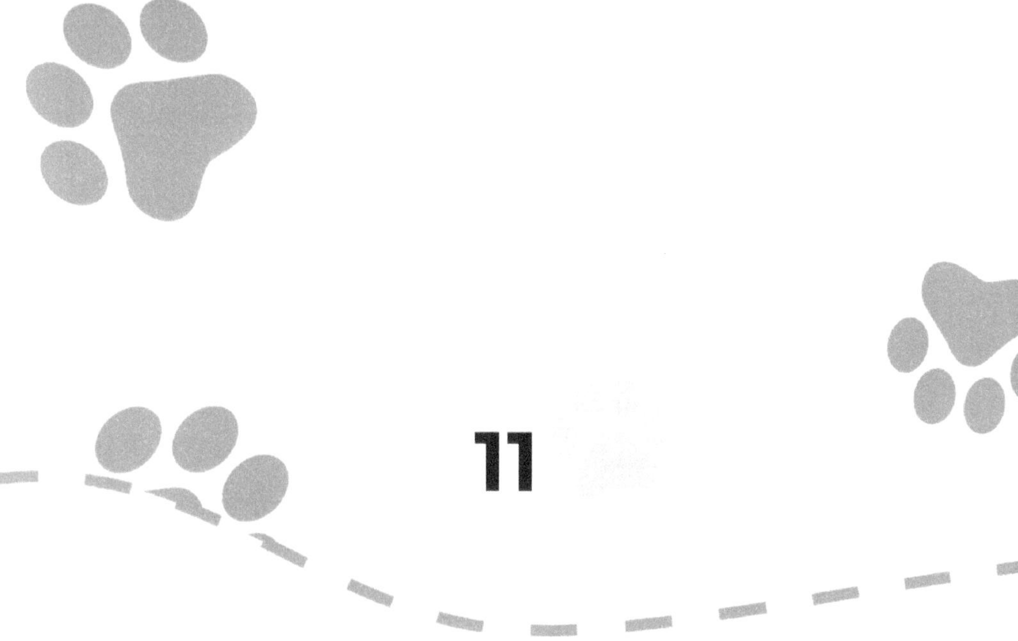

11

I was on my own that evening, thanks to Charles wining and dining an important corporate client. Luckily, I had lots of Nan's famous blueberry scones to fill my belly for dinner. We'd already discarded the batch I'd been responsible for making. Somehow I had forgotten to add the salt, which ruined the finished product much more than one might assume.

By now, the cats had finished their lessons for the day, which meant they all hung close to me—a small and demanding pride of mismatched house-cats.

We'd decided to snuggle up and watch *The Wizard of Oz* together, seeing as Charlene had never seen it, and we were just to the part where Dorothy meets the cowardly lion when my phone buzzed with a notification. I grabbed the device from the nearby coffee table and gasped when I noted what it was attempting to tell me.

Octo-Cat noticed me tense up right away. "What?" he asked, high-stepping across the couch and climbing onto my lap to bat at the phone. "What is it?"

"It's a new mess—"

"Angela, pause the movie first!" he cried with such astounding vigor it made me leap in my seat. I grabbed the remote control and clicked the stop button then revealed, "It's a new message from Charm."

Octo-Cat scrunched up his nose as if smelling something foul in the air. "Your bully? But I thought we figured out who it was, and UpChuck got them to stop. What now?" Ever since we'd returned from the honeymoon, Octo-Cat had gotten in the habit of calling my husband by that horrible nickname again. He claimed it was so as not to confuse Charlene and Charles, but I knew he just liked giving me grief.

"Was it really that nice girl Blaire? The one who adopted my mama?" Charlene mewled sadly.

"Unfortunately, yes." I hated this. Charlene was still far too young to have to deal with issues like this, to know how much bad there was out there.

"I have never met a human with so many problems," Jacques said, stretching forward to expose his hairless webbed feet.

"And our first owner was murdered," his sister added eerily.

"Yup, thanks for that." I avoided arguing with the Sphynx cats whenever possible. They could go on and on without reprieve, and I just didn't have the time or energy to meet them part way.

“Well, go on and read the message,” Octo-Cat prompted, rubbing his face against my phone impatiently.

“Right, okay.” I swiped to open the social media app and held my breath as I read the words silently to myself. As soon as I’d finished, I let out a long, happy sigh.

“Don’t just keep it to yourself. We’re all invested now,” Jillianne groused, then dragged her tongue across the wrinkles near her armpit. Those two were always pretending to groom themselves, but really I thought their feeble attempts just made them filthier than they were to begin with. It was why they got baths twice weekly, a chore that thankfully Charles took care of himself.

I turned the phone so Octo-Cat could read the new message from Charm and paraphrased for the others. “She says she’s sorry and just wanted to double-check to make sure I’m not going to sue her.”

“We *should* sue her,” Octo-Cat said, greed lighting his amber eyes. “We could use the money to buy stock in Little Dog Diner.”

“You’re not playing the stock market,” I warned immediately. “No freaking way.”

Octo-Cat flattened his ears against his head. “Well, could we at least get some lobster rolls then?”

I rolled my eyes at him. “We literally just had them yesterday.”

“Hey, the stomach wants what the stomach wants.”

“I don’t think that’s how the expression goes,” I corrected with a scowl.

"Can we please get back to the movie now?" Jacques snarled, then gingerly licked his fleshy thigh and added, "It's my favorite part."

"We will." I chewed on my lower lip as I worked through the flurry of thoughts that had just blanketed my brain. "First, can we talk about something real quick?"

Charlene jumped onto the back of the couch and crawled over to sit near my shoulder. Octo-Cat settled himself on my lap. The Sphynxes looked irritated, but offered no verbal argument, at least.

"This whole thing with Charm... Blaire... Well, it's got me thinking." I paused here, just in case any of the cats planned on complaining, offering commentary, or insulting my usual lack of foresight.

They remained blissfully quiet, and so I continued with my heartfelt plea for advice. "I became absolutely terrified when I thought some mystery stranger on the Internet would expose my secret. She seems to have backed off now, but what if it happens again with someone else? I got so keyed up when she messaged again today—so afraid. But what if I could avoid all that in the future? What if—?"

"You want to tell the world your secret," Octo-Cat interrupted, still poised on my lap. "As long as my life doesn't change in any way, I am all for it."

"I like that you can talk to us," Charlene offered in that cute squeaky voice of hers.

"We don't care what you do," Jillianne spoke up as a representative for both naked cats. "Just leave us out of it, and don't let any harm come to *our* human as a result."

The Sphynxes and I would probably always have a lukewarm relationship, but the same could be said of Octo-Cat with Charles —or as my cat preferred, UpChuck. Charlene was different since we had adopted her together, but our other pets were definitely one-human animals. Such was their nature; I couldn't fault them for that.

"Do you think I should come out on my own? You know, control the narrative?" I studied each of their unblinking expressions, trying to glean any insight as to whether this was a crazy idea—or a brilliant one.

Jacques was the one who spoke up first. "Again, don't care as long as our stipulations are met. Now can you put the movie back on already?"

I sighed and pressed play on the remote, bringing the cowardly lion's song-and-dance routine onto the screen.

"Angela," Octo-Cat said, pawing at my lap. "May I please see you in the kitchen? *Alone.*"

Uh-oh. Now I was really going to get it. Somehow I'd upset him without even trying. I was too focused on my own problems. I was—

"I had to play it cool for the others. You know, be a cool cat and all that," Octo-Cat whispered as soon as we both made it to the kitchen and he'd had the chance to hop up onto the counter. "But I think you should do whatever makes you happy. Lately you haven't been—happy, that is—and I don't like that at all.

You're much better company when you're not in a constant state of worry."

I reached forward to stroke his head between his ears. "But what will people say when they find out?"

"The ones who matter will be there for you, just like they always have. Screw the haters."

I glared at him. "Did you figure out how to turn off the parental locks on your iPad again?"

"So what if I did? That's not the point. The point is people live very small and complicated lives compared to us cats. A cat doesn't keep secrets or worry what others might think. A cat just is, and he's all the better for it."

I bit my lip to avoid pointing out that he'd just faked indifference for Jacques and Jillianne's benefit and only shared his true feelings on the matter once he had me alone. What he was saying made a lot of sense. I'd been keeping my secret for nearly three years and it was not easy. How much different would my life be if I simply stopped caring? If my secret was out in the open for all to see? Then it would be up to them to decide how they felt about it. The burden would be completely removed from my shoulders. I could finally rest.

"Well…?" Octo-Cat prompted when I still hadn't met his heartfelt words with a response. "Are you going to do it?"

"Tell you what, I'll sleep on it." I smiled as I stroked Octavius's striped fur. "But thank you for what you said. It means a lot to know you always want what's best for me."

"You're my human, and I love you." He let out a rumbling

purr before abruptly falling silent. "But your happiness shouldn't ever come at the expense of mine. As long as you understand that, we'll be good."

I let out a soft laugh at that. "You're good. We're good."

Now the question was *would I be?*

I guessed I'd decide in the morning.

12

Well, I slept on it.

And by the next morning, I felt pretty confident about what I must do. For my own sake—really, for all of our sakes—I needed to come clean to the world about my strange ability.

I woke up early that day to spend a little time with Charles before he left for work, and he promised to support me in whatever was to come, reminding me once again that this was what our marriage vows were all about in the first place.

One by one, I called all the people who already knew, or at least the ones I'd confided in personally. Nan's Internet friends didn't need a heads-up on what was to come, but my family definitely did.

"How are you going to do it?" Mags asked when I called to tell her the news.

As much as this new plan had been dominating my mind lately, I still hadn't worked out all the details. That was another reason for calling those in the know—to get their advice. "I thought about writing out a speech, but I'd really rather speak from the heart."

"No, I mean, *how* are you going to do it?" Mags insisted, her pale eyes wide with intrigue. "Post a video on your page, call up that reality TV crew that filmed your wedding? Oh, I could interview you for my YouTube channel. Wax Nation already knows and loves you. I'm sure they'd be very supportive!"

I thought about this for a second. "I don't know," I admitted at last. "It feels really big coming out to your millions of subscribers, especially when they all follow you to see cool candle videos. I can't compete with that. And on the flip side, my own page only has, like, ten followers. Nobody will even see the video if I post there."

"So then the reality show guys?" my cousin suggested with an expression that told me exactly what she thought of that idea.

I shook my head adamantly. "No, they were unfair with Sharon. I wouldn't do that to her."

"Then what?" Mags wanted to know. Heck, I wanted to know too!

"I'll think on it some more and let you know when I figure things out," I promised.

"Okey dokey, smokey." A giant smile split Mags's face. "That's a new catchphrase I'm trying out. What do you think of it?"

I returned her smile, but no doubt had a mischievous glint in my eyes as well. "I'll keep thinking on my thing, and you keep thinking on yours."

"Ouch. Burn. Love you, Cuz."

"Love you. Bye."

After Mags, I called Grandma Lyn. I'd already decided for myself that I needed to come clean, but talking to all the people who loved me most in the world only made me more and more confident this would be the right next step for me in my life.

"I'm proud of you, Angie," Grandma Lyn cooed once she, too, had heard the news. "Being true to who you are while not being sure how the world will react is very brave. Just make me one promise."

"Sure, what?"

Grandma Lyn didn't use FaceTime, so I had no visual clues as to what was coming next. "Find someone you can talk to. Someone who's available now and will be there for you whatever happens next."

"But I already have so many people I can talk to," I argued gently. "You're one of them."

Grandma Lyn chuckled at this. "Yes, you'll always have me, but find a professional, too."

"Are you suggesting I'm crazy?" I teased, but I guess my playful tone didn't quite come across the phone line.

Grandma Lyn sighed. "I wish I would have started therapy earlier in life. It should be a requirement for every human, and it's extra required for you and your extraordinary life."

I promised her I would find someone to counsel me, then

called Nan. It wasn't so long ago I would have told her before anyone else, but the added physical distance between us made everything so much harder these days.

Nan was, of course, incredibly supportive once I told her. I seriously didn't know why I ever doubted her.

"I think that's the right decision, dear, and if you think it is too, well, then there we go," she said with a warm grin.

"There we go," I repeated back. "Only I have no idea how I'm going to make my big reveal."

"Why, you'll do it on your parents' news show, of course."

Yes, of course!

My parents co-anchored a local news show, which was recorded and broadcast here in Blueberry Bay but served communities as far away as Massachusetts. It would be the perfect platform for what I needed to do.

I exhaled with relief. "Nan, you're a genius."

She clucked her tongue at this. "Well, yes, but we both already knew that, dear."

"And today we have a very special human interest story for our viewers," my dad announced, shuffling his papers on the news desk before him.

My mom sat at his side, her hair neatly curled and her lipstick perfect as she stared into the teleprompter with a charismatic grin. "That's right, Roman. We have a special guest in the studio, and it's none other than our daughter, Angie Longfellow."

I cleared my throat as the cameras panned toward me. Nan had wanted to dress me in some sparkly flapper-esque gown, but I'd insisted on wearing my favorite polka-dotted knee-length frock. Sure, it made me look a little like Minnie Mouse, but it also gave me the confidence to be myself, quirks and all.

"Hi, Mom. Dad," I replied with a huge practiced smile. That had been my parents' advice to me before we started the segment. *No matter what, just keep smiling.* So that's what I did now. I smiled so wide that my cheeks hurt. I even attempted to maintain my toothy grin while talking, which made my words come out somewhat muffled. "It's great to be here."

"Angie, tell us why you're here today," my dad enunciated far more clearly than I had, glancing quickly toward the teleprompter before he continued. "You have something you wanted to share with our viewers. Is that right?"

I nodded, swallowing down the freshly formed lump in my throat. I wanted to come clean with the world, but that didn't mean I wasn't incredibly nervous about finally voicing my secret aloud.

Apparently, I didn't respond fast enough because my mother spoke up next. "And you've brought somebody with you today, I understand."

That was the prompt I'd needed to shake myself free of the mental bonds that had immobilized me. "Yes!" I practically shouted, forgetting about my smile for a moment as I reached under the news desk and grabbed a plastic pet carrier.

I set it on the desk and opened the metal door. Octo-Cat immediately strolled out.

"Well, hello there. You're very handsome," Mom cooed even though she'd seen Octo-Cat a million times before. "What's your name, big guy?"

"Octavius Maxwell Ricardo Edmund Frederick Fulton Russo Longfellow," my cat introduced himself with his usual pomp and flair.

I repeated the name for the viewers at home. "You can't understand him, but I do. My name is Angie Longfellow, and I can talk to animals."

A beat of silence passed before I added, "I suppose I should tell you how it all began. Almost three years ago, I was working at the law firm of Longfellow and Associates. Of course, back then it was called Fulton, Thompson, and Associates. And, well, there was this coffee maker..."

13

"How'd I do?" I asked eagerly once I'd finished my segment. Mom and Dad had to get back to the news, and Grandma Lyn said my exposure brought back too many painful memories for her to be physically in attendance but that she'd be cheering me on from afar. Charles, Grant, and Nan had both taken the full day off from their usual activities to support me, and they all gave me enthusiastic thumbs up as I rejoined them backstage.

"I was the main draw, of course," Octo-Cat crooned from within my arms, having refused to get back in his carrier once I'd gotten him out. "I mean, look at me. Who wouldn't want to talk to me?"

I laughed and shook my head, filling the others in on what my cat had just said.

In public.

With other people around.

I'd never been able to do that before, and it felt great to be able to do it now.

"Should we go home and have some pancakes?" Nan suggested after clapping her hands together to draw our focus. Not a single one of us could argue with that idea, and so the four of us headed back to the old manor house to celebrate.

And, well, I guess that was it.

I'd done it. I'd like to say that I felt different, better somehow. But honestly, I felt the same as always. Who knew how many people would even see my brief five minutes of fame? And out of those how many would actually believe it?

Some might assume I was a comedian. Others may think I was a fraud looking to make some money. Either way, they would now know the truth about what I could do, whether or not they chose to believe it.

"This will be wonderful publicity for your business," Nan said later when we were all seated with heaping stacks of flapjacks in front of us. You can add 'As seen on channel seven' to your website."

"I don't really have a website anymore," I admitted. I'd stopped running the recommended updates months ago and when I'd tried to log in a couple weeks ago, the entire site crashed.

Nan shrugged off my concern. "Then you can add it to your page."

"Do you really think people will want to hire me now?" I asked, my eyes wide with wonder.

"I can certainly give a great endorsement based on all the help you gave us at the Christmas Festival," Grant added as he sliced into his steaming stack of breakfast cakes.

"That's not a bad idea," Charles caught hold of this thread and pulled on it some more. "You should get testimonials from as many former clients as you can."

"One problem with that. Nobody was really an actual client, except the former mayor and I doubt he'd endorse me." Heat rose to my cheeks as all eyes zoomed toward me.

"They're still people you helped. I'm sure most of them would be more than happy to say a few nice words, dear," Nan threw her two cents into the pot as well.

"I haven't been thinking about any of that stuff, although I guess I should now that my big confession has been made." I popped a bite into my mouth and chewed before adding, "There's no going back now. It's out there."

"How do you feel?" Charles asked.

"The exact same," I admitted after swallowing that delicious mouthful of sugary, buttery mush.

Nan reached across the table for the syrup. "Well, nothing about you has changed, I suppose. I am very proud of you though, dear."

Charles scooted his chair so close to mine that our hips touched. "Me too, honey. I'm very proud of you."

"And I'm a proud step-grandfather," Grant said with a kindly chortle.

My phone buzzed in my pocket. "Oh," I cried, setting down my fork and knife to fish it out. "I have a new message on my page."

Grant's bushy eyebrows shot up. "Already? Well, that was fast."

"I'm not even one bit surprised," Nan stated triumphantly.

Seeing as the room was filled with my biggest supporters, I decided to read the message aloud. "Saw you on the news. You look really pretty…" My voice slowed as I continued to read, not liking where this was going one bit. "I would like to be your—" I stopped altogether here.

"Your what, Angie?" Charles prompted.

My cheeks burned with the flames of blazing embarrassment. "Your sugar daddy," I whispered, immediately pressing the button that would block the user.

"What's a sugar daddy?" Charlene asked from beneath the table.

"It's a man who makes delicious cookies for his family," Octo-Cat answered confidently. Lord help me.

My phone buzzed again. This time I read the message to myself before speaking up: *You're the Pet Whisperer, right? Can you get my dog to stop eating its own poop?*

Uh, that's not really what I do, I typed back. *Try the Dog Whisperer instead.*

"Everything okay?" Charles asked, trying to crane his neck to look at my phone, too.

I handed him the phone and sighed.

"Well, it's natural for a few crazies to come out of the woodwork with things like this," he offered, returning my device to me. "The point is you're getting attention now. Eventually the right people will find you."

* * *

Charles was typically right about almost everything, but this time he was very, very wrong.

As time passed, I received more and more inquiries that had nothing to do with my actual business or abilities. I also received a few messages with photo attachments that were—ahem—quite inappropriate and completely unwanted.

As much as I loathed it, I could handle people picking on me; but what I couldn't tolerate was how many chose to bother Charles at his work. A handful of strangers showed up each day, hoping to gawk or even score a bit of one-on-one time with the "magic coffee maker" that had gifted me with my powers.

Some even booked new client meetings just to get a closer look at where it all went down.

The net result was that Charles became even busier than he'd been before. He tried to keep a good face, but I could tell all the negative attention was bothering him.

And that was just the crazies.

Soon the bullies emerged, and—boy—did they let us have it. Charles went from being the most respected attorney in the entire region to the husband of that crazy woman who believed she could talk to animals.

Because the truth was, despite that heartfelt introduction on my parents' news show, very few people actually believed me about what I could do.

By the time a still shot of my televised interview turned into a meme, I was about ready to reach out to Blaire/Charm again and beg to take her up on her earlier offer of management. The only reason I didn't act on that urge was because it had become abundantly clear that there would be no money in this for anyone—least of all me.

Still, every day I dutifully scrolled through my messages, hoping beyond hope that there would be at least one authentic inquiry amongst the dozens of dreck.

Can you help me talk to my dead guinea pig? One woman asked. I had a number of stock replies to send to people now, and chose to send her the one that read, "Pet Whisperer P.I. doesn't offer the particular service you're looking for, but we wish you all the best!"

The next message in my inbox informed me that I was a danger to myself and society and that I belonged in a mental health institution. That was the fifth one this week. *Lovely.*

Farther down, a local rescue organization informed me that they would be happy to find Octavius a more stable household while I grappled with my own issues.

They honestly thought the most spoiled cat in the entire world needed to be rescued, or at least removed from my care.

And that was the final straw!

I couldn't take all this negativity anymore. Whatever I had expected from coming out with my ability it wasn't this.

In a fit of fury, I deleted my entire social media presence and slammed my laptop shut.

There, now nobody could make fun of me anymore. Why had I ever complained about being bored?

This was so, so much worse.

Once again, I'd failed—and this time it hurt more than ever.

14

My head rested in Nan's lap as I cried my heart out.

"There, there," she said, slowly stroking my hair and making soft shushing noises.

I turned my patchy face to look up at her. "Why is this happening to me?" Nearly a week had passed since my big interview, and it had been less than two since I'd deleted my social media page and gone into hiding.

Charles had wanted to take a leave of absence to watch over me, but Nan had insisted she was up to the task. She brushed her hands across my cheeks to wipe away the tears. "The whole world's a stage, and they've only just realized you're a star," she offered sagely.

"I don't feel like a star." I sniffed. "I feel like a monster that's being hunted with pitchforks sharpened and torches lit."

"You aren't afraid to be different, to be yourself. A lot of people are threatened by that, I guess."

I sat up and swiped at my eyes. "That's where you're dead wrong. I'm afraid all the time."

"It will get easier," my grandmother assured me before slowly rising to her feet. "Let me go put on the kettle."

Normally, I'd follow Nan to the kitchen and stand with her while she prepared tea, but today I just didn't have the energy. Her little dog Paisley trotted after her to make sure she had company, but that left me alone.

The poor Chihuahua had tried so hard to lift my spirits, but my constant state of gloominess seemed to be wearing on her. Not that I could blame her. My emotions were cranked to the max, and every day they felt bigger, more unwieldy. Would I ever feel like myself again? I was seriously beginning to doubt it.

A knocking on the window behind me caught my attention, and when I turned I saw a familiar masked fur ball staring in at me.

I motioned for Pringle to move to the front door, then grabbed a tissue from the end table en route to the entryway.

Pringle stood on his hind legs, holding onto his tail and brushing his fingers through it nervously. "I'm sorry to bother you at home," he said with his head dipped in reverence.

I offered him a momentary smile as I waved him inside. "You're not a bother. Come on in."

The trash panda shook his head. "No, I'm not allowed in the house."

"Unless you're invited. Remember our new rule?"

Pringle's eyes lifted cautiously to meet mine, and I gave an affirming nod. I just didn't have it in me to smile at the moment. The first one had taken it all out of me.

I watched with interest as the raccoon sucked in a deep breath and then slowly moved one foot over the threshold, still holding onto his ringed tail like some sort of security blanket. He let out the breath he'd been holding and slid his other foot past the doorway.

When he looked up at me with shining black eyes, I nodded again and motioned toward the living room. "Come on. Nan and I were just about to have some tea."

"What's that, dear?" Nan called from the kitchen, her voice extra chipper to balance my melancholy.

"Pringle's here!" I called back. "Can you grab some extra snacks so he can join us?"

Pringle's eyes grew wide, and he reached for his tail once again. "Really?"

"Really. Now hop up here and tell me what's going on." I patted the couch beside me.

This time Pringle only hesitated briefly before acting upon my invitation. "I came to check on you because I miss you. You didn't come out to read yesterday or the day before, and I just want to make sure you're doing okay."

My heart swelled in my chest. The very thing I was now being ridiculed over was also the same thing that had brought me so much joy, that brought me such kind and caring friends like Pringle.

"I'm sorry. We'll finish Merlin's adventure soon, okay?"

The raccoon shook his head and folded his hands in his lap. "That's not what I mean. You just never miss reading time. It made me worry."

"I'm okay, Pringle. Promise." I held his eyes, daring him to question me.

"Excuse me for saying so, but you don't look okay."

I laughed through a fresh wave of tears. "Remember how you like secrets so much? And watching people do crazy things on reality TV?"

He bobbed his head.

I don't know why I hadn't told Pringle all this before, especially when we still read together every day—or at least we had, until I officially shuttered Pet Whisperer P.I. and became too depressed to leave the house, even for the backyard. I guess I just enjoyed our little world of magical cats and a guaranteed victory for the good guys. It provided a nice escape from my current reality.

But now that the raccoon had come asking after me, I needed to tell him the truth. "Well, I went on TV and told everyone my secret, and let's just say there's been a poor response."

Pringle gasped. "Bad ratings?"

I nodded subtly. "Something like that."

"I'm sorry people didn't like your secret. Which one did you tell?"

"What do you mean which one did I tell? I only have the one secret."

"Did you tell people you can talk to animals, or did you tell them about the baby?"

"Excuse me, what?" I exploded, causing Pringle to jump back in fright.

"Pringle, I'm not—I don't..." I didn't know how to finish that. Was I getting fat? Is that why the raccoon thought the impossible?

Of course, Octo-Cat chose this precise moment to wake up from his nap and join us in the living room. "You're not what?" he asked suspiciously, whiskers twitching.

I could barely speak the word. Charles and I hadn't been trying for a baby, but we also hadn't *not* been trying. "Pregnant," I choked out hardly above a whisper.

My cat appeared almost bored. "Oh, that? No, yeah, you totally are."

"WHAT?!" I boomed. "You knew and you didn't tell me."

He yawned as if this conversation wasn't completely and unalterably life-changing. "I thought you were waiting to make it some big reveal. I didn't realize you hadn't figured it out yet."

"May I?" Pringle asked before reaching out to press one hand to my belly.

And now Nan returned with the tea and a tray of assorted snacks from the pantry. Paisley jumped up beside Nan and growled, the hair bristling on the little dog's back. Let's just say Pringle hadn't always been the nicest to her, and even if she'd forgiven him for his past sleights, she had a very hard time forgetting. Paisley hardly weighed more than five pounds; the poor thing needed to stay on high alert to stay safe.

"What did I miss?" Nan asked, staring pointedly at Pringle. I don't think she'd ever seen me willingly allow him in the house before, so the sight of him cozy on the couch took her rather by surprise.

"Nothing," I shouted, then pressed my lips in a firm line and muttered, "I mean, nothing out of the usual."

Thankfully, she let it go. I couldn't get her hopes up until I knew for sure.

It took everything in me to act normally while we drank our tea and munched on our snacks. Well, at least I wasn't crying over my spoiled reputation anymore. I had a new problem to worry about now—no, not problem—a new *change*, and this one felt even bigger than revealing my hidden ability and closing my business.

Was I ready to be a mother?

That would certainly keep me busy, but not for another nine months or so. And when the time came, would I be able to survive all the work that came with a newborn while Charles worked practically one-hundred hours per week? If I had one baby now, would I just keep on having babies until my whole life became mommyhood? That wasn't necessarily a bad thing, but it was different.

And also very, very scary.

15

As soon as Nan and Paisley left for the evening, I threw on a pair of flip-flops and made a beeline for the nearest drugstore.

To buy a pregnancy test.

Me.

My heart had now taken up residency in my throat, threatening to cut off my air all together. Charles and I had decided to leave our family planning to fate, which hadn't seemed like that big of a deal when we'd originally discussed it. But now that I could be jobless and with child? I was nowhere near mastering my domestic lessons? In fact, I was but ready to give up on them altogether. And without a job, I couldn't justify hiring someone else to come in and run the household. That would make me entirely useless in my own disaster of a life.

I couldn't justify labeling myself a full-time stay-at-home cat mom, and even they had found plenty to keep themselves busy without me.

Where did that leave me?

And did I want this? Did I want it right now at this very point in my life?

One way or another I'd get on board, but it was hard not to feel completely overwhelmed as I plucked the pink and white box off the shelf and buried it in my basket beneath a healthy-sized layer of selections I'd made in the candy aisle.

This particular pharmacy didn't have a self-checkout lane, which meant I was at the mercy of the cashier. Hopefully, she wouldn't comment on the pregnancy test or ask any questions that I was not prepared to answer.

Just to be sure though, I pulled out my phone and pretended to take an important call. Sure, it was rude, but desperate times and all that.

Imagine my shock and embarrassment when the phone actually rang with an incoming call. Heat flooded my cheeks as I clicked to answer.

"Hello?" I muttered, avoiding eye contact with the cashier as I spoke.

"Angie," my husband sounded almost relieved as he shouted into the phone. "Can you be ready to go out in one hour? I'll swing home and pick you up for dinner. Wear something dressy. We're going to Fernando's."

My mouth salivated at this information. Fernando's was the swankiest restaurant in all of the Bay, one to which we almost never had cause to visit. Did Charles know I needed some extra TLC today? Whatever the case, it would provide the perfect setting to tell him about the baby—if there even was a baby.

I smiled as I handed the cashier my credit card. "I can be ready," I informed Charles.

"Sorry for the short notice," my husband continued. "I've had this thing planned for weeks. Only now he's insistent you come, too."

"Wait. It's not just us?" I felt like I was going to be sick.

"Oof, sorry. I thought you knew I had the thing with Richard Fulton tonight. He's up from Florida this week and asked if we could talk business. We set it up at the wedding reception actually. I put it on our shared calendar."

I took my card back from the cashier and grabbed my overstuffed shopping bag before hurrying back to the parking lot. "Sorry," I murmured. "I've just had a lot on my mind lately, and you've been so busy... But yeah, I'll be ready in an hour. See you soon. Love you."

I debated waiting until after tonight's dinner to take my test, but quickly decided that was stupid, that I absolutely could not wait to know the truth.

So I peed on a stick, and...

Yup, pregnant. With child. In the early days of motherhood.

Things were moving along quite briskly on the family front, even if they were dead in the water when it came to my career. It would be incredibly difficult to keep mum during tonight's dinner, but this also felt like the kind of news a wife should tell her husband in private.

I could share the news when we were getting ready for bed, right in front of our enormous bathroom mirror as we brushed our teeth side by side. Charles would be ecstatic. Of that, I had no doubt.

His enthusiasm would help build mine, and everything would be fine, just fine. I wasn't unhappy, just shocked. Bringing another life into this world gave me a ticking clock when it came to figuring out my own.

I sat motionless on the edge of the tub for what felt like hours as I tried to make sense of it all. My phone buzzed with a text from Charles stating that he and Fulton were leaving the law firm now. That meant I had about fifteen minutes to give myself a pep talk while putting the finishing touches on my look.

"You've got this," I whispered to my reflection as I dragged a coral lipstick over my mouth. "You'll be a great mom. I mean, look at Octo-Cat, he had no idea we'd be bringing Charlene home, and yet he's such a devoted dad. You'll be that too. Devoted. Not a dad, but a mom. A darn good one."

"I'm glad I could inspire you, Angela," Octo-Cat said from the doorway. I hadn't even heard him approach. "And you aren't alone in this. I'd be happy to give you parenting lessons."

"I thought cat lessons were supposed to be for cats only."

"I can adapt portions to fit the human experience. Just say yes and be grateful. You don't turn down Mozart when he's offering piano lessons."

I blinked hard at this assertion, although the analogy shouldn't have surprised me one bit. Octo-Cat had always thought highly of himself in the way all cats did. Now if I could just bottle that confidence for myself.

"I'd love some lessons," I answered as I breezed past him and headed downstairs. Charles would be here any minute, and I was ready.

I was so not ready.

I'd never been good at keeping secrets, but now I had to sit through the next two hours making small talk and pretending my entire life hadn't just changed in an instant.

Charles held my hand under the table and gave me the occasional reassuring squeeze. He could tell I was upset, but he thought it was about the other thing—about how I'd become a local laughingstock. Well, I was still rather unhappy about that, but it was no longer the star of my inner anxiety show. I'd just risked an awful lot to rid myself of one secret, and already I had a brand-new one clawing at my conscience.

It didn't help that I noted the curious eyes of the staff and other diners landing on me again and again; each time, muted whispers followed. They were talking about me, calling me crazy or a fraud. One person even brought me a print-out of the meme they'd made from my interview and asked me to autograph it. *Fabulous.*

"Is it true?" Fulton asked over the salad course. "Can you really...?" He dropped his voice and leaned in conspiratorially. "Talk to animals?"

I twisted the cloth napkin that lay on my lap and nodded meekly.

Fulton took a sip from his water goblet and asked, "Is that why you were so eager to adopt Aunt Ethel's cat, because you'd befriended him?"

I nodded again. "It's how I knew your aunt had been murdered in the first place. Octo-Cat told me." It was easier to just agree than to explain the long and tortuous road Octo-Cat and I took to truly become friends. Earning a cat's trust took work and lots of it.

Fulton leaned back in his chair. "Well, I'll be. I feel silly for not having noticed all that time, but how could I? It's not a very common thing now, is it?"

I glanced up at Fulton to find him watching me. "So you believe me?" I asked, then held my breath as I waited for his answer.

"Of course I believe you, Angie. I've always known you to be focused, kind, and smart as a whip. Why on earth would you lie about something like this?"

I let out a strangled laugh of relief. At least there was one person who didn't seem to think of me differently after finding out what I could do. Maybe it was a good thing I'd come tonight, after all.

"Now that we've settled in, allow me to tell you why I wanted to speak with you both tonight." Fulton traded his water goblet for a wine flute and raised it toward my husband. "Charles, you're the most brilliant young attorney I've ever had the privilege to work with, and I'd like to offer you a job. How would fewer hours with more pay suit you?"

Charles tensed beside me, but it didn't seem like Fulton noticed. "That sounds fantastic."

The other lawyer bobbed his head enthusiastically. "I thought you might say that. I've been asked to come on as a partner at my friend's very successful firm, and I agreed, provided I could nominate a junior partner to come with me. It's a slight demotion according to the official job title, but everything about it is bigger and better. They stick to the forty hour work-week there. No more drowning in overtime. You'll have time for a home life too. Imagine that."

I didn't know what Charles was thinking in that moment, but I was already imagining this new life just as Fulton had urged. I didn't care about the money, not really. We'd always had enough, thanks to my husband's brilliance and my cat's trust fund. But to have that time together? It would be a dream come true, especially with a baby on the way. I knew Charles was proud of the progress he'd made with his firm, but I hoped it wasn't so much that he would refuse to leave when given a better opportunity. I would definitely encourage him to take it, provided he didn't come to that conclusion on his own.

Everything was perfect, until the corners of Fulton's mouth turned down as he revealed, "There's just one catch. The job is out of state, and would require you to relocate."

16

"I'm not going to take the job," Charles told me once we'd dropped Fulton off at his hotel and had begun our drive home. "Your whole life is here. Your family. I can't ask you to give that up."

The fact that this new dream opportunity was in a completely different state sullied the offer a great deal. Fulton hadn't even told us which state it would be in, instead claiming that we shouldn't spoil our time together going over the finer details—not until Charles knew whether or not he'd even be willing to consider relocation. Fulton needed to know whether we were open to the general idea, and then he would put an official package together to offer my husband.

And already Charles was dead-set against the whole thing. I still didn't know exactly how I felt, but I did think it was worth proper consideration, especially once I gave Charles one very important piece of the puzzle that until now he'd been missing.

"It's true that if we move, I'll miss Nan and Grant, and Mom and Dad, and of course, Paisley," I admitted softly. "But right now I spend all day missing you. And working all those long hours can't be good for your health."

He shook his head, keeping his eyes on the road as he drove. "I'll bring on an additional partner. Share the load more."

"Which directly impacts your salary, and without me working right now, that could be a real problem," I pointed out. But these were all very generalized arguments, things Charles probably already knew. I needed to tell him what he didn't know, and unfortunately I'd need to do it before we got back home for the night.

"Look, Fulton's a great guy. I really like him, I do. But your happiness comes first, Angie. He reached across the car to grab my hand and hold it in his. "Always and forever."

"My happiness comes second," I whispered, seeing my opportunity and grabbing it with both hands.

"What do you mean? Of course I put you above me. I—"

"I'm pregnant," I chose that precise moment to reveal. "So I would think our baby comes first."

Charles accidentally tapped the brake causing the car behind us to honk an angry warning. My husband said nothing as he maneuvered into a strip mall parking lot and cut the engine.

"Charles? Is everything okay?" I asked, leaning forward to try to see his face.

He'd put both hands onto the top of the steering wheel and rested his forehead on top of them, his shoulders moved up and down but no sound escaped him.

"Charles?" I prompted again. This was not the reaction I'd expected. Was he upset? Overwhelmed? Frankly, I couldn't tell.

Finally Charles lifted his head, his entire face was red with emotion. "Angie," he whispered, his voice cracking. "Honey, I love you so much. And this is the best news ever."

He leaned forward to capture me in a kiss.

"I'll take this job if that's what you want," he said after we'd parted. "Or I'll take another job. I'll quit working altogether, and we can rent an RV and live off the land." He took a moment to laugh at his own ineptitude before continuing, "Okay, so I don't know what I'm talking about, but I do know that I love you so much. And somehow already I love our baby so much. I'll do anything, whatever it takes, to make sure the two of you have the best life."

"You'll be such a great dad." I reached out to stroke his hair, tucking an errant strand behind his ear. He'd been too busy with work to get a haircut, but I liked the shaggy look on him. "Let's ask Fulton to put that package together so we have all the information, and then we'll take a couple days to talk it over, think about what would be best for our family's future. The right decision will come to us. I have no doubt."

* * *

When we'd pulled off into the strip mall to talk things out, Charles had inadvertently ended up parking near my go-to pet supply store, Frank n' Beans. And since we were already there, I asked if he wouldn't mind me running in to pick up a few supplies for the cats.

Truthfully, I was still annoyed with Octo-Cat for knowing about my pregnancy and choosing not to share that little tidbit with me. Then again, animals did things differently—and cats, most of all. I suspected that in some warped way, he thought he was doing me a favor. Ha!

So now tonight we would tell the others, provided they didn't already know, and have an intimate celebration—just me, Charles, and our four favorite felines.

While Octo-Cat preferred his treats in the form of grilled shrimp and lobster rolls, the Sphynx cats loved creamed salmon, especially when they could lick it directly from a little tube rather than having me plop it onto a cold plate. And because I wouldn't have time to get out to Misty Harbor before the diner closed, I settled on an assortment of new treats, filling my basket to the brim with various kitty delicacies. It would be fun to try them all out and see who liked what.

"Please bring your final purchases to the register. We're just about to close," Frank called from the front of the store. I hadn't seen him when I entered. He must have been in the back, taking care of stock. Sometimes he moved around this place like a ninja.

I smiled as I approached the checkout counter. "Hi, Frank," I said as I plopped my basket down between us.

"Oh, Angie, hi." He immediately began scanning my items, glancing at me as we chatted. "It's been a long time. I was hoping you'd stop in again soon."

"Sorry, it's been hectic," I mumbled. I liked Frank, but I was also eager to get back to Charles and eager to share our big news with the rest of our household, which meant my tolerance for idle chit-chat was at a minimum.

"Yeah, I saw your interview. Really cool." Frank fumbled a bag of treats, then looked up at me askance. "Is it all true? You know, what you can do?"

I nodded and averted my eyes. "Yeah, unfortunately."

"Why is it unfortunate? If I could have any superpower, that's exactly the one I would want to have."

"It's not really a superpower," I hedged, even though I'd thought of my ability in that exact way too many times to count.

"It is to me," Frank enthused as he finished ringing up my massive quality of cat treats. He paused again. Even the massive Darth Vader helmet on his T-shirt seemed to wait with bated breath. "Um, I hope it's not asking too much, but I was wondering if maybe you could do me a favor? Or if you'd rather, I could pay you? I'm just in a pretty desperate spot with Beans. He's not eating, and he's been avoiding me, too. I'm really worried about him."

"That sounds like something you want to address with your vet," I answered briskly, hoping I wasn't coming across as too cold.

"I did, and there's nothing physically wrong with him. If I

could just understand what's going on in that fluffy little head of his—" Frank stopped abruptly and sighed. "I'm bothering you, I'm sorry. I wouldn't ask if it weren't of vital importance."

My hand drifted to my elbow to pick and twist at the skin, a nasty nervous habit. "It's just… I don't do that anymore," I tried to explain, soft yet firm. "I closed my business a couple days ago."

Frank's face crumpled in on itself. He seemed just seconds away from flooding the place with a hot wave of tears.

"But I can help you with Beans," I decided aloud. And really what choice did I have? Frank wasn't mocking me like the others. He truly needed my help, and I'd be a horrible friend if I said no. "Is Beans here now?"

Frank lit up, taking on an energy I hadn't seen from him before. "He's somewhere around here. Maybe he'll come out if he knows you're here to help."

I glanced toward the glass door before he could hurry off in search of his feline co-clerk. "Would you mind locking that to give us some privacy? I'm still kind of shy when it comes to showing off my ability, especially given the response I've received since going on the news."

Frank dutifully rushed over to twist the lock and then turned back to me with the biggest smile I'd ever seen in all my life. "Tell you what, if you can help, your order is on the house."

I gasped at his offer. "But, Frank, that's like two-hundred dollars' worth of cat treats."

But he just shook his head, continuing to smile like a man

who'd just had every last one of his dreams come true. "You're about to save my cat's life," he insisted. "The least I can do is spoil yours a little."

17

It took all of five minutes to discover that Beans had been avoiding his owner as a means of protest. Frank was a proud and vocal vegan. While he didn't exactly like his cat's biological need for meat, he understood it enough to allow him a seafood-only diet.

Except Beans absolutely hated it.

The first time I'd met the cat he'd bribed me into bringing him a raw steak in exchange for the information I needed to solve a mystery, one that landed particularly close to home.

Beans had then managed to sneak some more red meat a few weeks later at my wedding. Subsequently, he hadn't been able to stomach his "fish food" since and decided to mount a silent protest.

Upon learning this, Frank marched straight to the premium wet food and grabbed a can of the juiciest beefiest pate, which

Beans tore into with gusto, singing both our praises. My work there done, I insisted on paying for my wealth of treats, but Frank insisted even harder that it would be on the house.

Back at home, Charles helped me open up every single container of treats and sprinkle a few from each onto the kitchen floor for our eager team of taste testers.

"Tonight we're celebrating the new addition to our family," I announced once the cats had all gathered around.

"It's about time you celebrated Charlene," Jillianne chirped before lowering her face to inhale some salmon-flavored soft treats.

"No, not Charlene." I moved my hand to my abdomen. Was there really a baby in here? Gosh, that would take some time to get used to. "Charles's and my baby."

"I thought *I* was your baby," the kitten whined, her jaw dropping open and partially chewed treats spilling out onto the floor.

"Our human baby," I corrected with a serene smile. "But we can absolutely throw Charlene a party too!"

"It's okay," the kitten said with a shrug that suggested it might not be. "Besides we already knew about your baby, but Papa Octo-Cat told us not to say anything," she said before grabbing a cat nip crunchy and munching away happily.

Jacques turned his nose up at the assortment of goodies offered. I would have to break out a tube of creamed salmon for him, but only after we finished our conversation. "I, for one, don't see why we're celebrating now. Shouldn't we wait for you to birth the litter first?"

"Not a litter! Just one!" I shouted before the true horror of that scenario could seep in. "Believe me, one will be more than enough."

"I don't like these treats," Octo-Cat stated flatly. "Can I have a lobster roll?" He paused for a moment then added a snide, "Please."

But before I could respond, my phone rang in my purse. I grabbed it and headed to the other room for a bit of privacy—or to get a short break from the cats, take your pick.

"Christine? What's up?" I asked, when I saw who was calling. It was Grizabella's owner, which made the two of us in-laws, even though she didn't know it yet.

"Is it true?" the other woman asked pointedly instead of offering a greeting. "You can talk to animals?"

Oh, that again. Every time I tried to move on to something else, the chaotic mess that came from sharing my secret dragged me right back in.

"I'm sorry I didn't tell you sooner, Christine. I mean, it all happened really fast, and—"

"How long have you been able? Since before we met?"

"Yes," I admitted. "Again I'm really so—"

Christine interrupted me with a spirited chuckle that instantly put me at ease. "I'm not mad. In fact, I think a small part of me always suspected. But I always told myself you were simply a devoted pet owner. I'm glad I'm not crazy."

"Nope, you're not crazy, though I sometimes think that I am."

I paused for a moment before dropping the confetti bomb. "Did you know our cats are married?"

Christine let out another sharp laugh, and here I had worried she was mad at me when this call started. "Ha, I guess that makes us family!"

"Wait, how did you find out? Was it that horrible meme?" My stomach churned as I called up the unflattering image of myself that had taken the local Internet by storm.

My friend quickly put me at ease—or made things a whole lot worse. "Meme, no. There was an article about it on Buzzfeed. I called as soon as I saw it."

Buzzfeed? Great. That meant I was now getting national—possibly even international—attention. "I guess my secret's really out now."

And here I thought that the possibility of moving somewhere new would free me from the ridicule I'd received locally. Apparently not.

"The article was mostly click bait, to be honest," Christine was quick to explain. "There were a couple sentences about you and then the rest of it was a listicle about the top ten questions the staff wished they could ask their cats."

I let out a slow breath. "Anything good?"

"I'll send you the link," she promised.

An awkward pause followed, which led me to ask, "So you really don't care that I can talk to animals? Or that you had to find out the way you did?"

"Angie, I know things are different in your small town where everyone knows everybody. But it's different in the city. There's way too many people to keep track of here, let alone in the whole rest of the world."

"But people don't believe me." That was the one thing I couldn't get past. I was used to people thinking I was silly, but not a liar. And definitely not an unfit cat mother.

"So what if they don't believe you," Christine practically shouted. "At worst, you're a charismatic airhead, right? People will forget about it as soon as the next Florida Man article hits the news circuit. Maine Woman thinks she can talk to animals, cute. Florida Man wrestles alligator on a dare and loses big, now that's crazy."

I chuckled at this, wondering what it might be like to talk to an alligator, what kind of stories he might have to tell. "You definitely have a way of putting things into perspective. How are you? How are Grizz and the others?"

"We're doing just great, but it's not me I'm worried about." Christine's voice softened. "How are you handling the fallout?"

"It's been rough," I confessed and bit my lip.

"Maybe it's time you come for another visit. We'd love to have you!" It was true that Nan, Octo-Cat, Paisley, and I had enjoyed our last road trip out to see her and Grizabella, and I definitely wanted to bring Charles along for a future visit, but we simply had too much going on at present. And as much as I'd love to confide in Christine, I knew better than to share the news of the baby during the first trimester, and even more than that, I knew better than to tell her about our possible move within earshot of the cats.

"We'd love to have you have us," I said instead. "I've just got a lot going on at the moment, but I'll call you back soon, okay?"

"You better!" Christine chirped before offering a quick goodbye.

"Everything okay?" Charles asked as I padded back into the kitchen. Octo-Cat and Jacques had already dispersed due to their apparent dissatisfaction with the treats on offer, but our two female cats happily picked up the snacking slack.

"Yeah, that was just Christine. She saw an article online and wanted to check in with me," I explained.

"Word is really spreading, huh? Are you okay?"

"I will be," I said as my husband wrapped his arms around me.

Octo-Cat ran back in the kitchen so quickly, he had a hard time stopping himself from skidding across the linoleum floor. "Did you say Christine? How is my beautiful Grizz?"

"She's doing great," I answered without hesitation. I knew better than to suggest anything else or to confess that Christine and I hadn't even discussed her.

Octo-Cat swooned, dramatically flopping onto his side. "Ah, my lovely bride. Sweet, sweet Grizz. Our daughter looks more and more like her every day."

Charlene was a stray black kitten and Grizzabella was a pedigreed Himalayan, but okay. Whatever made him happy.

"Congrats on the baby, by the way. I'm glad Charles wasn't neutered like I was."

I practically choked on my own saliva, such was my surprise at that statement.

"Angie, are you okay?" Charles tapped me on the back until I stopped coughing. "What's he saying?"

"Let's just go to bed. It's been a long day!" I said before running toward the stairs, praying there wouldn't be any more awkward questions.

Such was life with cats. Never a dull moment!

18

It took two full days to receive the official job offer from Fulton, and when my husband shared it with me, my eyes practically bulged out of my head. "You've got to be kidding me!"

Charles laughed. "I know he said more pay, but I've got to admit, that number is way higher than I was expecting."

"Not the salary, the location," I insisted pointing at that detail on the computer screen. "It's a sign. Don't you think?"

I grabbed both of his hands in mine, this newfound certainty filling me with blissful release. "Charles, you have to take it."

Apparently, my husband didn't have the same confidence I felt. "What about Nan? And your parents? Your life here?"

"Well, that's why they make air travel and video calls." I flashed him a goofy smile, but he still appeared worried. I needed to take a different approach.

I moved behind him to rub at his shoulders, keeping my voice soft and even. "Just because we move away doesn't mean we have to be out of touch. Besides, this offer is incredible, especially as we start our family."

Charles turned to nuzzle my cheek, letting his warm breath fan over my skin. "Are you sure?"

"If you don't accept it, then I will," I half-joked. "Do you think Fulton will care that I don't have a law degree?"

Finally Charles's mood lightened, and he let out a laugh. "If there's one thing I learned early on about you, my sweet Angie, it's that you can make anything work if you want it bad enough."

He gave me a quick kiss before getting up to call and accept Fulton's offer, leaving me to my thoughts for a moment. I replayed my husband's words as I settled myself on the couch.

I could make anything work if I wanted it bad enough. What did that mean when it came to my P.I. business? Had I simply not wanted it? Or had it lost all appeal when Octo-Cat chose to retire to focus on his new feline family? Had some small part of me already sensed the new life growing within me?

I couldn't answer any of those questions with any real certainty. But I'd started to suspect that maybe I had to break my life a little in order to rebuild it. I needed to bring old adventures to an end in order to be ready for all the amazing ones that came next.

I may have given up my title as Pet Whisperer, P.I., but I'd taken on the equally compelling new ones of wife and mother.

Something good was coming to an end so that I could have something even better—something absolutely fantastic.

Charles returned and lowered himself gently onto the couch beside me. Our baby was hardly the size of a poppyseed, but he'd been extra careful around me since learning about that tiny seed.

"He's giving me a month to wrap things up here and even offered to help with the sale of the house. He said he had lots of interest after his aunt died, but when he found out you wanted it, he put them all off."

"That's really nice of him." I didn't think Richard Fulton realized how much he'd impacted my life for the better. He'd paved the way to my meeting both Octo-Cat and Charles, inarguably the two most important men in my life. Speaking of Octo-Cat... "I guess that just leaves one thing."

"Telling everybody," Charles agreed. "How do you think Nan will take it?"

"She'll understand. I'm not afraid about that. I do worry about Jacques and Jillianne, though. They've been uprooted so many times in the last few years, and now we're moving them again."

"What about us?" The Sphynx cats hissed in terrifying unison as they sauntered into the living room to join us.

"Well, speak of the devils," Charles said with a laugh.

"We might as well tell them all now," I decided, more than ready to get it over with. I had a pretty good idea of how Octavius might respond, but he often found new and irritating ways to surprise me. "Octo-Cat! Charlene!"

"Tell us what?" Jillianne rasped as she claimed a spot on Charles's lap.

"I'm coming! Hold your ponies!" Octo-Cat yowled from somewhere upstairs. I decided not to tell him how badly he'd butchered the expression, and instead waited patiently until we were all together.

Charles and I sat side by side, our hands laced together, as we presented a united front as heads of the family.

"Guys," I said slowly, unsure of the best words for conveying this life-changing news. "Something really important happened today. Charles accepted a new job."

Octo-Cat yawned. "How quickly you forget, Angela. We don't care as long as it doesn't affect us." *Oh, boy.*

"That's the thing." I worked hard to keep the nervousness out of my voice. This was big news, but good. Surely they'd see that once I had the chance to explain everything, right? I cleared my throat before continuing. "It does affect you this time. Very much so, in fact."

Charlene flattened her ears against her tiny head. "What's happening? I'm scared."

"No need to be scared. It's a good thing, I promise. It will just take a little adjusting for all of us."

Charles squeezed my hand. "What are they saying? Is there anything I can do to help?"

I squeezed back. "It'll all be okay. I've got this."

Octo-Cat's tail began to swish wildly behind him. "I don't like the sound of this."

Time to rip off the Band-aid. "The new job is pretty far away. We'll have to sell this house and move into a new one."

"Absolutely not!" Octo-Cat bellowed, poofing up like a cat on Halloween. "I refuse to leave this house. You know how special it is to me. It's where my former owner lived and died, and if you force me to leave, I will—"

I raised one hand to silence him, surprised when it actually worked. "Octo-Cat, you don't understand. The new job is in Boulder, Colorado. You know, with Grizabella."

The tabby's mouth dropped open, and all four cats stared up at me with wide eyes.

"I don't like it here," Jillianne said from atop my husband's lap. "Too drafty." She shook to emphasize her point.

"Yeah, we don't care where we live as long as we have each other—and Charles, of course," Jacques clarified as he resettled himself on the chair.

"And Charlene! We also need Charlene!" Jillianne quickly added.

"Will we really get to live with Mama Grizz?" The small black kitty cried, eyes shining with the potential promise of happiness.

"Not *with*, but *near*. We'll be able to spend lots of time together once we're settled in."

Octo-Cat still hadn't spoken since my latest reveal.

I lowered my face so that I was at his level and asked, "Well, what do you say?"

He closed his mouth, then opened it again like a fish gaping for water. When finally he spoke, it was to complain. "You nearly gave me a heart attack, Angela. You really need to work on your delivery. If you would have just rearranged the facts in a more pleasing order, I would not have had such a cloying response."

My chest unclenched as I let out an enormous sigh of relief. "I'm sorry for that," I said, reaching out to stroke his head.

Octo-Cat shook off my attempts to pet him, rose to all fours, and peered up at me with obvious agitation. "Well?" he shouted.

"Well *what?*" I asked, more than a little confused.

"How soon can we leave?" And with that he took off running toward the stairs. "I'm going to start packing!"

Looked like we were all on board.

Yes, including baby.

19

I'd expected a bit more protest, but everyone was truly happy for Charles and me about this new chapter in our lives, especially once I revealed my pregnancy.

"You better have a room for me, because I am going to visit all the time!" Nan declared the moment she found out. "I'm going to be a Great-Nan!"

"You're already the greatest," I said, saddling her with a huge hug.

Paisley was a bit harder to convince. "But you're my Mommy, and I'll miss you," she whimpered.

I picked her up and held her like a baby, gently rubbing her tummy as we talked. "I'll miss you too. In fact, I've already been missing you since you and Nan moved out. But you know Nan is your real Mommy, right? She's the one who rescued you from the shelter and has given you such a good life since."

The tri-color Chihuahua wagged her tail furiously. "I know. I guess I just always thought of myself as having two mommies."

"That's sweet, Paisley, and that doesn't have to change. No matter how much distance we put between us, our hearts will always be connected." I bent down and placed a small kiss between her huge triangle ears.

"And you'll come back to visit?"

"Lots and lots. I'll be back so often, you'll get sick of me," I promised, giving her a kiss on her pink tummy. And that's all it took for her to go back to being her usual spunky self, thank goodness.

* * *

The hardest person to tell, of course, was Grandma Lyn. We'd only just been reunited after decades of searching on her part, and now I was voluntarily moving away.

"Are you upset?" I asked her after I'd made my big announcement.

"No, of course not. As your grandmother, I want what's best for you, and you seem really excited."

"I am excited, but I'm going to really miss having you nearby."

Grandma Lyn cleared her throat and placed each of her palms flat on the table. "Actually, if it's okay with you, I think I'd like to come, too. I can get my own place, but I'd just like to be nearby."

"What about Mom? She'll still be here," I argued, even though I loved the thought of bringing her with us for our fresh start.

My grandmother looked me straight in the eye as she explained, "Your mother already lived so much of her life before I ever found her. You have too. I can't miss watching your little one grow up. It's like I'm being given a fresh chance, as if the universe is finally intent on setting things right."

"I like that. And I'd love for you to come with us."

As the days wore on, I found myself revisiting all my old haunts—small businesses I'd supported, restaurants I'd frequented, crime scenes I'd stumbled upon. My whole life had been lived out here in this place, and even though I knew I'd be back for frequent visits, I still felt like I needed to say goodbye to the places just as much as the people. As I ventured around the Bay, I attracted some pointed stares and curious whispers, but I also sensed that my little televised interview was starting to become yesterday's news. Christine had been absolutely right about that. Now I was just Maine Woman, and soon I'd be out of people's minds altogether.

For years I'd focused on hiding my ability to talk with animals. Hiding that secret had become just as big a part of my identity as the secret itself. Then I'd decided to come clean and the community's collective response had defined my existence for a brief time after that.

And now?

Now neither of those things determined how I lived my life. I did that. The people and animals I held dear helped, too.

When I first learned I could talk to animals, I had thought of myself as a freak, then I'd redirected all that energy into becoming some super-powered sleuth. Now I realized that, more than anything, the main thing my ability had brought me was more friendships, more love. A richer and fuller life.

I'd been able to help animals who might otherwise not have found any. And I didn't need an official title to keep on doing that. Even if I was no longer a private investigator, I could still put good in the world, still help bridge communication between human and animalkind, and—yes—even solve the occasional mystery that came my way.

I made my ability. It didn't make me.

It wasn't sharing my secret, but rather realizing that last bit which truly freed me.

Similarly, I realized it wasn't bricks and drywall that made a home, but the people who occupied it. I loved our old manor house, but not in the same way Octo-Cat always had. Other than the time he spent with his mother as a kitten and those few short months when I'd forced him to live in my former rental with me, this manor had always been his place of residence. It was where he'd met and fallen in love with Ethel Fulton, his first owner. That attachment was why he'd insisted I purchase this house on his behalf.

And now I would be forcing him to leave it all behind.

I needed to do something special to commemorate our time here, to honor all this home had meant to us, all it had given us.

And I knew just the thing.

* * *

I'd hardly seen Charles these past few weeks as he prepared his firm for the transition in leadership. Fulton had helped us take care of that pesky detail as well. His daughter Bethany, a former colleague of ours, would be moving back to the Bay to transition from Longfellow & Associates to Peters & Associates.

I couldn't have selected a better person myself.

So while Charles worked feverishly to catch Bethany up on the current client load, I took care of things on the home front. Yes, I still wanted a career of my own, but I no longer wanted to force it. The right job would come to me at the right time, and until that happened, I had plenty to occupy my time with both the move and the baby.

We'd be selling the house furnished, which meant our packing would be minimal. It also meant that I had no trouble finding what I needed in the garden shed.

A hand shovel.

Carrying my prize, I walked around the perimeter of the house until I found the exact spot I needed. *Here.*

This was the scene of one of my earliest memories at the manor, so it made sense that it would also be one of my last.

I lowered myself onto my knees, leaned forward, and began to dig, creating a small pile of dirt beside me. It didn't take long to find what I was looking for, and I gasped with joy when the tip of my shovel hit the small coffin.

Well, really it was a shoe box.

Quickly clearing the rest of the dirt away with my fingers, I then lifted the dirty vessel from the ground, taking care not to disturb the lid.

I already knew what was inside, but I also understood that it wasn't my place to open it.

With great reverence, I brought the box inside. Charlene was already occupied with her lessons from the Sphynxes, which was just perfect for my purposes. I wanted to have this special moment alone with Octo-Cat.

I let myself into his bedroom, closing the door behind me so that we wouldn't be disturbed.

Octo-Cat turned from where he was watching his fish swim about the tank. "I'm going to miss these little guys."

"I know," was all I said. Logistically, we just couldn't move a one-hundred-and-forty gallon tank across the country. Luckily, our friend Frank at the pet supply store had agreed to give Yummy, Delicious, and the others a new home.

The tabby's eyes grew wide when he spotted what I held in my hands. "What's that?"

"It's a present. For you."

His nose turned up in disgust, drawing his whiskers together. "Angela, I can't accept that. It's filthy."

"You don't have to touch it, but I wanted you to have it." I removed the lid and placed the box on the floor so he could admire its contents. Inside lay several large pieces of floral-patterned Lenox. It was one of the late Ethel Fulton's teacups. Sure, Octo-Cat still had the others, but this one was special to him. It's why we had gone to the trouble of throwing a funeral when it got broken, and it's why I wanted him to have it now.

Back then I had rolled my eyes at the ridiculousness, but now I couldn't imagine leaving it behind. This broken teacup had become an important part of our family history, and it would be coming with us.

Octo-Cat sighed happily. "My long lost Evian vessel."

I smiled as I watched the realization take hold. "Yes."

"But why did you disturb its eternal slumber?"

"I thought you might want to bring it with us."

"It's true I miss Ethel very deeply, but you're my human now, Angela. And you're taking me to live beside my dearest Grizabella, which is the greatest thing a cat could ever want. I appreciate the gesture, but I don't need this anymore."

Honestly, his response wasn't what I'd expected, and I didn't want him to come to regret it later. "Are you sure?"

Octo-Cat shook his head. "We should let sleeping teacups lie. Why waste time digging up the past when the future is right there for us to grab with both paws?"

And honestly, I couldn't have said it better myself.

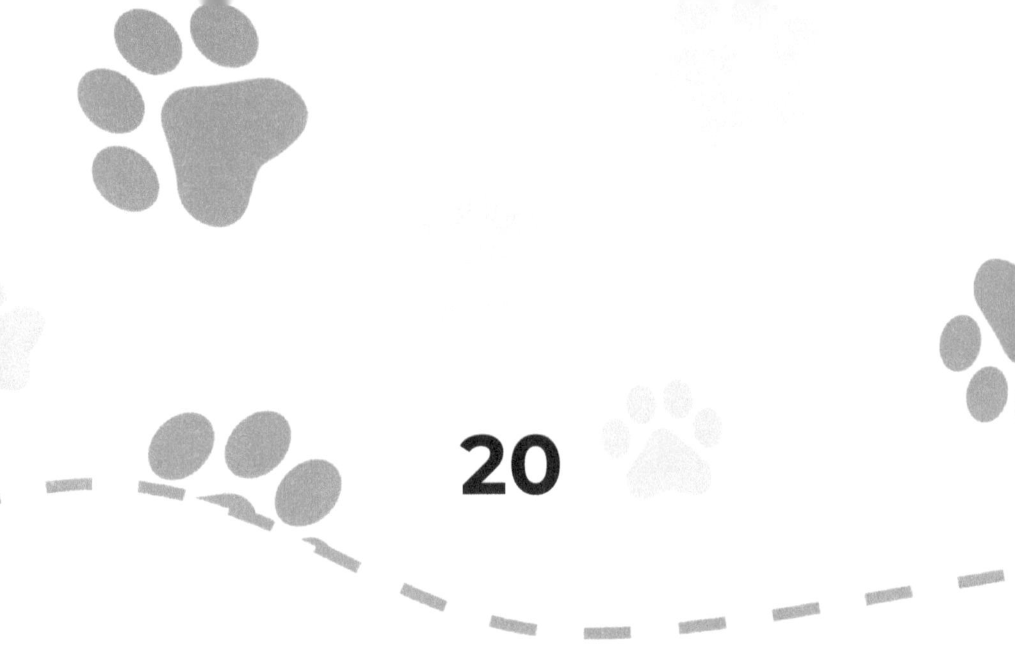

20

One week later, Charles and I flew out to Colorado, paying extra to bring the cats in cabin with us. Octo-Cat happily consented to medication to help bypass his nerves, which made the flight quite pleasant for the rest of us.

Charles had already worked with a dealership remotely to purchase a new car for each of us, having traded in our old models back in Maine. Which meant all we had to do now was to take a taxi straight from the airport to the dealership. I squealed with delight when the car salesman handed me the keys to my brand-new MINI Cooper. Charles had purchased a more sensible SUV, but I wasn't ready for the mini-van life just yet.

For years, both Nan and Charles had pleaded with me to turn in my junky old jalopy for something new, and given the logistics of our move plus my fast-approaching motherhood, I'd finally listened. Making me wonder why I hadn't given in sooner.

I guess I had wanted to earn it myself rather than letting my grandmother, boyfriend, or cat pay the way. Charles finally convinced me to allow myself this small luxury by offering me a new car as celebration for my new job.

Yes, I'd gotten a job, and it was in the most round-about way possible. In preparation for our move, I reactivated my social media profile and started looking into local businesses I could support once we'd relocated. I even changed my town to Boulder, CO, and wouldn't you know it, I started to get served local ads for the area.

One of the ads featured my meme along with the words: *Animals talk. It's up to you to listen to what they have to say. Join us for a special talk with animal behaviorist Meredith Greyson. Admission is free, but donations to our shelter are highly encouraged.*

I decided to message the page that was sponsoring the event, an animal rescue group. I told them who I was and asked if I could get a recording of the event since I wouldn't yet be in town when Dr. Greyson gave her talk.

They recognized me from my profile picture, and it all escalated rather quickly from there and before I knew it, I was hired—not just hired, but they'd created a whole new position for me.

It would be up to me to help match the shelter pets with their perfect forever homes. I would use my talents to create robust adoption profiles detailing exactly what each animal wanted from his or her new family. I'd also be present at any meet-and-greets with potential pet parents to make sure it was a match on both sides.

The position was volunteer for now, but honestly I didn't need the money. I just wanted the purpose, and this one was absolutely perfect for me.

I started next week.

That gave Charles and me some time to settle into our new home. We had a lot of furniture shopping to do to fill up our new neo-colonial domicile. We'd bought in an up-and-coming community of other young families. Sure, our house was much smaller than what we'd had before, but we absolutely loved it.

The manor house had always felt like it belonged to Ethel. This new construction was all ours, and as a bonus it was situated in a great part of the city with loads of entertainment options, both for adults and kids. Just past the city, we had gorgeous scenery that reminded me of back home in Maine, though we were in a whole new mountain range now. We even had a small garden that reminded me of the inn in Virginia where we'd first met Charlene.

Best of all though, we would already have friends and family close by. Grandma Lyn had ordered a new build on the other side of our neighborhood and would be joining us when it was ready. Christine and Grizabella, on the other hand, were already here. Not only were they a short eight-minute drive away, but they were also *here* here, waiting for us now in the driveway of our new digs.

"Welcome home, you!" Christine screamed, racing forward to give me a hug.

"Let me out of here! I need to lick my wife!" Octo-Cat screamed from inside his carrier.

I returned my friend's hug briefly before racing for the door. "Let's get the cats inside. They're eager to say hello."

Charles twisted the key in the lock and pushed the door open to reveal the spacious open-concept floor plan, and I loved the place even more now that I got to see it in person.

Yes, like our cars, we also bought our house sight unseen. Clearly, the builder's pictures hadn't done it justice. And now I twirled around, eager to take it all in.

"Angela!" Octo-Cat growled and shook his carrier, throwing himself against the metal door. "If you don't let me out this instant—"

I quickly stooped down to open the little door, and he flew forth like a madman.

"Um, Christine. You better let Grizabella out fast, or I'm not responsible for what Octavius does."

"Oh, yes, right." She held the Himalayan in a space-age looking backpack, which she easily maneuvered to one shoulder and unzipped.

Grizz hopped right out and ran to nuzzle her groom. "My darling! I can't believe you're really here!"

"Well, believe it, baby. I'm never leaving you again. I—"

"Octo-Papa?" Charlene's voice broke in, a soft and hesitant mewl.

Charles stood on the doorstep holding a small nylon carrier. I grabbed it from him and gently removed the little black kitten, setting her on the floor a few paces away from her adoptive parents.

"Oh, my sweet girl!" Grizabella cried and floated forward to slather her new daughter in sandpaper kisses. Both cats purred so loud, it was hard to hear anything else.

Until Octo-Cat came over and nudged me with his paw. I settled myself on the floor so that I could hear him, while Charles and Christine went outside to grab the Sphynxes.

"Would you look at the two of us?" he said, watching his two girls with obvious pride. "We did good, Angela. Real good."

I smiled as I scratched at the fur between his ears.

My heart felt full, but then he continued, "Honestly, I always knew I'd get my happy ending, but I didn't know whether you had it in you. I'm glad I was wrong."

I laughed and pushed myself to my hands and feet.

Charles and Christine had just released Jacques and Jillianne into the empty house, and the two hairless cats immediately ran upstairs to hide.

"Well, it may take them a little getting used to," I said, knowing I would do whatever they needed to help them accept this place as home.

I sauntered over to my husband and threw both arms around his shoulders, stealing a quick kiss. "Welcome home, Mr. Longfellow."

He kissed me again and said, "Welcome home, Mrs. Longfellow."

A light scratching at the door caused us to exchange a confused look.

"Were you expecting anyone else?" Christine asked, and we both shook our heads.

"Might as well see who it is," I announced as I padded toward the door and pulled it open.

A familiar masked bandit stood on my new porch step, stroking his tail and flashing a fanged smile my way. "You didn't seriously think you could go anywhere without me. Did you?" Pringle demanded, pushing his way into the house.

"But Pringle, how did you...?"

"I left early. The seagulls helped map my path, and from there, I just hitched rides in old truck beds. It's amazing how accommodating folks can be when they don't even know you're there."

"Well, I'm glad you're here," I told him. The trash panda had in fact disappeared days before our departure, and I'd worried that I'd never get the chance to see him again. Like Octo-Cat, I was glad I'd been wrong.

"We'd have brought you, but—"

"Yeah, yeah, it's illegal to own wildlife. Something about me being undomesticatable. Shows what they know!"

"I'd be happy to build you a treehouse out back," I offered. "But you know you can't stay in here."

"Just wanted to introduce myself as your new neighbor," he

said, offering a wave and moving back toward the door. "Let me know when that treehouse is ready for me!" he called as I held the door open for him.

I shut the door again, and almost immediately my phone buzzed with an incoming call.

"Hi, Nan," I shouted happily.

"How was your flight? Did you make it? You forgot to call!"

"Oh, sorry. Yeah, we just got here, and, Nan, it's beautiful. You'll love it when you and Grant visit next month." Yes, we'd already planned out an entire year of visits, and, no, it probably wouldn't be enough.

"That's lovely, dear. I've been dying to tell you the news." Her voice dropped to a conspiratorial whisper that was hard to hear over the phone. "Grant and I drove by your old place, and the new people are already moving in."

"That's good. I hope they love it as much as we did."

"No, that's not the news." She paused for a beat, so dramatic my grandmothers. "Something's off about them. I'm sure of it."

"Off how?" I nibbled on my lower lip to keep from laughing.

Nan, however, remained undeterred. "I don't know. It's just a feeling I get. That something isn't right. Angie, I think we have a mystery on our hands."

I chuckled at that. "Oh, no you don't. I'm out of the mystery business now, remember? I'm now a pet placement specialist for the local animal shelter."

"You may be done with the mystery business, but I don't think

I am," she revealed, making me wish this had been a FaceTime call instead of voice only.

"What are you trying to say?" I asked slowly.

"How upset would you be if I revived Pet Whisperer, P.I.?"

"Not upset, but Nan, that's a thing of the past. Besides," I reminded her, "you can't talk to animals."

"It's all about branding. You never wanted people to know you could either, dear. And besides, whether or not you like it, you've built up all this notoriety now. We can't just let that go. I know, how about Pet Whisperer, Incorporated? It's different but the same as all great business ideas are."

When I realized she was one-hundred-percent serious, I finally relented. "I think that has a nice ring to it. If you want it, it's all yours."

"Angie dear, I don't think I have a choice," came her immediate reply.

And that's how my business died and then came back to life under new ownership. I'd gotten all I needed from my years as the Pet Whisperer. I couldn't wait to see what my kooky nan did with the title.

WHAT TO READ NEXT!

Merlin is just your ordinary, everyday Maine Coon. Except he's a witch. With a human familiar.

In the sleepy Georgian town of Elderberry Heights, danger lurks around every counter but the laughs are never far behind. Join Merlin and his sidekick Gracie as they fight off evil ex-girlfriends, vicious ghosts, and even a horde of zombie squirrels.

If you love quirky humor and madcap magical adventures, then you do not want to miss this hot new series from a USA Today bestselling author. Here it is! This is your chance to binge read the full trilogy— Merlin Takes a Familiar, Merlin Fights a Ghost, and Merlin Kills a Zombie—in this special boxed collection... Enjoy!

The *Merlin's Magical Mysteries: Complete Trilogy Edition* is now available.

Get your copy so that you can start reading this series today!

SNEAK PEEK

MERLIN TAKES A FAMILIAR

I returned home physically exhausted and emotionally wrung out. Everything happened so fast after Harold collapsed. The severity of Officer Dash's implication didn't fully sink in until I finally escaped the coffeehouse and began my quiet drive home. Now that I had a moment to think, a few very important questions crowded into my mind. Why was she so sure that he had been murdered? And even more puzzling, why did she believe I'd done it?

True, lots of people disliked Harold, but nobody had a reason to kill him—least of all me. I mean, why would I when I could have just quit my job and never seen him another day in my life?

The whole thing made me sick... and terrified. All I wanted to do was wake up from this horrible nightmare and go back to my normal, if a tad unexciting, life.

So I changed into my favorite matching flannel pajama set even though it was still the afternoon and the outside temperature was well over eighty degrees. Sometimes I missed my hometown in Northern Michigan where it was chilly more often than not, and my jammies—along with the added help of an overworked tabletop fan—helped allay the occasional bout of homesickness.

Right now, I wanted my mama. It didn't matter that I was an independent twenty-something. I'd been hurt, and I was scared. And just because I'd grown up didn't mean I couldn't turn to my mother in times of great need...

The fact that she didn't answer the phone when I called, however, meant precisely that. I hung up instead of leaving a voicemail, then fired off a quick text asking her to call me back whenever she got the chance.

Fluffy meowed and jumped up on the couch beside me. His whiskers twitched as he tried to discern whether I had anything worth eating. When he didn't find any food, he sunk his teeth into the edge of my sleeve and growled softly.

"Good idea," I said. "Today definitely calls for some ice cream."

I scooped up some of our favorite flavor—plain vanilla bean—into one of my lesser used breakfast bowls, grabbed a spoon and the remainder of the gallon, and settled myself back on the couch. The bowl was for Fluffy. I needed the entire container.

As we ate together, I began to share the events of my day with my feline companion. “That cop was so mean,” I whined. “I mean, why would she just automatically assume I killed my boss? It was terrible. Just awful. To see the life leave his eyes. I don’t think I’ll ever forget it.”

Fluffy sat up straight and cocked his head to the side. Sometimes, in moments like this, it felt like he could actually understand me.

“Mew?” my Maine Coon asked.

“Oh, yeah. I guess I should start at the beginning, huh? Well, my boss at the coffee shop, Harold. He died today.”

“Harold is an awful name,” Fluffy rasped.

“I know. I never thought anyone in the—” I stopped suddenly and closed my mouth up tight, then just stared at Fluffy for a long moment. Was I really so worked up that I was now hearing things?

I laughed at myself. “Silly me,” I said with a deep breath out. “Thinking you’re talking to me, Fluffy.”

“My name’s not Fluffy,” the cat said, then hopped off the coffee table and onto the sofa beside me. “So don’t call me that anymore.”

“Wh-wh-what?” I sputtered, rubbing my eyes until I saw stars. “I’m seeing things. This isn’t real.”

Fluffy clucked his little sandpaper tongue. “You meant to say you’re hearing things, and no, you’re not. I’m talking to you, Gracie.”

I jumped off the couch and spun wildly around the living

room. “Come out, come out wherever you are!” I shouted with a mad laugh, not really sure who I was confronting here. “The joke’s up. Haha, you actually had me convinced Fluffy was talking. Yup, I’m crazy! You win! Now come out and fess up!”

Fluffy let out an enormous yawn, then settled down with his paws tucked into himself. “You are most definitely acting crazy. Also I already told you my name’s not Fluffy, so will you please stop calling me that?”

I gasped, then sunk to the floor before I could pass out and crash down onto it. “This is not real. This is not real,” I murmured, acting quite similarly to how Kelley had when she was balled up and rocking in that club chair back at the coffee shop.

“What’s not real?” Fluffy asked, jumping off the sofa and striding over to me.

“You can’t talk.”

“I can talk, but it seems you’re not very good at listening.”

“Are you going to hurt me?”

“Of course I’m not going to hurt you. I need you to feed me, don’t I? Silly human.”

“What do you want from me?”

“The aforementioned food and also for you to stop calling me Fluffy. I much prefer the name given to me by my ancestors, thank you.”

“Um… Okay. What should I call you?”

“The name’s Merlin, and I come from a long and noble lineage of wizards dating all the way back to King Arthur.”

"You're magic?" I asked with a quick breath in.

"Duh," my cat spat, and then I officially passed out.

***Merlin Takes a Familiar* is available as part of the *Merlin's Magical Mysteries: Complete Trilogy Edition*.**

Get your copy so that you can start reading this series today!

ABOUT MOLLY FITZ

While *USA Today bestselling* author Molly Fitz can't technically talk to animals, she and her three feline writing assistants have deep and very animated conversations as they navigate their days.

She lives with her child and their own private zoo somewhere in the wilds of Alaska. Molly will occasionally venture out for good food, great coffee, or to meet new animal friends.

Learn more about Molly and her books, and be sure to sign up for her newsletter at **www.MollyMysteries.com**.

ALSO BY MOLLY FITZ

Learn more about Molly's collected works, so that you can decide which book you'd like to read next...

PET WHISPERER P.I.

Angie Russo just partnered up with Blueberry Bay's first ever talking cat detective. Along with his ragtag gang of human and animal helpers, Octo-Cat is determined to save the day... so long as it doesn't interfere with his schedule.

Start with book 1, ***Kitty Confidential***.

MERLIN'S MAGICAL MYSTERIES

Gracie Springs is not a witch... but her cat is. Now she must help to keep his secret or risk spending the rest of her life in some magical prison. Too bad trouble seems to find them at every turn!

Start with book 1, ***Merlin Takes a Familiar***.

PARANORMAL TEMP AGENCY

Tawny Bigford's simple life takes a turn for the magical when she stumbles upon her landlady's murder and is recruited by a talking black cat named Fluffikins to take over the deceased's role as the official Town Witch for Beech Grove, Georgia.

Start with book 1, ***Witch for Hire***.

THE MYSTERIES OF MOONLIGHT MANOR (WITH TRIXIE SILVERTALE)

Sydney Coleman has it all—until she doesn't. No sooner does she launch her bed and breakfast, than a trio of ghosts turn up oppose her at every turn. They insist she solve the murder of their mistress, but Sydney is desperate for cash. If she can't book some guests fast, her haunted mansion is utterly doomed.

Start with book 1, ***Moonlight & Mischief***.

CONNECT WITH MOLLY

Sign up for my newsletter and get a special digital prize pack for joining, including an exclusive story, *Meowy Christmas Mayhem*, fun quiz, and lots of cat pictures!

Sign up: **MollyMysteries.com/subscribe**

Now, if you ever wished you could converse with cats, here's your opportunity! This is me officially inviting you into my whacky inner world as part of my Cozy Kitty Book Club.

For those who just can't get enough of my zany cat characters and their hapless humans, this book club will provide new content to devour and the chance to get to know my best author friends.

From exclusive stories, behind-the-scenes trivia to never-before-released bonus content, and monthly giveaways, there's a lot to love about the Cozy Kitty Book Club. Join today to find out what we're reading next!

Join: **MollyMysteries.com/club**

www.ingramcontent.com/pod-product-compliance
Lightning Source LLC
Chambersburg PA
CBHW030627310726
48979CB00003B/917

* 9 7 8 1 6 4 4 5 1 5 3 4 1 *